Unexpected Events

Judith Cuffe

POOLBEG

Published 2021
by Poolbeg Press Ltd
123 Grange Hill, Baldoyle,
Dublin 13, Ireland
Email: poolbeg@poolbeg.com

A catalogue record for this book is available from the British Library.

ISBN 978178199-4283

www.poolbeg.com

About the Author

Judith Cuffe lives in County Wicklow, Ireland, with her husband, three children and faithful writing companions Wilbur and Blue. *Unexpected Events* is her fourth book. When she isn't writing, she can be found walking the dogs, running, shopping online or drinking coffee (sometimes wine!) with friends. To find out more about Judith, follow her on Facebook (Judith Cuffe Author) and Instagram (@judithcuffeauthor).

Also by Judith Cuffe

When Destiny Sings

Sing Me Home

Lying with Truth

For Gertie – my littlest one – who remains the best unexpected event of my life. As a fellow youngest sibling, we understand each other. We're the fun ones, the bringers of luck! Always remember that the view from the bottom looking up can be even greater than that from the top looking down. x

Let there be room in your heart for the unimaginable —
serendipity has a way of showing itself just when you feel like
giving up.
    Nikki Rowe

Prologue

The air is heavy, so dense that she's finding it difficult to breathe. Her diaphragm is pressing against her lungs no matter how hard she tries to relax, to breathe through whatever emotion she's feeling. Before her eyes, the sky alters, morphing from purple to orange to yellow . . . to black. She reaches her hand out as if to touch it one last time, this dusky light – the end of one day and the start of another.

She'd been deceived by this place – its colours, its living fields, vineyards heavy with fruit, rows and rows of ripening grapes – deepening to almost black, ready to be freed from the vine and transported to the winery to be converted into rich red wines. The types that had so often sat breathing at her kitchen table, to be savoured over dinner with friends all those years when life was simpler. It made sense now that those wines should taste as they had: firm, earthy, tannic, with traces of blackberry, vanilla, cherry – strong and dark. She understood the process now, what it takes to work the land, to make something extraordinary from nature.

It takes blood.

Should she have known?

But then, how could anything so natural be less than it seemed? Here, the rustic beauty of the earth contrasts with sprawling structures of grandeur – the likes of which she'd only seen in books and on postcards delivered to her back home in Ireland. They still hang there, vision after vision, pinned to large corkboards, running the length of their little wine shop in Ballycross, next to the home they'd made – together. How strange that they'd never made the time to come here in person, to visit the very place around which they'd built their livelihood. In many ways, she'd felt as though she already knew it – or could imagine it, at least, from stories told. But, when it came to it, she'd needed to see it with her own eyes to understand why an entire slice of an existence had been kept secret. How different her memories would be if she hadn't endeavoured to decipher the mystery.

Now, she is connected to these people. And yet, still she can't comprehend it, no matter what way she looks at it. But then, isn't that the point? To accept that we aren't always meant to understand life's twists and turns, the unexpected patterns that can lead us along curious paths.

Masked in the shadows, trying to control her ragged breath, it's impossible to consider that *this* could have been part of the plan, that *this* was where she was meant to end up. From where she's positioned, near the gate, she can just make them out. As she has stood wondering what to do, whether to walk away or finish this out, the light has faded further, so now there's only a suggestion of orange in the distance behind the darkened house. For a moment, it appears as though it's ablaze.

They are barely shadows, the three darkened figures

gathered on the balcony, set above the imposing front door that no one ever uses. It's rarely opened, aside from when the rare busload of tourists descend, twice a year, for brief access to the ground-floor rooms inside one of the finest establishments on the left bank of Bordeaux in the Médoc region.

She can picture their faces upon seeing it. They'd mirror her own expression of wonder, the first time she'd seen it, when suddenly it had all made sense.

Advancing slowly along the tree-lined driveway, she can see the figures moving, gesticulating in typical French fashion. Raised voices travel across the deserted grounds. She's too far back to decipher the sounds. Pausing, she tries to muster the feeling of dread that enveloped her earlier as she roughly shoved her belongings into her bag to leave, glancing over her shoulder as she did so. For the first time in her life, she'd been petrified.

Once again, she glances up at the balcony, following the ornate black iron railings with her eyes until her head starts to spin. *No.* Turning, she creeps back towards the gate. That's when she hears it.

A scream. A shout. A name.

Her head whips back in time to see a single shadow falling to the ground. It's too slow – its limbs flail pathetically, attempting to latch on to the thick air.

Then a thud – silence.

At that moment, she is confident of two things: she should never have come here in the first place and, worst of all, she's sure that the body splayed on the gravel below the entrance to the chateau was meant to be hers. This time, there's nothing in the atmosphere left to breathe. Her legs falter momentarily, then she runs.

Chapter 1

I get the same feeling I often get lately as I drive the final stretch of road from Carrigbyrne to Ballycross – a sudden tightness in my chest, an unexpected lump in my throat. I reach for my bag on the passenger seat, pat it, feeling for the hard plastic shape of my inhaler tucked inside. It's there, just in case I need it. My asthma hasn't been bad in years, but I've become reliant on the presence of the small blue-and-navy device to loosen my lungs when I feel I can't catch my breath. It's on the checklist whenever I leave the house now. Nothing to chance, not any more.

It's a far cry from how I used to be, living openly in the knowledge that anything can happen. Anything used to happen to me all the time. Little positive twists and gifts landing from nowhere, making me feel like the luckiest person alive. Now, it's what I live in fear of – anything could happen. I've learned that "anything" isn't always good.

The road weaves its way along the river, where the river will open its wide mouth into the harbour, in a never-ending yawn. Sporadically, I acknowledge oncoming cars as I follow the meanders. It's a village thing – a full wave for friends, a hand lifted from the steering wheel for acquaintances. For strangers, two fingers, but in a polite way – a curt nod for someone who's got on the wrong side of you but you can't bring yourself to ignore. Luckily, I know the road well. Driving in Ballycross is as much about recognising the car, giving the appropriate salute, as it is about the destination.

"Sure, I only recognised you when you were past me!"

"I still don't know the new car! Hope you didn't think I was ignoring you."

You get to know the licence-plate numbers, so you can decipher who's approaching, be ready with your salute. It can be tricky, since so many drive very similar "mammy mobiles" in black or grey. Or white – lately, there's a lot of white, I've noticed that – a mix of five, some seven-seaters, depending on their needs, or indeed their fortune.

There's no hiding in my own ancient little white van with the name of the shop, "*Quelle Surprise*" on it – images of bottles of wine proudly emblazoned down the sides. We added a coffee cup and a picture of a croissant several years ago when we morphed into a patisserie shop to make use of the morning trade. Even in Ballycross, coffee has become a big thing. People stopping on the way to work for a takeaway blast of caffeine. Mothers meeting after the school drop-off. Tourists. The summer trade is always significant. Everyone wants coffee. "Bigger than wine," I'd enthused after reading an article on it in one of those boring industry magazines. At the time, I'd felt a bit like Richard Branson with my idea – ready to seize the opportunity and learn later. After all, a business has to adapt over time. Okay.

So coffee isnt't exactly revolutionary, but I was right. It boosted our income significantly and eradicated the need for me to walk across to Centra every time I felt like a caffeine hit. They go hand in hand, I suppose – coffee in the morning, until lunchtime, then everything tidied up, reverted to what we started off as: wine merchants.

Over the years, we've built up quite a name for being experts in our field, helping to plan the wine list to accompany the menus of many Cork restaurants. A career in wine, converting the family home into a wine shop is a million miles from what I ever thought I'd end up doing. It came as a considerable surprise – passion tailing passion. You see, the wine was never *my* passion – not really. Someone else's dream became mine over time. It's a way of life – a lovely one which has rarely felt like work, more like welcoming friends into our home, our world. For me, it was *all* about the people, something I used to be great at. Adding coffee and pastries was simply giving our loyal customers another reason to hang out with us. We'd had space in the shop, not to mention the time, and it took off quickly, making us busier than we'd ever been before.

I'd loved it at first. I've always been a morning person. There's subtle energy to the start of each day. Faster than when people come in later in the day to peruse the rustic-looking wooden shelves to find the perfect bottle of wine – usually French – again not my contribution. I'm about as French as a bowl of Irish stew. Regardless, all things French is our speciality, you might have guessed from the name of the shop.

Lately, I find the persistent morning chatter exhausting – like an act. That, and I can feel them watching me as they sit there, sipping from their white mugs, picking up

7

the last bits of flaky pastry from their plates and sucking it from their forefingers – wanting to ask how I am, but not knowing how. It's something I need to make a decision on – whether or not to continue with the coffee or revert to just wine. A lot has changed. Perhaps I should adapt back, simplify. Either way, I can't seem to decide. Choices have never been my forte. Until recently, I'd have looked for a sign – like that coffee article in the magazine, or a Frenchman sitting alone on a bench …

Then again, perhaps there had been a sign. A few months back, in a case of art imitating life, someone picked away parts of the croissant image on the side of my van, then proceeded to colour it in brown with a Sharpie pen. I have to admit it was a good job – realistic-looking. Now, my van bears the image of what a dog might produce along the river walk leading away from the harbour, over which the local councillors have a field day. There was an entire debate last year at the council meeting as to whether it sufficed to "stick and flick" canine excrement into the undergrowth. As head of the Traders' Association – a position that had "fallen" upon me – I'd had to go along to the meeting. It got almost as heated as the contents of one of those peach-coloured nappy bags that most people use to pick up their dogs' excrement, only to hang it from a tree to retrieve on the way back home. Mostly they'd forget, often leaving the "decoration" dangling for weeks before someone got irate enough to dispose of it on their behalf.

The bins they canvassed for were a welcome addition. After all, who wants to walk the river path, looking out at the boats moored uniformly to orange buoys – the wind turbines spinning in the distance, cows grazing the green fields on the other side – swinging the still-warm contents of that bag in their hand? The use of plastic, of course, is a problem in itself, but neither Rome, nor Ballycross, was built in a day.

It's much cleaner now. Only Marian Cummins from the dry cleaner's still refuses to remove Tiny's offerings and is allowed to continue to "stick and flick". She has an extreme gag reflex, as she argued herself at the meeting, putting across her point seamlessly whilst retching and gripping the back of the chair at the very mention of the act.

You might have thought it an excuse, but I'm not the only one who's witnessed Marian's attempts at removing her pet chihuahua's deposit. Seán Cooper from Centra, the local convenience store, spoke up for Marian, reiterating her point. He's good like that. Marian's watery eyes, profusely sweating brow and violent retches were enough to make her exempt from a possible fine or prosecution.

I've often offered to do it for her if I pass her on Tiny's toilet-run. The last time, both Marian and I had tears in our eyes. Her: from the kind gesture. Me: because contrary to his name, that dog can deliver.

"I've always said you're the nicest girl in Ballycross, Seren. I only wish you had better luck, but I'm praying for you." Marian had issued one of those sad smiles where you exhale, tilt your head, and squeeze your lips tightly together.

Marian had been a close friend of my mother's. Under normal circumstances, I'd have loved to stay and chat longer, but I'd had to change the subject when I felt the familiar tightness travel across my chest.

"You should really get that picture on your van fixed, love," she'd waved as I'd scuttled towards it. "Not good for business."

"It's on the list, Marian."

Marian's right. Who wants the thought of a French roast coffee accompanied by a plate of dog shit? Then again, it was precisely what life had delivered lately – a generous side of shit. I just need to decide whether to remove the coffee and dog shit from the van altogether, or get it fixed. I'll get to it eventually. To be fair, you might say I've been otherwise disposed. Actually, that would be an understatement, and I've always hated understatements. I'm far too honest to waste my time trying to play things down.

"Serendipity, you're an absolute scream! Talk about saying it like it is."

I've heard it a thousand times, matched it with my typical response.

"Well, I'm an open book. Sure, I'm named to be that way. Open to life and all its surprises."

It probably doesn't quite match their point, but I'm proud of my name, always ready to slip it in wherever I can. Although, most people, especially the older generation like Marian, call me Seren, or Sheren, sometimes Sharon. I get all sorts. But Seren is less of a mouthful than Serendipity, easier to manage with a thick Cork twang, where all five syllables have a tendency to blend into one. It had always sounded far nicer delivered smoothly with a slow French lilt. It's something I hang on to, though – my name – even if I no longer believe in its meaning. I cling to it like the old van, I suppose – the one I can't seem to bring myself to part with. Besides, I've never gone very far in it. Until recently, it's always been enough to make the bi-weekly trip to the cash-and-carry in Carrigbyrne. And I get to park outside the shop, also my home, right in the loading bay.

Not that anyone would ever stop me. I've been in that house since the day I was born. Imagine. I've never been more than two weeks away from it. Everyone knows me here, in Ballycross, where I've always lived in the grey house opposite the harbour, looking directly out at the yacht club. I'm as much a part of it as it is of me. Waking each morning to the grounding whispers of the sea or shouts, depending on the weather. The boat masts clink and ding reassuringly like a ticking clock in this place where the wind always breathes.

Coming through the village, over the bridge, past the B&B – more a hotel – I try to swallow the developing lump in my throat, and remember a time when this road felt as though I were edging towards safety. Up until recently, that's what Ballycross was to me: home – a little kingdom, right at the edge of the world. My world – small yet big enough in which to lead a full life, one that over my almost forty years here has developed wholly, despite the ten-mile radius.

It's where my parents had been born, theirs before that, where they'd died. It was where I'd been born and, in many ways, where I'd always expected someday to finish my journey. It happens a lot – more than you might imagine. Those born here rarely leave and if they do, sometimes by choice, at times forced, they usually come back. "Ballycrossers" like to think it's testament to the type of place it is. Nothing outside matches up to the beautiful seaside village, with its choice of beaches, its proximity to Cork city, while still making you feel as if you're miles from anywhere.

"You'll never find a sense of community like Ballycross," those who'd returned with growing families would often claim. "It's the people who make it."

I'd always felt the same. Strangely, lately, it's the people who make me feel like I'm suffocating.

I pull into the loading bay next to the shop, grab my

bag from the passenger seat and get out of the car. It's not yet midday – bright but not sunny. The wind is up, making my hair whip across my face, reminding me of another appointment I need to keep – another item on the list. The telltale signs of age are beginning to bleed from my roots down the front sections of my brown hair.

"Morning, S-heren."

I look up to see Bobby Cronin standing in his usual position, facing the harbour with one foot poised on the wall, watching the sea. The corner of my mouth twitches ever so slightly at the mispronunciation of my name. I've let it go for far too many years to correct him now. Bobby would likely die of embarrassment. Besides, I like how he says it. It's familiar.

"Choppy, today," he comments without looking at me.

"Will you get out later?" I ask.

"Looks like it's blowing across. I'll wait it out."

Bobby's one of the local fishermen – unmarried, no children. I have no idea how old Bobby actually is. He's looked the same for as long as I can remember. He had white hair even when I was a teenager, but his face is youthful, lined by the sea but still fresh. Bobby would often be invited to share Christmas dinner with my parents and me. He'd eat hungrily, say very little and be off just as fast. I once asked my father if he thought Bobby was lonely or sad.

"Bobby! Sad! There isn't a man more content. Sure, as Bobby says himself, he has the life. Him and the sea. That's all he needs."

It's how I once felt. That I, too, had "the life". But it wasn't the sea that kept me afloat, it was something else. Now, what I have is "a life". There's a gaping expanse created by those two words – "the" and "a".

Bobby's a real presence in Ballycross, if that's what you could call it. Always there to help. Whenever anything needs to be done, Bobby's your man. Tree fallen – Bobby. Boat adrift – Bobby. Car stuck in a ditch – Bobby. Life torn asunder … Bobby? He's a man of few words, which are chosen wisely. He turns to look at me, tilts his head, frowns.

"Are you doing all right?"

I smile. "I am, Bob. I'm okay." My face says otherwise.

"You know where I am if you need me. I . . . " Bobby thinks for a moment, opens his mouth, closes it, then says, "I still think about –"

Please don't say it. Please don't say it.

"Best be off. Mind yourself, S-heren."

"I will, Bob. Take care out there."

Relieved, I lock the car, glance over at the activity beyond. Ballycross is shaped like a horseshoe. All the shops gathered together at the end – nothing beyond but the Atlantic.

"Our house is on the horse's leg. See . . ." my mother used to point from our front door. "But we're close enough to absorb all the luck from that horseshoe. Sure, isn't that how I have you?"

My favourite story. How I came to be. I suppose the surprise of discovering she was pregnant at the age of forty-eight after she'd lost all hope was the reason my mother named me Serendipity. Then, of course, there was the added bonus that in the end I'd turned out just fine, despite her age and the concerns that the entire residents of Ballycross had had, that I'd be born another way.

"You were all I ever wanted. Then as soon as I decided I'd settle for a camper van, travel around Ireland with your father, along you came. Hope for one thing, get another."

13

I wish she was here now – more than anything, I wish she was here to tell me everything was going to be all right. Mind you, I knew from a young age that I wouldn't have her forever, nor my father, who was older again. In exchange, they'd spent every possible moment with me until it was their time to leave, equipping me for my journey ahead, or so they thought. It's only lately that I feel their loss more profoundly than ever before.

You see, I've done something. Something that I should be more sure of than anything before in my life. But I'm not. I've done something and, so help me God, now I wish I hadn't.

Chapter 2

I reach my hand towards the brass handle of the shop door, then whip it away just as fast. The memory darts up my arm. Me: proudly unveiling the much-sought-after antique handle and matching shopkeeper's bell unearthed at a car boot sale like I'm demonstrating the top prize on a game show. These episodes, snapshots into the past, happen a lot lately. In them, I'm so different that sometimes I wonder if it had really been me. Perhaps it was someone else entirely who'd once agonised over every microscopic detail when we'd first opened the shop, speaking of nothing else for months until we had it right. We were so proud of what we'd created, so optimistic for the future. We were always busy making plans, improving, painting something, moving something, and attempting to defeat the dodgy door.

It's slightly ajar now, as it always is during the day, where it rests on the thick rubber sill, put there as a last resort to prevent it from continually swinging open. The result is a steady stream of sea air or free ventilation, depending on your level of optimism. It was either that, leave the door to its own devices, or keep it bolted – not entirely conducive to footfall. We'd had several discussions over how to best tame the door that wouldn't remain shut. No sooner would our backs be turned after thinking we'd cracked it when it would creak open once more. "I give up. The ghost of cheap plonk doesn't want us here," I'd teased.

In reality, the door's failure to comply rested on the entire house being built at a slight angle, sloping with the footpath. That's my theory anyway. Mind you, if you asked me now, I'd say it is haunted, or maybe that's just me. At times, it feels like I'm the ghost.

From where I'm standing outside, I can see that the shop is busy. So much so that the windows have steamed up while I try to muster the courage to go inside. Through the crack in the door, I can hear muffled conversations, the clatter of cups and plates. The thought of hurling myself inside to witness every head in the place pivot towards me makes me shudder. Before, I wouldn't have thought twice. Back then, I'd already be in amongst them, spewing pigeon French as if we were in the thick of the Loire valley and not the arsehole of Cork. "*Bonjour.*" "*Bienvenue.*" It always secured a laugh from the regulars, who'd give it loads in return, throwing out whatever French phrase they could muster from schooldays. "*Voulez-vous.*" "*Je ne sais quoi.*" "*Un. Deux. Trois.*"

Each pitiful attempt would be met with a look of mock disapproval, a grin as lopsided as the house from the genuine article behind the counter. It only served to encourage us further, all part of the game. By now, I might have paused at a table for a quick chat, admired a baby, asked after an ill parent, complained about the bloody weather … Lately, I make people uneasy. My presence induces awkwardness, constipated-looking faces.

Braving it, I push the door, avoiding eye contact for fear that people will read my mind or see the truth. Of course, by acting suspiciously, I'm probably arousing suspicion. It's often the case when someone's entire demeanour changes practically overnight – bubbly to elusive in the blink of an eye. I look over their heads towards the shop counter. For a nanosecond, a single beat, I genuinely expect it to be someone other than Fi standing there. She's deep in conversation. When I see who with, I edge back, but not before Fi's eyes flash in my direction. It's enough to make Cathy, who she's speaking with, turn too, but by the time her head swivels, I'm already gone.

Back outside, I feel ridiculous. Today, of all days, I hadn't counted upon Cathy being here. Despite being one of my oldest, most-loved friends, we're avoiding one another without admitting it. Worse still, I know exactly why she's here.

I sidestep to the left and quickly open the door to the house. Once inside, I take a few calming breaths, then stare longingly at the wonky staircase. More than anything, I'd like to climb each step, then turn left towards my bedroom, lie on the bed, and try to process the morning's events. The view always helps. At the same time as doing up the shop, we'd made some improvements to the house. In what had once been my parents' bedroom, we'd painted everything white, even the floorboards, then had the bed specially made, so the mattress rests on top of a platform. Three steps up so that as soon as you open your eyes in the morning, you can see the sea. Not just the masts of the boats, as it once was, but the water. It had been cheaper than ripping out and replacing the crooked window frames. "Darn topsy-turvy house," my mother would often complain. When I was little, I'd marvel at how the stairs in the hall got smaller as you neared the upstairs landing: big step, big step, small, small, smaller. Mum used to say they were that way to help tired little legs get safely to bed. Over time, her grievances over the irregularities of the building became elements of my childhood imagination. The uneven door frames – pushed up by the giants of my father's bedtime stories. The undulating floorboards could make an all-day event of a single game of marbles. I'm glad now that I never gave in to a complete overhaul of the house. In doing so, I might have erased some of its flawed charms. Today, it still feels like where I grew up, an improved version – "A house in which you never know what you're going to get next," Mum would say. How right she'd been.

It used to make me think of her whenever I'd hear the bell chime over the door of Quelle Surprise. I'd lift my head, excited to see who was about to spill over the threshold. "That's it. Give that door a good old nudge. It deserves it," I'd encourage from my stool behind the counter. Then I'd watch them absorb the intentionally dark, relaxing atmosphere, the industrial-looking steel-and-wooden shelves, neatly stocked with all manner of wines to suit every palate and pocket. They'd invariably pause to read, then grin at the blackboards throughout, emblazoned with witty quotes about wine, life, sometimes both.

"I used to think drinking was bad for me, so I gave up thinking."

"One kind word can change someone's day. Wine!"

"Wine is the answer. What was the question?"

"Size matters. Who wants a small glass of wine?!"

Those who come daily for coffee, weekly for wine, or sometimes that in reverse order – it's not my place to judge – still smile at the quirky quotes. At one time, I used to change them almost every day. Lately, I'm doing well if I get around to it once a week. Watching people's responses to them used to amuse me. Now, they must know that my morose exterior cannot possibly match the quirky sentiments squiggled on those chalkboards. There's no quote smart enough to make everything better, nor a bottle of wine big enough in which to drown. Perhaps I should get rid of the sayings like I did the bell. Out of the blue, a few months back, I'd got up from my stool, walked over and unscrewed the antique bell from its bracket, then thrown it into the drawer beside the cash register. The shop is so small that I don't need to be alerted to a customer. Besides, I don't like surprises, not anymore.

"There you are! You were there one minute and then gone." Fi, my one and only staff member, or "friend whom I pay", as I lovingly refer to her, appears through the internal door that separates the shop from the house. "Everything okay? How did you get on?" She tilts her head in concern.

"Yeah, fine," I smile. "I just … sorry, I just remembered I needed … this." I pick up the first thing I see on the hall table, which happens to be an envelope, and wave it.

"Well, how was it?" Fi doesn't question why I'd vanished upon seeing Cathy, despite trying for weeks to get me to spill on the noticeable cooling of the friendship. Today, she's more interested in my appointment. For one terrifying moment, I can't remember where I'd told her I was going.

"Just the one filling," It comes to me in time. I accompany the lie by scrunching up my cheek in mock pain.

"*Ugh*. God, I hate the dentist. Sort of feel sorry for

them, though," Fi muses. "Imagine working away in a tiny office on big rotten teeth, sucking spit from mouths with that sucker thingy that makes it impossible to talk back. Like zero interaction all day long." She makes a face.

"Hello. Excuse me." A voice from behind interrupts her rambling.

Fi rolls her eyes. "I take that back. Mute customers might not be a bad thing. It's bedlam in there. They're all out today." She gestures with her head. "I could try stuffing croissants in their mouths to shut them up." She looks fussed. Her red curls are beginning to poke upwards from where her hair is slicked back, and her cheeks are worryingly pink. "I'd better get back."

"I'll be there in a sec." I remove a bobble from my wrist, and go to the mirror over the hall table.

"Are you sure? Will you be able?" She points at my face, and I frown.

"Oh. The tooth. God, yeah. Sure it was only a small filling. I'll be grand."

"Did you see Cathy just there?" she asks as I twist my hair into a bun and secure it at the nape of my neck. "She wanted to know where you were. I was talking to her when you came in."

"Were you?" I don't look at her.

"You know I was."

I glance at her and catch her shameless smile before she disappears back inside the shop. I hate myself for lying. It's all I do recently. Half the time, I can't remember what I've told whom. It's the reason I'm avoiding people. I'm less likely to slip up. Besides, what was the point in telling Fi where I really was unless I was sure there was something to tell? Only that, as of now, there *is* something

to tell. I push the thought aside and instead fix my top,
noticing how easily it slides into the waistband of my
jeans. I've lost more weight. It's the reason I'm wearing
this baggy old sweatshirt in the first place to hide it.
Funny. It's the same one I used to wear whenever I was
carrying that little bit extra, after periods of overindulgence
like Christmas or general contentment ... mostly that. At
one time, there was nothing I loved more than a delicious
home-cooked meal, followed by glass after glass of red
wine over conversation with my closest friends – friends
like Cathy and Jane – the original three.

We've been friends for as long as I can remember.
Christ, I miss it ... them ... us ... me ... those nights. We
named it "Saturday Service" – a quip dating back to our
teenage years. To a time when Ireland was still so bloody
Irish, and our parents would force us to go Mass for fear
that we'd burst into flames if we didn't. Attendance at
Saturday evening Mass used to fulfil the obligation to go
on a Sunday morning with the old people. We never
actually went. Instead, the three of us gave thanks by
hiding around the back of the church giggling and
smoking ten packs of Silk Cut Blue, then frantically
chewing gum and spraying our fingers with Impulse
body spray to cover the trail.

Years later, a twist on Saturday Service was reinstated
after we'd all returned to Ballycross from wherever the
wind had blown us after school and college. I'd travelled
more on a gentle breeze as far as Cork University and, in
the end, for only a short time. Cathy and Jane went
further to Dublin, but I always had faith they'd return.
There's no place like Cork, after all, even if we do say so
ourselves. Or perhaps it was because we simply couldn't
bear to be apart. Before long, we were spending every

Saturday evening together again: me, Cathy, Jane, and some additions who instantly doubled the size of our threesome.

Thinking of it makes my breath catch unexpectedly, and I grasp the edge of the hall table to steady myself before the image strikes. Oh, God, I can still see it so clearly. My head is thrown back, and I'm laughing so hard that my stomach hurts. I'm barefoot, dancing my way to the kitchen after a quick dash to the shop to grab yet another bottle of wine – "Just one more, I swear."

"Christ, Seren, we'll end up talking backwards for the week. Or upside-down in a bush outside."

Was it Jane, or Cathy's husband, Dermot? I can't remember.

"That was only the once."

Cathy. I'm sure.

All three couples are laughing now. That's the thing about memories: they blur, but you never forget how you feel, and I'm happy. For a moment, I can really feel it. Oh, God, the agony. I'm so happy.

"Swear to me," I close my eyes and whisper the words.

"I swear."

"You'll never leave me?"

"Never."

Opening my eyes, I stare beyond my reflection. "Liar."

Oh, God, what have I done?

Chapter 3

Almost as fast as the episode hits, I'm transported back to where I'm still gripping the hall table. Releasing my hold, I walk through the shop door and in behind the counter. "Here, let me." I take the coffee filter handle from Fi. "You clear up. I'll man Big Bertha." It's our nickname for the temperamental coffee machine. Bertha's mood swings used to drive me insane. Recently I've come to understand her.

"Thanks. Bertha's acting shirty this morning." Fi scowls at the machine and then leans towards me to whisper, "A bit like *her*."

I follow her eyes towards the table nearest the door to where, Derbhla, the doctor's secretary, is sitting perfectly still as if in sleep mode but with her eyes fixed open.

Derbhla, or "*Deeervlah*" as she pronounces it herself through her nose (making it impossible for me to say it any other way), is maybe mid-fifties, single, no children. Which is fine, except she acts and dresses like she's in her early nineties: set hair, a strong whiff of Lily of the Valley, wears wool everything, even blouses. She's here every weekday for her break, which should make her a valued customer, except she does nothing but complain. Both Fi and I do whatever it takes to avoid serving her, often ducking behind the counter, playing dead, feigning a sudden bathroom urge when she approaches. Fi claims that we'd make a fortune if we could somehow market Derbhla as a natural laxative. The fact that Derbhla is employed by Cathy, or Dr Catherine Clear, if you want to be all formal, is merely coincidental.

Cathy is the local GP in Ballycross. At work, she's super professional: pencil skirt, crisp shirt, impossibly neat blonde hair, really and I mean *really* expensive shoes. Cathy is what you'd call together or "anally retentive", according to Jane – in jest, of course. When we were sixteen, she'd bring a bottle of red wine, her own glass, and a corkscrew in her bag while the rest of us sipped cans of Ritz around the back of the sailing club before the underage discos. She's highly revered in Ballycross where she grew up right down the road from me, and now has her practice. Except nowadays she lives just outside Carrigbryne on the main Cork Road in what can only be described as one of the biggest houses I've ever seen. Did I mention she married a surgeon? Dermot, who is all heart, also mends hearts for a living. Yes, some people have it all. Locally, Dr Catherine Clear can literally do no wrong, but outside work, with us, she's just Cathy. The same old one who, believe me, has fallen backwards into a bush a lot more than once. Derbhla would be horrified if she knew the truth.

"Cathy, you do realise that Derbhla is a complete weapon," Jane had imparted one evening, years before, over a bottle of wine after hours in Quelle Surprise. We'd often made use of the perk of our own private wine bar. "You know she never tells you when I call, ever! Today, she actually tutted and said that I should phone back after hours if it was personal. The cheek!"

"She's tricky, our *Deeervlah*," I added, imitating her nasal twang.

Cathy wasn't phased. "Lads, seriously, I couldn't care less. She's good at her job, and she makes my life easier. I don't need another friend. Not when I have ones as honest as you pair." Cathy threw her eyes up to heaven, then primly tucked her hair behind her ear.

"She's like a medical crusader," Jane continued, undeterred. "Guarding you as if you're Christ's Chalice Incarnate. I'm surprised she doesn't stand outside your door in full chainmail brandishing a sword to protect the great doctor from streptococcus or ..." Jane started to laugh as she pushed her chair back and stood statuelike next to Cathy. "Ah, shite, I can't think of another infection."

"Syphilis," I rushed to her assistance. "Doctor is *verrry verrry* busy!" I sang, rolling the r's, in my thickest Cork accent. "Do you have an appointment? What *exactly* is it concerning?"

"It concerns ongoing vaginal thrush," Jane attempted the accent. "And piles. Massive ones, like a bunch of grapes. Here, I'll show you, Derbhla." She bent over, pretending to show us her behind.

"Christ, you're both so immature." Cathy batted Jane away. I could tell she was trying to be all pious while I snorted. "Her job is all she has, and I'm telling you, girls, she's good at it, and I *am verrry* busy, as you say." She smirked at last. "Keeping idiots like you pair at bay is not as easy as it looks."

"I can vouch for that." Jane raised her hand and sat back down before taking a slug from her glass.

"Here's to never employing a friend again!" Cathy lifted her glass and grinned.

For a short time, Jane had thought it would be a good idea to pack in her career as a chef and try her hand at something more conducive to raising her young family. Cathy had offered her the job, then promptly fired her a week later.

"In my defence, I thought I was helping," Jane justified herself.

"By asking patients if it was an above or below the belt issue? Seriously!"

"It made sense to me. I was saving the 'below belts' for the afternoon so as not to put you off your lunch."

"See! With you, it was always going to be about food! But thank you for caring." Cathy patted her hand.

"And thank you for firing me."

"It all worked out in the end." I grinned, waving my glass in the air. "All doing exactly what we should. A doctor, a chef, and …"

"Allow me," Jane offered. "The Saviour! Let's face it, without the wine and the laughs, we'd never have made it this far."

"What?" Cathy had feigned surprise. " All those years of studying and no points for the doctor?"

"Zero! Save your prescriptions, Doc," Jane had winked at me. "We've got all the medicine we need right here. To the one who never had a clue what she wanted to do, look at her now! God only knows where we'd be without the wine. And you, I suppose …"

She'd turned to where a figure had materialised at the door. Following her line of vision, I'd smiled broadly.

"The day she met you was a fortuitous one for us all." Jane's tongue had twisted endlessly around the word *fortuitous*, making Cathy spit her drink, and the laughter started again.

I'm not sure about them, but it was certainly true of me. Where would I have been without ... the wine? Mind you, without it, I definitely wouldn't be in this quandary. I sometimes ask myself: if I could swap those years of ignorant bliss to never have to feel the torment I now feel, would I? I can't, of course, so I guess I'll never know.

One thing for sure is that Jane had been born to cook. She thrived in the high-stress environment of a busy kitchen. Cathy craved order. And me, well, I'd been happy to let life dictate. At university, I'd settled on studying English on the premise that I could, at least, speak it. And French, following my seventeenth summer that had understandably piqued my interest in all things Gallic (or phallic as Jane would argue). I'd voluntarily dropped out at the start of the second year to help Mum after Dad got sick. I've no regrets. My parents had been everything to me and, as it turned out, studying wasn't. After Dad died, then Mum far too soon afterwards, I sort of floated for a while doing various jobs here and there before life dictated once more, and I found my true calling. Or it found me, you might say. Regardless, the three of us: me, Cathy and Jane, have always been there for each other, never judged each other's choices. Not until recently, that is.

"So, is Cathy going tonight?" Fi asks after returning to the counter laden with empty cups and plates. She's trying to act innocent, but I know she's fishing once again.

27

"What's that?"

"Cathy," she repeats, louder. "Is she going later?" She starts to load the dishwasher, then glances back at me for an answer.

"I thought she'd have told you earlier."

"She didn't mention it." Fi shrugs. "Do you think she is?"

Big Bertha saves me by frantically hissing out a cappuccino for an exhausted-looking woman holding a baby. The baby stares at me even more intently than Fi, waiting for my answer. For a moment, there's an unnerving stillness aside from a slow stream of saliva running from the corner of the baby's mouth as it eyeballs me.

Fi breaks the silence. "I suppose she must be going."

I hand the takeaway coffee cup over the counter to the now grateful-looking mother, take the cash, then wave the judgemental baby goodbye.

"Sure, of course she's going," Fi goes on. "No need to ask, I suppose. It's just you haven't seen much of her lately. Aside from today, I can't remember the last time she was in. You should lift the phone. Call her and see?" Her voice lifts at the end like a question.

"Maybe."

"Suit yourself." Followed closely by, "I just thought if you haven't seen her in a while, you should –"

I cut her off. "She's probably just busy, you know? Like with her business, her marriage, the kids. It's full-on. I'm a lot … freer." My eyes fall to the floor.

Fi doesn't notice.

"Jane has kids too and is about to open a restaurant," she says, "and she still comes in a few times a week."

I shrug. "I don't know, Fi, okay?" It takes a lot for me to lose my patience, but this conversation is undoubtedly veering in that direction.

"Okay." She opens her eyes wide, puts her hands up in surrender and goes to serve a customer.

The truth is, Cathy and I are more than avoiding each other. For the first time ever, we're not actually speaking. It's the reason Cathy now sends Derbhla to fetch her daily one-shot Americano and almond croissant instead of coming herself as she once used to. Even worse, she knows how much Derbhla annoys me. She's probably doing it on purpose. I suspect Cathy came in earlier to try and break the ice before tonight. The problem is, I imagine she was also here out of curiosity. To see if I've made any progress with what I'd told her – the very reason we're not talking. If it was any other day, and if I hadn't just learned what I had an hour before, I might have collapsed into her arms. But how can I face her now? She knows me too well not to know when I'm lying. At least tonight, with other people around, she won't be able to pry.

Fi's right. There was no need to ask if Cathy would be going later. Of course she'll be at the restaurant opening. We both know how hard Jane's worked towards getting her own place. Whatever problem we have with each other, we'd never do anything to ruin this occasion. After many years of manifestation, we'll be perfectly civil when Jane finally opens the doors of *Más* – Cork's first contemporary Mexican restaurant. *Más* will serve traditional Mexican cuisine with a twist, using as much locally produced ingredients as possible. Not only is it a way to support local, it's been great for publicity. Even before the big opening, I've already heard the name *Más* circulating.

The three of us came up with the name years before.

It means "more" in Spanish, pronounced "mass" – how very Irish! We'd been astounded by our wit. "It'll be the very first time we make it to *Mass* together! Get it? *M.A.S.S!*" Cathy had shrieked.

Immediately, Jane had scribbled the name on a piece of paper and held it up. "Take a picture, Seren. This is me asking the universe, trusting the process, and accepting."

I still have the photo on my phone. I'd always planned on getting it printed to give to her when it eventually happened, but I'd got distracted. I catch sight of my reflection in the curved stainless steel of the coffee machine. In it, I look like all my features have been squashed downwards, aside from my eyes. They look enormous, like a terrified cartoon character staring back. I look away.

Of course, Jane had noticed straight away that something was up between Cathy and me, but neither of us had been willing to tell her what.

"After everything, I can't believe that *now* we fall apart. When did you turn into such a clam, Seren? Cathy is just as bad. She won't bloody tell me anything. I could kill her. Actually, I could kill you both."

It drove a wedge between us all, but it's me Jane should be angry with. It's not that Cathy *won't* tell her, it's that she *can't* – that's the difference.

You see, I'd gone to see Cathy as my doctor. Upon hearing what I had to say, she'd sat on the other side of her mahogany desk, gawking at me with her mouth open.

"Does Jane know anything?" she'd asked finally.

"No."

"What! You have to tell her, Seren. Let's meet up after work, try and talk it through, like we always do."

"No." I removed a set of papers from the envelope resting on my knee and pushed them across her desk. "I just need you to sign these."

She'd picked them up, scanned them, then practically thrown them back at me. "And what if I won't?"

"Then I'll go elsewhere."

"Seren," she'd softened. "Come on. You can't take this back. Ever." She'd paused, looking crestfallen. "I don't understand."

"And how could *you* possibly understand?"

She'd shook her head. "Please, Seren. Don't do this. Not yet. Wait! Things will get better. Let me talk to Jane." She'd gone to lift the phone.

"*No.*" That time, I'd been firmer. "I'm *your* patient, Cathy. That makes this confidential. I assume that still stands. Or is that just for other people?"

She'd replaced the receiver and nodded slowly, wounded.

I hadn't meant to pull that card, to unblur the somewhat hazy line that existed between Cathy being my friend and my doctor. Up until now, she'd been both without complication. To me, it was normal.

Jane, on the other hand, hadn't shared my view. "There's no way I'm lying on your examination table, showing you my fanny," she'd told Cathy. "No thanks. Not that there's anything wrong with it, like. It's a lovely one, but no. No offence."

"None taken," Cathy had assured her. "It's a personal choice. I get it."

"But surely if there was something wrong, wouldn't you tell her anyway?" I'd argued. "What I'd tell Cathy as a friend, I'd tell her as my doctor. Sure we tell each other everything anyway. Don't we?"

No. It seemed we don't. No matter what Cathy said, I wouldn't listen.

"Please, Seren. Don't shut us out. You need us. And

31

we need you."

Except they don't need me, not anymore, not in the same way. In one way, I always suspected it would end up like this, as much as they'd assured me that it wouldn't. I drove by Cathy's house one Saturday evening a few weeks back, wanting to see for myself. Jane's car was parked right in the driveway, where I knew it would be. Without being able to see inside, I knew that two couples were sitting at the banquet-style table – two instead of three. Nothing is the same. Not me, not them, not our friendship. And soon, sooner than I care to imagine, it will change again.

Chapter 4

"So if it's okay with you, I won't drive later." Fi is chatting away again.

"What's that? Say again." I pick up a cloth and mop up some spilt milk. The place has mostly emptied out, all while I've stood hypnotised, lost in thought, robotically banging the coffee filter empty, filling it again, passing cup after cup across the counter to customers, trying not to engage. Mostly, it's Fi now who smiles, nods, enquires after their children, their jobs, remarks on the weather, listens to their everyday hardships: unruly teenager, holiday disaster, washing machine on the blink, flat tyre.

Before, I'd listen sympathetically, tut along with them, even issue a "Seren Special".

"You poor thing. See that bottle of wine there. Well, go home, feet up, and administer 150ml. With food! Tomorrow will be better."

Now, I find triviality challenging, often struggling not to issue a death stare when people catch me listening, then try to cover up by saying something like, "It could always be worse, isn't that what they say?"

I used to say things like that too. Until I realised people haven't one iota what it feels like when it actually *is* worse. Tomorrow isn't always better. More than once, I've caught myself wanting to say, "If you can't deal with your bloody car breaking down, you'll be rightly screwed if your –" But I don't, of course.

"I was just saying I'm not going to drive later. I know I said I would, but I've decided." Fi nods determinedly.

"Okay." I frown. I can't remember a conversation about who was going to drive. I hadn't thought that far ahead yet.

"Unless you still want me to. It's just …" Fi begins, then edges closer, so we're both concealed by Big Bertha, and lowers her voice. "It's just, it's still not happening, you know?"

I nod, hoping she won't realise that I really don't know. I've obviously missed something – hardly surprising, but I can't ask again. Asking Fi to repeat herself is all I seem to do. My perpetual state of distraction is nothing new, but today I'm notably absent.

Thankfully she continues, "Month after month and bloody nothing. I told Kevin last night I can't take much more."

Kevin is Fi's husband of five years – an adorable guy who is quite remarkable at everything, except making money, according to Fi. He's a boat broker who works down near the marina, *not* buying or selling any boats.

"Tricky business," I'd heard Bobby Cronin say on a few occasions. "You either make a bomb selling Gin Palaces and yachts to rich city folk, or you'd make more stringing seashells together."

Kevin is more one-man dinghies than Gin Palaces and,

even at that, business is slow. A while back, Fi confided that if the job here at Quelle Surprise hadn't come along when it did, they might have been forced to eat a dinghy. If nothing else, my misfortune was her fortune.

"Maybe it's time for Kevin to try doing something else?" I suggest, hopefully. "Find another way."

This time Fi looks confused. "What would you suggest?" She jerks her head back and frowns. "Stick it in my ear!"

My eyebrows knit. "Are you talking about Kevin's job?"

Fi stares at me for a moment and then snorts, "No! Jesus Christ, I thought you'd completely lost it there." She leans closer. "I'm talking about getting pregnant." This time she looks utterly forlorn.

"Getting pregnant?"

"Yes. You know when a man and woman love each other very much and –" Fi does a gyrating action, then makes an arc over her stomach with her hand.

I roll my eyes.

"Seren, sometimes I think you need a hearing aid. You should get that checked." Then she whispers again, "Yes, getting pregnant. Remember, I told you? We spoke about it a few weeks ago."

This time, I shake my head. "Yeah. Sorry. Of course." Had we? Perhaps I am going deaf. I try to focus, stop my mind from wandering once more. Already, I feel like the worst friend in the world.

"So, I counted back. It's been well over two years now," Fi says. "I'm sick to the teeth of horrific robotic sex. It's awful. I'm just short of saying 'Stick it in there, Kevin' while I watch the telly. And, believe me, I've tried to forget about it just like everyone keeps telling me but, the more I try, the more I can't stop thinking about it. I'm obsessed! Like, what if it sends me over the edge and I end up like yer one in that programme we watched who took a baby from the playground –"

I give a half-laugh. "Please don't steal a baby! You're no use to me in jail."

She manages a brief smile before her eyes well. "The doctor wants to send us for tests." She bites her lip to stop the tears.

I'm surprised. It usually takes a lot to upset Fi.

"You know I haven't touched a drop of alcohol in weeks. Kevin gave up the fags, even socially, and how could we ever afford IVF?" Her voice catches.

I'm lost for words. "Oh, Fi!" I place my hand on hers – her face caves for a moment, her eyes falling to her feet before she shakes her head.

"It's fine, really. I shouldn't complain. I've loads to be thankful for. Sorry." Fi glances up at me sheepishly. "What do they say? Not everyone gets everything."

I pause before I answer. This isn't a trivial complaint or a flat tyre. To Fi, this is obviously huge. "My mum used to say that." I smile sadly. "And of course I know it, but don't feel you have to play it down for me, Fi. This is important. If you want to talk about it, do." My stomach is heaving, but I push the feeling aside.

Fi smiles gratefully. "*All* I want is a baby," she gushes. "People keep telling me these stories. You know about someone they know who tried for years and then out of the blue got pregnant with sextuplets or something mad. I'm not greedy, Seren. I just want one. Christ, I want one so badly I ache." She closes her eyes and places her hand on her flat stomach. At the same time, her features morph. Instantly, I recognise the all-too-familiar look – yearning, pain, anguish. I had no idea Fi felt this way. The guilt hits me like a punch. If I could take her pain away, tuck it next to my own, I would. After all, what's a little more?

"You're only thirty-two," I encourage her. "There's still time."

"Not if there's something wrong. It doesn't matter how old I am then."

I nod absently. "I suppose not."

"Maybe it's a good thing." Fi forces a smile. "I'd probably be an awful mother. And we haven't a pot to piss in, so …"

Fi would make an amazing mother. She's young and happy and alive, unlike me who's dead inside. I put my arms around her, and try to hug away the fact that very soon, instead of helping, I'll be adding to her problems.

Fi pulls away. "So I've decided to stop trying! Leave it in the hands of fate. Instead, I'm going to get steaming drunk at Jane's do tonight. With you! On margaritas. How about it?"

I want to tell her that it sounds like the best idea I've ever heard. I almost say as much. "You know what? I'll drive," I hear myself say instead. "That way, you can drink *all* the margaritas, and I'll chauffeur you home. It'll save on the taxi."

Fi looks so grateful that my heart twists.

"Maybe you'll get pregnant tonight." I nudge her and wink.

"*Nah!*" She throws her eyes up. "Kevin's away looking at a boat. As far as tonight goes, you'd have more chance of getting pregnant!" Her hand flies to her mouth almost as soon as it's out. "Jesus, Seren, I didn't mean … Christ, I'm sorry … that was an idiotic thing to say. I –"

Her apology is broken by a cough. I turn towards the

counter to see Derbhla standing there. I glance back at Fi, whose face is puce.

"Fi, it's okay. Really. I know what you meant. Don't think about it again. It was –"

Another cough. "Now, Derbhla." I take a breath.

Once again, Derbhla has managed to be the final customer of the morning. I suspect she hangs around longer than necessary so that she'll be the winner of the brown-paper bag of leftovers. We bake what we need for each day. It's the reason we had the catering kitchen installed years ago. The pastries usually all sell. If they don't, I'm happy to give them to the last customer of the morning. More often than not, it's Derbhla.

Fi maintains that there's something Derbhla requires far more than the leftover pastries. She'd suggested it one day after we'd both witnessed Derbhla running her forefinger across the table, lifting it under her nose to inspect it and then, wait for it, take a sniff.

"Mother of God," Fi had snorted, "she's unreal! Do you what she needs? A good old-fashioned ride." She'd waved the handle of the coffee filter at me suggestively. It was one of the few times of late that I'd had to hold my stomach from laughing. We'd laughed on and off all morning, unable to stop, sporadically having to turn our backs for a moment to try and pull ourselves together.

"You've some laugh, Seren. I had no idea." Fi's shoulders had been shaking.

The smile had dropped from my face like I'd been caught doing something I shouldn't. Fi hadn't noticed. All I could think was how strange it was that she'd been working with me for almost two years and never heard me laugh that way – the way I used to. What was even more shocking was that she liked me anyway – this lesser version – the person I now am.

"Sorry to interrupt your little chat, girls." Derbhla is smiling like a ventriloquist's dummy. Her eyes flit towards the leftover pastries and, wanting to get rid of her fast, I catch Fi's eye and nod. Fi nods back and shovels the remainder of the treats into the bag.

"There are some extras for you today. Shame to see them go to waste," I say with a grin.

Derbhla pulls out the surgery debit card (of course), and Fi passes the machine across the counter. The card beeps and, as the receipt prints, Derbhla says, "Can I ask if you've changed the recipe for the pastries? They seem different lately. Actually, I've noticed it for quite some time now."

I tilt my head, stick my bottom lip out and shake my head. "No, not at all. Why do you ask?"

She sucks her cheeks in and squints. "The method, is it?"

"How so?" I frown as I move out from behind Big Bertha to beside Fi, wondering what today's complaint will be.

Derbhla pops the card back into her wallet, puts it in her bag and pats it before answering. "They seem smaller. And ... darker," she adds.

I narrow my eyes. "Do you mean burnt?"

"Oh, I don't want to insult. Maybe it's more the size. They're half of what they used to be."

Fi is trying and failing to stifle a giggle. I see her opening her mouth and, before I can stop her, it's out. "You know what they say? Size *does* matter, Derbhla. So, you like a big one, is it? And not too dark?"

Derbhla's mouth drops open, and her eyes grow round. I'm desperately trying not to laugh. It's the height of disrespect, I know, but she really has picked the wrong day.

Derbhla blinks several times. "Honestly! If you can't take constructive criticism, and you're happy to laugh at customers, then so be it. It seems to me that standards in this establishment have dropped. For well over a year, this place has been going downhill. It used to be –"

My face changes so suddenly that even Derbhla falters. "What did it used to be, Derbhla?"

"Well. It was …" Her head is vibrating, and she can't get the words out.

"And for how long has it being going downhill, Derbhla?" I urge.

Derbhla is blinking furiously, and no one is smiling anymore. I feel Fi's hand on the small of my back, trying to guide me away, but I won't budge.

Placing both hands on the counter, I lean forward. "Well?"

"I … I …"

I can feel it happening. I can picture myself inching towards her face in a parallel universe and shouting the words right at her. In that place, I scream them so loudly that I have to wipe the saliva from my raging mouth. Because I know the answer. I know what she wants to say. Instead, I inhale and slowly blow out.

Straightening up, I swallow, then woodenly ask, "Will that be all, Derbhla?"

Derbhla recoils as though she's somehow heard every syllable of my imaginary outburst.

I don't wait for her answer before I turn towards the door to the house and flee through it, taking the stairs two at a time, even though there's no escape. I can't outrun reality, nor the fear of ending up as miserable as Derbhla

with only her job and her sad little routines. She's alone –
like me.

Inside my bedroom, I stand panting, trying not to close
my eyes. If I do, the reel will start, and I can't bear it. It's
always there turning behind my eyes – like a strobe light,
alternating between me standing here against the
bedroom wall, and the other version – the screaming one,
keening like an animal. I try to suppress it for fear that
one day I might say aloud what I'd inwardly screamed at
Derbhla: "It's been one year, three months and twenty-
eight days. That's when the place started to go downhill.
That's when my husband left me. That's when the
fucking croissants got smaller. Because he's fucking *dead*.
He's *dead*."

Oh God, help me, André, my entire life, is dead and
there's nothing I can do to bring him back. Cathy tried to
warn me. Nothing will ever return him to me. My God, I
also ache, just like Fi, but not for a baby. I ache for
something else entirely. This time, I close my eyes because
perhaps I deserve the pain – the agony of my actions.

Chapter 5

I'm preoccupied as I pull open the door, knowing I'm late to collect Fi and I visibly startle when I see Bobby Cronin standing there on the front step with his arm extended to knock. I place the palm of my hand over my heart and exhale. "Jesus!" I smile then so as not to make him any more embarrassed than he already looks.

Too late. Bobby has already reddened from the neck of his thick navy sweater to the roots of his hair.

"Sorry, Bob. I wasn't expecting you."

"That's all right."

"What can I do for you?"

I expect he's been home to his cottage up on Dolphin Bay after a day on the boat and isn't long out of the shower. He looks well – smarter than usual – dressed in dark jeans and deck shoes. I remember being surprised once when I saw an ancient-looking tortoiseshell comb inside a chipped mug next to a few pens on the dashboard of his boat. I'd never thought that Bobby might be one to care about his appearance, but he's never scruffy – more windswept. Over time, I've noticed that Bobby has two looks – rugged seafaring and slightly-more-polished seafaring. The difference between those guises is subtle, but by how his still-damp hair is brushed neatly to the side, I'd say this is the polished version.

"Here." Bobby thrusts a bag at me. The opaque plastic is stuck in places to the scales of whatever fish is inside. "Mackerel. Caught them earlier," he clarifies, then looks me up and down, perhaps as surprised by my more refined appearance as I am by his.

After I'd calmed earlier, I'd stood in the walk-in wardrobe at a total loss regarding what to wear to Jane's event. Turning up in jeans wasn't an option. The past few years aside, she's spent a lifetime trying to get me to update my clothes. Forever telling me that "It's an out-and-out sin to waste that figure and a face that needs feck all make-up" – her words, not mine – "going around dressed like a teenager."

In the end, to appease her, I'd rooted out one of the two dresses I own – one that I once remembered her saying wasn't entirely dreadful.

Despite it being the nicest thing I own, the other one – the dress I'd worn to my husband's funeral – wasn't an option. Cathy had bought it for me on a hurried trip to Brown Thomas in Cork to find something suitable to wear to André's farewell. Knowing her, it had probably cost a small fortune. Knowing me, she'd already removed the tags before giving it to me. I knew she'd wanted to but wasn't permitted to say how good I looked after I'd slipped it over my head and tugged the stretch fabric over my frail body. Instead, I'd said it for her. "I am one hot widow." The unintentional joke, the absolute absurdity

43

of my new status, had initiated a fit of hysterical laughter before my face had crumpled.

"I can't," I'd pleaded.

"You can."

I did. Somehow, I made it through that day, armoured by the black designer dress. I'll never wear it again. What you wear weeping over the body of the love of your life is hardly something out of which you try to get more wear by teaming it with boots and a cardigan for a different look – one other than heartbroken. I should probably throw it away, but it remains the last thing I wore in André's presence. Not that he saw me in it. André was there but gone – his eyes unseeing, his senses vanished – laid out in a coffin wearing his favourite sweater, the infamous tweed cap in his hand. No, André never got to see me in the dress that hid the fact that I hadn't touched food in weeks. Its three-quarter-length sleeves concealed the bruises on my arms from where I'd dug my fingers into my flesh to prevent myself from disintegrating. So I keep it as if the dress somehow connects me to him or to that day. I know, it makes no sense. Then again, there's very little about loss that does. Some people chase white feathers, butterflies, robins, rainbows. Recently, I went a step further.

"Ah, you're very good. Thanks, Bob," I say now. "Give me a sec." I take the bag of fish and go back inside, desperately trying not to heave at the thought of what's inside. The memory of mackerel sizzling on the pan hits anyway – a dusting of flour, olive oil, a squeeze of lemon. "*Delicieux.*" André's voice echoes, and I laugh as he playfully grabs me from behind, dips me backwards, pretends to gnaw my neck. I brush him off as I prepare a salad, pour the wine, cut some bread to shove under the grill – our favourite supper.

Now, the imagined smell of the fish makes me want to hurl. I rush down to the kitchen, holding the bag as far away as possible, just like Marian Cummins with a sack of Tiny's shit. Tugging open the freezer door, I pull out the top drawer and push this bag on top of all the others – at least twelve. I know … but I can't bring myself to insult Bobby or cook anything that would remind me of André. For a second, I almost smirk at what André might say if he knew that the smell of mackerel was his legacy. Or that I was sinfully wasting such gloriously fresh fare. "Stop acting the maggot, *ma chérie*. Eat the fish, girl!" You don't get more Cork than adding "boy" or "girl" to the end of each sentence. After almost eighteen uninterrupted years in Ballycross, André had spoken what I'd labelled "Fork" – a mix of French and Cork dialect, at times making him sound as if he'd been born right here in Cork, instead of Bordeaux, France.

I'm back, slamming the fridge shut and swallowing hard as bile travels up my neck. I can't decipher if it's the thought of the fish or something else that has turned my stomach. All day I've felt strange, as though I'm walking on unsteady ground. I shake it off and head back towards the front door like a puppet controlled by strings through a trapdoor in the roof.

"Sorry, Bob. I just wanted to pop them in the fridge," I smile. "I'm off out to *Más* this evening."

Bobby looks surprised. "Right. Okay. Well, I suppose it's not unusual to turn to God, not unusual at all, S-heren."

"Not church Mass. *Más!*" I laugh. "It's the name of Jane's new Mexican restaurant. Tonight is the opening above in Cork."

45

"I see." He looks uneasy as if he wants to say more.

It's not like Bobby. Usually, he does his best to keep small talk to a minimum. It's odd, other than me, sometimes I think Bobby Cronin is the only person badly affected by Andre's death. They'd been really close. Of course, Cathy and Dermot, Jane and Frank, had suffered too. Afterwards, their lives had changed, but not in the same way. They still had each other. I suppose if Bobby Cronin is like the commanding officer of Ballycross, then André Dubois had been his second in command. If Bobby ever needed a hand with anything, it was André he'd call to heroically tow a boat that had lost its mooring, launch a boat, lift something impossibly heavy.

When André first returned to Ballycross, Bobby had rented him a room in his cottage. To some, André's sudden arrival with a single bag of his worldly possesions may have seemed mysterious. Only, he'd already spent a summer in Ballycross when he was nineteen. That was the first time I fell in love with him, at seventeen. I'd never expected to see him again until he materialised out of the blue years later. André used to say that Ballycross was the first place that crossed his mind to visit after his parents' death. I'd liked that. That mine, too, had recently died immediately set us on common ground. Like me, he'd been floating, searching for what to do next.

He'd found me and the view from Bobby's cottage across the sea. "Like therapy," he'd claimed, describing how he and Bobby would sit out back watching the freight boats coming and in and out of Cobh, chatting about nothing in particular.

"It was he who convinced me to stay here in Ballycross," André said once.

"Not me?" I'd thrown him a disgruntled look.

"*Mais, oui,* but Bobby said if there was nothing wrong with where I was, then why leave? To stop looking for life and start living. If I was 'appy, then I was 'ome. And I *am* 'appy." He'd put his arms around me and kissed me. "I *am* 'ome – not where I was born, but where I'm meant to be."

Despite his claims, for a short while I'd had this terrible fear that André might one day turn around and tell me he was heading back to France. The concern vanished after seeing how he'd anchored himself to Ballycross, immersing with abandon into the "'appy" life. André rarely spoke of France, aside from the wine, of course, and his evocative description of the land, the vineyards from where they originated. I think after his parents died, and with no family in France, he'd enjoyed the stability of Ballycross – with me, our business, his pastime – out fishing with Bobby at the weekends or during the long summer evenings.

"What do you talk about out there? Bobby barely speaks," I'd joked once.

André had pursed his lips and shrugged – so impossibly French.

"And he's so old!"

"Bobby? Old? He's not as old as you think!"

"How old is he then?"

"I don't know." The shrugging again.

"Ask."

"*Non!* You ask!"

"Maybe I will."

They were an unlikely friendship in one way, and in another they were perfect for each other – both unflappable, strong, kind, reliable, equally content in the world of Ballycross, with no desire to step outside it. No one (as they so often had with others) ever dared to call André Dubois a blow-in. Besides, I'd always had a sneaking suspicion that most people liked him more than they liked me. (Perhaps confirmed when people starting calling the shop *André's* instead of Quelle Surprise.) It hadn't really bothered me. In truth, I'd understood it. He was *that* charming, *that* nice, *that* amazing. In many ways, it still feels like I'm the one who's living in André's world.

"Never liked Mexican food much," Bobby announces suddenly.

Pulling my leather jacket around me further, I pick up my bag and jingle my keys as a hint that I need to go.

"All a bit busy," he went on. "Bits here and there, like. Seems like a lot of work, having to put it all together yourself and that. And what's that green stuff, like mashed potato?"

"Guacamole." I grin at his description. "It's not for everyone," I agree.

"You can't beat the spuds." He shakes his head. "Himself thought the same."

Even in the thick of grief, it's still funny. How André and the Irish potato had been a match made in heaven. That and the fact that there had been a hugely popular TV ad for Kerrygold butter in the eighties featuring a sort of ruggedly handsome French fella, also called, wait for it … André. In it, after spending the day at sea and catching a few "*poisson*", Frenchie lifts his tweed cap to a sort of sexy Mary Hick who's cooking the lunch in the kitchen with Mammy and asks, "Is there something I can 'elp?" And all coy, but there's a look of yearning to Mary, she answers, "You can put a bit of butter on the spuds there, André."

It was Cathy who remembered the famous ad after André rolled into Ballycross for a second time. Christ, we used to plague him over it. From that day on, whenever he'd ask anyone if he could 'elp, either Cathy, Jane, or I would have to stifle explosive giggles as we'd whisper the tagline.

Apparently, there were very few women in Ballycross who would have refused André's offer of 'elp, or so I was forever being told. I suppose if you think about it, I was the Mary Hick. I was okay with that. After all, it was always my spuds that got buttered.

"I'd better push on, Bob. I'm going to be dead late." I step outside onto the path next to him and close the door behind me.

"Sure, I won't keep you." He hesitates again. "I just, well, I … it's about *Sher-en-dip-ity* …" Bobby struggles with the word. "Not you, the boat like," he blurts.

Years before, André had treated himself to a decent-sized offshore fishing boat and christened her predictably.

"Is there something wrong with her?"

"No, she's grand. Well, she needs a bit of work, S-heren, and she's just sitting there. The lads from the marina have been on to me." Bobby shuffles from foot to foot. "The yearly fees for the berth are due and –" He holds his hand up to stop me interrupting. "I don't want to rush you and, if it's a financial thing, I want you to know I'll cover the cost if you decide to hang on to her, but I thought I'd better ask. It's been well over a year …"

I stop myself from throwing my eyes at the timeframe. Lately, it feels as though I've surpassed the allocated window for grief. It seems you're afforded just one year, twelve months, 365 days, a chance for each first milestone to pass before you have to come back to reality after you lose your entire world. That's when people start to push you. Besides keeping the shop going, I've failed miserably at making decisions in the aftermath of André's death.

"I'll sell it, Bobby," I say firmly.

He nods. "I think that's wise. I can look after it for you. Free of charge, that goes without saying. She'll fetch a day-cent amount."

"Actually, Bob. Can you give it to Fi's husband to sell? You know, the fellow down in the portacabin."

Bobby raises his eyebrows.

"They could do with a bit of luck if you know what I mean," I explain.

"Ah, I see. Right you are," Bobby hesitates and then adds, "I'm sorry to spring it on you."

"Life goes on, so they say, the sun keeps rising, the clock ticks." I walk over to the driver's door of my van and open it.

"None of us is getting any younger," Bobby adds, then turns to walk away.

I'm about to climb into the van when I stop and glance over my shoulder. "Hey, Bob!" I call after him. I'm feeling bold after making a decision without crumbling. He turns. "Can I ask you something?"

"You can."

"How old are you?"

He jerks his head back, amused. "I like people to think I'm older than I am."

I grin, amused too. "Why's that?"

He shrugs. "Makes them think I know more than I do." He reaches up and tugs at his fringe. "The hair helps. Runs in the family. Premature grey."

"Go on, I won't tell." I giggle suddenly.

"Fifty-one."

"Oh." I'm shocked. "You *do* like people to think you're older than you are. Not that you look it."

"*Hah.* I'll take the compliment." He laughs in a way that makes him instantly youthful and me giddy. His smile fades then, and he looks at me in earnest. "You're a good person, S-heren. About the boat – are you sure?"

"I'm sure."

Perhaps Bobby is afraid I'll regret my decision.

Until now, there's been only one phone call a few months back that made me respond as fast. Was it a coincidence that it came on a day when I'd never thought it possible to feel so low, so alone, so in need of … something … anything? I'm not trying to make excuses, but the voice on the other end of the line sounded warm and safe, as if it genuinely understood how I was feeling at that precise moment. Was that what made me do it? I'd listened to myself making the arrangement and fixing a time, and all along I couldn't believe that it was me speaking until I was there in front of them, and one thing was leading to another and then, "Are you sure?"

Again. "I'm sure."

Only I'm not. As I watch Bobby walk away, something stirs. There's a part of me that wants to call him back – ask him to come with me tonight. For a strange fleeting moment, I can picture him standing next to me. I close my eyes. Instead of the past, I catch a glimpse of how things might have turned out if I'd allowed life to dictate, as I used to. If I'd sat back on my hands and done nothing. Why the hell am I noticing now that Bobby Cronin has an honest smile and clear eyes? Or that he's not as quiet as I first thought or even as old. Or that for the first time in so very long, I've felt normal talking to him – like the old me. Why now, when it's too late?

I was wrong about Bobby, but he's wrong about me too. I'm not a good person. Giving Fi's husband a boat to sell isn't enough to make me the person he thinks I am. Opening my eyes, I take a deep breath, wishing I could reverse it all. But precisely like Cathy warned me months before, I can't. Only now do I finally comprehend what she'd meant and the actual consequences. This morning at my appointment, I'd sat staring ahead, trying to make sense of the words. I suppose I should be happy, but I'm filled with dread – terror mixed with regret in place of happiness.

Chapter 6

The name certainly works. *Más* is everything I thought it would be, only more. Straight away, I can see the goal has been achieved. Everything about the place screams Jane: the vibrant colours, the music, the energy. It's as if Mexico itself has glided over the trendy side street off Patrick's Street, sprinkling it with life. There's an enormous yellow neon sign behind the bar with the words, "Más is Más". *More is More*. It's what Jane always responds to Cathy's "less is more" mantra when she's trying to be all doctorlike and reserved. I grin at the pun before noticing, but then again, how could you miss it that the bar and waiting staff are dressed head-to-toe in black, teamed with Day-of-the-Dead-style make-up. If Jane's goal is publicity, she'll undoubtedly get it from this launch.

Fi and I are just inside the door, on the other side of the heavy black-leather drape that hangs ceiling to floor in front of the entrance. It's there to ensure that you can't see anything from the street until you're on the other side of the curtain. It's worth the wait. Think exposed brick, white subway tiles, dripping candles, shelves with every type of tequila imaginable, high tables, low lighting. The wow-factor has caused a backlog of people loitering near the entrance. Slowly, we're nudged forward.

A waiter welcomes us. With the heat, his skull facepaint has started to melt near his painted-on teeth. "Can I take your coats, ladies?"

"I'll hang on to mine," I say. I think he smiles. It's hard to tell.

"Plenty of flesh on his bones," Fi leans over and whispers to me, then shimmies her coat off and hands it to him. "Thanks, Skeletor." He winks, and she omits a high-pitched laugh. "Christ, it's all very sexy, isn't it?" She sucks in her cheeks. "Like we're not in Cork anymore!"

Slowly we're pushed forward into Jane's vision. She's spent years planning this and the whole year implementing it. I've been absent for the entire process. All the while I've been drifting in my bubble of despair, I can see she's been busy. Seeing it in the flesh, the enormity of what she's achieved gives me shivers: securing finance, planning permission, perfecting menus, drinks, staffing, builders, architects, interiors, suppliers. I know because we did it ourselves once with Quelle Surprise, only without kids, a mortgage, or big bills to pay. I'm not sure we'd have managed to overcome the same hurdles Jane has. Opening Quelle Surprise in the mortgageless house left to me by my parents and using most of the money André's parents had left him could hardly be considered the risk of the century. Granted, our budget hadn't been huge, so we'd ended up doing a lot of the work ourselves. Having less forced us to get creative, scrimping and saving where we could to ensure that our stock was top-notch.

We'd bought the floor tiles from a house renovation. Our shop counter was the ripped-out kitchen island from the same place, repainted by me. The shelves – reclaimed floorboards from the community centre. Plenty of people had chipped in offering us all manner of items for which André mostly found a use – the melamine "*armoire*" donated by Marian Cummins had been a stretch too far, despite her telling us how much she'd paid for it in the day. As Jane had pointed out, there was a reason why Marian wanted rid of it herself. Anyway, I soon discovered the difference a lick of paint can make to *almost* anything.

André covered in dust with a sledgehammer over his shoulder will be forever ingrained in my memory. As will me, wearing dungarees, splattered in paint and smiling from ear to ear – eating supper sitting on a cushion on the floor, sampling far too much wine, making love, falling asleep, building a dream, a life … all the more to lose in the end. They were good times. In many ways, we'd been lucky. In others, not so much.

A different waiter approaches, expertly brandishing a tray of icy margaritas. Fi's eyes widen as she seizes a salted glass from the tray. I'm about to refuse when I glance up to see Cathy standing at the bar. Her eyes briefly lock with mine before drifting past. Cathy is an expert at letting her gaze travel over you as if she hasn't seen you. When we were younger, she was always able to tell us precisely what lad was checking us out in the pub without making it obvious. Except I know her method too well. In about twenty seconds, she'll look back again. "It's the window of opportunity," teenage Cathy claimed. "Look away. They will too, and it will give you a chance to check them out before they look back."

I take a cocktail glass from the tray just as Cathy looks

back. I give her a nod. She twitches but nods back.

Fi glances at my drink. "I thought you weren't –"

"I'm not. I'll just hold it for you. For when you finish that one."

"God, you're clever. Good plan."

Fi's head is like a lighthouse, rotating on her neck to get a good look around. "Oh, look. It's Cathy!" Fi shamelessly gestures to the bar, where Jane too has materialised from the kitchen.

Despite feeling intensely guilty about how I've let things get in our friendship, I can't help but smile when I see her. She looks utterly bonkers, dressed like a modern-day Frida Kahlo wearing a black off-the-shoulder dress with fabric flowers stitched all over the skirt. Her dark hair is plaited and knotted on top of her head, perfectly finished with a floral garland. Her signature hoop earrings are there, as always, as is the red lipstick. Knowing Jane, I imagine she rushed into the shops last night, bought the dress right before closing, then sped home to sew the flowers on herself. As usual, she's pulled it off.

My smile widens as she catches my eye. Instead of looking away, as Cathy just has, her face lights up. She's about to walk towards me when she's interrupted by a panicked-looking chef tugging at her arm from behind. Before Jane disappears to deal with whatever problem has arisen, another emotion pierces her smile. It's ever so brief, but her brow knits. She places her hand on her heart, bobs her head a few times, then blows me a kiss. Catching her drift, I try to ignore my stomach dropping. I blow a kiss back in response to her silent acknowledgement that André should be here and nod once that it's okay. Then she's gone, dragging Frank with her for support. Before he turns, he waves at me and exaggeratedly throws his eyes up to heaven. I smile back. It's impossible not to picture André where he might have been standing with his arms slung around Dermot and Frank's shoulders. Me: tucked next to Cathy and Jane, rolling our eyes ar their antics. It's not okay. It should be the six of us here.

"I was in school with them!" Fi exclaims suddenly, pointing at a group in the corner. "Is it okay if I go say hi?"

I nod profusely. "Of course. Go! Enjoy yourself, Cinderella. You have until midnight before your carriage departs."

Fi kisses my cheek then rushes off, leaving me standing alone, holding the untouched margarita. A sudden longing for everything to be how it once had been balloons inside me and, taking a breath, I squeeze past a group of people and advance towards Cathy.

Before I know what's happening, Dermot hauls me into one of his famous bear hugs. Dermot is a hugger. He hugs like he means it. He's obviously missed me, as this evening's hug is even more vice-grip than usual. Despite a sudden lack of oxygen, it relaxes me. Letting me go, just before I faint, he holds me at arm's length and grins down at me. "*Seren-pippery!*" It's what their daughter, my godchild, still calls me, even though she's now twelve. The cutest mispronunciation stuck. "We've missed you." He leans in. "I'm not prying, but please, *please*," he says out of the corner of his mouth, "sort out whatever's going on. You know what they say – happy wife, happy life. My wife is miserable without you and, in turn, *I'm* miserable. Don't we all know life is too short?" He hugs me again, releases me, picks up his bottle of Mexican beer from the bar, and steps aside so that Cathy is smack-bang in front of me.

57

"Hello." Cathy's face is tight, like a disappointed headmistress.

"Hello," I mimic. "You look lovely." I'm trying to appease her, but she really does, dressed in a black-leather pencil skirt with a fine black knit. Her blonde hair, as always, is perfect. I glance at her feet. "Nice." I nod approvingly at her impossibly high red pointy ankle boots.

"New." She's still clipped.

"Cost enough to educate half of Cork?"

"All of Cork." This time, there's a smile. "You look lovely too." She looks me up and down. "If I recall, the last time you wore that dress, you got yourself wedged into the Little Tyke's police car at our house."

Despite myself, I laugh. "That's right! I forgot about that. André practically had to dislocate my leg to get me back out. It was touch and go whether I'd have to give up the wine shop and veer full-time into toddler law enforcement."

She softens at the mention of his name and places her hand on my arm. "I'm sorry I haven't been on. I did call into the shop today. I just … well, the last time we spoke …"

What I should say is: You mean when I totally compromised our friendship and threw a grenade at my life? Instead, I raise my eyebrows and grimace. "I didn't mean to spring it on you. I should have … I don't know … phrased it better."

Cathy takes a breath, goes to say something then stops. She puts her arm around me.

Giving in, I exhale and rest my head on her shoulder for a moment. Before she can ask more, I say, "What about all this? Jane's done well, hasn't she?"

"Isn't it fab?" Cathy looks around. "I'm glad you came."

"Of course I came. Why wouldn't I?"

"Well, I thought … sorry. Of course. It's good to see you is all."

We're both being cautious, cagier than usual, but it's a start.

"Knock that back." Cathy points at my glass with a glint in her eye. "I'll get us another. Let's get pissed."

I know what she's doing. If asked, I'd tell you the colour of my knickers with a few drinks on board. It's not going to work tonight. I look uncertainly at the glass in my hand, then back at her. "Actually, I'm driving."

Her eyes flash up. "Oh. How come?"

I can't meet her eyes. Instead, I gesture at Fi, who's in full flow with her friends. "Ah, Fi's been having a hard time, so I said I'd drive. She doesn't have the money for a taxi."

"Yeah, but you do." She's quick.

"You know what?" I say. "You're dead right. I think I'll leave the car and have a few. Good plan."

Cathy looks appeased and grabs another couple of margaritas from one of the skeletons and hands one to me.

The conversation is cut short by the distinctive sound of Mexican mariachi. We glance towards the kitchen to where three men wearing sombreros march through the door, singing and playing the guitar. The place erupts as Jane follows, swishing her skirt and clapping. Unsurprisingly, the press photographers are lapping it up. Behind Jane, a line of waiters emerge, holding trays lined with taquitos, tostadas, bowls of nachos – a small taste of what to expect when *Más* formally opens next week. As people converge to tuck in, I'm pushed out of the circle at the bar. I take the opportunity to put down both drinks. I have no intention of drinking them – it's not worth the risk. Grabbing a prawn taco off a passing tray, I examine it.

"Not your poison, either?" I turn to see Hazel, Jane's aunt, next to me. "These aren't bad." She picks up one of the discarded margaritas and takes a slug. Hazel is honestly a lovely person, but let's just say she isn't someone with whom you'd want to get trapped in a lift. For as long as I can remember, we've called her "Hiking Hazel" since it's literally all she does, and mostly all she talks about. Her husband left her years before for his secretary. The cliché bothered Hazel more than him leaving. "A blessing in disguise," she'd told me in the queue for the bathroom at Jane's wedding. "I get far more thrills from the hills."

I place the taco back down. "I ate before I came out," I lie.

"All a bit much, isn't it?" Hazel looks about. "Bit dark. Nothing like the light at the top of Sheep's Head in Bantry. Have you been up?"

Usually, this is where I'd make my escape, but right now, I'm happy to let her chat away and drink my drinks for me. While Hazel details said mountain light, I catch Cathy watching me again. Tonight, she's as alert as the *Skibbereen Eagle* logo, keeping an eye on me. Hazel's already on the second drink, so I pick up the other now-empty glass and wave it at Cathy. Then I turn my eyes in and stick out my tongue to convey that the margaritas are taking effect. Cathy gives me the thumbs-up.

"So, anyway ..."

I tune back in to Hazel, who has hiked on without me.

"It's like I always say, as soon as I learned to use the compass and the map, well, there was no holding me back."

I'm just thinking how a compass is precisely what you'd need to stay on track with this conversation when Hazel narrows her eyes.

"You stepped out with him, didn't you?" She points to where Jane's brother, Simon, is standing alone near the entrance, looking deeply uncomfortable.

Simon catches my eye, looks away quickly, and then does that thing where he reaches up and unconsciously scratches the back of his head. His hair is thinner now, I note. Surely that must help his itchy scalp.

"Briefly," I answer.

"Terrible drip. I probably shouldn't say it, him being my nephew and all, but he was an argumentative little fecker even as a child. Terribly mean too. Apparently that's why the wife left him." Hazel hasn't lowered her voice in the slightest for the revelation.

Simon glances over again, and I fix my eyes on the ground.

"He'd ration a tomato if he could."

I laugh. "Actually, we were engaged once for about three weeks."

It was shortly after my parents died. Simon was ... well, there. The entire experience was akin to being trapped in an endless round of Simon Says. You know that children's game where "Simon" issues a list of instructions preceded with "Simon Says". He'd actually use those very words. "Simon says, pass me the remote." "Simon says, make me tea." He tried it once during sex, then tried to claim he was joking. He wasn't.

When I finally saw sense, it gave me immense satisfaction to yell, "*You forgot to say Simon says!*" on the day I ended our relationship, and he shouted after me to

"Come back here right now, or you'll be sorry!" I know now that all Simon wanted me for was my house, a comfortable life, a pliable wife. Despite his chronic psoriasis and demanding I massage lotion into his flaky scalp, I almost fell for it. Serendipitously, or whatever you want to call it, died shortly after we'd got engaged I unexpectedly ran into André down by the benches near the harbour – entirely out the blue. Within about twenty seconds, I knew I'd have to finish with Simon. An hour later, I was single. Mind you, not for long.

It was, in fact, the second time André saved me from Simon. The first was when I was seventeen. For some bizarre reason that no one, least of all Cathy or Jane (his own sister) could understand, I was obsessed with Simon that summer. That is until I met that French student. If it wasn't for André, I would have spent that entire summer pining after Simon, who wouldn't give me the time of day. If it wasn't for André showing up again years later on his travels, I might have spent my entire married life wondering how to ditch Simon without destroying my friendship with Jane. I needn't have worried. Apparently, the thought of socialising with her creepy brother for the rest of her life had terrified her.

"Good Lord," Hazel says with a nod. "I remember that now. A lucky escape! I was sorry to hear all about that other business."

I assume she's referring to André's death.

"I bet you have all sorts saying stupid things like it's better to have loved and lost than never to have loved at all?" She tuts. "It isn't, of course. It's far worse, but I suspect you must know that."

"I've heard it all," I agree.

"And how is life? I imagine it's a great big pile of shit."

I shrug. "It's okay. You know, I used to love my life, but it doesn't seem to fit me anymore."

Hazel tips the remainder of *my* drink back. "You know what I did when my trousers no longer fitted in my forties? I hiked on! Talking of hiking, I'd better find the loo. I suspect it's avocado-shaped or something bizarre." She's slurring slightly. "There's a world outside Cork, you know, Seren? You're young. You've no appendages."

I hope she means children.

"Go find yourself."

I watch Hazel weave away, thinking of her trousers metaphor. Never have I ever considered leaving Ballycross and existing elsewhere. Travelling, wanderlust, the need to escape isn't something I've experienced. André and I never even visited France! I know, it sounds insane not to have seen where he was born – the country around which our entire business is based. I've thought about it a bit lately, why we never went when we had the chance. All I can come up with is that we'd been happy in our bubble here. André always insisted that Ballycross was his real home, that without family in France it wasn't the same. And I suppose having the wine shop, open seven days a week, tied us. But Hazel's words have rattled me. The sudden need to unfasten, find something new that fits my life is overwhelming. Perhaps if I'd spoken to Hazel before now, she might have made me see that what I needed was a change of scene. But how can I leave Ballycross now after what I've done? Then again, how can I stay?

I scan the room. Fi is nowhere to be seen, Jane is schmoozing, and Cathy is scrutinising me while keeping her distance. An intense feeling of paranoia washes over me. Cathy knows. Deep down, I know she does. I suppose I should get used to it. Sooner rather than later, an entire village will be studying me.

Chapter 7

"I just want to talk." Cathy's drunk.

"What the hell are you doing skulking after me? You frightened the shite out of me." I'm still pointing the car key like a knife from where I've turned suddenly to startle my "attacker". My other hand is on my heart.

"Where are you going? You can't drive. You've been drinking."

We're up the road from the restaurant next to where I parked the van. I can see by how Cathy is standing with her hands on her hips, leaning heavily on the tilting heel of her left boot, that Jane's cocktails have unleashed "Contentious Cathy" – born after a phase of drinking whiskey with Coke in our twenties. At her tipping point, Cathy would end up starting these impossible, twisty-in-every-direction debates that made her sound like a boozed-up politician. She'd always win. Not because she was always right, but because she was relentless.

"Well?" she asks again.

The heel of her boot gives way, but she manages to

right herself.

I almost laugh. "I'm really tired," I sigh instead, dropping both hands to my side.

"You can't go now. It's still early. Why are you leaving?" Cathy persists.

For a moment, I consider telling her that I've come out to get something from the van to get rid of her, but then I'm so desperate to get home that I can't bring myself to continue the charade. After speaking with Hazel, the evening hadn't got any better.

"I just had enough, okay?" I say truthfully, then before I can stop myself, "It was the speech."

"The speech?" She frowns at me like I have ten heads. "Jane's speech?"

"Ah, come on, Cathy."

I know I wasn't the only person to have interpreted it as I had. Hazel, too, had sought me out and rolled her eyes in solidarity. One or two others had turned to see where Jane was directing her words. From my shocked face, it wasn't hard to deduce that I was the one connected to "the one person who isn't here tonight but should be". For this part, Jane had fought and failed to hold back gulping tears. "Without him, we might not even be here. He made me realise how short life really is, that *today* is the day to follow your dream. And this restaurant is *my* dream. To André!"

"I don't think she was trying to upset you," Cathy says. "You know she gets a bit philosophical when she's had a few. She probably thought she was doing something nice. And André *should* be here. *We* miss him too, Seren."

"I know that. It's just … it's hard to explain."

"André's death affected us all. *All* of our lives will

never be the same. You have to know that."

I close my eyes and swallow. "I do. It's not that. It's –
"

"Well, what? Explain it to me." She comes closer, taking both my hands in hers.

I look up at the sky, trying to find the words, then back at Cathy. "It's just, do you know how many people have told me that André dying changed their lives … for the better?" I give a short, sharp laugh. "People have given up smoking, changed jobs, had a reality check, opened restaurants …" I raise my eyebrows. "Hugged their wife, had sex with their husband, vowed to walk the dog more often, watched their children sleep, counted their blessings, booked a holiday." I pause. "Thanked God it was me and not them." My shoulders heave with the words.

"Oh, Seren."

I inhale, then release it with a shudder. "Like *he* had to die so everyone else could see how short life is. So they could fix their lives or relationships or whatever. Why did it have to be André? Why not me? He was a better person than I am. He never hurt anyone, ever, and he wouldn't be standing here saying horrible things like I am." My chest deflates as I finish.

"Seren. You *are* a good person. Please don't say that," Cathy begs, suddenly incredibly sober. "We know how you must feel."

I don't argue but, truthfully, they've never mourned more than the loss of a family dog or Jane's obese hamster. Don't get me wrong. I'm happy they haven't because someday they will. Until then, they can't know how I feel. Both Cathy and Jane still have their parents. Before André, I'd already lost mine. I knew the hollow ache of loss, the emptiness that eventually dims but never really leaves. Arrogantly, I'd believed I'd never have to face it again, at least not so soon. Never, not in a million years, could I have guessed what would happen. It hit me with the intensity of being run over by a train. If having André felt like compensation for my parents' loss, losing him felt like punishment for something terrible I'd never done. It blindsided me.

"I know." I try to smile. "Maybe I'm just sick of being the widow in the room, you know? I'm like a dried-up hag with facial warts and black teeth."

"You couldn't be further from a hag, Seren. You could never see what other people see, could you? You're sunshine."

"Covered with clouds."

"It's still so new, Seren. Give it time. You still have so much of life ahead. This isn't the end." She pauses while I digest her words.

That's precisely what I'm afraid of – an enormous expanse of life ahead, with nothing to fill it.

"I'm glad you reconsidered that other stuff," she continues.

My stomach drops.

"I understand what you were trying to do, but it wasn't right. I know you know that."

My eyes drop to my feet. I can't meet her glare. If I do, I might give away that I reconsidered nothing. It's already done.

"Come back inside," she urges. "We can have another drink, a giggle –"

I shake my head. "I really am tired."

"Come on. Just one more, as you say yourself! We can all share a taxi later."

"Honestly, Cathy. I have to go. I'll chat with you

tomorrow." I turn towards the van.

"I can't let you drive, Seren. I'd never forgive myself. Those drinks are lethal. Come back inside and call a taxi at least." She truly is relentless.

"It's fine, really. I only had a few."

"But what if you're stopped? It's really not worth it. Look, twenty minutes, and you'll be in a cab. Come on." Cathy takes my arm and tries to lead me back towards the restaurant.

Something inside me snaps. "Can you just let me go, for Christ's sake! I didn't drink, okay?"

Cathy stops suddenly, jerks her head to where I've abruptly pulled my arm away, and then slowly meets my eyes. "Why not?" Her tone is frosty.

"I wanted to be able to leave if I wanted, okay?"

"Why?"

I shake my head impatiently. "Can we not make a big deal out of this? It's nothing. I'm tired, that's all."

"*Is* that all?" Her eyes bore into mine. "Because earlier I had this weird feeling when I saw you that …" her eyes flit down, "but then I thought I was wrong. But I wasn't, was I?" Her hand flies to her mouth. "You're pregnant, aren't you?"

I bite the corner of my mouth and let an approaching couple pass before I answer.

"Yes."

The word hangs in the air.

"Oh, Seren!" She puts her head back and blows out loudly, then shakes her head in disbelief. "I didn't think you'd actually go through with it. I honestly thought you'd come to your senses." She pauses. "How long?"

"A few months," I answer robotically.

"When did you find out?"

"Today," I shrug.

"Is that where you were this morning?"

I nod.

Earlier, I'd sat across from the doctor with my mouth hanging open, barely been able to understand the words "Congratulations, Seren. You're pregnant". All day, they've been playing on my mind, yet it still doesn't seem real. All while Fi was telling me how much she longed for a baby – *Seren, you're pregnant.* While Derbhla was complaining about my substandard croissants – *Seren, you're pregnant.* While Hazel suggested that I hike off and find a new life – *Seren, you're pregnant.* While Jane was honouring my dead husband – *Seren, you're pregnant. Congratulations. Congratulations. Congratulations.*

"Why didn't you come to me?" Cathy looks hurt, then furious. "Jesus Christ, Seren!" She exhales again and looks at the ground. "I don't even know what to say."

I fold my arms and squeeze the flesh with my fingers. "I don't *want* you to say anything." My voice is quiet. "I haven't decided what I'm going to do yet." Cathy's head shoots up so fast that my face twitches. "If I'm going to keep it, I mean." This time, it's barely audible.

"Did you just say 'keep it'?" she snaps. "*Keep it?*" Her voice grows louder. "I fucking hope you're joking." Cathy never curses, so the word stings like a smack across the face. She goes to walk away and then pivots back. "Why go to all this trouble if you're planning on having an abortion? What do think André would say?"

"I didn't say I was planning on having an abortion. I said I haven't decided. Don't bring André into it. It's my choice, isn't it? My body?"

"I don't even know what to say right now," she repeats, despite having already said more than enough.

"Well, stop speaking then!" I snap, holding the palms of my hands out. "It's none of your business, anyway. You can be so superior, Cathy. You always have been. What you said earlier about knowing how I must feel … well, you don't. Okay? You have no idea how alone I am. There's nothing ahead for me." My voice breaks. "I thought … I thought …" I can't finish because, truthfully, I'm not sure what I'd thought. That a baby would heal me? Give me a reason to want to live? I'd never pushed for children, even when I was married. If they'd come along, I would have gratefully accepted it, but it had never been top of my list. It was André who'd started talking about children, quite a lot actually before he'd died. Apparently, it was *all* he'd ever wanted. I hadn't listened until it was late.

Cathy's face softens. "Couldn't you have waited?"

I shake my head. "I'm almost forty years old, Cathy."

"Forty isn't old, not nowadays. And I'm saying that as a doctor. Sure, look at your mum. She was forty-eight having you."

I smile sadly. "Yeah, and Mum was gone by the time I was twenty-two. And now, look at me."

"Okay," she says with a nod. "So you're pregnant. This should be good news. You can't seriously be thinking of terminating it? Do you realise how that sounds?"

"Please, Cathy." I close my eyes to shut out her words. "I can't discuss this now. Except to say, I thought I'd feel differently. I was so sure, but now …"

"What?"

I run my hand down my face. "How can I raise a baby this way?"

"You have us," she reminds me. "We'll help. It's natural to panic."

71

"It's not that."

"Well, what then?"

I shrug my shoulders. "What right do I have? Not to mention that half the time I don't want to be in my own sad life, let alone make another human suffer through it. I thought I was doing something … Oh, Christ. What the hell have I done?" I'm shaking.

"Seren, please, breathe. It'll be okay. You're still in the throes of grief. It's barely more than a year."

I smile sadly. "I thought a year was all I got to grieve – now that a year has passed, it feels like everyone wants me to get over it – but I don't want to forget him –"

"No one wants that, Seren. We only want to help you, but I'm sure we say the wrong thing all the time. As I said before, I think you should speak to someone who knows how to say the right thing. At least, let me tell Jane. She's good in a crisis."

She's right. For someone who appears to have their head in the clouds, Jane can be really practical.

I shake my head. "She has too much going on. Maybe in a few weeks."

"You don't have that long, Seren. How many weeks pregnant did they say?"

"Nine … and a bit …"

"You only have until twelve weeks to decide, and you'll start showing soon. Did you not notice something before now?" Her eyes flit to my stomach. "Are you not sick? Are you …" She glances over her shoulder to see what has distracted me.

"Please don't say anything, Cathy. Not tonight. I don't want to ruin it for her. Please," I whisper.

"There you are!" Jane's floral headband is slightly askew, but she's grinning. "I came out for some air and saw the pair of you. What's going on?"

Cathy looks at Jane and then back at my pleading eyes. "I was just walking Seren to her van. She's up early tomorrow for work."

"Yeah, sorry," I say. "Duty calls. Fi was supposed to work in the morning, but she'll be in no fit state by the looks of things. Will you make sure she gets home, Cathy?"

Cathy nods woodenly.

"I'm so proud of you, Jane," I gush to distract her. "The place is amazing. I'm so sorry I wasn't more help to you with it all. Really."

"Stop! Would you go 'way. We're all busy." Jane throws her arms over our shoulders. "You guys are the best. I miss this. It feels like we're never together anymore." She pulls us in for an embrace. "Promise we'll go away for a weekend soon. When things have settled in a few weeks."

"Absolutely," I lie. God only knows what state I'll be in in a few weeks. "Now, is there anything I can do to help out with the restaurant?"

Jane thinks, then holds up one finger. "There is, actually. Reviews! It's all everyone keeps saying. Get as many online reviews as possible. Obviously, I can't review myself. But if I could, I'd give myself five stars!"

"I'll do it tomorrow. First thing!" I promise. It's the least I can do to alleviate my guilt for not being there for Jane more. "Listen, I have to go. Us entrepreneurs need to look after our businesses." I jog around to the driver's door of the van and blow each of them a kiss. "Get back inside. Go!"

I get in, start the engine and wave as I drive off.

In the rearview mirror I see them link arms and walk back towards the restaurant.

Cathy turns to glance over her shoulder. Even from here, I can see the look of pity. It's the same way she looked at me months before. I'd already decided before I went to see her that day. The visit had been merely a formality. Despite her protests, she'd given in for the sake of our friendship – put her signature to the form claiming that I was of sound mind. I wasn't, but she signed it anyway. Every time she looks at me, I know she wishes she hadn't. I know this because I wish she hadn't either.

Chapter 8

My head is spinning despite having abstained from drinking at the restaurant earlier. I lie back, pull the bedclothes up and attempt to empty my mind. I've left the curtains open, so I can hear the sea, the reassuring clinking of the masts. I won't sleep tonight. I already know that. For an instant, I consider retrieving the small brown bottle of sleeping pills from where they're hidden behind a tube of hair-removal cream in the bathroom cabinet. Lately, they've both gone unused. The tablets are heavy-duty ones, prescribed by Cathy after deciding that my face was the same pale grey as her Farrow & Ball painted kitchen cupboards. "You're Elephant's Breath," she'd lectured, fishing her prescription pad from her handbag and scribbling something illegible. "And while you'd look lovely teamed with a deep navy, you need sleep. Only take them for a few nights." They'd worked. After three nights they'd managed to break the chronic cycle of insomnia after André's death. Now, I save them for dire circumstances as Cathy made me swear. "While they might improve your pallor, they could actually knock out an elephant."

I wonder if tonight would qualify as a dire situation until I remember that the tablets are no longer an option. Nor is alcohol, shellfish, soft cheeses, smoked meats. That said, the thought of most items on the prohibited list that the nurse handed me this morning makes my stomach churn. It's strange. Even though I still can't get my head around it, as soon as the doctor confirmed the "happy news", the feeling of being pregnant had hit me like a lightning bolt. As if him saying the words had made it happen, and not the act itself, weeks before.

Then again, perhaps I've been experiencing it for weeks without realising. I close my eyes and try to think back. I've been tired, more so than usual. It makes sense now that, at times, it's felt like I've been trudging through bogland wearing flippers. I wonder if feeling like you're persistently knee-deep in marshmallow fluff is the tiredness I'd often heard Cathy and Jane describe when they'd been expecting. Had I not been so caught up in hiding it, perhaps I could have asked. I may also have confused the anxious churning in my stomach with morning sickness. Come to think of it, what I've been experiencing isn't all that different from how I've felt ever since André died. Who knew that pregnancy and grief had so much in common? In both cases, you're carrying something alien. Granted, one instance should make you far happier than the other.

The heightened sense of smell has been there too. I'm reminded of Bobby's earlier offering, and I shudder. Perhaps it wasn't the memory of André cooking fish but my aversion to the smell that almost made me retch. Indeed, I've been revolted by plenty of foods that I usually like, note the weight loss … Yes. Now that I know, all the signs were there, and yet I was beyond confident that there was no way I could be pregnant. In my defence, what threw me most was the fact that I'd had a bleed about a month before. It was light, but still enough for me to mistake it for a period. It's why I never bothered to take a pregnancy test or keep my scheduled appointment at the clinic. I genuinely believed *it* hadn't worked. "It" being the procedure. Or perhaps by then, I'd been hoping it hadn't worked.

Despite myself, I smile ever so slightly at the word "procedure", but not in the way I would have before when it wasn't me having one. Jane maintains that a "procedure" always describes something below the waist and above the knee. "Otherwise, why wouldn't you just say what is is? Like you'd say 'I'm having an ingrown toenail or a mole removed'. I'll tell you why," she'd tapped the table with her finger, then glanced at her lap, "because it relates to your downstairs." In hindsight, Jane's probably right.

My "procedure" had an average success rate of just 15-20%. Teamed with my dire levels of fortune, I was convinced it wasn't going to work.

"The majority of women will conceive after the first two to three cycles. We do everything at your pace. Nice, slow, controlled," the doctor had assured me after the initial consult. His voice had been incredibly soothing, like a verbal massage. Actually, everyone who works at the fertility clinic speaks in dulcet tones. It must be a prerequisite to getting the job that you have to sound like Barry White speaking the lyrics of a love song.

"After forty, though," he raised his eyebrows and looked across the desk, "the success rate declines, so we have a window here." He clicked the top of his pen as he spoke like a beat-timer or a biological clock. "After that, we can discuss other options."

"Other options?"

"Donor IVF." He shifted in his chair. "We have only two vials of your husband's sperm. After that, we move in another –"

"That won't be necessary." I was quick.

"I see." He put the pen down and leaned forward. "Seren, I want to make sure that you understand exactly what you're doing. After a loss, some women initially want to ... how can I put this? Conceive soon after a partner's death. It can be a way to ..." He stopped as if he didn't want to say it.

"Keep him alive?" I offered helpfully.

He coughed. "Help with grief." Again he raised his eyebrows. "We offer counselling."

"That won't be necessary," I'd assured him again, pushing the forms that Cathy had already signed, confirming I'd been counselled by my doctor, across the desk.

"Are you sure?"

"I've thought this through. I'm sure."

I had thought about it. I'd thought of nothing else since I'd got that phonecall – the one that spurred me into action. It was the reassuring voice on the other end of the phone that had started it all, offering me an appointment to come in and discuss my options. I remember it well because, that day, for the first time ever, I'd felt like I wanted to die. I couldn't see anything ahead, no hope, no one to love or be loved by. When the phone rang – a courtesy call from the fertility clinic – it felt like a sign. All they'd wanted was to ask if I wanted to continue with storage. It was coming up to two years. There was a cost involved. It wasn't even that much, but it wasn't about the money. I'd started to ask questions, and the voice had been so calm, patient, non-judgemental that suddenly I'd felt a wave of … purpose.

"There's absolutely no rush," it had assured me. "We can carry on as we are if you'd like. Or I can make you an appointment?"

"Please. The sooner, the better."

I'd hung up with a warm feeling in my stomach – the same one I used to get when a teacher would praise me in school. Gradually, I convinced myself that I was doing the right thing, that there was something of André that still existed out there, albeit at well below room temperature. Thinking of it now makes me squeeze my eyes shut and visibly cringe. Is it any wonder Cathy thought I'd lost my mind when I sat in her office afterwards trying to explain how I believed that my dead husband's frozen sperm deserved a fighting chance – a final lap of honour through my cervix?

Over and over, I assured myself that it probably wouldn't work anyway. But at least I'd have tried, and that would be it. The plan was to do it only once, then put it behind me, and live out the rest of my days as the haggard widow. In hindsight, if I'd wanted to ensure it worked, I would have gone for IVF. Instead, I chose IUI – Intra-Uterine Insemination – as a way of letting fate decide. It was all relatively simple, not terribly expensive, or invasive. I'd take a tablet to stimulate my ovaries to produce eggs. Twelve days later, they'd perform an ultrasound. I'd get another medication to trigger ovulation, then the procedure would take place the next day in the clinic, all while Fi thought I was at a health spa.

An hour before the main event, they'd prepare the

79

sample in the lab. In other words, defrost André's little swimmers, then Dr "Barry White" would suck my dead husband's sperm up into a catheter, insert it into my uterus, and I'd lie there. When it actually happened, as odd as it sounds, I remember feeling like André was alive again, for a few minutes at least, and I was finally giving him the chance to leave behind some form of legacy.

"Any regrets?" I'd asked not long after the final diagnosis.

"*Juste un*." Only one.

"Maybe I can fix it."

"Not unless you're a miracle woman."

"Tell me."

"I wish we'd had a child," he said, at last. "You know, someone to share my wisdom with?" he joked, then turned serious. "Someone to carry on my name. Flesh and blood, mine and yours. It all ends with me." It felt like a knife through my selfish heart. It wasn't the first time he'd brought it up. "I can see her, you know." He was lying back on our bed, with my head resting on his chest. "A girl just like you. Or a boy, I'm not fussy." The nonchalant French shrug. "But I always imagine a girl. Your smile. My eyes. Your hair. Perhaps my French charm! Clever, talented, a musician or something like that …"

He'd described her in such detail that it was clear that this imagined daughter had resided for quite some time in his consciousness.

"Instead, I leave behind my pastry recipe. Don't mess it up!" André had remained upbeat until the very end, smiling despite the agony. He'd described it to me only once: sharp, blistering pain. Funny, it was only after he was gone that I'd been able to understand his description. It's how I've felt every day since.

"Promise me you'll live, Seren. Meet someone else. Please, *chérie*."

I'd shook my head, still trying to deny what was going to happen.

"Hey, look at me. We had the dream, *non*? You, me, Ballycross … It was perfect, huh?"

By then, time to continue our idyllic life, time to do all the things we said we would – time to use the frozen sperm in the fertility clinic, was up.

"The word *deposit* is right up there with *procedure*, isn't it?" Once again, Jane's sensitivity had floundered upon hearing what we'd done before André started treatment. "Far too clean a word to describe what it involves." She'd considered this while we sat around the table eating dinner. "What they actually mean is that you were at yourself, looking at slutty yokes with their legs akimbo in one of those magazines?"

"For Christ's sake, Jane!" Cathy shook her head in dismay while I held my breath for André's reaction.

"I've had worse Saturday afternoons. Some of those women would make super gymnasts. Very athletic." He winked while the rest of us exhaled with relief.

"See, told you," Jane confirmed while everyone laughed.

Everyone except Cathy. I'd caught her eye, and she'd smiled stiffly. God, I should have known. I should have bloody known by her that it was more severe than I was willing to believe. But then, you hear what you want to hear. But none of us, not even Cathy, could have imagined that just one year later, André would be dead.

Almost to the very end, I'd had faith that he'd get better, or have longer, at least. Gradually, gentler terms like "area of concern" changed to "slight increase", "make comfortable", and finally "sort your affairs".

There'd be no time for sorting affairs, let alone babies. There was no time for anything other than being with him, watching his body shut down, his mind grow restless, confused, and panicked.

My eyes fly open suddenly, and I push the bedcovers down as if they're attacking me. I'm warm, agitated. I don't like thinking about that part. My hand travels over my stomach, and I press to see if I can feel anything inside, trying to picture the bean-sized existence of flesh and blood that I know is now there. The doctor at the fertility clinic had been thrilled at the rare success. "Someone must have been smiling down on you," he'd enthused. Did he mean André?

I try not to think of Cathy's earlier question: "What do you think André would say?"

Instead, I try to imagine how different it would be if he was still here with his sallow hand resting protectively on my belly. Of everything I miss about him, it's his hands I crave most – his reassuring touch contrasted with rough hardworking skin.

"*Bonjour, chérie.*" The hair on the back of my neck stands up, and I shiver. Sometimes, if I listen closely enough, I can hear him. I hunch my shoulders in pain. "I don't think I can do this," I answer.

He doesn't respond. I sit up, swing my legs over the side of the bed, and walk to the window. No. I don't think I can do this. I don't think I can go ahead with this pregnancy. I try not to think of Fi, aching for a baby. I try not to think about what Cathy had really meant to say earlier. *What kind of monster gets pregnant this way and then aborts it?* She's right. Despite ticking the box on the forms,

I don't think André ever anticipated that I'd do this without him.

"Would you like the gift of my sperm?" André's hand, holding the pen, had been poised over what he'd just read. It was the day we'd visited the clinic after he'd been diagnosed and we'd been advised that chemotherapy could affect fertility.

"What?"

"Here on the form. Let me read. It says … In the event of my death or becoming mentally incapacitated I wish my thawed sperm to be donated to my partner to decide their fate." He was grinning, still sure that everything would be okay in the end.

"*Mais oui, monsieur,*" I'd said with a wink. "It's not going to happen, but still it would be a terrible shame to destroy such potential virility."

"Consider yourself the proud owner of my finest specimens."

No. I'm certain André would never have expected me to do what I have done. I hadn't planned to do it either, until I was given the choice. More worrying still, he'd be horrified by what I plan to do next. I knew my husband. Inside and out, I knew everything there was to know about him, and I know what he'd say. But he's not here, and I don't want this baby. I *can't* have this baby. I turn and pad towards the bathroom, pull open the cabinet, push the hair-removal box aside and pick up the bottle of sleeping tablets. I examine the label, then glance up at my reflection in the mirror, willing myself not to look away, to face it. My mind reels as I try to think of my options. No matter what I decide, someone will hate me. Fi, Cathy, Jane … me. I'm cornered.

My heart pounds in my chest. Opening the bottle's lid, I pour the contents into my hand and close my fist around them. What difference will it make now anyway? I'd wanted to do something … anything to make life make sense again, but I was wrong. I can't bring my husband back, and I can't bring his child into the world already missing the greatest gift I had to offer – André Dubois – the most perfect, honest, generous, unexpected event of my life. He was the best thing to ever happen to me. It hits me like a blow. It's time to accept that there's nothing ahead for me – nothing that can ever come close to before.

Chapter 9

Marie-Hélène

No matter what way Marie-Hélène tries to reason it, André Dubois was still the worst thing to ever happen to her. Encountering him had destroyed her life. Leaning back in her chair, she shakes her head, admonishing herself for letting her thoughts wander. All the while, her cigarette has burned down so that when she takes a drag it bites her lip. She touches her mouth with the fingers of her other hand, winces, then leans forward, twisting the butt into the makeshift saucer ashtray on the metal table in front of her. Straight away, she's tempted to light another, if only to mask the sour stench from the industrial bins lined up next to the fire door at the back of the Bordeaux restaurant.

Glancing at her watch, she once again leans back in the plastic outdoor chair, crosses her legs, adjusts her black work skirt and folds her arms across her stiff white shirt. There's still twenty minutes before she's due back. Despite the chill in the air, she'll wait it out. Already she does far more than for what she's paid – but not tonight.

Tonight, she has other things on her mind. It's almost time. She can feel it closing in, as it has been for weeks now, edging nearer, so it's almost within her grasp. Time was always going to be her greatest challenge, learning to be patient, day after day, year after year, watching, anticipating, existing. She's tired now. She's ready.

Closing her eyes, he appears immediately. Sometimes she can go for months without giving him a second thought, then all of a sudden he leaps into her mind, residing there for months. At these times, there's barely a moment where she isn't trying to conjure his face, his voice, his laugh, how he'd once made her feel. The familiar stirring in her blood makes her shiver. My God, he was handsome: charming, refined. But what had captured her most was the generous twist of manliness. Before that, she hadn't been with many men, had never encountered the unique combination of gentleness and masculinity, nor has she since. For that, she supposes, she should be thankful.

Opening her eyes, Marie-Hélène leans forward and lifts the coffee cup next to the ashtray. She wipes the remnants of her pink lipstick from the rim. The black liquid has gone cold, but she takes a gulp, then cradles it as if it will somehow provide warmth. Tilting her head to the side, she narrows her eyes and chews her lip.

In hindsight, it was André who'd chased after her. At first, she'd tried to refuse, but she hadn't stood a chance against him. From the first moment she'd allowed herself to dissolve in his eyes, deep down she'd known he'd be a part of her life. Just how significant a role she could never have anticipated. She hates him for it, and yet …

Setting the cup down, she lifts the cigarette packet to her mouth, grasps a filter with her lips and lights it. Years before, someone told her she resembled Brigitte Bardot: brown eyes, tousled blonde hair, cigarette. At one time, she'd felt like her too: young, free, beautiful. Now she feels old – far beyond her forty-four years. Old and tired, with spidery lines around her mouth from years of drawing hard on those little brown butts. Excessive drinking hasn't helped either. She rarely admits it, even to herself, but for more than a decade she has drunk far more than she has eaten – to numb the pain, quench her anger. Now, when she looks in the mirror, her skin reminds her of a scrunched-up brown-paper bag.

A few weeks back, she'd been horrified when a table of men – more ignorant pigs – had abused her for the entire evening while she'd served them, laughing and whispering insults under their breath. When she'd tried to tell her overweight obnoxious boss, Julien, he'd howled laughing, repeating the taunt over and over, while clutching his fleshy gut. *"Anus mouth. Anus mouth!"* She'd run to the bathroom with hot tears stinging her eyes. Hurt to her core. She'd stared at her reflection, pathetically trying to smooth out the lines carved into her upper lip. Worse of all, she'd been able to see what they'd meant.

Usually, she wouldn't have batted an eyelid, but that particular insult had stung. Then again, being ridiculed at work is nothing new. Chez Julien, one of the most legendary restaurants in Bordeaux, owned by three generations of Juliens, attracts a specific brand of privileged asshole. She's never understood their interest in the dingy overpriced restaurant with the old-fashioned bistro bench seating (there since the first Julien, she imagines) and low lighting to hide the dilapidated interiors. Nonetheless, Julien's is an institution. Although not much to look at, Julien can cook. All the same, the clientele are the very reason she's been working here for the past year. It's certainly not for the love of Julien and their on-again, off-again relationship. Mind you, on-again was never much more than after-hours drinking and fucking. No, she stays because, after many years of waitressing, she learned that rich pricks tip big as a way to demonstrate how wealthy they really are.

The emergency exit door flies open, and Julien pops his bulging face through it.

"We need you." He rubs his hands down his apron. His face is puce from the heat of the kitchen.

"I'm on my break."

"*Marie-Hélène!*" he sings her name. "Do you want me to put you over my knee?" He smirks, then snorts. "I know you like that."

"I'd rather eat shit."

Julien narrows his bulging eyes. "What's that? That's not what you said before. Or don't you remember? Too drunk? Or will I put you straight on the bar like last time," he sneers, humiliating her back into her place.

"Ten minutes," she scowls, trying to forget, or indeed remember.

"Five. And those things will kill you." He points his stumpy finger at her.

"What would you care?" She takes a defiant drag on her cigarette and blows it out in a long, thin line at where Julian has vanished back inside. For the past few weeks, she hasn't been in the mood for after-hours activities. Her mind is elsewhere, on what lies ahead.

She takes another drag. No one smokes anymore. Even the French, once synonymous with it, gave in. Those who still do huddle outside next to stinking bins like they've something to hide. Smoking is the least of her worries, not when she has far more pressing things to conceal. No one knows her secret. Not one single person. Not Julien, or those pigs she fawns over in the restaurant to make them feel like they're someone. All while they treat her like she's nothing.

Screw them all. Soon enough, they'll know – then it will be different. She won't have to endure them for much longer or endure their abuse. Indeed, if they'd known her back then, they wouldn't treat her as they do now. Back then, she'd been beautiful. *He'd* certainly thought so. She still does her best – wears make-up, keeps her now darkened roots at bay by dying her hair over the sink in the bathroom. Still, sometimes she catches a glimpse of herself in a shop window or a passing car and startles at the wizened woman she sees looking back. After everything, all she was forced to do, is it any wonder she's different? She's struck by sudden fury at the injustice.

Why should André remain unchanged in her mind – forever frozen in time – still beautiful instead of hideous like her? She can still picture him leaning against a wall, watching her – the curl of his lip, his slightly crooked nose, his hooded eyes. *My God*. She's doing it again – letting herself drift back. But then, no matter what she does, he'll always be with her – his face, actions, and expressions. There's no escape. Perhaps it's a good thing so that she doesn't forget the pain. Sometimes, to make sure she can still feel it, remember what life should have been, she takes out the photo hidden under the drawer of the television cabinet. He's staring straight at the camera with his arm slung over her shoulder, and she's looking up at him like there's no one else in the entire world. It must be a nice feeling – being adored, having done nothing to deserve it.

Despite how he materialises in her thoughts, she knows from the second photo of him hidden in the drawer that André has changed with the years. He's older, of course. She purses her lips and tries to remember when she'd received that photo – it must be about a year and a half ago now. The image had been taken from afar so that both subjects are somewhat grainy. Regardless, she'd known straight away that it was him.

Examining it, Marie-Hélène had found herself inexplicably drawn to the woman next to him – his wife, Seren, she'd discovered. She was staring at André in the same way Marie-Hélène once had. They were outside, sitting on a bench, holding hands. There were boats in the background, the sea, houses, mountains. The scene had instantly reminded her of Port de Centuri in Corsica, where she'd lived for sixteen years when she'd first left Bordeaux.

Yes. André is older, still handsome, if not a little frail-looking – to be expected by all accounts. His wife is pretty. They make an attractive couple. Or is it now made? Marie-Hélène isn't sure how to refer to him – past or present tense? Indeed, by now, it must be past tense. The note accompanying the photograph suggested it was heading in that direction. Is Seren now a widow? In one way, Marie-Hélène feels sorry for the youthful-looking woman with wavy brown hair and a smiling face. In another, she'd love to know how much André told her of his past, if anything. After all, it would be hard to articulate. Perhaps the wife knows absolutely nothing, is entirely ignorant of the events of Bordeaux eighteen years before when her life detonated.

Subconsciously, she clicks her fingers. Sinking back once more in her chair, she throws the still-lit cigarette in the air and watches it arc to the ground. "*Boom*," she whispers as it falls. She should go back inside now, wash her hands, straighten her blouse, reapply her lipstick. But for what? So she can listen to the customers' piercing laughter, their indulgent stories, all while she tries to refrain from slamming her fist in the centre of the table, sending their beef bourguignon flying. She wonders how many of them have had their lives ruined, let alone their overpriced meal, by someone else's hand?

By now, André must also know what total obliteration feels like – to have your future stolen. Perhaps he's floating above her now, able to read her thoughts. Maybe now he knows the full story. Glancing up nervously to check, she chuckles at her absurdity. Learning André had terminal cancer should have felt like retribution, except she'd already believed him dead. Everyone had, it seemed, from the story she'd found online seven years after she'd first fled Bordeaux. It was only then, close to a decade later, that Marie-Hélène began her research, after seeking impartial counsel one evening from a wise holidaymaker in Corsica. The conversation with the older woman came about so unexpectedly that Marie-Hélène started to believe that it had been a sign – more than being in the right place at the right time.

How had she not known before then that André was dead? Then again, why would she? Despite who André was, the story of a man presumed drowned following his daily swim was hardly big news outside Bordeaux, let alone in a practically comatose fishing village in Corsica.

Reading the article at the time, she'd felt dissatisfied that André had reached what seemed a sort of pitiful end after everything. It had almost made her want to forget the entire thing until it struck her that she had no recollection of André ever swimming, and certainly not daily or since he was a boy, as the article claimed. There'd been several heartfelt quotes from his beloved mother. That's what had planted a seed of doubt. It remained dormant for several years until Marie-Hélène unearthed a second article, and further suspicion began to sprout. That particular piece of news helped to confirm two things. One: contrary to what she'd first thought, André being deceased was, in fact, fortuitous. Two: what she needed was proof. You see, unless there's a body – more concrete evidence than a pair of shoes, a towel, and a wallet containing a driving licence – then there's hope, and where there's hope, there's life.

It didn't take long to find life. André Dubois had not met his end in the sea years before but had resurfaced in a town called Ballycross, southern Ireland, where he was alive and happily married with no children. The detective's thorough account that accompanied the photographic proof had contained several useless tidbits of information, like that the village of Ballycross is teamed with the French town of Beglés in Bordeaux. How very apt! That the happy couple run a wine shop. No surprise there. And that André is held in high esteem by the residents of Ballycross. At first, Marie-Hélène had been furious reading it until she'd reached the final statement: *Several accounts from locals confirm that André has cancer, recently described as incurable.*

André wasn't dead, not yet. So all Marie-Hélène had to do was wait. While she waited, she had time to reflect. It bothered her that if she'd been able to find André with relative ease (and the use of an extortionately priced detective that she could ill afford), how had no one else? Or had they never tried? At first, it didn't make sense, but it soon did. That's when she'd decided to return to Bordeaux to wait it out – being near to where it had unravelled years before only helped to drive her desire further.

The door swings open once more, startling her.

"There's someone here to see you." The new waitress holds the edge of the metal door. "Oh, and Julien said that you could finish up early tonight if you're too tired. I have to stay to clean up. The perks of being the new girl!" She rolls her eyes and smiles.

Marie-Hélène smiles back. "Okay. One second."

The door bangs shut. Julien must have realised that she wasn't in the mood to play games tonight, not with him anyway. Perhaps she should warn the new girl that later Julien will produce the Cognac to impress her before taking something entirely unimpressive from the zipper of his trousers. No. Let her figure it out alone. There was never anyone to warn her about ulterior motives.

A slow smile spreads across her face as she recalls the very moment she deciphered the mystery and what it made her want to do. *Revenge is a dish that is eaten cold.*

It's been a painfully slow process, but it's time now to make contact, move to the next stage. As soon as she gets home, she'll send another email. She's already sent one to the address provided a few weeks before, but it's gone unanswered. Maybe André is too busy fighting for his life to respond, or perhaps he's already dead. It shouldn't be too hard to find out either way.

Walking back inside, Marie-Hélène spots her, standing there, blissfully unaware. She must have finished her shift early. They've arranged to meet here so they can walk home together.

"Nicole?"

Her face clouds when she looks up. It's like a knife in Marie-Hélènes's chest.

Nicole hates it here in Bordeaux, so far from Corsica, the only place she's ever known. She says it all the time, how she feels no connection whatsoever to this place.

"I'll just close off, get my things. Can you wait?"

The corner of Nicole's lip lifts ever so slightly, and she nods. Marie-Hélène has let her down by growing obsessed by it all. One day Nicole will understand how hard it was to let it go. There's no guessing who's to blame.

Without a doubt, Marie-Hélène had loved André Dubois until she'd learned what he was. It sickened her to her very stomach. It took everything she once felt for him and twisted it into something vile and unimaginable. Now it's time to slay as she was slain. She'd toyed many times with turning up unexpectedly in Ireland to witness the shock on his face. Perhaps it's still an option. No. It's better this way. This journey goes far beyond André's life. Still, it doesn't stop her from picturing how he'd have reacted. She wouldn't have forgotten her manners. Before anything, she'd have thanked him for bestowing upon her the greatest gift he ever had to offer. Now, she has something that no one else in the entire world possesses – his power.

Chapter 10

In the end, I'd slept. Not because of the tablets I'd poured into my hand the night before in panic, but because I'd been plain worn out – physically and emotionally. I'd love to say that André had saved me by appearing to me in my moment of need, asking me to put the tablets down and step away, but he hadn't, of course. Instead, I'd squeezed my eyes shut, wrestled with my conscience for about five seconds, realised that the tablets wouldn't be enough anyway, then flushed them down the toilet.

So I'm still here. I'm drained, but I've slept. I know this because I've awoken, and in doing so must endure the awful moment where reality caves like quicksand. It never lasts long, but for those few seconds, I forget before I remember. Since that day, there hasn't been a single day where I don't slide my hand across to the empty space in the bed to pat where André should be but isn't. It's never a bad dream. I never discover his sleeping form, nudge him awake, thankfully put my hand to my heart with relief, then tell him that I had the worst dream. One in which he got a form of brain cancer with the most ridiculous name that no one could pronounce. He's never sitting up with his arms behind his head, smiling as I recount it. I don't tell him how he started getting headaches and began forgetting simple things like taking the bins out. How the next thing, he was in surgery, having a tumour removed. Then there was chemo, radiotherapy. We don't get to laugh that he got bald and sort of fat from the treatment, then rail-thin. I don't go over the massive seizure he had at dinner in Jane and Dermot's, or that the very next day we were told that all that remained was a matter of weeks. But most of all, I never get to say, "My God, it was so real. Please don't die on me, André. Swear to me."

André never answers. He swore once before. It was a promise he couldn't keep.

Every day, it shocks me that it wasn't a dream, even today. The only difference this morning is that I have to remind myself of three things. One: André is dead. Two: I'm pregnant with his child. Three: I'd decided to terminate the pregnancy.

I take a minute extra for the subsequent revelations, then reach for my phone. Tapping out a message to Fi, I tell her to stay in bed and offer her the afternoon shift in the shop instead. She won't see it for a few hours, it's still early, just after five, but I know she'll be pleased. Besides, I'm awake now, and the likelihood of further sleep is slim. Getting out of bed, I pause in front of the full-length mirror and pull up my T-shirt. Turning to the side, I run my hand over my stomach and jerk my head slightly when I notice a slight swell.

Surprised, I rub my hand over it in a circle. Again, I have to push away the image of André standing behind me, placing his hands over would have grown over the months to become another missed opportunity – that of André as the expectant father. I manage a smile. I know exactly the type he'd have been: a Mozart-playing, vile-smoothie-concocting, poring-over-every-pregnancy-manual Daddy-to-be.

"*Serendipity.*" I hear his throaty pronunciation of my name as if he is standing next to me, and something stirs within. I shake my head and bite the corner of my lip, then pad towards the bathroom. I go to the loo, wash my hands, and splash my face with cold water. After I dry my face, I stand there holding the towel in my hands. My head tilts to one side as I muse on all the things no one tells you about loss – like how you'll miss physical contact, having someone there to hold your hand. But more than that, no one warns you that you'll crave intimacy and being touched. How sometimes you'll still get turned on thinking of him, how you'll yearn to make love, to kiss, to have someone wrapped around you.

I told Jane about it once.

"I have a theory on that," she'd said. "So, ideally, if life was fair, you're meant to be really old and crusty when you lose your husband or wife. Like eighty-five or something. See, by then, you should be completely over having the flah on a Saturday night."

How I loved Jane's way with words, and how she'd taken the time over the years to painstakingly educate André on Cork slang – everything from *flah* to *shifting*.

She'd placed her hand on mine. "But life's not fair, is it?"

"No." I shook my head sadly. "Lusting after a dead man. Not normal behaviour, really. Let alone fair."

"No. But of course you miss it. You're still young, and

you, Seren, lest we forget, were one of the lucky ones. You were *actually* in love. Not 'in-tolerance' like I am most of the time." She made speech marks with her fingers and laughed. "Personally speaking, for me, zero sex would be a blessing in disguise. Like I'd rather cook a Clonakilty pudding than have one fly at me on a Sunday morning." She'd paused then. "No. It's not fair. While I'd do anything to bloody avoid it, all you want is a good old-fashioned, totally legal, nothing-to-be-ashamed-of ride from your husband."

Of course, I'd laughed. But I do still struggle with the injustice of my husband's death, especially when I know that there are some out there who might think, "Would it really be so bad?" Not that you'd ever be allowed to admit that you might like the peace.

I shake myself back to present, brush my teeth, wipe my mouth with the back of my hand, and walk back into the bedroom. Once more, I stop in front of the mirror and lift my T-shirt. The swelling is still there. I put my hand on my stomach again.

I'd often overhear other women complaining about their husbands in the wine shop. "Bring the kids to the park? Would you go away! He wouldn't wipe his own arse if he could get away with it."

"Wouldn't spend Christmas."

"Never bloody listens."

Sometimes, I'd join in. After all, who wants to be judged by the smug wife who sits tight-lipped, pretending to examine her nails. Except mostly, mine had listened until one day he'd stopped. It's how I first noticed that André was acting differently – the forgetfulness, but mainly because he stopped listening. Before that, he'd paid attention. I could have been telling him that I'd terrible trapped wind, and he'd nod along earnestly as if I was reciting Joyce. I know what you must be thinking, that I'm looking back through rose-tinted glasses, remembering it differently. My mum used to mock those types of women – the ones who'd conveniently forget.

"He never gave her a bloody penny nor lifted a finger at home. Oh, and he was well able to give the poor young fella a clip around the ear when he felt like it. And there she is like the wailing widow as if no greater man ever walked the face of the earth!"

Of course, André hadn't been perfect. No man is. He'd had his moments, but the rest, well, it had been as good as it gets. I'd been lucky. I stop staring at my stomach, grab my jeans off the chair, and pull them on. As I do, I glance out the bedroom door to the landing. I'd never considered the concept that you only get a certain quota of luck in life before it runs out. Not until I'd heard Cathy and Jane discuss it.

"She was lucky … I mean, of course, I love mine, and I know you love yours too. But she got what we all wanted, didn't she? Like, is there anything sexier than a man who adores his wife? He was just a good man – nothing weird about him. I'd say he even had decent toenails. You were his doctor. Did he?"

"Jesus, Jane. I never saw his toenails."

I'd heard Cathy laugh, then sigh.

"You're probably right, though. The fact I never saw them would suggest they were decent. Christ, it's not fair, is it? No one's ever looked at me the way he looked at her."

There'd been silence then. I'd almost called out to let

Cathy and Jane know that I was still awake and that I could hear them. They'd been sitting outside my bedroom, keeping watch over me after the funeral.

"I just wish she'd taken the time to prepare more," Jane said. "You know? For the inevitable. She's so shocked! It's as if he drowned or got run over. As if she wasn't expecting him to die."

"Maybe she thought love would conquer all."

I'd been able to hear Jane exhaling loudly.

"Cancer doesn't work like that," she said, "She still has no idea what's ahead. It's so unfair. She'll never find that again, you know? What she had with him. You don't get that lucky twice. No one does."

Slipping on my shoes, I wrap my arms around myself and shiver. It's chilly this morning. I look away from the memory replaying outside my bedroom door and towards the window. The sun isn't yet up. The new day hasn't quite dawned, but it will.

In the same way, it had dawned on me that day that I'd had my luck in life. What I'd had with André had been a once-in-a-lifetime love. I'd never find that again, even if I wanted to, but I'd always have my memories – even the final painful and beautiful ones. Teetering in the place between life and death is incredibly unique. Walking that line with André, we'd shared other-worldly moments throughout the horrors of chemo and radiation where no subject was off-limits, no revelation would have mattered.

"Do you ever wonder what my final words will be?" André had asked one time with a cheeky smile.

"I'd really prefer not to think about it, thank you."

"Humour me."

"Something like 'cancer is a dick'?" I'd raised my eyebrows smugly.

"*Le cancer.*" He rolled his eyes. "I never understood why the word is masculine in French. It should be feminine. I'm sure cancer is a woman."

I shoved his arm. "Very funny. A woman would never be as sneaky as cancer is. It's a man, for sure."

André laughed. "I wouldn't waste my final words on something so horrible. Instead, I think I'd remind you how lucky you were to have such a handsome, wonderful Frenchman in your life." His smile faded then. "Or I might tell you that you've given me the greatest life, that I'd do it all again in a flash, without changing anything. That you made me believe in real love without deceit or –"

"Deceit?" I interrupted, physically trying to draw the tears back in. "That's very deep. Is there something you're not telling me? Christ, you don't have a lover somewhere, do you? Tell me you never buried anyone under a patio, or –"

"I love you, Seren." For once, he wasn't laughing at my attempt at a joke.

"But you would tell me, wouldn't you? If there was something that you wanted to confess ... It was you who broke the hoover that time, wasn't it?" I was babbling. "Hey." My smile faded when I saw his eyes fill. "I love you too, André." This time, I allowed the tears to roll freely. We'd held each other for a long time before he'd broken away.

"So now you know." Then he'd clapped his hands together suddenly. "Moving on. Ah, yes. Funeral song. I'm thinking ... 'Another One Bites the Dust'."

"I'm warning you, André!"

"Okay, okay, but we have a lot to cover here. Right, last meal?"

101

"If you say bloody mackerel, I'll kill you right now."

I walk into our closet, bury my head for a moment in one of André's sweaters, still where they always were, nothing moved, then grab one of my own and tug it on. In the end, Andre's last meal had been administered via a tube, and his final words, well, let's just they were light-years from what he'd imagined they'd be. No matter how hard I try, those words still flash into my mind from time to time. I don't think I'll ever understand their meaning. They'd made quite the impact – like a slap across the face. The doctor had tried to reassure me, saying that there can be hallucinations, acute confusion, and agitation in the final stages. Still, they'd hurt. Knowing there'd be no answer, I'd attempted to ask André what he'd meant, but by then they'd upped the morphine. By then, keeping him comfortable took precedence.

I grab my phone off my bed and make my way downstairs to prepare for the day ahead. At least that's one thing for which I can be ready, unlike how I'd failed to equip myself for grief. Again, Cathy was right. I was ill-prepared for everything that lay ahead. Perhaps it's my tragic flaw. My positivity, my stupid belief that good will prevail, let me down. Maybe if I could treat my personal life as I do my business, leaving little to chance, always being ready, then I'd be in better shape.

At the end of the stairs, I turn left into the shop where I'll prep the pastries, switch on Big Bertha, mop the floors. My father used to say that there was great joy in mundane victories, that the happiest of people found joy in the ordinary. He was a wonderfully realistic, unindulgent sort of man. As a schoolteacher, I suppose often dealing with teenagers who tell lies and make mistakes, he had to be. It had made him fair, unjudgemental, always urging his students and me to not worry about the past. "We can do nothing about what is done. We can only solve what lies ahead."

I can hear his words now as I switch on the lights, flick switches, fill the bucket with boiling water. I wonder if it's a sign that I'm thinking of what my dear old dad might have said in light of my recent blunder. Truthfully, last night, after I'd finally settled myself back in bed before my eyes gave in to rest, I thought I'd made a decision to terminate the pregnancy. I'd decided not to tell Jane or Fi and hope that Cathy would eventually come around. Then I was going to book myself onto a cruise, where perhaps I'd meet a troop of eighty-five-year-old fellow widows who'd take me under their wing. I'd return six months later refreshed and wise, wearing a tunic, slacks and a golf visor, with a new outlook. All would be forgotten.

Except, this morning, I feel different. I don't know why. Had I stumbled upon the turning point, stubbed my toe off rock bottom? Or maybe, deep down, I always knew what I'd do before my mind caught up. In hindsight, perhaps I'd already twigged that I was pregnant before they'd confirmed it yesterday. It would explain a lot – the blazing internal battle, the constant self-judgement, avoiding people.

While I mop the floor, I realise I was a fool to jump head-first into getting pregnant so soon after his death. But I'm an even bigger fool to think I could get rid of André's baby. Not when I'm still so furious about him being wiped from the world. How could I extinguish him further? It's what André would say too if he could. This decision is irreversible, and now it's time to bow to the inevitable, as I once failed to do. What's coming is coming, there's nothing I can do it stop it, but I can prepare. It's time to face all I've been avoiding – clear away some of André's belongings, get a decent car instead of hanging on to the battered old van because we'd bought it together, simplify my life, stop indulging in my sorrow.

I place the mop against the wall and head down the three steps to the back kitchen. After switching on the lights, I turn on the ovens and get out the ingredients. André used to prepare for the day ahead like a dance. Music on. Eggs cracking. Flour in his hair. Hips going. It was his way, and he did it so well, but I can do it too. I've already been doing it since he became too ill to get up in the mornings. With Fi's help, I've kept this place afloat throughout his illness, even after his death. Perhaps I'm stronger than I realise. Maybe with the help of Cathy and Jane, I will be able to raise this baby. Who cares what people think about what I've done? In time, like every piece of small-town gossip, they'll forget.

It's a good thing that Fi is off this morning. I need to be alone today, to face people and prove that I can be ready. Later, when Fi comes in, I'm going to take myself up to Church Bay and clamber down to the swimming area, overlooking the colourful houses on the other side of the bay. It's the same place where I'd run as a child when something had gone wrong. I'd sit on the throne-shaped rock and wait for a sign. Today, I'll do the same, except I won't be waiting for guidance. I'm going to make a plan for this baby – our baby. It's the first time I've thought of it in any way other than André's child. But this is my child too and, for the first time, amidst the cloud of flour, I think I glimpse her – the girl he'd once described, the perfect mix of him and me. The daughter André already loved, without ever having known her. Like André, this child will have no other family on earth but me. Perhaps the responsibility is what I need. Maybe I should start feeling more grateful for the gift I've been given – that of life, of André's flesh and blood.

Chapter 11

I spend the morning lost in work, mentally constructing a list of tasks on the quest to pull myself back together. It's busy without Fi, but the hiss of activity is what I need. There's little opportunity to exchange more than a greeting with customers or worry about being observed. Today, I'm oblivious. I have no time to notice anyone mouth to their companion that I'm the poor girl who tragically lost her husband. The rhythm feels like a fast-paced choreographed dance, and for once I'm enjoying it. The chatter, the gurgling of Big Bertha, the clattering provide the white noise to help me focus. Even spotting Derbhla scuttle into the shop and queue up for takeaway doesn't irk me. Even she has the grace to look coy.

"To go today, Derbhla?" I ask, at the same time as reminding myself to add 'Do not get fussed by people who don't matter' to my list.

"Yes, please. We're *verry* busy. Oh, and can you make that a two-shot Americano for Doctor, please?"

I stifle a grin. Cathy's head must be throbbing for her

to veer towards a heart-rate-raising double hit of caffeine. Then again, I'm hardly surprised. If not for my utterly sobering revelation, she mightn't have made it back inside the restaurant without breaking an ankle. Earlier, right before I'd pulled open the shop door to the eagerly waiting builders, suits and joggers, already in desperate need of sustenance and coffee, I'd checked my messages. There'd been one just after 2 a.m. In it, Jane has swapped her floral garland for an outsized sombrero. Her arms are spread wide as she serenades Cathy, who's standing on a table, thankfully no longer wearing the break-neck red boots. Staring at it, I couldn't help think that if things were different, I might have been there, lying chorus-girl-style sideways on the table with one leg thrust in the air. As soon as I'd read the words beneath the image, my eyes had welled.

Not the same without you. Charlie has three angels.

I'd stuffed the phone back in my pocket, swallowed the tears and pulled open the front door to a chorus of "Mornings" from the queue of people outside.

Only now, when the shop stops heaving for a moment, do I take my phone out, open the message and run my finger over the image of teeny Jane and Cathy. Mum used to call us Cork's answer to *Charlie's Angels* because of our childhood obsession with the seventies show. We spent every Saturday watching reruns. Cathy always insisted on being the blonde one. I was the one with the wavy brown hair, which begrudgingly left Jane as the one with the ugly pageboy hair. We nearly fell out over it one Saturday until Mum pointed out that the bowl-haired one was actually the prettiest. Jane was further reconciled when Mum went on to say "You can always grow your hair, Jane. It's much harder to change a face!" It became our mantra of sorts over the years, reminding us not to sweat the small things. "Hair will always grow."

It came in very handy when Jane decided to cut a very full fringe after her first baby and when I ended up looking like Colm Meany from *The Snapper* after trying to recreate Baby's hair from *Dirty Dancing*. There wasn't a person alive who wouldn't have put me in the corner while I waited for it to grow out.

I give a short sharp laugh. We've been through so much together – a whole life almost – far too long for me to continue pushing them away as I have been. Perhaps since André died, being around them reminded me of who I used to be, and it hurt. I shake my head as I tuck the phone back in my jeans pocket. Leaning against the counter, I look up at the ceiling. Or maybe I was angry because it happened to me and not them.

God, I'm a despicable person. Perhaps it's time to face that it's me who's been avoiding them, and not the other way around. I'm the one who's checked out of the friendship. Is it any wonder they've started holding Saturday Service without me? Sure the time Dermot mistakenly put out six plates instead of five, I'd acted as if he'd gone out and trampled all over André's grave, making him feel as though he was single-handedly responsible for my sorrow.

Standing here now, I add Cathy and Jane and fixing our friendship to the very top of my list of tasks. I'm going to need them, now, more than ever. They're closely followed by Fi. I'll try and make her understand that this pregnancy is not an attack on her, and I'd never do anything to upset her.

"Well, well, well. Good night?" I grin at Fi when she

comes through the door an hour later, wearing dark sunglasses and some form of grey onesie that makes her look like she's come to work in her pyjamas. She leans dramatically on the door handle and pulls a face like she's about to retch before inhaling and then blowing it out slowly.

"Jesus wept," she manages at last. "You're no friend. Why? Why did you let me destroy myself last night?"

I laugh and thrust a coffee cup at her as she makes her way behind the counter, laden with a Centra bag packed to the brim. Before taking the coffee, she bends, stuffs the bag onto the shelf under the counter and comes up huffing and puffing like an old lady.

"Supplies." She gestures at the bag, swiping her hair to the side. "There are about six bags of synthetic crisps in there, a two-litre bottle of Coke, a share size bar of chocolate, trashy celebrity magazines – and, if they don't work, I'll order pizza." She forces a smile, then salutes me. "Fear not. I shan't let you down, sir. I *will* make it through the day." She takes a sip of the coffee. "Ah, thanks. That's better."

She immediately busies herself, tidying up the remnants of the morning's work. "Also, thanks for the lie-in. I was absolutely wrecked." She barely pauses. "Guess what? I only had my picture taken like a thousand times for *RSVP* Magazine. It's going to be in the 'Movers and Shakers' column next month. Famous!"

"Go, you! I'm glad you had fun. You deserve it. Now, I hate to be the bearer of bad news, but I've a few bits to do this avo, so you and your crisps must survive alone."

She glances up, terrified. "Sweet Jesus, Seren. Please don't leave me. I'll never make it alone! This is a hangover like no other. My senses are very much in question."

I lean over and give her a sympathetic hug. "Sorry. I've places to be." I grab my bag from next to her hangover-first-aid kit. Unlike hers, mine is filled with everything I need for an afternoon of getting a grip – notepad, pen, water, snack, blanket in case it takes me far longer than I anticipated, and I'm forced to take up permanent residence on a rockface. "You'll be fine," I assure her. "Sell as much wine as you can. Hell, go wild. Drink some if you like."

"Stop! I'll barf. I'm never drinking again." She puts her hands on the hips of her onesie and narrows her eyes. "What's going on here? You seem different. I want to use the word … *chirpy*, but that's not it. I want to say … No. It couldn't be. Seren, are you … *happy*?"

She raises her eyebrows, but I dismiss her with a wave of my hand.

"Of all the stupid things you've ever said!" I say with a grin. "Don't be ridiculous, Fi. I'm a widow. Widows are miserable. We hate all people, life, fuzzy puppies and … " Unconsciously, I'd been about to say babies, but I stop myself in time. "Actually, I have been thinking. There are going to be some changes around here, Fi."

Her brow furrows, and she puts her hand on her chest. "Please don't fire me. I'll go home and put on proper clothes if you like. I'll even apologise to Derbhla about what I said yesterday. In hindsight, it was far too risqué for morning trade. I swear I didn't mean it that way. And all is pure to a pure mind. I can assure you my mind is as pure as snow. Now, if you picked up another meaning, that's your problem."

"I have no idea what you're talking about, Fi." I feign innocence. "Besides, putting Derbhla in her place is, in fact, cause for promotion, my little mouthy employee, which is what you might just be getting."

"Shut up!" Her eyes are wide.

"Well, I've been thinking of ways to work smarter. Maybe earn some more money. As much as it makes me sad, we should start doing more separate shifts. I know, not as much fun but perhaps necessary. Also, maybe bring back the wine-tasting evenings …"

Fi fake-retches again. "Please, not the wine again. Not today. But, yes. On any other day, this would excite me very much. Those evenings were epic. I loved going to them before –" Fi stops. "You know what? You and I could do them just as well. I know we could."

I smile and nod. The wine-tasting evenings had always been André's gig where groups of friends, corporates, birthday parties would come to be captivated by his knowledge. (Or depending on the group: his looks, sexy French accent, however you want to put it.) Even after hosting hundreds of them, I'd still loved listening to him speak about wine. When he got sick, we'd stopped doing them. And since he'd died … well, I hadn't been able to bring myself to imitate one of his much-appreciated presentations. Not that I wouldn't be able to. I knew André's spiel by heart. Through osmosis and by drinking plenty of it, I also knew wine. Fi was right, together we could easily replicate them, but I'd had a better idea.

"I actually thought that maybe you and Kevin could host them together. He could sell packages to companies on the side of his own work and take a cut. It could be a way of making a little extra money."

This time her eyes light up. "Are you serious? That would be amazing, Seren. I think Kevin would be fantastic at sales." She grimaces. "Well, not boats, but you know what I mean. And this is a no-brainer … Christmas parties, hen nights. I have so many ideas." She sounds like I used to.

I splay my hands. "See." Perhaps I'd invented the idea to take the sting out of what I had to tell her soon, but it also makes sense.

"Look at you being all positive," Fi smiles broadly. "I'm proud of you, pal."

"I just figure, you know, maybe it's time to …" I can't say the word.

"Try?' Fi offers.

I'd been about to say "live" – live for my unborn child. "Yes, try," I agree. "But don't get too excited, okay? I still *hate* everything. This is going to be –"

"Baby steps?"

This time I can't meet her eyes. Instead, I nod. "I'll see you later, Fi. If I'm not back, lock up. You do tomorrow morning, and I'll do the afternoon."

"Got it, boss."

Once outside, I'm about to set off towards the bay when I notice Cathy and Jane coming in my direction. There's nothing beyond my house except the yacht club, so unless they're after a quick boat trip it's me they want. I'm so focused on my planning afternoon ahead that I consider diving back through the shop door to hide, except that Jane is already waving enthusiastically. I wave back, roll my eyes and wonder what's about to happen here. I'm suddenly aware that Cathy, fuelled by Mexican rocket-fuel the night before, may already have divulged my news to Jane. I had meant to text Cathy to tell her that I'd had a change of heart about the termination and to stop worrying but, with everything else, I'd forgotten. As I try to come up with a plan, Jane is still waving. Christ, her arm must be exhausted, but it means she's happy and, more than likely, still in the dark about my situation. In contrast, Cathy looks even more pinched than she did last night.

"Hey, you," Jane folds me into her arms. "We thought we'd surprise you with lunch." She dangles a greasy-looking bag from the chipper in front of my face. They must be just as hungover as Fi.

Cathy hugs me next, clinging to me for a moment too long. "You're telling her now," she whispers as I pull back and frown.

"Open up," Jane clucks. "If I don't eat something soon, I'll die. Sorry." She grits her teeth. Jane still can't use the word *death*, *dying*, *die*, around me without apologising.

I pretend not to notice, begrudgingly take my keys from my pocket and unlock the front door. Immediately, Jane dashes to the kitchen, where I can hear her taking out plates.

"*I've eaten!*" I call after her while Cathy removes her coat.

"Here." I offer to take it from her, but she grabs my arm.

"Seren. *Please*, tell her."

I nod. "Okay."

She looks relieved, and I'm about to walk away when she pulls me back and wraps her arms around me again. She makes a strange noise into my hair, a sort of muffled sob, and for the first time I hear her anguish.

"I've been so worried. Tell me you've reconsidered. What's done is done now, but this should be happy news. This is a flip-it situation."

Another of our sayings. "Flip it." First established when we weren't allowed to curse as children. We found

113

a way around it by using "flip" instead of the prohibited F word. It later morphed into taking a shite situation and turning it on its head, making the most out of the dealt cards. It's been utilised many times with break-ups, fights with parents, general disappointments, and now it's being applied to getting pregnant with your dead husband's sperm.

"It's okay, Cathy. I've decided to keep the baby, but let me tell Jane everything my way, in my own time, all right?"

Cathy nods and swallows.

"Come on, you two," Jane mumbles from the door. Her mouth is already full. "Oh, and get that laptop of yours, Seren, will you? We need to get those reviews up. And wine! Fuck it. Get wine too. This feels like a celebration, doesn't it?"

"On it!" I call back, wondering if she'll still feel the same when I tell her my news. "I'll get the laptop. You get the wine," I say to Cathy.

Before I run up the stairs, Cathy reaches her hand out, places it on my stomach, and leans down to my belly. "You are going to be more loved than any other little French baby in the world, ever," she says, then stands up and looks me straight in the eye. "Because he or she had a wonderful father and *has* a wonderful mother."

My chest caves, but Cathy has already walked away.

As I go upstairs, I feel as if a weight has been lifted from my shoulders. Everything's going to be okay. I can feel it. Grabbing my ancient laptop off the chair, I pause, then go to the drawer next to the bed and take out André's laptop, along with the rolled-up power lead. If Jane needs reviews, then reviews are what she'll get.

When I walk into the kitchen, Jane is sitting at the

table, practically making love to a burger, and Cathy is popping the cork of the wine. Taking out three glasses, she pours me a tiny amount accompanied by a little wink.

"Right." I place both laptops on the table, reach over and plug them in.

Jane and Cathy exchange glances.

"I just thought that in André's absence, the very least he can do is to write the most glowing review that ever had the chance to glow," I say.

Jane puts her hand to her heart. "I love that, Seren. Straight from heaven. We can say whatever we like on his one. Totally big-up *Más* as the best restaurant in the universe. I know André would approve."

I nod once, then take a deep breath. "And then ... I'm going to ask you both to help me shut down his online accounts." I pause. "And after that, I need to tell you something." My voice wobbles.

Jane looks from me to Cathy, who gives a little headshake indicating not to ask.

"Okay." I sit and open the laptop. "André's first. Start constructing what you want me to say while I log in."

"Definitely something about the cocktails being mindblowing." Cathy raises her eyebrows.

"And the prawn tacos. We have to mention them." Jane is excited.

I'm half-listening, keeping an eye on various notifications popping up on the screen as the laptop starts, suddenly distracted when I notice something flash up. Trying not to react, I click on the email notification and begin to read. It's in French, so I take my time.

As I get to the end, I gasp. *"What the hell?"*

"Seren?"

Jane says my name first, then Cathy, but I don't hear

115

them. Instead, my hand flies to my mouth as I read the name on the screen.

Marie-Hélène.

My blood runs cold. It's the same name André called for over and over on his deathbed. The last thing my husband would ever say. Blinking, I look up at Cathy and Jane, then once more at the screen. This time I register a second name.

"Gigi Dubois-Challant," I whisper.

Reading the word next to the name, the air exits my lungs, then my chest tightens, and I'm gulping for air. Then everything goes black.

Chapter 12

Gigi

Gigi Dubois' eyes drift from the laptop towards her assistant Camille, who is waiting outside her office door, leaning against the glass wall. She watches as Camille tugs her maternity underwear up over her ever-expanding stomach, then in an action that cancels the first, reaches behind and pulls the fabric from her bottom.

Gigi rolls her eyes and refocuses on the laptop. At times like this, she deeply regrets the decision of an all-glass office expansion. It hadn't taken much for the architects to convince her that the vast ultra-modern structure was the way to go. It had been something like "blending old with new in a symbiotic battle of modern versus classic, lulling the vista inside the building". Or some such rubbish. Despite the vista of the Bordeaux hills, for her work transparency had been the goal. Gigi had wanted to see everything, anticipate what was going to happen before it had. Running an operation this size, at various times of the year employing over 300 people, visibility is the only way to maintain control. Leaving nothing to chance is how to survive.

Her eyes fall on the fifth item on the agenda for this morning's meeting. She sincerely hopes H.R. have managed to find a suitable replacement for Camille, preferably a man this time – one who won't be getting pregnant any time soon. Although nowadays, not even that would surprise her. Gigi hates that Camille is pregnant. Not least because she's excellent at her job, but also because her current predicament is a constant reminder – one that has been playing on her mind lately.

She drums her fingers impatiently on the desk and then glances at what's really bothering her. The Public Relations department are once again pushing for her to do the blasted interview with *French Vogue*. It's been coming for months since she was named one of France's top fifty businesswomen. Ever since then, Gigi has felt restless. The stupid girl from P.R. has it as her only item on the agenda, followed by several insolent-looking exclamation marks.

"It's an enormous honour, madame. This is *French Vogue*! Any woman would give her right arm to be featured in the social pages, let alone on the front cover," the typically bubbly, fashionable P.R. girl, probably right out of college, had implored her months before. "They want to know the woman behind the wine dynasty."

"And what about a man?" Gigi's eyes had shot up, then narrowed. "Would any man give his right arm to be featured on the cover of a *fashion magazine*?" She'd said the words like they were dirty.

"Well … I … it's a great opportunity for the business – a huge compliment. I'm sure it's because you're so stylish. It would make us a household name –"

"Don't try to flatter me, and we're already a household name."

"Yes, but people want to know more about *you*."

"All they need to know about me is that I'm head of Chateau Challant. *The end*. When this business stops being about wine, my dear, that's when we have a problem." Gigi had stood then, trying to appear taller than her five feet, and stared the girl down.

That should have put an end to it, but it appears the girl hadn't got the message. She'd be firmer today. There was no way Gigi was going to splash herself all over the cover of any magazine, regardless of whether it was *French Vogue*, all because she'd been blessed with good looks and knew how to put an outfit together. Getting to where she is today had never been about fame or praise. It had been about proving to herself that she could. Besides, she'd read enough "life" features to know that they wanted to know every little detail, and if you didn't give it they'd dig for it. Dirt sells. Of course, Gigi had a story that could see millions of magazines, but there was no way she was going to give it to anyone, ever. She'd sworn that eighteen years before.

"It's eleven o'clock, madame." Camille shuffles forward, puts her head around the door, and reverses back outside.

Moving only her eyes, Gigi can see the others beginning to make their way to the coffee station and then towards the boardroom, where they'll await her entrance. She'll wait a few minutes to give them more time to mentally prepare. She can't stand it when they run over their allocated time slot. In business, especially this business, it's all about timing – the right timing. Mess that up, and the entire harvest is doomed. She is always surprised more people don't realise that.

Camille is now rubbing her stomach in huge big

circular motions and wincing. Gigi wonders, if asked now, would Camille still claim to be happy? The girl can barely walk.

"Was it planned?" she'd asked Camille when she'd first announced her news.

Camille's eyes had grown wide at the blunt question.

"Ah." Gigi had raised her eyebrows. "I suppose that's something I can't ask?"

"Well … I … no, I mean. No, it wasn't planned. Not really," Camille answered eventually, looking at the ground. "But we're very happy."

"Congratulations."

"It's a boy –"

"Can you please get the distrubutors on the line?" Gigi had interrupted.

Barely a few months later, Camille had come to her again.

"You see, I have this condition called symphysis pubis dysfunction and –"

"Please, Camille," she'd held up her hand and flared her nostrils, "remember. No details, just facts."

To Gigi's horror, Camille had limped forward as though all the bones in her legs had fused together. "I'm so sorry, but I'm going to have to take early leave. She'd paused to hoist her knickers.

"Which is when?"

"In two weeks, madame. But I'll be back as soon as I can. I really, *we* really, need this job and I –"

"And when is as soon as you can?"

Camille held up both hands. "Ten weeks after the baby is born."

"So, ten weeks after the birth of your son, you are

expected to return to work? And who said that?" Gigi barely flinched, although she'd been utterly shocked. She didn't usually deal with this sort of problem.

"Human Resources, madame. I get sixteen weeks altogether. Since I have to take early leave, I get six weeks before, and ten weeks after."

"You won't be okay by then." Gigi went back to typing.

"I will, madame, I swear. I have to be."

"It took me a year afterwards before I felt able to –"

"You have children, madame?"

Gigi had stopped typing and stared ahead. For one instant, just one, she'd had the most tremendous urge to sit Camille down and tell her everything she knew about motherhood … life … loss … Instead, she'd ignored the question.

"That's all, Camille."

"Will it be okay then, madame? If I leave in two weeks?"

"Yes. Fine."

Of course, it wasn't okay. None of it was. Gigi knew only too well that it wasn't the slightest bit okay to have your body turned inside out in childbirth, only to be handed an infant to care for after the ordeal. And then, ten short weeks later, with raw nipples and a stomach that still requires the knickers that wouldn't stay up in the first place, be expected to return to work. No, that wasn't justice, but then Gigi didn't make the rules. There was no guessing who did. Indeed not a woman. For no one, but someone who'd never experienced pregnancy, childbirth, or motherhood would be so cruel. Because of it, Gigi would have to either have Camille placed elsewhere, make her position redundant, or force her to leave. Gigi is too busy to have a post-partum balloon bouncing around the office, showing off baby pictures, complaining that she'd had no sleep. That said, she'll miss Camille's professionalism, her discretion, but this isn't a charity. This is real life, and as much as Gigi is an advocate for women in business, her business comes first. It's all she has.

"I'm going to shatter a myth for you ladies," she'd often say at various lunches where she'd be asked to speak. She didn't mind speaking at these events. Unlike with magazines, she was able to control what she said. "You *can't* have it all. Somewhere along the way, you will be forced to choose. Something will suffer, and it's either your job, your family, or you." She'd point around the room while she spoke. "Being a successful woman is knowing how to prioritise. Make sure you choose wisely."

It was always met with raucous applause. Perhaps because it subtly alluded to the tragedy Gigi had suffered many years before. Notoriously private, she never discussed it, although many had heard whispers. The sensitive nature meant that no one pressed her further or asked what choices she'd made. They'd be disappointed to learn what she'd prioritised. In truth, from the day she'd set her sights on running the family business, she'd chosen it over everything else. She'd learned that motherhood and ambition are only companions to a point before they must part ways – before you must choose.

"They're ready for you, madame," Camille insists again.

"I'm coming."

Gigi stands up, pushes her chair back, and opens the bathroom door to her left. She needs a moment of privacy to pull herself together, in preparation for sorting all the little problems her staff are about to present. In an industry like this, so often reliant on nature, there are constant issues, ultimately falling to her. Of course, fixing things is where Gigi has always flourished. Now, at fifty-nine, she's still sorting things, still doing what needs to be done. At times, it makes her feel as old as the chateau beyond the vast stone wall on the other side of the offices. Sometimes she feels she's lived a thousand lifetimes instead of just this one. Not that she looks it. Her grey hair is the only thing that belies her age, yet it somehow makes her face more youthful, accenting her unlined skin and clear eyes. Although she's worked hard all her life, there have been other people to take care of life's menial tasks. It's been a very long time indeed since she made a bed, washed a floor or cooked a meal.

To this day, people baulk when she reveals that she was married at eighteen. Even more so when she elaborates that it was to a man almost thirty years her senior – back then, France was still France and more liberal, a little more accepting. She never tells much more, but she's heard the rumours of how she fell in love, then charmed and quickly married Henri – a poor orphan girl done well, or so the story goes. It's a poetic tale, but it's not true.

What is true is she'd been reborn the day she'd first arrived here. Now, she feels it's as much hers as if it were her blood running through the vineyards beyond. Those who'd worked here under her husband – when he'd almost run it into the ground, she might add – are long gone, dead, erased. So that now, when people see the name above the door, it is synonymous with only her – a new generation, a modern female-led establishment producing the finest wines in the world.

Closing the bathroom door behind her, she exhales as if she's been holding her breath all morning. She swallows hard. Her reflection in the mirror is as it always is – understated, current, professional but with a twist – one that says she knows exactly what she's doing. She always has. Behind her pretty brown eyes, determination burns. Within her beats the heart of a woman who has been wronged as much as she has wronged. Now wouldn't that tagline sell plenty of copies of *French Vogue*? Except this is *her* life. No one else needs ever know what she's endured for it.

Looking into her own eyes, the agony erupts. For one instant, she feels as though her heart has stopped, and her hand flies to her chest to check. No. It's still beating, as it always is. Not once, throughout everything, has it given in. Nor has she. Gripping the edge of the sink, she takes a breath. All morning, she could feel it coming, bubbling to the surface, as if he was silently announcing his return. As soon as she closes her eyes, he appears immediately, as he always does. She knows there's no way to stop his visits. It's better to get it over and done with fast. "*Hello, maman.*" His voice is strong today. For a second, her chest swells, and she smiles. "Hello, André," she whispers the words, then her features contort.

She gives in for a moment before her eyes flash open suddenly, and she turns the tap to cold to run her wrists under the water. She doesn't have time to battle emotions today. Instead, she dries her hands, wipes her face, pulls the door open and strides towards where Camille is still waiting outside.

Camille begins to talk straight away as they head in the boardroom's direction. "You have a meeting at two fifteen as requested, with Marketing. Then at four, you are expected back at the house. The doctor wants to speak to you about your husband's medication. Then ..."

Gigi rolls her eyes at the mention of his medication. Perhaps she should ask for some herself. Whatever they're injecting him with must be more potent than kryptonite to have kept him alive this long. She tries not to picture him where he now resides on the fourth floor of the chateau, clinging to life, lying in a hospital bed next to the window so he can look out on what he built.

In reality, Henri had built nothing. He'd been handed it by his father and his father before that, generation after generation of chauvinistic, unloved, unloving primogeniture men. She'd had to research the word – the right of succession belonging solely to the firstborn son. Oh, they would turn in their graves if they saw someone without a dick taking what they'd built from strength to strength, in a direction her husband could never have envisaged.

Passing the rows of photographs that hang on the curved wall ahead of the boardroom door, she slows to almost a stop as André appears again. This time, in a photo next to his father, Henri, on the steps of the chateau. My God, André was a beautiful child, as beautiful as the chateau that has stood for centuries. Except, unlike it, André had been weak.

"Is there anything else? Today is my last day," Camille says as they reach the boardroom door.

Gigi pauses, again fighting the urge to take the girl aside and offer her some advice. More than anything, she wants to tell Camille to give in to motherhood instead of trying to fight it – to say to her that it can be enough. "That's all," she says instead. Besides, Gigi suspects Camille already knows what lies ahead. Camille will choose wisely. After all, becoming a mother in your thirties must be very different from what Gigi had experienced.

Sometimes she wonders what sort of life she might have had if she'd given in, settled for what life had mapped out for her, in place of battling against the constraints. She'd been heartbreakingly naïve. But then, she had been only a child herself – a child with a child. Was there any wonder that it hadn't come naturally? Or how she'd been so shaken by how it came about at all? Back then, the act itself had frightened her to her core, sickened her, and then, nine months later, the torturous birth. Never again, she'd sworn.

Walking into the boardroom, she takes her place at the head of the table, facing the vast rolling vineyards beyond. After this meeting, she'll throw on her old boots and walk the paths between the vines as she does every day, inhaling the Bordeaux air. It still astounds her to think that the best vintage the house ever witnessed had been produced on her watch. The reviews stated that you could taste that a woman had created it. They'd used words like *intense, smooth, balanced, generous*. Now, when she stands in the vineyards and looks back at the estate, the winery, the chateau – her home – she feels triumph. That it came at a cost is no surprise. It always does.

It could well have been André sitting here in her place, making the decisions she's made for so long, except André hadn't wanted it. He'd made that very clear. If he had, he'd have fought harder. The sun catches her eye as she half-listens to the latest sales figures. It's hard to believe he's gone eighteen years now. It took Gigi a long time to accept that he was never coming back. Throwing herself into the business all those years ago had been the only way to distract herself, to cease the constant questions, the regrets, the shame, the guilt.

Still, although he's not here, he'll always be a part of her. But he's nobody's business but hers. She keeps him locked inside now. Despite his many shortcomings, from the day André Dubois-Challant was thrust into her arms as a defenceless and needy infant, she'd loved him. But as much as André often claimed he'd been born into the wrong life, so too had she. Indeed she hadn't been born to be his mother. As a mother, she'd let him down. Gigi often comforts herself with the idea that in one way André got the one thing he'd always wanted, his freedom. Truthfully, it was Gigi who'd been born to be Head of Chateau Challant. It's who she is now, and she'd challenge anyone who dared suggest otherwise.

Chapter 13

I'm slumped on the whitewashed floor of our dressing room amongst ruin. Earlier, as soon as I was alone, I'd flown upstairs, rushed into our bedroom and stared about helplessly, trying to locate a target for my rage. Seizing the first weapon I could find off the chest of drawers, I stormed into the dressing room, pulled André's suits and shirts from their hangers, then swiped the rest of his clothes off the shelves below. For once, I let myself go, screaming and growling while reality, mixed with several once symmetrically folded Aran sweaters, tumbled to the floor. I'd raged for several minutes then sank to my knees after them.

"Bastard," I mutter now, picking up one half of the tie that I'd eventually managed to sever with the less-than-lethal nail scissors from the chest of drawers. In hindsight, I should have known they wouldn't provide the anticipated relief. They were entirely the wrong tool with which to vent. By the time I'd managed to cut through the fabric of his favourite tie, the moment had passed.

Nevertheless, what I needed far more than the fabric scissors in the drawer in the kitchen downstairs, was an explanation. Cutting up André's belongings, when he wasn't even here to witness the act, wasn't the answer.

Spying the rest of the tie poking out from under a shirt, I pick it up and hold it against the other half. It could never be repaired now. Much like the memories of my life with André, it's ruined. I rest my head back and squeeze my eyes shut, willing him to appear so that I might ask the questions that swirl in my mind.

"Did you know?"

"Why did you lie to me?"

"Who the hell are you?"

All of a sudden, my real-life biography feels like a work of fiction. Despite the anger, I ache for him to be here with me, to set it right once more. Grabbing a pile of clothes from the floor, I bury my head in them. His smell is still there, packed into the fibres – a small hint of the man I thought I knew. Until a few hours before, I'd believed I knew every inch, inside and out, but if what I've read is true, it's a lot more than an inch of information I've missed. It's hectares.

I stand shakily and move to the bedroom to lie on the bed, so tired and stressed that I can't think straight in amongst the suffocating mess I've created. The only person I've hurt by disrupting it all is myself. There's no one else here to witness my outrage. Only me, stuck in a life that keeps going from bad to worse. I'm the one who'll have to clear it all up, attempt to reassemble the remnants of the man I used to know. Now, André feels like a stranger. I hate him. I hate him so much that if he wasn't already dead, I'd kill him with my bare hands.

Earlier, I'd spewed every insult I could muster while

Jane and Cathy gaped at me aghast. I'd ranted until the words dried up, and then I'd stared ahead in a trance, allowing everything to slow around me until all I could hear was my heart pounding in my ears.

It had felt like one of the bad dreams from which I never wake until I'd heard Cathy say, "Seren, I think you should lie down. Try and sleep it off. We're going to nip home and sort the kids, and then we'll be back. Okay?"

"One of us should stay," Jane said.

"No." I'd swallowed and shaken my head. I wanted to be alone. "I'll be fine. You're right. I'm tired. What about the shop?"

"Let me."

I'd listened while Cathy spoke to Fi at the internal shop door, asking her to lock up early for the day and put a sign on the door citing an electrical problem, "or something, anything", anything but the truth.

I don't want them to come back later. I can't bear to rationalise the situation further as we'd tried to earlier. No matter what scenarios Jane and Cathy had imagined, nothing helped. I need to figure this out alone. Whatever lies or stories André had spun, I still wasn't ready to hear anyone else make assumptions about him. "You can live with someone your whole life and never truly know them," Jane had said. It sounded like something my mother might have offered. Right now, the reality that I hadn't known André at all feels as devastating as his death.

Right after reading the email earlier, I'd been struck by an asthma attack. The shock and the loss of oxygen had made me faint, slumping forward for a moment. Cathy had caught me, given me my inhaler, pushed my head between my legs, hunkered down beside me and spoke to me until my breathing calmed. I'd sat staring at the floor with my mind racing. None of it made sense. Nothing was familiar, except, of course, the name.

I say it aloud now, *"Marie-bloody-Hélène"*, through gritted teeth. I'd never told Cathy or Jane about André's incessant chanting of her stupid name so close to his death. I'd wanted to forget I'd ever heard it, push the silly thoughts I was having from my head. I'd actually thought he might have had an affair at some point. By then, I hadn't wanted my marriage to unravel. It was ending anyway. Only, I still can't bear for it to fall apart now.

Perhaps I should take comfort in the fact that he hadn't been unfaithful. At least I know that much now. It's a small mercy, I suppose. Indeed, I also know that it all took place before he even met me eighteen years before. I squeeze my hands into fists as I try to conjure her face. *I hate her.* I hate this Marie-Hélène, almost as much as I hate André. I hate the words she wrote to him. I hate her claim to him, her declaration that he was the love of her life. André was the love of *my* life, not hers.

Where was *she* when he lay dying? There was no sign of her when I was trying to absorb his suffering, take away his pain. It was me who'd held his hand, kissed away his tears. Not this woman who claims that they were once secretly engaged. Engaged! It was the first I'd heard of it. In fact, until his final days, I'd never before heard her name. She can't have meant that much to him. Staring at the ceiling now, I allow the word *"bitch"* escape my lips. Why now? What the hell did she want now, after letting so many years pass in between? And why did I stumble on it today, of all days, when at last I'd decided to try my hardest to move on?

After I had recovered from the asthma attack, Jane had

131

reached across me, expertly copying the text from the email before opening Google. Within seconds, I'd been staring at the English translation of the words. At least, while it had been in French, there was an outside chance that I'd skewed the meaning. I hadn't. In fact, in English it sounded worse. Once again, I'd read it while Jane and Cathy studied it from behind, each with a hand on my heaving shoulders. As soon as I'd reached the end, I'd roughly pushed back my chair and headed for the shop.

"Seren?" Fi had frowned upon seeing me stalk past her, zombie-like, in the direction of the French wine.

"Seren, what are you doing?" Jane's voice from behind.

Then from Cathy, "Okay. Let's just take a step back here."

I'd turned to glare at them through hooded eyes before seizing the almost-black bottle of Cabernet Sauvignon with the fancy cream and gold label from the top shelf, letting my knuckles turn white around the neck of the bottle.

"What about this one?" I could remember saying while perusing the stock catalogues before we'd opened the shop. "Chateau Challant is a staple."

"Is it?" André hadn't looked impressed. "I've always found Challant old-fashioned. There's a really strong aftertaste."

"Some people like old-fashioned, André."

"I don't."

"Well, don't drink it then. But it stays in. We have to sell what people want, not just what we like."

"True, my love."

"Besides, look at the house. My God, It's stunning. Are they really like that, the chateaux? That big?"

"Bigger. I saw it once. But my family worked on smaller farms."

"*Liar!*" I spat, smashing the bottle to the floor, quickly reaching for another, and doing the same. Since reading the email, André Dubois, poorly son of a vineyard farmer, has morphed into André Dubois-Challant – son and heir of Chateau Challant. His lies were as robust as the overpriced wine the vineyard produces.

"*Christ on a stick!* What on earth?" Fi had catapulted past me to shove the shop door closed, then pull the window blind down so no one could saunter past to see the owner seething at the liquid seeping across the wooden floor like blood.

"What the hell did I miss?" Fi's mouth hung open. "Also, might I suggest a slightly cheaper vintage?" She pulled a bottle from midway down the shelf and attempted to hand it to me. "Or are we only mad at the expensive bottles?" She glanced nervously at Cathy and Jane for guidance. "Because that's about 200 euro on the floor there."

With a look of defiance, I reached up and grabbed a third bottle before Fi snatched it from my hand.

"Jesus, my nerves! Please stop. What's happened?"

No one answered. No one knew how. For a moment, I stood breathing like a bull before Jane and Cathy tentatively approached and led me away.

"Don't worry!" Fi called after us. "I'll salvage what I can. I'll try and scoop some into a glass, suck it up with a sponge, a straw. Leave it with me."

They steered me towards the living room and sat me on the sofa. Jane plonked down beside me while Cathy reached into the cupboard and pulled out a bottle of brandy. Pouring a small shot into a glass, she handed it to me and nodded for me to drink.

"I need to see it again," I'd spluttered from the shock of the burning liquid. "What did it say?" I'd looked from one to the other. "My God, what did it say?"

Jane had run to the kitchen to retrieve the laptop, and once more, I'd sat reading the message dated a month before.

My dearest André,

It's been a very long time, has it not? I still think about you every day. Is it the same for you? I've thought of so many ways to write this message to you. In fact, I've agonised over it. The summer you asked me to marry you was the greatest time of my life. I loved you, André. I suppose, in many ways, I still do. Maybe, I always will. What we had, as you said, was like nothing you'd known before. You told me you'd never love another woman in the same way. Have you? Was there someone else afterwards? For me, no. I was not surprised to hear that you were in Ireland. You always said one day we would go.

The electronically translated version made it stiff so that it was impossible to picture who might be behind the words. Someone who André had loved like he'd never love again? Hearing her describe it that way made me want to take his laptop and smash it against the living-room floor.

"Are you sure he never mentioned her? Are you sure he told you his parents were dead?" Cathy asked as I stared at the screen.

"Yes. I mean, I think so. No. Yes. I'm sure."

"Okay, let's start from the start." Jane rubbed her temples. "So, he told you his parents died. His father was a vineyard manager. Well, that's sort of true, I suppose. I mean, you *do* have to manage your own business. Are you sure he didn't say *owned*?"

"Of course I'm bloody sure. It's a pretty big thing to get wrong. You guys know this. His father worked on small vineyards. He was a bloody farmer. His mother baked. They died. It was the reason he came to Ireland. You heard it from his own mouth."

Both nodded.

"Maybe there was a family feud? Maybe it was all too much for André, living in a castle?" Jane suggested hopefully.

"But why lie? It's a pretty big deal to say your parents are dead when they're not," I argued.

"Maybe they disapproved of this woman. This Marie-Hélène," Jane tried again. "Christ, I'm sorry, can we call her something else? It's a tough one to say, isn't it? Marie-Hélène." She overly pronounced it, gurgling the name in her throat. "Maybe M.H. was a gold digger?" She reached over and took the laptop, minimised the incriminating email and once again opened Google.

She tapped away and then stared at the screen while repeatedly muttering, "*Holy shit*".

The photographs of Chateau Challant did nothing to help, only serving to make it all the more unbelievable. It was so far removed from the country-like idyllic French childhood André had described, or indeed invented, that it was laughable.

"It just doesn't make sense. Maybe she's a psycho?" Jane proposed. "Maybe he left all that because of her. For all we know, she's a nutjob stalker. This could all be nothing."

"I hope so. I really hope so," I whispered.

"See if you can find anything about the family, Jane," Cathy directed.

For one moment, I allowed my eyes to close, hoping Jane would find an explanation. When the hollow tapping of the keyboard ceased, I opened my eyes to see André staring back at me from an article Jane had found. Releasing a sob, I instantly recognised the same youthful face, the same longish hair with which he'd arrived in Ballycross eighteen years before. The same crooked smile. My André. Except in this picture, he was standing stiffly on the steps of the enormous chateau flanked by his parents.

"'*Henri and Gigi Dubois-Challant pictured with their son, André, heir to Chateau Challant Vineyard*'," Jane read before moving to the body of the article, which elaborated on the email, citing that André had gone for his daily swim and never returned. In it, the police were asking for anyone with information to come forward. The family would not stop searching for André until he returned, dead or alive. There was no evidence of foul play. It ended by saying that André was set to inherit the Chateau Challant Estate – one of the wealthiest estates in Bordeaux.

"Look at the date!" Cathy pointed. "By then, he was already here in Ballycross."

"Fuck. Look at the mother." She zoomed in on her face. "She looks so young. And his father is ancient-looking, even there, and that was what? Eighteen years ago. Could he still be alive?"

I stared at the faces of the people I'd already believed were dead.

"Google the mother," I commanded.

The tapping recommenced, then stopped as Jane

clicked into a recent article about women in business and the troupe of Frenchwomen now behind some of the best wines in France. Gigi Dubois-Challant was sitting with one elbow resting on a vast modern desk in the photo, her chin cupped in her hand. In the next picture, she was standing in the vineyard examining a vine. The article claimed that she'd taken over the business following her husband's ill health. Apparently, he was still alive but now took a back seat.

"Mother of God. They're both alive. What the hell? Doesn't look too concerned about her missing son there, does she?" Jane sniffed, then checked herself. "Christ, Seren. I don't know what all this means. But I do know this – André loved you. You have to remember that. We'll figure it out."

"Sometimes people's lives are complicated," Cathy assured me. "Maybe he wanted something simpler."

I shot her a look. "Slumming it with me, you mean?"

"I didn't mean it that way, but think about it. Even you have to admit, there were parts of André that were … how can I put it … I mean he was very well-educated. Refined. Spoke English perfectly. Even before he came that summer to learn, he already spoke English better than we did. He was posh, like. You know that. He knew everything. Remember the way he used to set the table, his taste in food. It makes sense that he came from something like that."

I had known all that. As much as I'd wanted to fight Cathy's words, I knew what she was saying was true. André had been all those things. I used to think it was because he was French. Now, it was becoming evident that it was because he'd been some form of a French aristocrat.

My face had crumpled then, and I'd begun to sob, then curse, then stare. That's when Cathy convinced me I should lie down. Instead, my anger had erupted once more.

Cathy and Jane will be back soon, and I still can't come up with one possible reasonable explanation as to why my husband lied about his past or what I'm now feeling. Despite all the rest, it was the second part of the email that stung most, that has left me feeling empty.

I wonder if your mother had not told me what she had about you, would it have been different? I might not have left as I did. But it sickened me to my stomach to hear it. I thought you were perfect, and she made you a monster. So I left. I went to Corsica. I stayed for a long time there, but I'm back in Bordeaux now, where I belong.

It wasn't long ago that I discovered that you went missing – presumed dead. I can't imagine they looked very hard for you if I could find you as I have. There's no easy way to tell you, André. Perhaps, it won't come as too much of a surprise, but you have a daughter. I'm sure you can figure out that she's seventeen. Her name is Nicole, and she is so like you. I'm sorry I waited so long to tell you, but like so many others, I thought you were dead.

Perhaps we can talk. Gigi Dubois-Challant, 'your loving mother', has a lot to answer for. I read that your father is ill. Maybe it's time to come home and take your place as heir to Chateau Challant.

Marie-Hélène

André lied. But worst of all, André was a father. My heart sinks like a stone when I realise there was already a living, breathing part of André out there. There was no need for me to have done what I have, trying to bring a piece of him back to life, attempting to honour his name. It already existed. *She* had already existed – the daughter of whom he'd dreamed, except she isn't mine. She's him mixed with a stranger. I sit up suddenly as a wave of something I don't understand hits. This woman described my husband as a monster. What the hell did she mean? And what if I've created a monster of my own. For the first time, I know what I'm sensing: fear. Cathy and Jane have instructed me to do nothing, not to answer the email, call the number at the end, or even think about any of it until they return. I already know I'm not going to do what I've been told.

Chapter 14

"Seren?" He looks shocked to see me but not necessarily displeased.

Standing on Bobby's doorstep, I realise it's been years since I've been here.

"Bobby, hello," I manage before the words dry up.

Leaving the house not twenty minutes before, I'd been confident this was where I should come. Now, I'm unsure. I suddenly feel as awkward as he'd looked yesterday evening standing at my door. The thought that it's been less than twenty-four hours since we'd last spoken strikes hard. How can so much have happened in such a short space of time?

"Are you all right, Seren?" he asks, and I nod vacantly. "You look a bit …"

I imagine *depressed* the word for which he's searching. It's the stage that closely follows anger in the five stages of grief. Cathy has them drilled into me: *denial, anger, depression, bargaining, acceptance.* Although now I know they can be applied to almost any regrettable situation.

"I wanted to … I needed to …" My shoulders drop. What the hell was I doing? If I hadn't known the truth about André, there was no way Bobby did either. André had lied to us all. "I'm sorry, Bobby. I don't really know why I'm here."

Meeting Seán Cooper on my way here had thrown me. Before that, I'd been purposefully marching up the road filled with intent, anger steaming from my ears, ready to confront Bobby. I'd been mentally running over the plan to get him to talk when I'd heard my name and turned to see Seán chasing after me. Seán's a big man. Speed isn't his ally.

"*Whoa!*" he'd come to a halt, puffing as he did. "Not as fit as I used to be."

"Seán," I'd sighed impatiently, hoisting my bag up on my shoulder.

Immediately he'd looked as though he regretted exerting himself to catch up. "A few of us were trying to get a hold of you, Seren." He grimaced apologetically, reading my body language. "It's about the trader's association. The AGM is coming up, and …" Another pained expression.

"I'm so sorry, Seán," I softened. "With everything, I just –"

"Please, Seren, don't apologise." He held his hands up. "I feel terrible even asking, but it's over a year … well, we have summer plans and, to be honest, we need to get them started."

"Seán, could you take over for me?" I asked urgently. "I think I should step down. I just don't have the headspace, and actually I'm in a bit of a rush –"

"Say no more, Seren. You were a wonderful contributor. We're all very grateful."

"Thanks, Seán. Take care."

I'd dashed away, but already my anger had dissolved. *Darn it.*

Turning right towards the bay, I'd tried not to think of how quickly my entire life had crumbled, how I'd lost touch with so many people and everything that used to mean something to me. How just a few short years before, I'd had the world at my feet. I'd felt so proud the day I was Head of the Trader's Association. André had made a fuss, even opening a bottle of champagne to celebrate. All evening, I'd spoken about my plans to put Ballycross on the map, filled to the brim with ideas for Christmas Fairs, Farmer's markets, Halloween festivities.

None of them transpired – not one single plan. Soon afterwards, André had taken ill. All I could think as I walked up the hill to Bobby's house was how pathetic I must have sounded, knowing, as I do now, from what sort of life André came. My God, I must have seemed like a small-town hick with my small ideas, my small life, my small world. It's what I feel right now – small.

Bobby stands back. "Right so. Well, you'd better come in, Seren," he says, opening the door and allowing me to pass.

I startle when I catch a glimpse of myself in the mirror to the left of the front door. There's a coffee stain down my grey sweatshirt, and the collar of my utility jacket is tucked down the back of my neck. I'm a mess. Pausing, I smooth back my hair, wipe the traces of mascara from under my eyes, try not to think that I look like I've been on a three-day bender. If Bobby has noticed, he doesn't react.

"Sit down." He gestures towards the sofa next to the fire. Even though it's late spring and not yet six, a fire is crackling in the hearth. In the open-plan kitchen beyond, something is sizzling in a pan.

The tranquillity is far from the chaos I'm feeling inside. I jump when a small grey dog materialises and hops up beside me, settling itself and resting its head on my lap.

"Go 'wan. Get down." Bobby moves forward to shoo it away.

"It's okay." I put my hand on its back. "Who's this then?" The dog shimmies to get comfortable and lets out a satisfied grunt.

"That's Nora." Bobby goes over to the stove and removes the pan from the heat.

"Sorry, Bobby. Am I disturbing you from your dinner?"

"Ah, just a bit of steak. It can wait."

"Nora is some name for a dog," I say as an afterthought, smiling as I pat her head.

"She's sort of a nosy yoke, as you can see. I knew a Nora at school who was the same."

The thought of little Bobby in school getting fussed by Nosy Nora is minorly amusing. For a moment I want to forget the real reason I'm here and instead absorb the calm, the mindless chat. Here, in this cosy cottage, with a smiling dog by my side, it feels like what life should be – uncomplicated – but it's not why I'm here. I need to refocus.

"So, were you passing?" Bobby breaks the silence, sitting down on the wooden arm of the chair opposite.

I omit a short exhalation. It's not quite a laugh. "No. Not really."

He nods once, gets up and goes to the fridge. "Want a beer?" He waves a green bottle at me.

"No, thanks, Bob."

He cracks it open and takes a swig. "Tea?"

143

"Tea would be good." I nod. It will give me time to remember my earlier plan.

Setting the beer on the counter, he busies himself, giving me a chance to gaze around. Not much has changed since André lived here with Bobby after first returning to Ballycross. Not that I'd paid much heed to the interior of the cottage back then. It's sort of eclectic – earthy but clean. In a way, the mish-mash looks intentional, even though I know it isn't. Bobby's strange collection of furniture and rugs somehow works. Not that different from how we'd kitted out the shop – I imagine most items were accumulated over the years from people getting rid of things and asking Bobby if he'd like them.

Back then, when I used to call here to collect André in my banger car – the one I'd owned before the banger van, Bobby would often be sitting where I now am. We'd never exchange more than a few pleasantries about the weather, the state of the roadworks, that sort of thing – whatever had been going on in the village at the time.

I glance at the door next to the kitchen leading to what had once been André's room. I close my eyes for a second to see if I can still picture him emerging through it, smiling back at me like he hadn't seen me in days when more than likely it had probably been hours. I can, but today I'm not smiling.

"Off out, lads?" Bobby would ask while André and I beamed at each other. Usually, we'd been "off out" to stay in, heading back to my house to make plans for what would become the wine shop.

"You know André proposed to me out the back of the house here, Bobby? Overlooking the bay," I say, absently.

"Is that right?" Bobby doesn't turn from where he's getting out a mug, putting a few biscuits on a plate.

* * *

"I've never done this before."

André's hands had been trembling. I'd never seen him that way before. His apprehension had been entirely unnecessary since I'd already been nodding in agreement before he'd even finished his spiel.

"So, I want to make it right because I never plan on doing it again," he'd said, dropping to one knee. "One time only, for the love of my life." He'd produced the box from inside his jacket and opened it.

I'd gasped (obviously).

We'd been together for less than a year, but it had been enough to know that it was for life.

"*Till death do us part.*" I've said it aloud without realising.

"What's that?" Bobby looks over his shoulder.

"Nothing." I shake my head, then lean over to where I've set my bag down. I feel a flush of anger once more, and suddenly my mind is obstinately clear. I need to do this. Testing the waters,

I reach inside, pull out what I've brought with me, and silently place it on the wicker-and-glass coffee table in front.

"I still remember what he said. Well, not word for word exactly. It was something about how we were both orphans, with no families of our own, and had somehow found each other. All very romantic. He said he'd never felt so much at home in a place. That although France was where he'd been born that here with me in Ireland was his home. He told me you said to stop searching." I'm looking at my hands now. "Funny, I never once questioned

145

anything he told me about his life before here. I mean, why would I?"

I look up and fix my eyes on Bobby. He's opposite me now – tea in one hand, a plate of biscuits in the other, his eyes on the bottle of wine I've placed on the table.

"Would you prefer a glass of that? I can open it for you if you like." He gestures at the wine, then places the mug and plate next to it. "Sorry, I don't have any in the house myself. Not much of a wine-drinker. All a bit fancy for me." Something in his face has changed.

"No, thanks, Bobby. I brought that one for you. I know you don't drink wine, but I thought it might help jog your memory."

Bobby blinks nervously, and I narrow my eyes. So, he does know something. It had occurred to me earlier as I lay on my bed at home that if anyone knew something about André, it was Bobby. Before leaving to confront him, I'd texted Cathy and Jane to tell them I was going for a walk to clear my head and that I'd call them as soon as I got back. I don't have long before one of them comes looking for me – in particular, Cathy. Currently, I'm what she might describe as high risk – pregnant, grieving, unhinged, and recently scorned.

Bobby's still eyeballing the bottle of wine. "Jog my memory?" he asks cautiously, then breaks his gaze. He walks over to the kitchen counter to retrieve his bottle of beer, then sits back down on the arm of the chair.

"That's right."

Judging by the developing colour of his face, I can see I'm making him uncomfortable.

"About what?" He crosses his legs and rolls his head like he's strained his neck.

"Can you think of anything?" I lean forward, disturbing

Nora, who gets up and goes to Bobby's side. Perhaps the dog can sense the hostility in my voice. To be fair to Bobby, I'm acting cryptically.

It suddenly dawns on me that he might know nothing and that his uneasiness has to do with me behaving like we're in a live recreation of *Poirot*.

"I'm sorry, Bobby," I shake my head, snapping myself out of it. "I've had a real shocker of a day."

"Is this about André?" he asks suddenly. He glances at the wine bottle, then at the ground. I've positioned it so that the label is facing him.

"I don't know. Is it?" I sit forward again.

"Well, I assumed since you brought a bottle of wine and you were talking about when you got engaged." He's acting cagey. "Has something happened?" He stands, puts the empty beer bottle on the table and wipes the palms of his hands down his jeans. He goes to the fridge to get another beer, opens it, then almost drops it.

He knows something. Right now, I'd be willing to bet that if I hooked Bobby Cronin up to a lie detector, he'd fail miserably.

"Do you want to know something bizarre, Bob? Do you know that I've never been to France?"

"That right?"

"Yes. That's right. Don't you think that's odd?"

"Not really. Never been myself." He takes a slug from his beer.

"But if you were married to a Frenchman who grew up tending vineyards with his father, who was a farmer, and his mother who was a pastry chef, then would you think it was odd? Especially since our business was wine and then pastries. Wouldn't you think he'd have wanted to show me where he grew up?"

147

I look at the wine bottle and then back at Bobby, who shrugs.

"Not much of a traveller myself. Got everything I need right here. I suppose André felt the same."

"Unless there was something in France he didn't want me to know about." Bobby can't meet my eyes. "I thought that maybe he might have told you something, Bob." I reach forward and pick up the bottle. "Something about this place. Chateau Challant. Did you know it's one of the top Bordeaux vineyards? And see that that tiny little picture of the enormous house?" I point to the label. "That's what it actually looks like. I looked it up on the laptop earlier. Some of their wines sell for 100 euro a bottle. Of course, in the last number of years, they produce a cheaper version too – one more accessible to the masses. Clever move. One that you might attribute to someone new running the business. I read an article online today – one about a woman running a vineyard. A woman whose son in his mid-twenties went for a swim one day and never came back. I believe his name was …"

There's an agonising pause. It takes everything I have not to break it as I usually do. I need him to feel it, so he'll speak.

"André," Bobby finishes, after what feels like weeks.

He doesn't look surprised, but I do. I'm so stunned that I almost drop the bottle in my hand. Carefully, I place it back on the table, then clasp my hands together to stop them shaking. Bobby has stopped jiggling around like he needs the bathroom and is waiting for me to speak, but however hard I try the words won't form. I need air. I need it so badly that for a brief moment I feel like I'm choking. The heat in the room, both the fire and the tension, has soared. I get up and move towards the back door, fling it open, and rush outside.

Once there, I grip the railings surrounding the patio until my knuckles turn white. I'm panting, almost as heavily as Seán Cooper had been earlier. Poor Seán honestly believes that the Trader's Association matters. How I long to be like him again. How I yearn for stupid, pointless worries to mean something once again.

I fill my lungs, slowly counting as I do. In and out. In and out until I begin to feel like I'm getting oxygen enough, so I don't collapse. The sea beyond is flat calm – the waves casually rolling in, then back out over the jagged black rocks below. It doesn't match how I feel. Right now, the water should be raging, crashing to the shore, bubbling over the cliffs. I sense a presence behind me, and I close my eyes.

"Right over there." I can hear his voice clearly, feel his body behind mine. "*La France.*" André had pointed over my shoulder. "So near and yet so far."

"Don't you miss it?"

"*Non.*"

"Why here? Ballycross must seem boring compared to France."

"Not really. The world is what you make it. It's not so different."

I felt him shrugging behind me.

"Here, by the sea, is as good at it gets."

"Will you take me someday?"

"*Oui.* Someday. If we can ever afford to go anywhere again after finishing the shop." He was laughing good-humouredly.

"I suppose we're stuck in Cork so."

"How about I promise to take you to France every

single day right here in Ballycross. How does that sound, *chérie*?"

"Sounds cheap! But I'll take it. Promise though, that someday we'll go?"

Had he promised? I can't remember now. Opening my eyes, I turn.

Bobby's hands are in his pockets, and his eyes fixed on the ground.

"You knew?" I ask.

Eventually, he nods. Slowly, his eyes meet mine. "I knew some."

"*You knew!*" I repeat. This time it isn't a question. My eyes are dangerously narrow, and I'm shaking my head in disbelief, tutting and huffing all the while.

"Come back inside." Bobby reaches his hand toward me.

I stare at it in disgust, then whip back around to face the sea.

"Please." Bobby tries again.

I'm still shaking my head, holding the railings, willing myself not to turn and angrily thump his chest. Or even worse, fold my body into his arms to find comfort.

Instead, I whisper, "Tell me."

For a moment, Bobby doesn't speak, and I think he's gone back inside until I see his hand resting next to mine on the railings.

"As I said, I knew some, not much," he repeats, then exhales. "What happened?" He turns to look at me. "What did you find?"

His voice is so full of concern that I have an urge to wriggle my hand under his for solace. Without meeting his eyes, I begin to explain. The only thing I don't tell him is that I'm pregnant, but the rest tumbles from my mouth. While I speak, I can feel his hand burning next to mine, millimetres from my skin. I'm so confused by what I'm feeling for Bobby, so angry at André, so in need of compassion. All I want is for Bobby to make it better, fix me like he fixes boats or punctured tyres.

I keep talking, explaining how in the space of a day I'd felt a little brighter about the future – perhaps ready to start living again. For this part, I'm sure I see some look cross Bobby's face, his eyes widen slightly, one side of his mouth lift, but I don't pause long enough to let it mean anything. I tell him how I'd been trying to do something nice for Jane to make up for neglecting our friendship. How I'd thought it would be a good idea to do a review from André's account.

Bobby's so quiet that I have to glance up to see if he's still listening. "Go on," he urges.

"It was supposed to be funny, I think." I put my head back and laugh humourlessly. "I think I was trying to show that I was moving on or something. I don't know what the hell I was thinking." I pause and observe him as I say it. "Then I saw the name *Marie-Hélène* pop up."

Bobby's jaw tenses. It's slight, but enough. My eyes flick towards where his hand is resting on the railings. He balls it into a fist and then flexes his fingers when he sees me watching. Slowly my eyes travel back to his, and I hold his gaze.

"You knew about her, didn't you?"

Bobby shakes his head. "I didn't." His eyes are blinking.

He's lying. "Bobby?" I say his name like a schoolteacher, waiting for a pupil to own up before the rest of the class goes down for his actions. "Bobby?" I try again and then lose my patience. "*For fuck sake!*" I exclaim, and he

151

startles. "I know you're a man of few words, but this is pathetic. You're lying. You can't even look at me." I turn and take a few steps away.

"You have to understand …" Bobby finds his voice. Running his fingers through his hair, he grips it at the crown, closes his eyes for a second and then puts his hands back at his side. "André was my friend." He says it like he's trying to convince me. He exhales loudly again and repositions himself back at the railings. Looking out to sea, he says, "He confided in me, and I swore, no matter what, I'd take it to the grave."

Chapter 15

It takes me a few moments to register that Bobby isn't going to elaborate further. "*But you did take it to the grave, Bobby!*" I shriek, throwing both hands in the air. "*André's dead!*" My voice is shrill. "*He's fucking dead!*"

Bobby whips around to look at me, then thumps his chest with his fist. "*My* grave, S-heren. I swore I'd take it to *my* grave." He looks genuinely torn, but I'm all out of sympathy.

"You're fucking kidding me?" Again, silence. "Wow!" my voice catches. "Typical! How incredibly honourable of you." I clap sarcastically. "And what about me?" I mimic the chest-thumping. "Do I not have a right to know the truth?"

"It's not like that. You're getting worked up over nothing." Bobby kicks some imaginary dirt and tucks his hands into his pockets.

"Over nothing? Really?" I walk back towards him. "So, today, I get the news that my dear husband was the heir to a vineyard dynasty. That he was engaged to someone else before me – a woman he never once mentioned. And then I find an article claiming that he drowned! His family thought he was dead before he was even dead. Christ, even I'm confused. Is he really dead this time? Perhaps we should dig him back up to check. Or is he inside there, Bobby? Are you hiding him?" I'm completely out of breath. "What is it, Bobby? Please."

"S-heren, stop. You're talking rubbish. It's not what you think."

"Really. Am I? I'm completely in the dark. Do you know how that feels?" I put my hands to my face and exhale loudly.

When I drop my hands, Bobby squeezes his eyes together and winces like he's in pain.

"Please." I move closer to him so that we're almost touching. "I'm begging you, Bobby. Everything I knew about André has just been ripped from under me. Please," I implore. "Tell me what you know."

This time Bobby throws his head back and emits a pained growl. He takes a step back. "Ah Christ, it's not like that, Seren. It's …"

"What is it, Bobby? Please."

"Okay. Yes. André was their only son, so yes, I suppose that made him an heir if that's what you want to call it to that French place. But he didn't want it. It was all too much. They wouldn't leave him be, so he left. All he wanted was a simpler life."

"So everyone keeps saying." I roll my eyes.

"Well, maybe they're right? Maybe you should bloody listen," he splutters.

My eyes widen. It's the first time Bobby has ever sounded anything other than even.

"I'm sorry," he says immediately. "I didn't mean to raise my voice."

My eyes fall to my feet.

"Look, what does it matter where he came from? A man is entitled to a past. He wanted a fresh start. André was who you thought he was. He'd do anything for anyone, especially you. He loved you."

I look up at Bobby. He places his hand on mine and pats it reassuringly, and for a moment I soften. Perhaps there is a perfectly reasonable explanation.

"Ah, I'm not one for this mushy lark, but he did, and rightly so. Now, I'm asking you, S-heren, leave it there." He removes his hand and stuffs it back into his pocket.

My head jerks. "*That's it?*" I spit. "Leave it there? Leave what where? What the hell happened, Bobby?" This time, I fail to hold back my frustrated tears.

"It was all nothing."

"Well, then tell me. Why did he lie about his parents? Why did he tell me his parents were dead?"

"I don't know."

He makes to walk away, but I grab his arm.

"Please, don't put me in this position," he says.

"What bloody position? Just tell me. Why did he leave France? Please, Bobby. Can't you see? If I don't know who he really was, it ruins everything we had. You're acting like he murdered someone." I'm sobbing now. "Please." My legs wobble, and I let go of his arm and grab the railings. Peering over, I think how catapulting myself over the edge seems like a very viable option. Nothing could be more torturous than this exchange.

"He didn't murder anyone, S-heren. It's nothing like that." He's beside me again.

"What then?"

"It was nothing. A disagreement with his folks or something, and he wanted a change. That's all." He's nodding encouragingly.

My eyes are flat as I stare at him, and it dawns on me that he's not going to divulge anything. Bobby is going to remain loyal to whatever André was hiding. I straighten up and take a deep breath.

"Did he fake his death?"

"No!"

"Did he love *her*?" I give it one last shot.

"Who?"

"Marie-Hélène."

"I don't know. There was a relationship. It was nothing."

It wasn't nothing. I can tell from Bobby's face. "Did his parents know that he was still alive?"

"I don't know."

"Great."

"All he said was that that part of his life was over, and he wouldn't be going back, ever." He can't meet my eyes.

"I'm none the wiser, am I?" I laugh bitterly. "I didn't know him at all."

"You did. Just forget it. It's the past."

"And you won't tell me anything else?"

"There's nothing to tell. He told me where he came from, that's all. That there was a girlfriend. They broke up. Nothing else."

This time I look at him in disgust. "You're a liar. Bobby Cronin. You were perfect for each other, the pair of you. Both liars! Out fishing, plotting whatever while you were out there. I thought we were friends too, but you've made it clear we're not. Take your little secret to the grave and, while you're at it, do me a favour and never look in my direction again. Shame on you!"

Bobby looks utterly taken aback by my outburst, even more so as I continue.

"I never took you for cruel. I always thought I could count on you, but you've just kicked me while I'm down."

"Ah, come on now. That's not fair." Crestfallen, he reaches for my arm and then decides against it. "I didn't expect –"

"What? You know what I didn't expect? I didn't expect to find out that André has a *daughter*." I pause to gauge his reaction. For the first time, he looks genuinely shocked. "Judging by your face, you didn't know about that part. Now, all I have to figure out is if André knew." Without waiting for him to respond, I brush past him and head back inside to grab my bag from the floor beside the sofa. He follows. "You can keep the wine, Bobby. Think of it as a parting gift. I hope you choke on it."

"S-heren, stop, will you? I'm not good at confrontation. I *am* your friend. I just –"

"Just what?" I haul my bag over my shoulder.

"You're upset. Sit down awhile."

"Are you going to tell me the truth?"

Again, no answer. It takes all my reserve not to swing my handbag at Bobby's face. Instead, I head for the front door, then whip around to face him one last time.

"Thank you for the information. Your generosity truly sates me. Don't worry, Bobby, I'll find my own way."

"What do you mean find your own way?"

"None of your fucking business. Have a nice life." I open the door, storm out, and slam it behind me. "*Fuck you, Bobby!*" I shout at the closed door, berating myself for having considered that Bobby Cronin might ever become something more to me than the man who delivers the unwanted mackerel. "*And fuck you, André.*" I glance at the sky. "*Fuck you all.*"

157

As I make my way back down to the village, I can feel my phone buzzing in my bag. I pull it out and answer gruffly.

"You okay?" It's Jane. "Cathy said you went for a walk. Honesty, Seren. Now really isn't the time to be getting your steps up."

I'm about to tell her about Bobby, but I can't muster the energy to repeat it, not yet. "I needed air."

"But you're okay?"

"As well as can be expected."

"So, I rang my mother."

"Oh, God, Jane, why?" Jane's mother has never forgiven me for ending the engagement with her beloved son, Simon.

"Don't worry – I didn't tell her anything. I just asked did she remember anything about when André came to us as a student that summer."

I'm suddenly alert.

"First, I had to listen to the health status of every person she knows. In brief, two deaths, one heart attack, one hip replacement, two knees, a fall and mole removal. Anyway, it was done through an agency. Mam used to take a student, and it would pay for all the uniforms, ugly school shoes, books etc. at the end of the summer. She said she never heard from André's parents directly, but she was able to tell me that she got paid about three times what she usually gets. Which I can vouch for. Do you remember I got the oxblood Doc Martens, for sixth year in school? And at the end of the summer, she was sent this crate of wine. All packaged up in those wooden boxes. Mam said it was the most disgusting wine she'd ever tasted, so she gave it to whoever she didn't like. She remembers it had this sharp –"

"Aftertaste," I repeat André's original description.

"Come to think of it, Mam probably handed out a 1000 euro worth of wine to her arch enemies. Does any of that help?"

"It proves he was a Challant, but we already knew that. Oh, God, Jane, my head is melted."

"I'll be over soon."

"Do you know what?" I rub my temples. "I'm exhausted. I just want to sleep. I'm down by the Centra now, so I'll be home in a few. I'm bushed. Can you call Cathy and tell her."

"Are you sure?"

"I am."

Jane does what I ask her. A few minutes later, I get a text message from Cathy.

Just sleep. We'll make a plan tomorrow. It's going to be okay.

I try to lie down on the sofa back at the house, but my mind is working on overtime. Starting from the beginning, I try to order my thoughts – go right back to the start, to where it all began. Taking a breath, I'm there.

I'd been outside Centra after a morning swim up near Bobby's house. An old friend of my mother's had stopped me to congratulate me on my recent engagement to Simon. I can remember not being able to muster the appropriate enthusiasm for the happy news. She was banging on about how proud my parents would have been that I was finally settling down. In reality, Mum would have been turning in her grave if she knew I'd decided to "settle down" so very young with someone as wet as Simon. I'd promised Mum that I'd go back to college after Dad died, but then she'd passed away not

159

that long after him – a stroke, followed by a heart attack. It had been a shock, one I still hadn't come to terms with.

After talking to the woman, I sauntered over to the grass area in front of the shops. Families were playing on the beach beyond, couples walking, friends sipping coffee on the stone wall, and I stopped to take it all in. I'm not sure if the next part happened as profoundly as I recall, or if I've altered the memory over the years to fit, but I do know as I stood there, clutching a small brown-paper bag with a single scone inside, I felt lonely. It had begun to dawn on me that it was unlikely that Simon and I would ever make it up the aisle, together at least. Simon didn't like me, let alone love me, and I didn't either. I was dreading breaking it off, having broken the cardinal rule of dating a friend's brother – crapped on my doorstep, so to speak, crossed the invisible line. In reality, I cared far more about my relationship with Jane than I did about Simon. Nevertheless, at that moment, I imagined there wasn't another person in the entire world as lost as me.

That's when I saw him.

He was sitting on a bench, leaning forward: his elbows on his knees, hands to his face. At first, he looked very much like someone who'd been on an all-nighter: dishevelled, tired, until I clocked the hold-all bag beside him. He was a tourist, perhaps, and yet there was something strangely familiar. He lifted his face from his hands then, massaged the back of his head, then circled his neck a few times. I stood watching with my head still facing the beach ahead, allowing only my eyes to move in his direction.

Then I saw him get up and pick up his bag. The height – a little taller than me, not much. The hair – medium brown, floppy. The face – stubble, tanned. As he neared,

I dropped my eyes, crossed my arms, pretended to be interested in something over to the right until he passed. Then I whipped my head after him and found myself staring straight into his eyes.

"Serendipity?" Recognition flooded his features.

"André? Is that you?" I smiled back admiringly. He was even better-looking than I remembered. "Are you here to learn more English?" I joked.

"Something like that."

"Are you just passing through?" My God, I could hardly breathe.

"I'm not sure."

"Oh. Well, it's good to see you."

"You too. You look really good. How long has it been?"

I pretended I was trying to think – that I didn't already know precisely how long it had been since he'd first kissed me around the back of the tennis courts, then spent an entire summer repeating it. "Well, I was seventeen," I blush. "Almost eighteen," I corrected.

"Hah. Yes, I remember that detail was crucial. So," he moved his eyes from side to side, thinking, "over six years?"

"Yes. And here you are. So what brings you back to Ballycross? Tennis?" I flirted.

He didn't laugh. Instead, his eyes fell with his shoulders.

"Sorry, André." I shook my head. Attempting to read his features, I had to resist the urge to reach over and smooth out his furrowed brow. "I didn't mean to pry."

"No, no … that's OK. I … I wanted a change of scene. There's nothing for me in France any more … my parents … they …" He stopped abruptly, unable to finish.

"Oh, Christ, André. I'm so sorry." I placed my hand on his arm. "Really. And there's no need to explain, unless

161

you want to, of course. My mother died last year, my father the year before that. Sometimes it's the last thing you want to talk about."

"I'm sorry for your loss, Seren." He looked up at last, forced a smile.

"Yours too."

He nodded once, then clapped his hands together. "Would you like a coffee, for old times' sake?"

His face was open again, and I felt a flutter of something unexpected. For old times' sake, I would have liked to haul him up to the tennis courts, let him press me and my denim halter-neck against the green fencing. Right then, I'd have gladly suffered through my mother's inquisition as to what the diamond-shaped marks on my back were.

"I'd love a coffee. Or is it too early for wine?"

"Never too early for wine. It's good to see you, Serendipity. I was hoping I would. And just like that, you appeared."

And just like that, it shatters. From this perspective, the memory seems different. Had André told me his parents were dead, or had I put the words into his mouth? Was it I who'd given him the idea to lie? If I'd said nothing, what might he have told me about his parents? Because he had been about to reveal something, but what? That they'd had a falling-out? That he'd gone through a break-up? I wish I could go back and prevent my presumptive words from escaping my lips, let it play out as perhaps it might have.

A few weeks after that, I'd asked him more. He'd told me the full story of how his father had died first – cancer. Then his mother – a stroke. His pain was so convincing that there is still one thing of which I'm sure. During those first months together, André had been mourning something. If it wasn't the death of his parents, then what was it? It hurts that he hadn't felt able to confide in me. I would have understood whatever it was, wouldn't I? Then again, look at my reaction now.

What happened in France to make André lie? Did he fake a disappearance? It's too far-fetched to fathom. If it's all nothing, as Bobby claims, why wouldn't he just tell me? And who the hell is Marie-Hélène? Does André have a daughter? There are far too many questions swirling inside my head.

My mind flits back to the email. Marie-Hélène said something barbed about André's mother. That she'd told her something about him that sickened her. What if she knows something about André and is trying to blackmail him? Could this be about money? Nicole can't be his daughter. I don't know how I know it, but I do. I need to reread the email. I stand to fetch the laptop off the sideboard where Jane left it earlier. Clicking back into the inbox, I almost faint when I see a new email. As I position the cursor to open it, my heart thumps in my ears. I do as Jane had earlier, taking no chances, and copy the text into the translator app, then I read it.

André, I see that you read the other message. Perhaps you are shocked. I want you to know that I don't want anything from you. I assure you of that. If I had, I would have come sooner. All I want, and I believe this is fair, is for the Challants to sponsor Nicole's college education. Please call me, and I can explain.

Clicking on the accompanying attachment, I wait for it to load, then gasp at the realisation that I'm wrong. Marie-Hélène isn't looking for money, well, nothing beyond reasonable. Especially since there is absolutely no doubt that the girl in that picture *is* André's daughter. It makes me wonder what else I have wrong. Immediately, I reach for my phone.

Chapter 16

Nicole

The sudden vibration of the phone against the coffee table startles them both. Nicole watches Maman reach for it, look at the screen, then frown. Her mother untucks her legs from under her on the sofa and stands. Holding the phone out, she stares at it blankly. It stops abruptly, then moments later starts again. Nicole observes Maman bite the corner of her lip, move her eyes from side to side, then take a breath.

"Hello." A pause. "Yes, this is Marie-Hélène."

She's speaking in English. Who can it be?

There's silence while Maman listens. Nicole goes back to her drawing but looks up from her sketchpad in time to see Maman's eyes widen.

"Can you hold for a moment, please?"

Holding the phone against her chest, Maman walks over to the dining table and lifts her purse. She takes out fifty euro and waves it at Nicole. "Here. Go and meet your friends. Go on. Quick." Nicole stands, tucks her sketchpad under her arm, takes the money and grabs her leather jacket and bag off the arm of the chair without arguing. "Have fun." Maman is behind her, ushering her towards the front door of the open-plan flat. Before Nicole even opens it, Maman turns and walks back towards her bedroom. Over her shoulder, she sees Maman put her hand over her mouth and say, "My God." Then she's sure her mother whispers the word "cancer" before her eyes flash at Nicole and she disappears inside her bedroom.

Nicole shakes her head, stuffs the money into the pocket of her denim shorts and pulls the door of the flat shut behind her. Outside, she takes a gulp of the Bordeaux air and sets off. *Who was on the phone?* Normally she wouldn't bat an eyelid, but something is going on. Then again, Maman's friends often phone in the evening and Nicole is sent to her room. There, she sits with her back against her bedroom door, listening through the thin plywood to her mother's undulating tones – giggling, whispering, followed by high-pitched laughter. It's principally about men, or lovers, as Maman calls them. From what Nicole can gather, the conversations about them last longer than the lovers themselves. Mind you, the friends don't last long either. Nicole is accustomed to people sweeping into their lives in an all-consuming way, only to flit away as fast. Over the years, there's been a stream of spontaneously close female friends. One minute they're there all the time in the flat, doting on Nicole, drinking and partying with Maman and the next they're gone.

"Nothing is forever. Always remember that, Nicole. Nothing is forever," Maman would explain if Nicole ever asked. Eventually, she'd stopped asking.

Nicole pulls on her jacket, throws her bag over her shoulder, and wonders where she should go. Truthfully, she doesn't have many friends here in Bordeaux. She'd only been at school here for her final year. By then, the others in her class had already formed their alliances. Although they were friendly, they were nothing like her friends back home.

She keeps walking, allowing herself to drift, see where the evening takes her. Actually, it's been a while since Maman has had anyone in the flat, friend or otherwise. Although she's never met any of the men, a few times Nicole has found remnants of them: two glasses in the sink instead of one, a forgotten sweater, a tie, a lingering smell of aftershave. Nicole sometimes wonders if Maman keeps them to herself because she's ashamed of the men she dates or embarrassed by Nicole. Either way, she'd have liked to have met one of Maman's boyfriends. It might have felt normal to have a man as part of their lives – someone to ask her about her art or interests.

Passing the Pont de Pierre bridge, she is reminded of a story she'd heard a while back. Apparently, the police had been called when one of her classmates stood on the edge threatening to throw herself off it after her mother revealed she was getting a divorce. What Nicole found odd was that the mother's husband wasn't even the girl's father. It wasn't until another girl from their class explained it further that Nicole began to understand. "She'll be alone with her mother now," the girl had clarified, "a fate worse than death." Having been alone with her mother for close to eighteen years, Nicole conceded the girl's fears. The difference is that Nicole realised a long time ago, in her mother's words, that nothing is forever.

Finding herself near the subject of her latest sketch, Nicole advances and settles herself across from the building. She'd been so deep in thought that she can

167

hardly remember how she ended up here. Sitting down, she crosses her legs, rests her sketchpad on her right knee, and poises her pencil. She's about to begin, but instead she tilts her head to one side, then flicks to the last page of her pad and lifts the portrait. Even when she closes her eyes, she can still see the outline of the face, the curve of his cheek, the lines in his forehead. She knows the face by heart.

Yes, she supposes she would have liked a man, any man, to be part of their lives. At home, in Corsica, she used to observe how her friends' fathers and brothers would do "manly" things around the house like taking out the bins, changing a lightbulb, lifting heavy grocery bags in from the car … hugging. In truth, it was the hugs that fascinated Nicole most – the rest they could manage alone. Something used to catch in her throat when she'd see her friends hugged by their fathers. Maman always said that the smartest thing a woman can do is to learn to never need a man, but more than once Nicole felt she'd needed one of those hugs – one that could make you disappear inside a pair of arms, vanish beneath a strong chin.

Flicking back to the sketch of the building, Nicole narrows her eyes. She can't concentrate. *Who was it on the phone earlier?* By the startled expression on Maman's face, certainly not someone she'd been expecting. Whoever it was, Maman is hiding something. And she'd spoken in English.

Something is coming.

Deep down, Nicole has always known it. Lately, she can feel it closing in, inching closer from where it has lurked her entire life. She can't explain what it is exactly, but it's there. Fortune or misfortune? Nicole isn't entirely sure, but it has always loomed, ever-present in the strange little things her mother says. For as long as she can remember, Maman has incessantly spoken in that manner. "It wasn't meant to be like this." "Great things will come." "Be patient." More than once, Nicole has wanted to scream back, *"What? What is coming? What the hell are you talking about?"*

Only lately, there's an added slant to Maman's cryptic messages. For a start, Maman is quiet, curiously calm. She's started talking about the old days in Corsica, lecturing Nicole on how brave she must be for the future. And then, of course, she appears to have stopped drinking. It's hardly surprising after the last time.

She'd tumbled through the door of the flat, staggering backwards and forwards, waking Nicole and then insisting on telling her how Julien, her boss, and actually all men, were after only one thing.

"They won't stop until you give in," she'd slurred while Nicole removed her shoes and tried to lie her down on to the bed.

"Well, don't give in then," Nicole had snapped.

"But if I hadn't given in, then you wouldn't be here," she'd mumbled, wagging her finger. "I'm so bloody tired. Tired and sick of it. I'm glad I don't have much longer left in this life. Soon, Nicole …"

Maman remembered nothing the next day, but her words have been playing on Nicole's mind ever since. "I don't have much longer … " It all goes towards confirming Nicole's suspicions.

Maman needn't worry. Nicole isn't frightened of surviving alone. Besides, she's practically been alone her entire life anyway. Nicole already knows where she'll go when it's all over. She's been saving all the money from her job at the pizza restaurant to make it happen. She

169

doesn't need much to survive, and she's almost eighteen. She knows enough people in Corsica to pick up a job, one that will allow her to continue drawing. It's all she wants to do anyway. The day they left was the worst day of Nicole's life. Even with all its grandiose buildings, Bordeaux doesn't come close to the places in Corsica where she could perch all day, sketching the curved lines of the fishing boats, smiling faces, rolling landscapes. Unlike here, where you'd be just as well drawing with a ruler, everything is so straight, uniform, and symmetrical.

Someone stops to glance over her shoulder at the building she's sketching. Without being able to help herself, Nicole turns to look right into the man's face. He smiles awkwardly, nods before edging away. Still she does it – stares directly into the faces of strangers, in the hope that one day it might be him. She's been doing it since she was eight years old. Of course, she's old enough now to realise that there's little chance of her father idling past her on the street. Still, there's more hope of it happening here than there ever was in Corsica. You see, she's originally from Bordeaux. Maman has told her that much, at least. It must mean that he was from here too, or nearby anyway. He might still be here.

Bordeaux is prettier at night when the city is illuminated. In daylight, everything is too real – the dirt, the dust, people rushing about. After dark, it's quieter, cleaner, mythical beneath the artificial lights. Looking down at her sketchpad, Nicole shakes her head in dismay, then gazes across at the buildings of Place de la Bourse. It's one of Bordeaux' most famous sights. She's been attempting to draw it for weeks now but can't seem to get it right. It's harder at night when the lights reflect off the shallow water on the concrete slabs in front, creating an exact mirror image of the building. It's as magical as it is challenging to depict. Looking at it often makes Nicole think she could walk into the reflected building on her hands, and once inside, everything would be inverted. Perhaps it wouldn't be that different from normal. Life already feels upside-down.

Her mind flits back to Maman, and her stomach flips. Perhaps she should head home now. She has a feeling Maman is going to tell her tonight what's going on. How should she react? She hesitates for a moment before closing the sketchpad, gathering her things and standing.

She ambles back towards the Pont de Pierre and this time she walks across it. Reaching the centre, she stops to peer over the railings, trying to muster up how desperate you'd have to feel to want to throw yourself over and be swallowed by the water.

Thankfully, she has no desire to experience it, not when she can sense what lies ahead – freedom. A pang of guilt hits. She cares for her mother, of course she does, but there's always been a gaping expanse between them, nothing to bridge the gap. Maman alone has never been enough to make sense of all the things about herself that Nicole has never understood. Like why her nose is a little crooked, her skin so sallow. Why she adores the sea when her mother can't abide it. How she's able to draw like she can. Where she gets her high I.Q. from. Her father must be the missing link. If she could meet him, even once, or at least know his name – anything more than the one visual she has of him – the same one she sketches over and over at the back of her sketchpad. Years before in Corsica, she'd found a photograph of her mother with a man. He'd had his arm slung over her shoulders, and she was smiling at him. Maman looked different, happier.

171

Nicole knew straight away who he was. She'd stared at the photo for hours, then held it next to her face in the mirror.

When she'd asked Maman about it, she'd told her it was an old friend and accused her of snooping. When she'd snuck back the next day, the photograph was gone. She's never seen it since, yet still she can recreate his face – so like her own. She will find him. She's confident about that. Sooner rather than later. She's been planning it for years. Once or twice, she'd actually typed the words **"Who is my father?"** straight into Google. Google hadn't delivered. Instead, she'd happened upon an article on fatherless daughters. According to it, as one Nicole should have self-esteem issues, find it challenging to build and maintain relationships, have an eating disorder, be prone to depression, be sexually promiscuous, susceptible to addiction. The article could have been written about Maman. She was a fatherless daughter, too, just like Nicole.

Reaching their building, Nicole takes a deep breath. She must be strong now – be the clever young woman her mother claims she is. Gifted is how Maman describes her to people. School was never much of a challenge for Nicole. Even moving from Corsica to Bordeaux and changing schools for her last year hadn't phased her academically. She'd have the results of her final exams soon. She already knows she's aced them, but she won't be going to college. Aside from not being able to afford it, she doesn't want to. She'll never study medicine like Maman keeps suggesting. She can barely stomach the sight of blood as it is. Maman says it would be a shame to waste her abilities – the same ones that have always seemed to surprise her mother far more than necessary.

"Imagine, there was a time I feared you'd never even walk, let alone speak," Maman had said once. "A constant worry."

"Why? Was I sick?" Nicole had no recollection of being poorly as a child.

"No. You were fine."

From outside the front door, Nicole can hear muffled crying. Trying to remain calm, she unlocks the door. Maman looks up from where she's sitting on the sofa. Her tear-stained face looks even more gaunt than usual. Nicole goes to her and puts her arms around her, smoothing her hair like a child. "It's going to be okay, Maman." Her mother nods once. "I'll be with you every step. You don't need to be afraid."

Maman's head jerks up suddenly. "Afraid?"

"Of dying."

"Dying?"

"You're not sick?" Nicole frowns.

"Why would you think that?" Maman stiffens.

"I … I … I thought … you said you didn't have long left … I heard you say."

Maman raises her eyebrows and laughs hollowly. "When did I say that?" She tuts.

"It doesn't matter. I thought … earlier on the phone … I thought you'd got bad news."

Maman takes Nicole's hands. "Silly girl. Imagining things again." She touches the tip of Nicole's nose. "I'm not going anywhere, but there has been bad news."

As she listens to the summary, Nicole fixes her eyes on the floor in front of her. Even still, she can tell Maman is selective with the information. She's not telling her everything.

"André?" Nicole looks up at last. "Was that his

173

name?"

"Yes. André."

It suits him, Nicole considers. The name fits the face of the man who will never materialise from one of her drawings. She's never going to find him now, nor the answers for which she's been searching.

"I know this is all hard to take, Nicole, but sometimes the unexpected makes us who we are."

For an instant, Nicole wants to reach up and slap her mother's face for making yet another ambiguous observation, for destroying the only ambition she's ever had. Instead, she closes her eyes and tries to picture him once more. Is it possible to love someone without ever having known them? She already knows it is. Nicole loved her father almost as much as she now hates her mother. As the image of her father dissolves, so too does the shortlived sympathy for Maman.

"There are great things to come, Nicole. I promise you that."

The words feel hollow. What great thing could happen now when the worst thing imaginable had occurred? Suddenly she knows precisely how that girl must have thought standing on the edge of the Pont de Pierre. Nicole had been right. Something was coming, but she could never have anticipated that it would be this, nor how vehemently she wishes that her father's fate had befallen her mother instead. Now, she's the one trapped in a fate worse than death.

Chapter 17

Despite a fluttery sensation in the pit of my stomach, I feel something I haven't in a while – freedom. Only now do I understand how smothered, observed and judged I've felt, unable to escape the constant noise in my head. Aside from a pair of eyes in front appearing sporadically to spy, for once no one is watching. A tiny triumphant smile spreads across my face as I glance about and exhale. Even the butterflies in my stomach are somewhat more pleasant than the pregnancy nausea, the sensation of sitting on a rocky boat despite being on dry land, the metallic taste in my mouth. Those symptoms have mostly abated now. I'm safely in my second trimester – the place I swore to Cathy I'd get to before making any more "rash" decisions. It's almost amusing. I used to be famous for my indecision, now I'm considered infamously obstinate. Despite my vow, we both knew what I'd do as soon as I could.

Enveloped in white noise, the plane's hum is soothing, as is being surrounded by people who couldn't care less who I am or what I've done. To the other passengers, I could be absolutely anyone. I could be flying to France to meet my lover, going on a business trip … emigrating. Not one other person on this plane knows my business, and it feels good, like wiping the slate clean. Of course, I've walked away from quite a shabby slate back home. It seems everyone who matters is either angry with me, disappointed in me, surprised by me, or suspecting of me.

"You've lost your fucking mind" – Cathy.

"So, Cathy knew all along – well, that says it all, doesn't it?" – Jane.

"What do you mean you're leaving?" – Fi.

"There's something different about you … if I didn't know better …" – Marian Cummins.

"Please, S-heren. I … I … I …" – Bobby.

I'd had enough. I'd had it up to my neck with awkward conversations, unsolicited advice, friendly curiosity, falling out with people. First, Bobby, then Jane. I had to get the hell out of Ballycross before the entire village caved in on top of me.

"If I don't, I'll end up sitting in my bedroom, picking the legs off spiders, wearing my wedding dress and covered in cobwebs like Miss Havisham," I tried to explain to Cathy, referring to the Dickens novel we'd studied at school. She'd been unamused.

Perhaps as soon as André died, my life in Ballycross had ended too, but it's taken me this long to realise it. I've taken Hazel's advice. I'm hiking on.

Before I lean my head back, I wink at the little boy who is peeking up once more over the seats in front. He sticks his tongue out at me cheekily. I do the same. He wrinkles his nose and disappears behind the seat. Closing my eyes, I try not to think of the past few weeks.

* * *

"What do you mean you don't know how long you're going for?" Cathy had looked shocked.

"I don't know. I might stay until after the baby is born." Truthfully, I was afraid of what people would say when they found out I was pregnant. I could imagine what they might say because it was precisely what I kept telling myself. *Trying to bring him back to life. Selfish girl – denying the poor child a father.*

"Where will you stay? What about a doctor? Christ, Seren. People will only talk for a while. So what, you're pregnant, who cares! You don't have to explain it to people. Stick your bump out with pride. Please. You can't move away and have the baby alone. What the hell are you thinking? What have we done to you? You're being really selfish."

I hadn't been able to find the words to explain it to Cathy.

I open my eyes to look around before my emotions take over. To my right, there's a young girl, not more than eleven, sitting on her own. Like me, she has the row of seats to herself. She's wearing headphones and colouring one of those intricate mandala patterns on the table in front. Around her neck, she's wearing what looks like an all-area access card, but judging by the way the air-hostess keeps swaying down the aisle towards her, it probably means she's being chaperoned by the airline. Perhaps I could have put myself down for a similar service – one for crazed widows. It might have been nice to have someone who didn't really give a hoot ask if I was doing all right. If I was scared of what I was going to find in France. If I knew what I was doing.

Just as fast, the fleeting feeling of freedom is replaced by crippling doubt. Maybe it would have been better if I'd been seated next to some astute person, who'd have impartially listened to my troubles and responded with something terribly profound to put my mind at rest. I can't even have a glass of wine or one of those little bottles of vodka to calm my nerves for my first solo plane journey. It's sort of pitiful. Then again, so is being a heartbeat from forty, thirteen weeks pregnant and flying to a foreign country with no plan and no intention of returning home anytime soon.

I'd rushed into Cathy's office first thing the morning after seeing the photo of André's daughter.

As soon as Derbhla saw me running up the stairs into the reception, she'd tried to stop me.

"Doctor is *verry verry* busy, Seren. There are others ahead of you. I'll have to –" She'd dipped behind her desk, putting her hand under the lip of the table, and pressed something.

"Did you just press a panic button, Derbhla?" I'd ignored her alarmed expression as I pushed open the surgery door.

Luckily, Cathy was there alone, looking none too pleased by my ambush.

"Sorry. I won't take up much of your time, but look!"

"What's this?" Cathy took the piece of paper from my hand and examined it. "Where did you get this? Is that her?"

"Yes. You can see it too, can't you?"

Cathy tilted her head. "They do look alike, all right, but how can you be certain? It could be a coincidence."

"Look at it!" I punched the printed image with my finger. "*And* I spoke to her."

Cathy's head jerked back. "To the daughter?"

"No. To *her* – Marie-Hélène."

"Christ, Seren," she groaned. "I thought we were going to be a little more … cautious this time."

I ignored the superior tone. "She was nice, Cathy – normal. Not what I was expecting at all." I slumped into the chair opposite her and exhaled loudly. "It was brief enough. There was so much I wanted to ask her, but I didn't want to bombard her."

"Like she bombarded you?" Cathy raised her eyebrows.

"I had to tell her André was dead regardless," I justified. "She was upset. Shocked by his death. She cried, quite a lot actually."

"And?"

"Well …" In truth, already, the conversation was sort of a blur. I'd still been in a state of shock after seeing the photo, after getting the email earlier and following the dispute with Bobby, but I didn't want to admit any of that to Cathy. "It's sort of innocent, really, not as weird as I'd imagined. She was working at a restaurant in the village next to the vineyard one summer. They met, became involved, she got pregnant. There was a disagreement, and she left."

Cathy frowned. "That's it? Like what sort of disagreement? Did he know she was pregnant? Does she know why André left France? The little thing about him being presumed dead?"

I shook my head. "We didn't get to everything."

Cathy lifted her hands to circle her temples with her fingers.

"Maybe he just wanted a change," I attempt chirpily, echoing Bobby's words from the day before.

Cathy eyed me cautiously. "Have you slept, Seren?"

One eye twitched tellingly as I shook my head. "Not really. But I'm fine."

"You're not fine. You're wired." Cathy paused. "I was thinking, Seren. Would you chat with Bobby Cronin? He knew André better than anyone."

"Better than me, you mean," I snapped.

"I didn't say that."

"I already spoke to him."

"When?"

"Yesterday evening?"

"Wow, again – you kept that to yourself!" She tutted. "Well?"

"He knew nothing," I lie. I didn't want to tell Cathy that Bobby knew much more than he was letting on but had refused to share. I wasn't ready to have anyone turn on André, not until I knew the facts myself. Anyway, it's not like she'll ask Bobby. As the local doctor, she rarely digs too far below the surface with people.

"Okay."

"That girl *is* his daughter," I repeated.

"If you say so. So what does she want?" Cathy asks.

"Who?"

"This Marie-Hélène."

"Nothing from me. She thinks I should write to André's parents and tell them he's dead, which of course I'll have to do. She wants them to put Nicole through college – she wants to be a doctor, like you."

I thought that might please her. She didn't look impressed.

"Is unversity in France not free?"

I flinched. "Maybe not all. It still costs money. Anyway, I offered to pay."

"*What?*" Cathy stood up suddenly, crossing her arms.

"It's okay, Cathy. She refused." My eyes dropped to the floor. "It's what André would have done."

Cathy exhaled again, then starting pacing the room. "But you're not André, and let's not forget he didn't even know about his daughter. Oh, God, Seren, something isn't right about all this. This woman could be lying. Maybe you should –"

"She's not lying. It sounds like she's had a hard life. From what she told me about her, Nicole is so like André, not just in looks.I know André would want me to know her. I can't explain it, Cathy, but it feels like he's sent me –" I managed to stop myself in time. I knew if I mentioned signs, Cathy might lose it altogether with me.

"Seren, there's so much all this could mean. I thought about it all last night. Something must have happened, and I think you should be really careful before getting involved. Did she say what it was the mother had told her – remember that weird part in the email?"

"I was afraid to ask."

Cathy pursed her lips, then sat back down. "I think you need to find out all sides of the story first."

I nodded back. "You're absolutely right, and I know just how to do that."

As the plane bumps and jolts, I put my hand to my stomach and rub in circles. I haven't told Marie-Hélène that I'm coming, nor have I revealed that I'm pregnant. I've replaced my usual skinny jeans and T-shirts with loose-fitting flowy tops and leggings to hide my burgeoning shape in the past few weeks. No one would guess (not yet anyway) that I have a neat little bump beneath the airy fabric, especially not someone I've never met. Until I know that Marie-Hélène is genuine, I'll play my cards close to my chest. Being mothers to André's children connects us, but I'll tread carefully until I know she's someone I want to be eternally associated with.

I'd spoken with Marie-Hélène twice more since the first time. During the next conversation, she'd asked if we'd had children.

"No." It wasn't a lie, since technically I don't, not yet.

"A shame. Nicole is lovely. André would have produced a lovely child for you."

I'd almost crumbled there and then, but I'd managed to stay firm.

"And you really knew nothing about where he came from, his fortune?" She'd sounded shocked.

"No. Nothing. Do you know why he didn't tell me?" I'd felt stupid asking, as though admitting we'd had a bad marriage.

"Perhaps it was better that way," she'd sighed. "It's a beautiful place, but there was no love there."

"What do you mean?"

"Money isn't everything. All I want now is to give Nicole a good education. She's clever, you know? Hugely so."

Marie-Hélène had a way of avoiding giving a straight answer to any of my questions. I put it down to difficulty communicating over the phone. I'd tried to call her several more times after that but hadn't been able to get hold of her. When I eventually did, she'd been pushed for time and hadn't been able to chat.

"Have you written to the family yet to tell them about André?" she'd asked.

"No. Not yet. I thought I should go in person." There'd been a long pause.

"*Non*," she'd insisted after a while. "They're not nice people, Seren. It's the reason André left. Talking to you now, I can see why he never went back."

Then she'd said something about being sorry for taking up so much of my time, wished me luck for the future and hung up. Afterwards, I'd felt strangely hurt, cast aside. Had I wanted to build a friendship? I suppose as far as she was concerned, there was nothing tangible to link us. Would she feel differently if I'd told her that I was pregnant?

One thing I'm sure of is that I want to meet Nicole. I feel an inexplicable connection to her familiar features, despite never having met her. It's more robust than the tie I feel towards my unborn child. She's André's flesh and blood, I can't deny that. I also need to find out what happened in France all those years ago.

I'd tried one last time with Bobby, but he'd been as insistent, if not more, than before. "It's not my place, S-heren."

Afterwards, I'd turned on my heel, walked back home, then returned twenty minutes later – this time in my van. Bobby had opened the front door and watched aghast while I'd emptied a black refuge sack full of frozen mackerel on to his doorstep.

"And it's not my place to accept anything else from you ever again, Bobby."

I hadn't given him a chance to respond. I haven't seen him since, despite him calling my phone for days on end. In the end, I'd blocked his number. I'm done with him.

Jane is a different story. When I finally got around to telling her that I was pregnant, she'd reacted really badly. I think it had more to do with the fact that Cathy knew before her and that I'd excluded her. And then I'd refused to listen to her when she'd pleaded with me not to go to France. Jane made it clear that she doesn't agree with me having André's baby. She thinks I'm young enough to have met someone else, that I'll never get over his death now. I'd tried to explain that I never would, anyway. To think I'd reckoned Cathy was the judgemental one. Jane had far more to say on the subject. She hadn't held back. Neither of us had ever spoken to the other the way we had that day. It had hurt.

Her reaction put me off telling Fi that I'm pregnant. I couldn't face her hating me too. Instead, I'd said to her that I was taking a few months off to find myself. She was upset at first, but when I'd asked if she and Kevin would move into the house and run the shop for me, she was somewhat appeased. "Christ. I haven't slept in anything other than a boat since I've been married. Don't come back, okay?" Of course, she'd been joking, but there's a big part of me that thinks I might never come back. I have no idea what's ahead of me, how Marie-Hélène will react to my appearance in Bordeaux, or indeed André's parents, but it feels like I'm doing the right thing. When it came to it, no matter what happened between them, I owe it to André to tell his parents in person that he's dead.

Last week, when the sonographer squirted cold jelly onto my stomach and ran the ultrasound wand over it, I'd felt the tiniest spark of hope.

"Will Daddy be coming along to see Baby today?" she'd asked gently, pressing my flesh and looking at the screen.

"No. It's just me. I'm… it's just me."

She'd smiled and nodded knowingly. "Well, you're doing a wonderful job. Baby looks lovely and healthy."

She must see all sorts. Indeed, I wasn't the first "geriatric" brave single woman to go it alone.

"He's dead," I'd blurted. "He ... he died."

"Oh, God." She'd paused to look over at me. "I'm so sorry."

I hadn't elaborated on the fact that he'd been dead for far longer than I'd been pregnant. "You know what?" she'd said after a moment. "You're not alone. You have this baby, and babies bring luck. Would you like to know what you're having?"

"Please, Seren. The pregnancy? *This.* Heading off to France on your own? It doesn't make sense," Cathy had said, holding her hands up in exasperation earlier.

We'd been sitting in her car in the setdown area of Cork airport with about sixty seconds remaining before the man in the high-vis jacket rattily knocked on her window again. Despite being wildly disapproving, she'd still agreed to drop me at the airport.

"I know." I'd nodded. "But since the day André was diagnosed, nothing makes sense, Cathy. Nothing. I have to –"

"You don't know what you're doing." She'd whispered this time.

"But what if I do know, Cathy? What if I'm the only one who does know what I'm doing? What if everything I've lost has made me realise what I need? Please, Cathy, just let me go, wish me well."

"I'm here, okay? If you need me. Just pick up the phone, and I'll get on a flight. Do you hear me?" Her voice had broken. "Can't you see? You're breaking all of our hearts."

"Tell Jane goodbye."

"She'll come around. As soon as you see sense and come home."

I'd nodded. I allowed my body to fall towards hers, where I'd rested my head on her shoulder for a moment before silently exiting the car.

So here I am. Lucky Seren, on my way into the unknown – alone, but not alone. There's no one to judge me, nor try to make me see sense, and it feels right. For the first time in a long time, something feels right. Sitting here, I try to picture André and how he might have felt leaving France eighteen years before. Perhaps, like me, he'd needed a different life. André had found me. I wonder what it is I'll find? I caress my stomach again. I have to find out the truth before I give birth. I need to know everything there was to know about André and his past in order to create the right future for his son.

Part Deux

Chapter 18

I adjust my new scarf, take a step back and tilt my head. Smiling, I extend my arm and imitate shaking hands, imagining what sort of impression I'll make. Yesterday, the woman in the exorbitantly overpriced shop convinced me that the designer scarf was all I needed to transform any outfit to chic. She spent an eternity showing me how to nonchalantly knot it around my neck, through the handle of my handbag, around my head. Not only could it be worn as a belt, but if I was feeling "directional", I could twist it around my wrist like a bracelet. I half expected her to turn it into a fruit basket before my eyes or do a magic trick by stuffing it into her closed fist and making it vanish. She put so much effort into the sale that I could hardly leave without it. In truth, I'd been trying to distract myself, kill time – the experience had undoubtedly delivered in that respect.

It looks pathetic on me. I squint once more at my reflection in the mirror, then untie the pink silk scarf and fling it onto the hotel bed behind. I'd thought it might draw the eyes away from my middle section, but all it does is make me look like I'm trying too hard. Who am I kidding? I'm not French, and it's going to take more than a jaunty square of silk to get me through the afternoon ahead. Plonking down on the bed next to it, I roll my eyes. Clearly, I'd been had. Imagine spending that much on something so tiny. I suppose it might come in handy later to sob into or stuff in my mouth to stop the screaming after I learn whatever there is to know about André.

I lie back with a thud. The bed is low and so ridiculously pliable that I almost roll on to the plastic-looking wooden floor. This is my fourth day in Bordeaux, in my new tiny little living space. Thankfully, the room is spotless, but not a bit what I'd expected from the exterior of the traditional-looking building. The website had said a small, quaint hotel, right in the very centre of the city. I wish now I'd paid more attention to the interior photographs. I stare up at the white ceiling and attempt to focus my thoughts. It's the only serene part of the space. The rest is like an acid trip. For some reason, someone thought it would be a good idea to mix lime green with red. It's like I'm trapped inside one of the *Doctor Seuss* books I used to read to Jane's kids when they were little. That said, my current predicament could be considered just as farcical as *The Cat in the Hat*. Perhaps, I could write a new version: *The Widow in the Scarf*.

The sudden thought of Jane makes my stomach twist. I turn my head to the left, trying to picture her lying next to me, laughing uncontrollably at how much I'd paid for the scarf. She certainly hadn't been laughing the last time we spoke. "It's like you're trying to destroy yourself and everyone who cares about you. I can't believe you kept this from me. I can't believe you did it in the first place."

I still haven't heard from her.

I'd texted Cathy when I first arrived to tell her I was alive, that the reception on my phone wasn't great, but that I'd text again in a few days. I'd accompanied the lie about the phone reception with a second one, saying the hotel was beautiful and that I was utterly relaxed – that this was just what I'd needed. I'd watched the three text dots moving on the screen to indicate she was responding. They'd flashed on and off for at least ten minutes before she'd sent a thumbs-up emoji. She must have known I was lying. Initially, I'd planned to take a week of rest before I started digging about into André's past, but the days move slowly when you're in a foreign place alone – even more so than they had back in Ballycross.

Getting to my feet, I glance in the mirror again and brush my hair into place with my fingers. I look better without the contrived-looking scarf. Besides, I'm wearing one of my new pregnancy-concealing outfits. She'll never guess. Anyway, I'm Irish. Just because André was French doesn't mean I'll ever manage to master the undone-chic look that the women here do so well. It's not a myth. They really are stylish – the men too. I've spent the past few days admiring them as I drift through the streets of Bordeaux. Although it's absurd, once or twice I've found myself gazing into the faces of strangers in the hope that one of them might somehow turn out to be André. Or, at the very least, that one of the teenage girls I saunter past might be his daughter.

Of course, it hasn't happened. Honestly, now that I'm here, I'm not sure anything will turn out how I'd imagined. After an initial elation at being in France, I'm deflated. This city doesn't echo André, as I thought it might. I can't picture him here, although I know he'd often spent time in Bordeaux, describing it as a mini-Paris. I've tried to envisage him meandering the pedestrian streets at the centre of the city, staring up at the grand buildings as I've done. It's beautiful, I can't deny that. In fact, under different circumstances, I can see myself, Cathy and Jane, here on that long weekend they'd continuously suggested after André died and I'd vetoed. Bordeaux has everything you might expect of a vibrant, modern city – shops like the one where I bought the insanely versatile scarf, restaurants like the one where I'd sat alone eating the most delicious steak I'd ever tasted. Cafés serving pastries – ones I'm happy to report are not dissimilar to those we do in Ballycross. The river is magnificent, the bridges, the architecture – it's intricate, elaborate, everything I imagined it would be … but it's not André.

The André I knew preferred sea air and small talk with the villagers to this fast-paced city where the people can be so abrupt. I'd asked André once why the French were often considered impatient with tourists. He'd been anything but with the customers in our own shop – I'd never been able to shut him up. André thought it was because the French don't like to speak English.

"They do so out of respect when they need to, but tourists often don't make any effort to speak French."

"But that's because English spoken with a French accent is charming. French spoken with an Irish lilt – not great!" I'd argued.

"Come now, chérie, I love it when you tell me how to get to the train station in French!"

My spoken French never reached too far beyond what I'd studied for my Leaving Cert French oral. I'd never get lost in Paris. I could still recite clear directions to the

Centre Pompidou from just about anywhere in the world.

In truth, I haven't spoken to many people since I've arrived – the odd waiter, the receptionist, the scarf connoisseur. They're not exactly rude, more completely disinterested. The irony isn't lost on me that the very thing I'd been craving – space to breathe, anonymity – is just as displeasing.

I pause to take my sunglasses from my handbag on the street outside the hotel and put them on. It's bright today, the heat as warm as expected in July, making it difficult to breathe. Without hesitating, I pull my inhaler from my bag and take a robust puff. As always, it helps, despite feeling sure that it's nerves and not asthma making me feel this way.

We've arranged to meet at a café near the cathedral – one I'd passed the day before. I'd suggested it. I hadn't understood the dry laugh until I'd hung up from the call and googled it. "Cathédrale Saint-André de Bordeaux – a Roman Catholic church dedicated to Saint André," I'd read aloud to myself and then smiled. Perhaps it was fate.

Patting my bag, I curse when I realise that I've forgotten something back in my room. I turn and head back inside, past the receptionist, who looks up briefly. I smile and make some stupid gesture at the lift as if trying to explain what I'm doing back so soon. She looks away.

"My husband is French," I'd told her when I was first checking in.

"*Très bien. Votre mari se joindra-t-il à vous?*"

I'd had to stop her. "Sorry. I don't speak much French. Well, I do, a little, but we live in Ireland, so you know?" I'd shrugged.

"I asked, will your husband be joining you, madame?"

193

She'd effortlessly switched back to English while I scolded myself for not even trying.

"Oh Christ, no." I'd laughed hysterically at the receptionist's perfectly reasonable question. "That would be a miracle."

That time, she'd studied me as if I was truly insane. I'd felt a far cry from the mysterious woman of the world I'd thought I was just a few hours earlier on the plane.

I take out my case back inside my room, remove the padded envelope, and spill its contents on to the bed. I'd found them a few weeks before leaving for France. They'd been right there under my nose all along. After making contact with Marie-Hélène, I'd rifled through André's belongings, studied receipts, opened envelopes, stared blankly at scraps of paper, looking for clues that it was all a strange coincidence. Even with the articles that Jane had found online, Nicole's photo, and hearing from Bobby Cronin's mouth that André was connected to Chateau Challant, I was still hoping it would turn out to be a mistake.

As a last-ditch attempt, I'd stood on the stool in our walk-in wardrobe and jabbed an umbrella at the top shelf until I'd felt something. Then I'd used the handle to hook the shoebox and pull it towards me. Clambering down and sitting on the stool, I'd opened it to find André's original French passport nestled between an old pair of boots. Inside the small burgundy book was the passport photo of the man who'd asked me to join him for coffee, then wine, then dinner, then life, all those years before. Biting my nails, I'd tried to think how it was possible that I'd never seen it before. But then, we'd never travelled outside Ireland together, nor gone for a mortgage or taken a loan. It was me who'd initially set up the bank accounts for the shop. Looking back now, for André, knee-deep in dust and timber with the renovations, me tackling the administration must have felt like a godsend. Of course, eventually, he'd had an Irish driver's licence. It took him four attempts and a plethora of French cursing to pass the test. Racking my brain, I'd tried to think of times when he'd needed a form of photo ID, but it was a blur. Had he used his driver's licence? I couldn't remember. At the time, it's not something you focus on. Perhaps I should have paid closer attention.

I'd sat there staring at the passport, looking for answers, noticing how it had expired ten years after he'd come to live in Ireland. His birth certificate had been there too, confirming his full name – *Dubois-Challant* and not just the Dubois that he'd used. I'd run my fingers over his parents' names: *Georgette Dubois-Challant* (that must be what Gigi was short for) and *Henri Dubois-Challant*.

And then, there'd been the photo.

He'd looked different in it, foreign to the André I'd known – more assured, worldly, with his arm slung over the shoulders of a girl who was staring up at him. Together, they looked impossibly well-suited, at ease, as if they were exactly where they should be at that moment. Her: blonde, pouting, sexy. Him: tanned, handsome, smiling. It had felt like a knife. Not because he'd been with someone before me, but because it was apparent they were in love. I knew straight away it was Marie-Hélène, even without going to fetch Nicole's photo to compare all three faces. I had, anyway. I'd ran to retrieve it from next to my bed, holding them together so I could fully appreciate the beauty that they'd obviously created.

I hadn't wanted it to be true – but it was. André had existed before me – not in the way he'd described, but in another way – one of which I knew nothing. He'd had a secret life and a love that he'd left behind, but why, and for what? Indeed, not for me. At that moment, I'd turned to catch a glimpse of my tired, wan, jealous face in the mirror. What had happened to turn the André in that photo into the one I'd known. I wondered if, all along, I'd been married to the ghost of his former self?

I select a few of the items from the bed now and tuck them into my handbag. I've included other photos of André from more recent times – one of our wedding day. That day, we'd been just as handsome as the couple in the picture I'd found. Everyone had agreed. I wonder if it's petty to take it? As if I'm trying to prove ownership. My hand hovers over the other envelope containing his death certificate, but I leave it where it is. Before I confirm his death, I first need to verify his life. Shaking my head at the surreality, I exhale loudly and, once more, exit my room. I don't want to be late. I want to be sitting at the table outside the café so I can be the one to watch Marie-Hélène approach. So it can be me to get the measure of the beautiful blonde in that photo. I want to call the shots. After all, I was his wife, not her.

Ever since speaking with her yesterday, I've felt on edge. Perhaps I caught her off guard, but she was unfriendly to the point of being ignorant at the news of my unannounced arrival in France.

"Is this really necessary?"

A far cry from previous conversations, the exchange had made me feel like a slighted child. She's coming alone. She'd made that very clear.

"I don't have long. I work evenings, and I really wasn't expecting this," she'd said for the third time.

I'd wanted to reply that I really hadn't been expecting

her to appear in my life and rip it apart either, but I'd held my tongue. "I didn't mean to surprise you, but I needed to see for myself."

"I can't talk now," she'd cut me off, making me feel like an idiot.

It took all my reserve not to phone Cathy and plead with her to get on a flight and accompany me. Only, I didn't want to admit yet that perhaps Cathy had been right again, and all was not as it seemed.

As I approach the cathedral, I'm blown away by its splendour. It's a far cry from St. Mary's of Ballycross where we'd been married. Glancing left, I clock the café and study the people already sitting at the small round tables outside. Getting nearer, I can't make out anyone who might be her. I still have about ten minutes before we're due to meet. Enough so I can settle myself, order a coffee, whisper a silent prayer to Saint André that she agrees to let me meet André's daughter. After all, I've come all this way. Yesterday I'd been far too meek, but in person I can be more assertive. As I advance, I can feel myself nervously fidgeting, adjusting my bag, pushing up my sunglasses. I aim for a table at the edge of the café. I may even attempt to speak French as a sign of respect, anything to assist my cause.

As I pull out the chair and sit down, I briefly smile at an older woman at the next table. I look away and stare up admiringly at the cathedral opposite.

"Beautiful, isn't it?"

It takes me a moment to register that the woman is speaking in English.

"Yes," I answer, glancing at her again and then blinking.

"I recognise you from your photo." Her accent is thick, her voice gravelly.

My eyes move from her to the image she's holding up. My breath catches as I gaze at a grainy photo of André and me sitting on our bench in Ballycross, overlooking the harbour. For a few seconds, I vanish inside the memory as if I've been sucked underwater. I can recall precisely how I'd felt that day, what we'd faced. It hadn't been long after we'd been told there was nothing else the doctors could do. Then I remember where I am. Resurfacing, I'm lost for words as I look up again.

"The private detective sent it to me," she explains.

"Marie-Hélène?" I try not to look too stunned.

"*Oui, c'est moi.*"

It's on the tip of my tongue to say that I, too, recognise her from the photo tucked inside my bag, but I can't lie. Tilting her head, she smiles, and I glimpse a faint hint of a likeness. Oh my God, it *is* her, or a version at least. As I nod, I'm struggling to stop my hand from covering my shocked mouth. Whatever, or whoever I was expecting, it wasn't this. My God, what could possibly have happened to the woman in that picture to change her so much? What had callously sucked the life from her? Because something did, or someone, that's for sure. With a sinking heart, I acknowledge Cathy *is* right. Something is very amiss.

Chapter 19

Marie-Hélène

"Mind if I smoke?" She lifts a cigarette between her lips as Seren gets up from her table and moves across.

It's lit before Seren shakes her head that it's okay.

"Go ahead," she says anyway, followed by an awkward silence that neither jump to fill. "Listen, I'm sorry if I caught you unaware yesterday ... surprised you," she clarifies when Marie-Hélène frowns at the phrase.

She doesn't answer, takes a drag from her cigarette and blows it above Seren's head.

Seren looks up as it disperses, then fixes her eyes on her clasped hands resting in her lap. "It's just ... well, I suppose since finding everything out," Seren lifts her chin in the air and looks at the sky, "it's turned my world upside down."

Marie-Hélène attempts a smile. Forced to stare into the other woman's tormented eyes, this time she nods slowly. "I'm sorry," she says, resting her elbow on the table before pulling on her cigarette.

Seren smiles and looks over at the cathedral while

Marie-Hélène regards her.

She is even prettier in the flesh than she is in her photo. Aside from being swathed in an ageing, floaty ensemble, she's irritatingly youthful. Marie-Hélène tilts her head and squints. Pared-back, perhaps in something more fitted, or coupled with a neckscarf, Seren could pass for any young Frenchwoman.

"I see now why you laughed when I suggested we meet here," Seren gestures her head at the cathedral. "Saint André."

"Saint André indeed." Marie-Hélène flashes a glance at the imposing building then back at Seren, who swallows in a way that looks like she's ingesting an entire croissant in one go. She can see that beneath Seren's outward smile, her warmth, there's far more. From her jittery gestures, her quivery voice, she can sense her fragility. She'd recognised it, even when they first spoke on the phone. For some reason, she'd experienced an uncharacteristic maternal obligation towards this total stranger. She'd tried to dismiss it, but now, here in person, she feels it again – an overwhelming need to protect her. Deep down, she knows she has no right to feel that way, mostly when she's failed at being a mother of any merit to her own daughter. Still, she has no real desire to hurt Seren, to unexpectedly turn her life upside down. What right does she have to detonate someone innocent? Unless, of course, they deserve it.

"You must think I'm mad turning up like this uninvited." Seren grimaces. "I know everyone back home does." She emits a high-pitched laugh, making the two women at the next table startle. Upon noticing, she blinks several times, swallows again, adjusts her brown wavy hair, then tucks both hands between her crossed legs to stop them shaking. Marie-Hélène's might have been the same had she not poured a large helping of vodka into a mug and downed it before leaving her flat.

Up until then, she hadn't had a drink in well over a month. As soon as things had started to progress, she'd wanted a clear head. Not that she feels the better for it. If anything, she feels worse. She feels wired without alcohol, with nothing but her cigarettes to distinguish one minute from the next. Still, she'd been able to give up at the drop of a hat, discrediting all those alcoholism leaflets that Nicole continuously leaves around the flat. Despite the month-long success, Nicole still sceptically eyes Marie-Hélène's mug of tea in the evenings when they're home from work. "Here, I'll put it in the sink for you," Nicole offered a few times, taking the mug and walking towards the kitchen with it. Marie-Hélène had seen Nicole lift it to her nose to check if the herbal tea was laced with something more.

Today, she'd awarded herself an exemption of one drink to calm her nerves. Now she'd like another. Seren is making her nervous. Her showing up in France hadn't been part of the plan. Then again, neither was how deeply shocked Marie-Hélène felt when she discovered that André was actually dead. Hearing it from Seren's mouth that night had shaken her.

"My name is Seren. I'm André's wife. I read your email. He's dead."

The voice had sounded robotic, stilted. Then again, delivered any other way, Marie-Hélène might not have understood the words. Although she'd been expecting it, it had felt like a blow straight to the stomach. She'd been even more taken aback when she'd heard herself crying.

201

Strangely, it was Seren who'd ended up comforting her.

"And you really knew nothing? Nothing about his parents. Chateau Challant?" Marie-Hélène kept asking because she hadn't been able to believe it.

She'd thought André might stretch the truth all right, but he'd gone so far as to tell Seren that his parents were dead. Seren had been so distraught at André's dishonesty that Marie-Hélène suffered an instant pang of guilt for falsifying the poor woman's memories. In reality, Seren was better off not knowing the real story – she'd already lost enough. But that's not the main reason Marie-Hélène hadn't wanted her to come to France. She didn't need Seren involved, complicating everything when she was so close to the finish line. Now that Seren is here, she'll have to tell her something, find out what she wants, and then send her on her way for good.

"It's so odd, but since André died –" Seren puts her hand over her mouth as her eyes suddenly fill. "Oh, God. Sorry, Marie-Hélène. I was really nervous about meeting you. I'm a complete disaster. Maybe I shouldn't have come."

Surprising herself, Marie-Hélène reaches out and places her hand on Seren's arm. "It was a surprise. *Oui*. But you're here now." She tries to act aloof, but the blatant agony etched into Seren's face is far too familiar. She has also been there – trapped inside a place where it's impossible to hold back tears, where you cannot conceive how everyone else around you is functioning when you're so fractured.

"Yes. Here I am," Seren says as the waiter approaches, interrupting them.

"Wine? Food?" Marie-Hélène suggests brightly. She needs a drink, something to lift the atmosphere if she's going to get through this. Sensing that perusing a menu might be futile, she turns to the waiter and in French orders bread, some salad and a bottle of red wine.

"Thank you," Seren says when he leaves. "That sounds perfect. I couldn't concentrate on the menu."

"You speak French?"

Seren frowns then laughs. "I speak pidgin-French. I understand more than I speak. I'm great at asking directions!" She throws her eyes up. "André used to tease me about that. There was never really much need for me to speak it. This is my first time in France, and André's English was –"

"Perfect," Marie-Hélène finishes. "You've never been to France? And you never thought that strange? Interesting." She raises her thin eyebrows and smiles smugly. Then without giving Seren a chance to answer, "André often spoke of a summer he spent in Ireland learning English."

Seren's scowl at the first comment turns to a smile. "It was already flawless when he arrived that summer."

Marie-Hélène jerks her head.

"He was a student at my friend's house," Seren explains. "I was seventeen. He was my first proper boyfriend. A lifetime ago."

Marie-Hélène's eyes are wide. "I didn't know that part, but I knew he loved Ireland. In fact, he always said he was going to take me there, you know … someday … "

Seren's face falls.

"I'm sorry. Is this making you uncomfortable?"

The waiter arrives with the wine and Marie-Hélène tastes it, nods at the waiter and he pours both glasses.

"It's all just so strange," Seren says after the waiter

leaves.

"Yes. But then so is life." Marie-Hélène's tone is more bitter than whimsical.

"That it is." Seren lifts her glass and waits for Marie-Hélène to do the same. "Anyway, *chin-chin*. It's nice to meet you."

"Is it?" Marie-Helene takes a gulp. "I can't imagine anything about this is nice."

Seren considers. "No, it's very unexpected." She takes the tiniest sip and places her glass back down as the waiter brings the food.

There's an uncomfortable silence as both pick at their salads, then attempt to make small talk for several minutes until Marie-Hélène puts her fork down suddenly.

"Can I be direct?" She proceeds without pausing. "Why are you here?"

Seren's eyes widen. "Well, I …"

"It seems unusual, *non*? Wanting to meet your husband's ex-fiancée? The mother of his child? If André was alive, maybe, but in these circumstances," Marie-Hélène laughs, then takes another large gulp of her wine. Mixed with her earlier drink, she can feel the effects of the alcohol taking hold. It's comforting. It's exactly what she needs.

Seren sets her fork down too. "Being in France has reminded me of how direct the French can be. Mind you, clearly, André wasn't. In fact, he couldn't have been more indirect about his life." She puts her shoulders back and straightens her neck. "Firstly, I'm here because I want to know why he lied about his past." She pauses to give Marie-Hélène a chance to elaborate. When she doesn't, Seren continues. "I loved my husband, Marie-Hélène, and the truth is I trusted him. I suppose I'm not ready to give up on that just yet. If André lied, I believe there was a good reason. I want to know what that was."

"And secondly?" Marie-Hélène raises her eyebrows.

"Let's start with the first."

The confident way she says it makes Marie-Hélène's stomach flip. Seren's entire demeanour has changed. Perhaps she's not the pushover she first thought she was. Maybe she's something else. Marie-Hélène is suddenly afraid. For the first time, it occurs to her that perhaps Seren's motives are not too dissimilar to her own. If so, it changes everything.

"Can I ask you something?" Marie-Hélène says, at last, asserting herself.

Seren nods. "Of course."

"Was he good to you? Was it a happy marriage?"

"Very."

"Are you sure you don't want to leave your happy memories alone?"

Seren narrows her eyes. "I'll take my chances."

"Okay," Marie-Hélène agrees, leaning back into the high-backed wicker chair, glass in hand. "Ask me what you want. I'll answer what I can, but you might not like what I tell you." Although she's trying to maintain control, her voice wobbles. There's silence while Seren thinks and Marie-Hélène refocuses. All she has to do is deliver a version of events to satisfy Seren's curiosity and quench her desire to know more. Taking a deep breath, she prepares.

"I just want to know what happened between you? Are you the reason he left France and never went back?" Seren asks eventually.

Marie-Hélène grins. "Maybe I am. He's certainly the reason I went to Corsica, pregnant and alone. But before

205

every tragedy, there is something wonderful. *Non?*"

Seren frowns. "I suppose."

"Love is complicated. We were in love, Seren. I know that must be hard to hear. I know it in my heart. If things hadn't gone wrong, I believe it might be me in your position now."

Seren scrunches her eyes shut for a moment before composing herself and looking up to hear more.

"I was doing some travelling at the time, taking some time out. I ended up renting a room and working in a restaurant in Margaux – the village next to the vineyard. He came in one evening alone. We got talking. It really was that simple. We met by sheer chance, and we fell in love." She laughs hollowly. "Actually, I fell in love with everything in Bordeaux, but mostly him. He was wonderful. So sexy, so mysterious. But there was also something very magical about that place – the countryside. At first, I had no idea who André was. He told me he worked as a vineyard manager. Of course, I had no reason to doubt it. Why would I? There are hundrerds of vineyards there, *and* he used only the name Dubois."

Seren nods. "That got me too."

"I didn't know who he was for a long time after we were together. It was months before he finally told me, took me to see the vineyards. We started spending more time there, mixing with the summer workers in the evenings. It was fun. Before long, he suggested I move in with him to save on rent. Shortly afterwards, I got pregnant. I was happy about it. After all, I was a couple of years older than André." Marie-Hélène smiles genuinely for the first time. "Scandalous, *non*? I wasn't exactly a teenager, so I was ready to be a mother."

"Do you think he purposely kept from you who he

really was?"

Marie-Hélène purses her lips and shrugs. "I suppose. Maybe he didn't think it was important until our relationship got more serious. They were an insanely private, paranoid family. When he finally told me it was his family's business, he spoke about it like it was a curse. He genuinely hated everything that went with it, except the land and the wine, but the rest … the wealth, the pomp, the ceremony. It wasn't him, and honestly, I didn't understand the level of wealth, not when André was so understated."

Seren nods along.

"He used to say it was like a prison sentence. It came with conditions. When I found out who André really was, and then I got pregnant, it changed everything."

"How?" Seren leans forward.

"Because I wasn't good enough for him. They thought I was a gold-digger. Men like that need a certain type of wife. One who looks a certain way, comes from a certain family …"

Seren is shaking her head. "Come on! Surely not in this day and age?"

Marie-Hélène shrugs. "I thought the same, but no. When I met Gigi, she made it very clear that I wouldn't do. Straight away, she put a stop to our relationship. She came to see me, and we argued. After that, I was practically removed from the premises."

"Did André know you were pregnant?" Seren asks suddenly.

"Yes," Marie-Hélène says and eyeballs Seren. "He didn't want anything more to do with me. His mother took care of the rest."

Seren shakes her head again. "I can't believe that. As

you said, it wasn't like you were teenagers. Why didn't he stand up to her? André was strong. He didn't give a hoot about money, and I know he wanted children –"

"Not with me, it seemed. He wanted his money more. He let his mother pay me off on the condition I had an abortion. Forced me, in fact. I understood if he didn't want me, but to turn his back on his child ... it's despicable."

"But you didn't go through with the abortion?"

"*Non.*"

"And you took the money and never tried to find him. Not until now?"

Marie-Hélène shakes her head sadly. "I was furious with him for being so weak, for picking his family over me. Because of it, I thought I didn't want his baby, but when it came to it I couldn't go through with it, so I went to Corsica. I did try to reach out to him many years ago, but then I found out he'd disappeared. I assumed, like everyone else, he was dead."

Seren is silent. Marie-Hélène knows what's coming next, and she's ready.

"But what would make you think otherwise? What made you believe he wasn't dead?"

"Because I thought André wanted to escape too. That maybe he only found the strength after losing me. You don't understand about his mother. Gigi is a dangerous woman. Even though he loved Bordeaux, in the end he wanted to be free." As an afterthought, she adds, "I suppose he found freedom with you."

Seren narrows her eyes. "If it was so simple, why didn't he just tell me? If his family, his mother was horrible, I would have understood."

Marie-Hélène leans forward. "Only André can answer

that and, since that is now impossible, I'd say he was ashamed about what he did – abandoning his child and me. Perhaps he did try to find me, who knows? But he found you instead." Marie-Hélène picks up the wine bottle, refills her glass, takes a slug and leans back. "Finding out he's dead has been hard on Nicole and me. She always thought she might meet her father someday." She pauses for a moment. "She deserves more. It's the reason I want them to sponsor her with college. She's so bright."

Seren nods, then changes her mind and shakes her head. "But if his family are that awful, why would you want anything from them? Why not let me help on behalf of André?"

Marie-Hélène shrugs. "I don't want anything from you, Seren. This isn't your problem. In reality, we're not really connected. Apart from being loved by the same man, you're a stranger. We'll manage like we always do." She pauses, closes her eyes, then opens them and laughs humourlessly. "Maybe you're right. Perhaps I should forget about asking them. You see, when you have a child, you forget about pride. Your child is the only thing that matters."

"But I *want* to help. Let me talk to his family at least. With the news of André being dead, they might be happy to have a granddaughter."

"*Please!*" Marie-Hélène spits. "Not another word." She throws her chair back and stands suddenly. "I don't want Nicole near them, ever. Do you understand?"

"Okay." Seren puts both hands up to calm her and glances left to right at people at the other tables who've turned to watch. "Please, sit."

Marie-Hélène sits back down. "*D'accord*. You have to understand, I'm no longer interested in the past. What's

209

done is done. André is gone. All we want to do now is move on, as you should."

Seren nods. "Okay."

"It was hard. I had no family but, in the end, I had Nicole." She pauses, then asks. "What will you do now? Return to Ireland? You must want to get back. It is hot and busy in the summer here." She picks up the empty wineglass and tilts it back, allowing a solitary drop run slowly into her mouth.

"Yes. I'll be going back soon. The summer months are busy in the shop."

"What is it you sell again?"

"Wine." I don't elaborate further.

"That's good." She lifts the wineglass as if to toast her, notices there's nothing in it and puts it down.

"I was planning to take a drive to Chateau Challant, but I'm not going to now."

"You should do what I said and write them a letter. Believe me. His father is very sick, and you won't get to see his mother."

Seren nods. "Talking of seeing people, that brings me to the second reason I came to France."

Marie-Hélène is eager for the meeting to conclude. She's tired now, and her thoughts are starting to feel muddled. She can hear Seren continuing to talk, but it's all beginning to sound the same, like white noise. Lighting a cigarette, she tries to focus but is distracted by the waiter. She summons him by holding up the empty bottle of wine and waving at him as a signal to bring another. She should celebrate, she thinks – today went well. She hadn't had long to prepare, but she'd managed it. She, too, had been nervous about meeting André's wife, but she needn't have been. Seren seems satisfied with what she's heard. It had all sounded plausible, and Marie-Hélène has avoided involving her further than necessary. That was important to her, but so is this next part. After today, she never wants to see Seren again, for both their sakes.

"I'm sorry," she slurs, at last, waving her finger like a conductor as she answers the question Seren just asked, "but that's never going to happen."

Chapter 20

I can't get away from the café fast enough. I'd felt so nervous earlier, meeting Marie-Hélène. Now, I'm furious. As I rush off, I wonder if all French people are liars or just those connected to André. It hadn't taken long for my initial compassion towards my husband's haggard-looking ex to wane, as soon as it became apparent that it was booze, and not something more sinister, that had embezzled her looks – sucked the life from her, making her appear at least a decade older. She'd done it to herself.

I speed past the cathedral, panting as I go. It takes all my reserve not to stop at the steps in front and let rip at Saint André for sending me right into the unfocused, drunk-eye of the storm. My God, I'm an idiot.

Because of a raving alcoholic playing the victim, I've taken an impromptu trip to France to listen to an utter deluder tell me about *my* husband – how in love they were, how he must have gone searching for her, but instead found me! For that part, I'd wanted to stuff my entire fist into my mouth to stop from screaming. Perhaps

I should have brought the silk scarf with me after all. At first, Marie-Hélène's story had seemed plausible, but once she'd begun to open up I'd realised that I was on the receiving end of explosive verbal diarrhoea. Now that I've met her, I imagine André must have been seeking asylum from her in Ireland. Or perhaps Andre's mother had wanted Marie-Hélène to leave in order to save the vineyard – to prevent her from siphoning the maturing barrels and drinking them dry. Honestly, I'd never seen a thirst like it. I felt dehydrated just looking at her. She'd guzzled two bottles of wine without noticing that I'd barely taken a sip from my glass. I should have known to make my escape after the first bottle when she'd picked up her empty glass and practically wrung it out.

"I'd like to meet Nicole." I'd had to say it three times before she'd heard me.

By then, she was already sloshed – hardly surprising, given she must only weigh seven stone and definitely had something to drink before leaving the house. She'd been trying to catch the waiter's attention by very nearly smashing a bottle of wine on the ground.

"I think André would want me to know his daughter," I'd tried again. "Maybe I could tell her about him, show her some pictures. I brought some with me if –"

"I'm sorry, but that's never going to happen." The answer, although slurred, had sounded well-rehearsed. "I did ask, but she made it very clear that she wants nothing to do with anyone connected to her father." She'd shrugged. "Nicole is … how can I say it … difficult? You can hardly blame her when she was abandoned like that. A child needs both parents, *non*?"

Non! I'd wanted to scream back. *Not if the one they have is enough.* And difficult? If Nicole is contrary, with a

213

mother like Marie-Hélène, I could certainly see why.

Earlier, I'd tried to object when she'd told me that André had known she was pregnant and shirked his responsibility. Indeed, the André I knew might have walked away from Marie-Hélène but not from his daughter. I can't accept it. She'd been adamant, claiming that André's mother had paid her off, practically forced her to have an abortion. Had she held a gun to her head? Marched her to the doctor herself? Come to think of it, for all I know, Marie-Hélène could have demanded the money. Deep down, I have a sneaking suspicion that all this relates to money, despite her insisting that she hadn't understood the level of his wealth. Had Marie-Hélène got pregnant to trap André when she found out what he was worth? Then when he wouldn't stay with her, threatened him somehow?

I shake my head at the thought. Do people really do that sort of thing? It seems ridiculously far-fetched. Or perhaps I'm naïve. But if she had needed money, why struggle alone all those years when she could have made a maintenance claim at least? In her original email, Marie-Hélène said she was contacting André to get his family to pay Nicole's college tuition – not André. It makes no sense. Marie-Hélène didn't know André was dead when she wrote that email – so why would she believe that André's parents – regardless of how wealthy they are – would be responsible for educating *his* child? That was another thing. These vineyards often had a tendency to haemorrhage money rather than making any. I'd seen it myself over the years, heard stories of it in the wine trade. There was possibly no substance behind the façade of Chateau Challant.

I stop walking suddenly as I hear my parents' words.

214

"When money is involved, that's when you get a real measure of a person." My mother had said that all her life. And my father: "If you want it, work for it. If you expect to get handed it from somewhere, you'll have to pay something in return. What that is might not unfold for a long time, but there's always a cost." Marie-Hélène must be after money and perhaps much more than college fees.

"Please don't mention Nicole again. She doesn't want to meet you. I can't make it any clearer," Marie-Hélène had finished in her gravelly voice as the second bottle of wine arrived.

Unfortunately, the second bottle appeared to generate a second wind, veering the conversation towards the farcical. "André was a wonderful lover. *N'est-ce-pas?* We did it everywhere," she'd giggled, like a schoolgirl with a desperate throat infection, while I cringed. I never imagined that I'd end up sitting in a Bordeaux café, listening to my husband's bedroom antics with another woman. She'd made André sound like a horny teenager, chasing her up and down the vineyards, dry-riding her against the grapes. If it wasn't so absurd, I could imagine myself laughing with him at the skeleton with flesh that had slipped out of his closet. Now that she was out, she'd be impossible to put back in.

Once or twice, while she spoke, I'd caught a trace of historical beauty behind her bleached hair, sunken eyes, and lined face. She'd sucked on cigarettes for the entire meeting like a granny in a nursing home. One cigarette was only out, and another was lit. She'd barely touched her meal and, to add insult to injury, I'd ended up paying. That said, it was a small price for not having to sit around and wait for her to drink a third bottle. God only knows

215

what way it would have gone after the hat trick. I saw her order it as she weaved towards the bathroom. The waiter issued me a panicked look over his shoulder, at which I shrugged. She wasn't my problem, not anymore, not now I suspected she was dishonest. I might have felt sorry for her, except she was also unpleasant, almost purposely insensitive, and I'd felt belittled by her. Whatever had happened in her life, I now felt confident she'd brought it all on herself.

It was evident that Marie-Hélène didn't have to go to work that evening like she'd claimed over the phone the day before – another lie. And if she did, the diners at the restaurant would be getting far more than they bargained for. It briefly crossed my mind that the more inebriated she became, the more willing she might be to tell me the truth, but by then she'd been speaking gibberish. She was concealing the truth as tightly as blasted Bobby Cronin. Except, unlike Bobby, she spoke incessantly in nonsensical riddles, mixing English with French to further skew the meaning.

More than once, she'd hooked her finger like the witch from *Hansel and Gretel*, beckoning for me to come closer. I had, in the hope that I was about to bear witness to a moment of honesty. Instead, she'd delivered several baffling proclamations.

"I did the right thing keeping Nicole."

"I knew it would end well."

"Patience is key. Key!" She'd tapped the table with her hooked finger on that occasion.

She's a liar. There are more holes in her story than the crochet blanket I'd knitted at school during the life-skills module.

I'm shaking with anger as I cross the busy road to walk

along the river in the hope that the water might calm me like it does at home. I have to remind myself that I'm pregnant and that stress isn't good for the baby. Thank God I'd decided not to reveal my secret. The only thing that Marie-Hélène had managed to clearly convey was that she doesn't want me in her life. I don't want her in mine either, but I still want to meet Nicole.

Or do I?

What if Nicole isn't actually André's daughter? Perhaps I've been forcing myself to see the similarities between their faces. Could it be a trick of the light, a coincidence? Like the picture Cathy took where I look like Julia Roberts. I'd had it framed immediately. To this day, I pass where it hangs in my living room and smile. From a distance and through practically closed eyes, I could see it too.

André had taken it off the wall to keep next to his bed whenever he was in the hospital. "I love that one of you," he'd told me.

"That's because I'm Julia." I'd squinted again at the photo before opening my eyes to see him doing the same.

"I think I can see it."

The everyday memories are even more wonderfully ordinary next to Marie-Hélène's wild story of André. André was not the man she'd described, and Marie-Hélène hasn't told me everything, I know that for sure.

Even how she'd recounted the hardship since discovering André was dead seemed weird. After eighteen years of not seeing someone, indeed it's sad news but not to the extent she'd claimed. If Nicole is André's daughter, then maybe it's a connection that never fades. It's hard to tell. One thing for sure is I've gone about this all wrong. I should have gone to his family

217

first. I'd been put off by how savagely Marie-Hélène spoke of them, but perhaps they'll be more forthcoming with the truth, whatever it is.

Pausing, I rub my temples. The thoughts are going around and around in my head as wearily as I walk. Truthfully, it was the draw of meeting André's daughter – his flesh and blood, that led me to the city first. Clearly, it was a mistake, an utter waste of time. Now I'll never get to meet Nicole, and it's unlikely I'll uncover André's side of the story. How can I? He's dead. Like Cathy had suggested, all I can do now is try to get all their points of view and perhaps, in doing so, summon André's voice. As long as his family aren't as deranged as Marie-Hélène, there's still a chance I can find the truth. I begin to move faster, trying to outwalk it all before I start to lose my breath and have to slow my speed again.

Spying a bench up ahead, I head towards it, sit down and put my hands to my face. I'm exhausted – nervous about breaking the news of André's death to his family. I suppose I could always pop a letter in the post like I'd told Marie-Hélène I was planning to, but it wouldn't feel right. If the situation was reversed, André would go in person. What will they tell me about him? More negatives like those that Marie-Hélène revealed? And yet, I still can't imagine what could have made him want to disappear. An unwanted pregnancy? Hardly. I gulp suddenly as the thought strikes. What if André actually did something wrong, something illegal? Again, my head throbs. Regardless, his family have the right to know that he's dead and buried in the hilltop graveyard, next to my parents, awaiting the day when they hurl my coffin in on top. I'm so exhausted that right now it sounds like the rest I need.

I try to think. Compared to what I've just encountered, I currently have a soft spot for André's mother, Gigi, no matter how vehemently Marie-Hélène had spoken about her – mostly through flared nostrils omitting smoke like a dragon. Perhaps Gigi isn't the villain. After all, she had the foresight to send Marie-Hélène packing. Considering it, I think I'd do the same for my son. Maybe she was protecting André.

Nodding to myself at the only thing that makes sense, I straighten and look out at the river. My anger is settling. If everything was how it once had been, I'd currently be phoning Cathy and Jane to tell them about my meeting with "Mad Marie". Right now, I'd probably be hysterically laughing at how André had impregnated the actual witch from *Hansel and Gretel* and how I'm currently carrying the witch's daughter's brother. It couldn't get more complicated! Exhaling, I picture their faces as if they'd been there at the table with me today. It wouldn't have been long before they'd have hooked their hands under my armpits and air-lifted me out of there.

I could hear what Jane might say. "Christ, you can see why André legged it to Ireland. She'd make you want to jump off the top of the Eiffel Tower, naked, onto a bed of nails. Maybe even on national television, without your legs shaved, and still carrying the Christmas weight!"

God, I miss them. An intense pang of longing for Ballycross hits me square in the chest. I miss my life. I miss my café. I miss Fi … but most of all, I miss André. Squeezing my eyes shut, I repeat it to myself. I miss my husband. What the hell am I doing here in this stupid city with its traffic and tourists and complicated stupid roads and weird pedestrianised streets? Despite the stifling heat, it's concrete and cold. I don't have to do this. I don't have to stay to find out what happened before I met André. What does it bloody matter? He loved me. Me! Not the drunken version of Debbie Harry that I've just met. I can go back to Ireland with my tail between my legs and try again, make an effort at happiness – fake it until I make it. "Would you like that, baby?" I place my hand on my stomach and look down. The baby doesn't answer. I have to decide alone.

"In Nicole's words, you're not actually family. Nor will you ever be," Marie-Hélène had said earlier. The unkind words had jolted me. I'd almost wanted to tell her my secret to spite her – to reveal that in less than six months we'd be forever linked.

"Tell me about Nicole at least. Do you have any more photos?" I'd asked instead.

"Not with me," she'd said, lighting another cigarette.

"Not even on your phone?"

She'd shook her head, then blew a thin line of smoke almost directly at my face.

Coughing, I'd fanned the air. My patience was gone.

"I do have this," she'd said eventually. Rooting in her bag, she'd pulled out a sheet of paper that looked as though it had been torn from a sketch pad. Unfolding it, she'd placed it on the table and smoothed it out.

It was a sketch of a very grand building with a mirror-like image below. Aside from a frustrated-looking pencil scribble at the edge, it was perfect.

"I found it in the bin this morning. She throws away whatever isn't good enough. She'll spend weeks and weeks sitting at the same place drawing." She'd pointed at the page, carelessly dropping ash from her cigarette on to it. By then, she could hardly focus her eyes. "Such a waste of time when she could frame this one and sell it. I keep telling her we need the money."

"Wow!" I'd brushed the ash away and touched the pencil drawing.

"Nothing is good enough for Nicole." Marie-Hélène leaned back in her wicker chair then, absently picking a fleck of tobacco from her lip. "Sometimes I think all I've done won't even be enough."

I reach into my bag now and take out the drawing. I'd slipped it in there earlier when Marie-Hélène had wobbled off to go to the bathroom.

When she'd returned, the farewell was brief. "He must have loved you, Seren. Deep down," she'd patted her chest, "maybe he was a good man, but not to me. Or to Nicole."

Staring at the sketch, I bite my lip. The girl who produced this picture is a talented artist. Drawing was obviously her voice. I study the lines, the details, the shadows and the squiggles at the edge, trying to hear what they say. Closing my eyes, I imagine Nicole quietly drawing it, thinking while she does. Is she picturing her father? Is she angry that she'll never get to meet him? She must feel rejected by him. Has Nicole listened to her mother slight André as she'd done today? If she is his daughter, I want to tell Nicole about the real André. My eyes fly open. André *was* a good man. I know he was.

I stand suddenly when I see a pleasant-looking girl approach. "*Excusez-moi.*"

She stops, and I show her the picture in my hand.

"*Ah, oui. La Place de la Bourse.*"

Moments later, I'm there. If I'd simply continued walking, I would have happened upon it myself. I stand staring at the astounding beauty of the buildings from Nicole's drawing. I wonder, if I persist with this journey, will I also happen upon the truth? In a day or two, when I feel strong enough, I'll venture towards the Medóc region to deliver the news of André and to see the vineyards and chateaux for the first time, alone. But for now, I need to catch my breath. Being here, I feel a sudden sense of peace wash over me.

My voyage isn't over yet. I can feel it. Sauntering along, I watch while artists skillfully depict the buildings. I pause behind a man sitting at an easel to admire his likeness. In truth, it's not nearly as good as the one I'm still holding in my hand. I move on, lost in thought, paying little attention until I glance down and startle, instantly paralysed. So much so that I can barely breathe. My eyes widen, and my mouth slowly opens as I stare mutely at him. His is the last face I expected to encounter here. He looks suddenly older, earnest, his features more shadowed than usual, but it's him. My limbs hollow as I reach my hand towards him and whisper, "*André*."

Chapter 21

Nicole

Scrambling to her feet, Nicole snatches her bag from the ground and leaps backwards. She's about to dart away, but the woman, in a gesture you might make to a spooked animal, cautiously puts both hands out to indicate she means no harm. The artist next to them turns to watch the silent exchange with interest, then raises an eyebrow at Nicole, who nods back that she's okay.

"Can I see it? Please." Speaking in English, the woman gestures to the sketchpad in Nicole's hand. Her eyes are pleading, brimming with emotion as if she might cry.

For a moment, Nicole stands frozen, her eyes assessing, darting from side to side before she slowly holds up the sketch.

Reaching her fingers towards the image, the woman whispers "*André*" once more, furrows her brow and looks curiously into Nicole's eyes.

It makes Nicole gasp, and she exhales louder than intended. It's the same name that has played non-stop in her mind after learning it a month before. Since then, she mumbles it, again and again, unable to stop repeating it to her reflection when she passes the bathroom mirror, the mirror in the lobby of their building, the mirror at work … any mirror. It swirls in her mind as she floats through the city, more lost than she's ever been before, still attempting to summon the impossible. Nothing has worked. Not until this moment. Only the face that has materialised isn't the one she'd tried to conjure.

"It's good." The woman nods reassuringly, then half-smiles. "It looks just like him. You're talented." Carefully, so as not to startle Nicole further, she opens the folded sheet of paper in her hand. "And this is yours too?"

Nicole glances at the drawing and frowns. "Where did you get this?"

"You're Nicole. Am I right?" The woman hesitates. "Your mother showed it to me."

"Who are you?" Nicole squeezes her eyes closed for a moment and shakes her head. When she opens her eyes, she's scowling. She already knows the answer.

Knowing more, or at least the tidbits that Maman has slowly spoon-fed her has done nothing to satisfy Nicole's hunger to learn about her dead father. Whenever she asks for more information, she can see Maman growing agitated, but she can't seem to be able to stop herself.

"I can't bring him back, Nicole. He's gone. I tried to find him, but I was too late. You're acting like this is *my* fault." Maman alternates between anger and intense sorrow as if she too is mourning something that will never come to pass. Maman doesn't understand. How can Nicole make her see that the one thing that could have made sense of her life is gone? She doesn't even understand it herself. Now Nicole is afraid that she'll always feel this way, this hollow, this ravenous for something that can't be replenished. Before, there'd always been a chance, a belief that her father would … what? Come and rescue her? Even Nicole knows fairy tales aren't real. Once or twice, she's wondered if her mother is lying. Perhaps he's still alive. Maybe she'd guessed that Nicole had planned to leave Bordeaux and search for him. But deep down, Nicole knows that he's dead. She knows it because she can feel it in her heart as if a little piece of herself is gone too.

At least her mother had known him. At least she can create moving images of him, his voice, his mannerisms, more than the same flat picture Nicole draws over and over again. "What did he sound like?" "Was he funny?" "Was he clever?" "Did you love him?" Maman had humoured her at first, managing, as only she can, to answer without delivering any form of information. In reality, all along, the digressions had led to the one question that burned.

"Did he know about me?"

How the answer had stung.

"I'm … I was André's wife." The woman answers with an abashed smile. "I'm Seren. I was your father's wife."

Nicole looks her up and down in disgust, then snaps her sketchpad shut. So this is her. Here's the reason she never knew her own father. Maman had told her about the wife in Ireland who'd wanted André all for herself, preventing him from being where he should have been, with his daughter.

"Were you following me?" Nicole narrows her eyes.

"God, no." Seren frowns and shakes her head. "No. I wasn't following you. I … I suppose I was looking for you, though. I've just come from meeting your mother. She showed me this picture, and I asked someone where it was, and I thought, well, you never know – that you might just be here and –"

"Here I am." Nicole splays her hands out and smiles sarcastically. "Bravo." She swings her canvas backpack over her shoulder, smooths down the curled-up ends of her denim shorts, and tucks her sketchpad under her arm. "Nice meeting you, Seren. Goodbye." She waves, then turns and strides away.

She's so fast that Seren has to run to keep up with the fishnet-clad skinny legs. Nicole glances behind and rolls her eyes exaggeratedly when she notices that she's being followed.

"What do you want?" she groans impatiently over her shoulder.

"I just want to talk."

Nicole whips around and indignantly runs her fingers through her long dark hair. "About what?" When Seren fails to immediately answer, she takes off again.

"*Jesus Christ, Nicole!* Can you give me a second, please? I'm not as young as you, and clearly I'm ridiculously unfit, and … and … I have asthma. So stop, please."

Nicole halts but doesn't turn around.

"And it's hot," Seren exhales loudly. "Christ. I know this isn't what I should be thinking right now, but how on earth are you wearing a leather jacket? Don't get me wrong, you look really cool – edgy, is that what they say? Sorry. I was never great at fashion. I suppose it goes hand in hand with being artistic like you are."

Nicole turns slowly, still shooting daggers, while Seren roots in her bag, then pulls out an inhaler. She holds it to her mouth and presses the button, at the same time rolling her eyes and grimacing as she inhales. "I was never great with the heat either. The Irish never are," she continues, fanning her face with Nicole's drawing.

"Then perhaps you shouldn't be in France," Nicole says drily.

Seren gives a hollow laugh. "You know, I was starting to think the same thing, but then, strangely, I've just walked right into the very reason I came here. I'll take it as a sign."

Nicole hesitates, then taking the sketchpad out from under her arm, she rips out the drawing. "Here. Take the picture." She thrusts the page at Seren. "Is that what you want, the drawing of him – my devoted father?"

Seren smiles sadly and shakes her head. "No, Nicole. That's not what I want. Please." She exhales again. "I know this is weird. I really do, and it must be such a shock for you." She pauses and rubs a hand down her face. "Christ, you're so like him. Do you know that? When your mother sent me the picture of you, it was like staring straight at him." This time she puts her hand to her heart. "Except, of course, you're a girl. A very beautiful one."

Despite trying her best to be angry, Nicole's lip starts to quiver. "He's dead?" She says it like a question as if she needs someone other than her mother to confirm it.

Seren swallows and nods. "He is."

"Well, that's it then. There's nothing more to say." Nicole makes to turn again, but this time Seren grabs her arm.

"Please. I've come a really long way. André *is* dead. Believe me, I'm so sorry he is, Nicole. For you, as well as for me, because I know," Seren presses her hand to her chest again, "he would have done anything to meet you."

Nicole crosses her arms and fixes her eyes on her

boots.

"Let me buy you a coffee."

"*For what?*" Nicole spits. "Maman told me about you. She said you made it clear that you didn't want to meet me."

Seren jerks her head. "If that was true, why would I be here?"

"I don't know."

"But *I* do. I'm here because of you. As soon as I found out about you, the very minute I saw that photo –"

"Found out about me?" Nicole narrows her eyes.

"Yes. I couldn't believe it. I kept thinking all this time you've been out there and –"

"You're a liar. You already knew! You both did. *He* knew. André knew." Nicole is breathing heavily.

"No." Seren raises her eyebrows. "I only found out a month ago. André didn't know –"

"He did. Maman told me he knew." She begins outraged, then falters. "He didn't want me."

For the third time, Seren places her hand on her heart. Nicole follows it with her eyes. She doesn't want to believe this woman, but there's something honest about the action.

"I swear to you, Nicole. I didn't know, and I'm willing to swear on my life that André never knew about you. I knew my husband and, if he had known, Nicole, I swear to you, he never would have left France."

Nicoles's shoulders heave. "Then, why?" She shakes her head. "Why would *she* tell me that? Why?" She sounds almost panicked.

"I don't know, Nicole, but I'd like to find out. I think André wanted me to come here on his behalf. Yes, he's dead, but you're very much here, and I know it sounds crazy, but since he died I've felt like there's something that isn't done. Please, I'm not insane, even though I must seem that way. Perhaps we should call Marie-Hélène and ask her to come ... I don't want to go behind her back, but she told me you didn't want anything to do with me."

Nicole jolts. "I never said that. I told her I wanted to go to Ireland to see where ... I wanted to find –" She stops. If Seren is telling the truth, then that means Maman is lying, but Nicole already knows that. She can sense it. "How can I trust you?" she asks eventually.

"Because I don't want anything from you," Seren answers. "Only to talk to you, nothing more."

Nicole nods. It's a good response, the opposite of how her mother might answer. Nicole is suddenly frightened – not of the woman in front of her, but of Maman. The thought strikes again – the same one she had the night she found out her father was dead. There's *still* something coming. It's more than the discovery of her father's death – it's something for which her mother needs her. She's sure of it, like a pawn in a game that's yet to begin.

"Why would she tell me that you didn't want to meet me?" she asks again, rubbing her forehead.

Seren shrugs. "Maybe she was trying to protect you. I don't know. But I promise all I want to do is talk, tell you about him. André was a good man, Nicole." She pauses then and bites her lip as if trying to decide what to say next. Looking down, she speaks. "Your mother told me the same thing. She said that you didn't want to meet me but, deep down, I was still hoping she'd got it wrong. I feel like I was supposed to find out about you. That I was supposed to meet you." Then she grins and splays her hands. "Come on, like, what are the chances that I walk past you? And yet, here you are."

Nicole nods earnestly. All her life, she's been waiting to be found. At last, it's happened, but it's the wrong person. It was meant to be him. "I don't want to involve my mother," she says, finally. "I'm eighteen next month. I can see you if I want to. I don't need her permission. Do you know where he was born? Do you know about his family?"

"I know some. I'm hoping to find out more. Did your mother tell you who he was?"

"André? You mean what he worked at?"

Seren shakes her head. "Where he was born, who his family are?"

"No. All she told me was that they worked together, that he knew she was pregnant when she left and moved to Corsica. She found him a while ago by hiring a private detective."

"A while ago?" Seren purses her lips and frowns. "Do you know when?"

"A year, maybe more. I'm not sure exactly. But she said she knew for some time where he was, but she hadn't decided if it was the right thing to tell me. She was waiting until I was old enough or something." Nicole laughs bitterly. "If she'd contacted him before now, I might have …" She pauses. "*Ugh!* I could have met him just once."

"I'm so sorry, Nicole." Seren looks genuinely upset. "I can't believe she knew for that long. I wish she'd reached out sooner too. I wish you'd met him."

"Did you really come here for me?" Nicole softens.

"Yes." Seren smiles softly. "I have photos. Right here, in my bag, and on my phone and videos. I'm happy to tell you everything I knew about him." Once more, Seren reaches her hand towards Nicole's arm. "There's a lot I

didn't know about your father, but I want to find out
before –"

She stops suddenly, making Nicole's stomach flip. *Before
what?* There it was again. What was going to happen?

"I need to know too," she agrees while Seren grimaces.

"At first, when I found out about you, I had my
doubts," Seren explains. "It was so out of the blue, but it's
clear now that you're André's daughter."

The words send a chill up Nicole's back.

Seren roots again in her bag and this time removes a
photo from an envelope.

"How did you get this?" Nicole takes it and stares at
it. "This is the one my mother had."

"It was in his things. They must have both had a copy.
I found it a few weeks ago." Seren takes her time. "You
know he told me his parents were dead? They aren't."

Nicole's eyes grow wide. "I have grandparents?"

She nods. "They live here, outside Bordeaux. I want to
find out why André left France and why he lied to me."

Nicole grows silent for a moment, then looks up at
Seren. "My mother did something, didn't she?" She
searches Seren's eyes before they fall to the ground.

"I don't know."

"What's my full name. What would it have been – I
mean, if they had married?"

"You don't know?"

"*Non.*"

"Dubois-Challant."

"Nicole Dubois-Challant," she whispers to herself,
then laughs. "Like the wine, *non*? You've heard of it? It's
very famous."

Seren nods slowly. "We ran a wine shop in Ireland. It
was André's passion."

231

"Hah," she laughs again. "There must be something about the name."

"No, Nicole, it *is* the name. It's who you are."

Letting herself into the flat, she tiptoes past where Maman is passed out on the sofa. After much goading, Seren confirmed that Maman had been drinking at lunch. Right now, Nicole couldn't care less. Gently closing her bedroom door behind her, she falls back on to the bed and stares at the ceiling. They'd spoken for hours, eventually moving away from the square at Place de la Bourse to a café, where they'd pored over photographs. Nicole learned about her father's obsession with food and wine. How everyone in Ballycross had loved him. How André had loved his boat and fishing, their friends. It all sounded so … warm. Then Seren told her how he'd got sick, how she still couldn't believe he was gone.

"And then, I get an email from Marie-Hélène. Finding out he wasn't exactly who he said he was felt like a kick in the teeth. So was finding out about you, I must admit." She'd smiled.

"I'm sorry," Nicole had apologised. "If I ruined it for you."

Seren had put her hand on hers. "Never say that. I'm glad I've met you. I kept thinking that there was still a part of him out there. I'm happy it was you."

After that part, they'd just chatted about everything and nothing. Seren was as youthful as she was honest. She'd made Nicole laugh, telling her the funny things about Ireland, and life, her friends, even about grief. More than a few times, Nicole had found herself imagining what it might have been like if someone like Seren had been her mother, or her stepmother, at least. Perhaps there might have been summers spent in Ireland, holidays, maybe more.

"I think he dreamt of you. Before he died, he told me that his one regret was not having had children – that he'd pictured a daughter – it was always a girl. She sounded like you."

Seren spoke to Nicole like an adult, covering everything from music to art to what Nicole really wanted to do with her life.

"I don't want to go to university. Not yet, anyway. Maybe not ever."

"So, you don't want to study medicine?" Seren had seemed surprised.

"That's Maman's dream for me."

"And yours?"

"I don't know. For some reason, it's like I can't see that far ahead."

Closing her eyes now, Nicole exhales. She'd ended up telling Seren a lot about life with Maman and how she longed to leave.

"Why do *you* think André left France?" she'd asked Seren. "You must have a theory."

Seren had smiled. "I can't seem to come up with one. I'm hoping his family can tell me more."

"Do you really think he tried to fake his death?"

"God, I don't know. It sort of looks that way." She'd laughed then. "I mean, I'm just this really normal, boring person. These are things you read about in books or see on TV. All this," she'd gestured, "is crazy! Vineyards, people presumed dead, mental mothers … no offence."

"It's okay. It's true."

"I might be wrong, but it feels like there's more to this than meets the eye."

"Like … ?"

"I'm not sure. I'm so nervous about going alone to see his family."

Nicole's face had lit up far too quickly. "Then take me with you, Seren, please. Let me come."

Chapter 22

Glancing to my right, I try to imagine what it would be like if I'd said yes, and Nicole was beside me in the rental car as I make my way towards uncertainty and the outer city roads. I'd almost agreed. I'd very nearly squealed "Road trip!" and high-fived her across the table before managing to reel myself back in. Although some moral support, a partner in crime, was precisely what I needed, a teenage one wouldn't do, and certainly not one so emotionally involved. Her intense connection to André – how she'd yearned for the father she'd never known had both saddened and shocked me in equal measures. As had her fragility, albeit mixed with an unquestionable inner strength. Nicole is special. I'd known it straight away.

I'm drawn to her. I feel an intense need to protect her. That need was the precise reason I'd denied her request to come with me. Despite Nicole appearing wise beyond her years, I'd had to remind myself that she is still a minor. Not only that, but the task ahead wasn't pleasant, the knowledge that she might face yet another rejection.

She'd begged, but for once I'd stopped myself from doing the wrong thing. Lately, there'd been far too much of that to make yet another knee-jerk blunder. Besides, the last thing I need is to be pulled in by the French Police and arrested for abduction before I even make it to Chateau Challant.

I jump and jerk away from the driver's door as another car zooms past at high speed, and I omit a pained noise in anticipation of it hitting me. Thankfully, it doesn't. Why hadn't I taken a bus? Instead, I'd decided that a rental car, the very smallest one possible, would be my preferred mode of transportation. Driving here is utterly terrifying, but at least the dread of imminent death is distracting my thoughts somewhat. I'd never heard of the Citröen model that the woman in the rental shop recommended. Upon seeing it, I'd been reminded of Noddy's car from the Enid Blyton book series I'd devoured as a child.

"Is there something missing off the front there?" I'd asked yesterday as the sales lady pointed at the compact yellow vehicle. I'd decided to wait a day after meeting Marie-Hélène and Nicole before driving to the Medóc. I needed to rest and a chance to organise myself.

"Like what, Mademoiselle?" she'd asked.

"Like the bonnet?"

No, apparently, it was all there. It seemed some people enjoyed having nothing in front of them but a steering wheel and a very short distance to the road.

If nothing else, at the very least, the entire vineyard would witness my arrival. Perhaps the whole family might rush from the chateau to greet Noddy sans Big Ears arriving for tea. I grin to myself. At this stage, there's absolutely nothing about this trip that would surprise me.

The car, driving on the wrong side of the road, fearing for my life every time another one passes, only adds to the increasingly bizarre situation in which I find myself.

Meeting Marie-Hélène and then Nicole two days previously had been nothing less than eventful. Mind you, I'd enjoyed the second encounter infinitely more than the first. Nicole is so like André – her looks, her voice, her mannerisms. It is as comforting as it was bittersweet. We'd ended up chatting for hours. Her English was almost as good as André's had been. She told me that growing up near a holiday resort, most people spoke English well. In truth, I hadn't wanted it to end, nor it seemed had Nicole. At the last minute, she'd called her friend from the pizza restaurant where she worked and asked her to cover her shift.

"Should you call your mother?" I'd suggested again, despite knowing that Marie-Hélène was more than likely passed out somewhere, hopefully at home. Nicole had asked more than once if her mother had drunk more than coffee at lunch. Eventually, I'd admitted that she'd had a few, playing it down to save her feelings. I hadn't wanted to reveal that by the end of the encounter she'd been barely able to string a sentence together.

Nicole had shaken her head. "There's really no need. She won't notice." She'd paused then. "I'm sorry again for being rude earlier." Her initial agitation upon encountering me had quickly faded.

"Honestly, don't worry. I took you by surprise."

We'd sat in a café sipping coffee while I'd shown her photos of André throughout the years. She'd stared so intently at each one as if trying to place herself in them.

"I keep thinking how different my life would have been if I'd known him. If he had been with Maman, and we were a family. Sorry!" She'd grimaced innocently. "Then he wouldn't have been with you."

"It's okay. I understand what you mean."

At first, Nicole had only hinted at what type of life she'd had in Corsica. By the sounds of it, she'd loved the island and the people. "I liked it there. Everyone knew us. I think they felt sorry for me." She'd grimaced again. "My friends' parents always asked me for dinner or invited me to their parties and celebrations. I used to draw them pictures to say thank you and make frames out of old fishing rope." She'd shrugged. "It sounds silly."

"It sounds lovely. It sounds like something your father might do if he'd been able to draw, which he wasn't." I'd laughed. "His form of communication was wine and food. His art was on a plate."

After a while, she'd opened up about her mother's drinking, how she was alone a lot growing up.

Slowly, I'd found myself delving a little more. "Nicole, I know we've only just met so please tell me to take a hike if you want, but … your mother … was she … did she … " I hadn't known how to phrase it, or even what exactly I was asking.

Nicole had lifted a corner of her mouth knowingly, and I'd felt my insides twist. "*Non*," she'd answered straight away, shaking her head. "She never hurt me. She was … how do I say … there, but not there. Even when she was there, she wasn't there, you know? I got any family life from wherever I could. When Maman told me we were leaving Corsica, my friend's mother asked if I could stay with them and finish school – that she would look after me. Maman said absolutely not – that Corsica was only ever supposed to be temporary."

I'd nodded. "Would you like to go back?"

She'd shrugged again. "I thought I did. It was always my plan, but now I'm not sure. At first, my friends stayed in touch, but lately I don't hear from them so much. I suppose people forget after a while. I guess I'm afraid of turning up and feeling like an outsider."

"I bet that wouldn't happen. As soon as they'd see you again, it would feel normal. You should call them. Friends are important." As I'd said it, I'd thought of Cathy and Jane, but I'd put them out of mind as fast.

Nicole's words had felt like daggers. To think that all along there'd been a little girl out there who'd needed her father. She'd needed André, and there we'd been obliviously living what I'd considered a dream life while she'd been trapped in a nightmare. The saddest part of all was that it hadn't been so bad that someone had come to rescue her from it. No, she'd been expected to endure it, to take what affection she could from others, to understand as such a young person that people had felt sorry for her.

I'd been flabbergasted when Nicole had mentioned that Marie-Hélène had known for longer than a year where André was in Ireland and had failed to contact him. To think that Nicole could have had the chance to meet him! It would have brought André such comfort towards the end when everything had seemed so very pointless. Although I know I have to stop thinking this way, it might have prevented me from doing what I had at the fertility clinic. It's something else about Marie-Hélène's story that doesn't quite add up. Why would she have waited so long? A few weeks is plausible, but over a year? What was she playing at? Then again, her mind must be distorted.

"She's an alcoholic, you know? It's called a

functioning one. The worst kind, apparently. They're able to work and live and –" she'd paused to find the word, "function! But they're just not really there. You know what I mean?"

I'd been taken aback by her adult knowledge. "I do know. Bad but not bad enough," I'd responded.

"*Exactement!* I tried to help her. I used Google," she'd said with a grin.

"Ah, so that's your secret resource!" It made sense.

"Yes, I looked up ways to stop her drinking, printed out information, but Google only does so much. Anyway, it wasn't all bad in Corsica. I learned to draw while she was at work. I'd draw myself a family, a dog, a father, as you saw!" She'd raised her eyebrows. "A life. And I'd study. I was good in school …" She'd trailed off, tucking her hair behind her ears. "Can I ask you something?"

"Anything."

"Did Maman say anything about me being sick when I was little?"

"No. Were you?" Christ, it couldn't get any bleaker.

"I'm not sure. Maman's not very clear. She makes it very hard to get information."

"I noticed that," I'd said, nodding. "But why would you think you were sick?"

"She says things sometimes. Things like she didn't think I'd live or walk – weird things. When I was younger, I used to get scared that there was something wrong with me, but then the older I get the more I wonder if her memory is mixed up. That she's confused from being drunk for so long."

Only that Nicole is the picture of health I'd wanted nothing more than to tell her to go and get her things immediately, and we'd disappear like André once had.

But I know I can't do that.

"When are you eighteen?" I'd asked suddenly.

"Five weeks. And then I can leave."

Again, I'd wanted to tell her that she could come to Ireland with me. Picturing Cathy and Jane's faces if I arrived back to Ballycross with André's teenage daughter in tow had been enough to stop my exuberance. After all, Nicole and I have only just met. I want to take my time and get to know her slowly over the coming weeks. Still, I already know that I'll fall head over heels for this beautiful, talented, gentle girl.

I have to keep asking myself how it's possible for her never to have known André but be so like him in both looks and demeanour – her movements, her glances, her smile, her spirit were all so familiar that while they hurt, they're exactly what I need. Nicole is what I've been missing – the link to André, the reason to keep going that has eluded me since his death. Thinking back over how the day had started so horrendously with Marie-Hélène, only to turn out so well, makes me feel lighter. I want to help Nicole as much as I need to help myself, and the best way is to find out the truth.

The roads are quieter now as I find myself flanked by lush fields. The scenery has changed as dramatically as meeting André's past had moved from hopeless to promising. Last night, I'd dreamt of André and Nicole together. I was there too, with our baby. It was like I'd sketched it, as Nicole had described, illustrating the life I wanted. I couldn't draw the life back into André, but perhaps I'm heading in the right direction with myself. It certainly feels that way. It's so peaceful on this stretch of road, exactly how I imagined it would be. I've estimated that the drive will take another forty-five minutes or so, probably longer in my yellow car, but I'm in no rush. Every so often, a vehicle approaches from behind, and I move in to let it overtake. I do the same now, pulling the car onto a grass verge. This time, I switch off the engine for a break. The closer I get, the more I can feel nausea growing.

I'd checked out of my hotel this morning. It was probably a stupid thing to do. Depending on the reception, there's every possibility that I could find myself doing a three-point turn in the driveway of the chateau and heading straight back to the city. But there'll be a guesthouse that I can check into close by, at least for one night. In one way, I'm hoping that André's mother is as left of centre as Marie-Hélène. That way, I can quickly conclude that he'd had no choice but to get the hell away from them all.

Then perhaps I can get back quicker to Nicole and finally tell her that I'm pregnant with her baby brother. I'd badly wanted to do so, but something had held me back.

I take my phone from my bag and glance at the screen. There's another message from Cathy. I quickly tap out a reply telling her that I'm okay – still exploring and relaxing. I don't feel like going into the ins and outs while I'm still processing everything. There's still nothing from Jane. It must be hard to understand what I'm going through and how I need to do this before the baby is born, but that's their problem, not mine.

I open the car door and get out to stretch my legs. Holding my hand up to shield my eyes, I survey the landscape. There's nothing but fields for miles and miles with nothing separating them from the road, no fences to lock them in. The rows of vines are right there in front of me, so close that I could reach out and touch them if I wanted, amble between them. In line with the time of year, the vines burst with greenery and clusters that will start to change colour and ripen in the coming months.

"It's called *véraison*," André had explained once.

I'd repeated the word, "*Vay-ray-zun*".

"*Très bien, ma chèrie.*"

I can hear him almost as clearly as I can see it all before me. *Why did we never come here, André? What were you hiding?*

I hold my face up to the blue sky, close my eyes and take a breath. Being away from the city feels good. Already, the air feels cleaner, bursting with life. It's how I thought Bordeaux would be. Soon, Google maps will direct me up more winding roads and towards the village of Margaux. Last night, I'd sat on my bed and tried to make sense of the aerial route. Chateau Challant isn't far from there.

"Are you just going to turn up? Won't you frighten them?" Nicole had asked, looking concerned. "They must be old. *Non?*"

I'd laughed. "Well, your grandfather looks old, for sure. From what I can tell, he's not well. And André's mother, well, unless there's a serious amount of photoshop going on, she looks young. In fact, she looks really young. I'm not sure whether to call first or just show up. Perhaps you're right. Maybe I should warn them."

Before getting back into the car, I walk up and down a little and then take a quick selfie with the vineyards in the background and send it to Nicole with the message: *I'll be in touch soon.*

I know she's as eager as me to find out the truth of her

243

beginning. She's promised to keep an eye on Marie-Hélène's movements while I'm gone. I doubt she'll have much to report. I'd imagine wetting her whistle the day before yesterday will only make Marie-Hélène thirsty for more.

Before saying goodbye to Nicole, I'd asked if it was okay if I gave her a hug. She hadn't hesitated before throwing her arms around me. For a second time, I'd had to restrain myself from asking her to come with me today. Instead, I'd hugged her back, then held on to her arms as I looked her in her eyes. "I swear if André knew about you, he'd have been in your life. Don't even think that no one wanted you. Okay?"

She'd nodded and scrunched up her nose to stop the tears.

"Thank you." Then she'd given me her number. "Promise me you'll come back to the city."

"Hell, I could be back by tomorrow night if Gigi tells me to get lost."

Nicole had laughed and then turned serious. "What if it's something bad? What if André did something?" She'd looked as afraid as I now feel as I approach the village ahead.

"I know he didn't."

"Well then, what if it was Maman? What if she did something?"

I'd shook my head. "I don't know, Nicole."

"She told me something was coming. Something good …"

I'd tried to smile reassuringly. "And maybe she's right. I've met you now, and that's good. Don't worry. It's probably a family feud, something that snowballed."

My stomach is churning as I take the turn for

Margaux, so much so that I have to swallow to prevent myself from retching. On the other side of the village, just 2km away, is my destination. The village itself is small and somewhat nondescript. Right now, I wish it was more significant – that there was some traffic, a market, anything to delay the inevitable. There's another possibility in all this. What if neither André nor Marie-Hélène did anything wrong? What if I'm willingly driving towards something from which I won't be able to extract myself. I focus on Nicole's face – sweet, lovely Nicole to whom I feel a maternal connection so strong it frightens me. The list of people I need to protect is rapidly growing. But from what am I shielding them? Or from whom? I breathe to calm myself as I see the granite wall on the road develop into gateposts, then enormous black iron gates. I gasp when I see it. Unlike the others, this vineyard is fenced in.

Chapter 23

Gigi

Gigi's eyes gravitate towards the sheet of paper next to her laptop. Although it's been there for the past two days, she can't stop glancing at the name, hoping that when she looks back, the letters might have unfurled and reconfigured into someone else. She'd always believed coincidence to be a foolish notion, but there's very little else to explain the appearance of that name, this week of all weeks. Picking it up, she reads it aloud, reciting the telephone number beneath, then scrunches it into a ball and throws it in the wastepaper basket by her feet. She isn't going to award it any power or allow it to distract her further. Opening the drawer of her desk, she pulls out the manila file nestled inside. It's been there for far longer than two days. Last week she'd drawn an asterisk above today in her personal calendar, with the letter "A" next to it. Then she'd circled it several times so that the paper had begun to split. It's not like her to avoid a task but, suffice it to say, this particular set of paperwork is something that she's been dreading.

Years ago, she'd been told the process would take far longer. When André first went missing, the law stated that they'd have to wait twenty years before applying for a presumption of death declaration. Twenty years! She'd been outraged, arguing that by that time they could all be dead. The length of time was excessive, especially since it was coupled with pathetically limited police support. She can still remember the detective's exact words after André's shoes and wallet had been discovered near the cliff where he used to swim.

"People have a right to disappear, madame. They do so every day."

He didn't need to tell her that. Not when she too had disappeared once upon a time. Except in her case, no one had tried to bring her back.

"We need to decide which cases are suspicious and which are voluntary." His voice had been monotone as if reading straight from a manual. "Does your son have any enemies? Did he owe money?" For appearances, he'd flicked open a notepad but then forgotten to write anything down.

"Money is not a problem," Gigi had snapped. "And André is popular." It wasn't a lie. He was well-liked wherever he went. No, there were no enemies. She wouldn't have phrased it that way – only mistakes.

"Was he in a relationship?"

"No," she didn't hesitate.

"Did he suffer from depression?"

"Not that I know."

"Drugs?"

"Never."

"Any family disputes?"

"No."

"Has he any siblings?"

"No. It's only André." She'd been growing impatient. "He's been gone ten days, detective. The shoes, his wallet, his …"

The detective had shaken his head and shrugged. "But no note? If there had been a note …"

Gigi had glared at him. "André would never do what you're trying to suggest," she'd uttered at last. "He must have got in trouble in the water. It happens, no?"

He'd pursed his lips. "Yes, it happens. Usually, when a person drowns, the body washes up in time. I know this is hard to hear, but you have to be patient. He's an adult man in his twenties. Is there money missing … have his cards been used?"

"No. Nothing. Please, can't you search the sea? Is there nothing you can do?"

"Madame, we would be searching for a needle in a haystack. Besides, he may turn up. André has a huge reason to come back." He'd looked around admiringly at the reception room of the chateau. "Maybe he's just having a little fun. Maybe all this was too much ..."

To this day, Gigi maintains the detective rolled his eyes as he suggested it. He may as well have said, 'Poor little rich boy'.

There'd been several further communications over the years, but as far as Gigi was concerned the door had been firmly shut on the police investigation. There was nothing suspicious other than André going for a swim and never returning – tragic but apparently not that rare. People vanished – the end.

Lost in thought, Gigi flicks mindlessly through the file,

then sinks back into her seat and exhales. After a few years of aimlessly waiting for André to return from "having a little fun", the law had changed somewhat. Apparently, it was due to the aftermath of the Indian Ocean tsunamis. In brief, if your son had fallen victim to such a natural disaster, you could file for a declaration after one year. In André's case, they'd halved the original time to ten years. They've far surpassed that now, and yet Gigi continues to drag her feet with the legalities. In truth, there hadn't been much need until now. It amazes her that they're almost at the original twenty-year requirement mark. Back then, it had seemed light-years away. It actually passed faster than she'd thought it might. Her lawyer is confident that the eighteen years they've accrued, coupled with legitimate reason – her husband's illness – will suffice to finally declare André deceased. Gigi's breath catches suddenly as she experiences a stabbing pain in her chest at the idea.

Just last week, the doctor's confirmed that Henri Dubois-Challant is in rapid decline with only a matter of weeks left to live. Gigi had almost smirked at the use of the word *rapid*. It certainly hasn't felt that way to her. She could never have imagined that her husband would live so long, well into his nineties. Henri had begun his descent even before André disappeared. After he vanished, Henri slowly began to lose further interest in work, then general life. He'd seemed sad. At first, his devastation infuriated Gigi since he'd never been involved in his son's life even when André was around. She'd soon concluded that Henri, then in his seventies, was getting on in years and was unable for the stress of the vineyard. What began as mild depression gradually morphed to forgetfulness, and then … well, let's just say

249

that finding him naked and circling the fountain at the back of the house had sounded the alarm that something wasn't quite right.

All in all, it took many years for Henri to thoroughly check out of logic and therein lay Gigi's biggest regret or oversight – the one detail that she'd allowed slip through the net. At the earliest sign that Henri was too old to work, and with André gone, she'd jumped in. She'd been so wrapped up in succeeding in the business where Henri had failed that she'd noticed too late that he'd completely lost his marbles. Had they spent any length of time together, it might have become clearer sooner. By the time dementia was diagnosed, it was too late for Henri to sign a power-of-attorney form. Much as Gigi had tried to convince the doctors that he was fine, it was quite apparent that Henri had lost mental capacity when he'd insisted on calling her "Maman" and attempted to sit on her lap.

Because of it, Gigi is still trapped within the antiquated legal constraints of the past. While she was free to work in the business and take it from strength to strength, Chateau Challant, in its entirety, despite having no surviving family, would never be hers, at least not until she completed these darned forms. With Henri's death imminent, it was time to break the constraints once and for all, and there was only one way she could do that.

Besides, it's what André would want. If anything, she was doing it for him.

Scanning the rest of the forms, her head begins to throb. According to her lawyer, the paperwork is merely a formality. They meet all the criteria, so much so that he's assured her he should be able to rush the declaration through. Still, it feels as though she has to go through it all over again, relive the agony. Over the years, Gigi was careful to accumulate everything they might need, like proof that she'd hired numerous private detectives to conduct searches. Since the day he vanished, there's been absolutely no communication from André or anyone connected to him. That is, until two days ago. Why now?

Impatiently, Gigi bends to retrieve the ball of paper from the bin. Testing herself, she recites the number and then smooths out the paper on her desk to check if she has it right. She does. "Clever isn't enough," her mother used to tell her. "You have to be smart." Sitting up, Gigi rests one elbow on the desk and puts her chin in the palm of her hand. Why is she thinking of her mother? A woman of no ambition, no drive, happy to take whatever scraps life threw her way. To this day, the thought of her still angers Gigi. Despite her own willingness to float through life, her mother had always pushed Gigi to do better. As a child, Gigi had been top of her class until the unforeseen happened. Her mother immediately gave up on Gigi and disregarded her as stupid and, in doing so, extinguished her future like a cigarette burned into flesh.

Tilting her head to the side, Gigi wonders if it's stupid to ignore the unwelcome surprise in front of her on the desk? Perhaps she should deal with it. She pushes her chair back, stands and walks towards the bathroom door. Pulling it open, she steps inside and throws the paper into the toilet. She presses the button on the wall and watches the paper twirl, then vanish. Sitting back down at her desk, she tries to focus.

In a month or less, she'll be a widow with a confirmed dead son if she can get to the end of these blasted forms. Mind you, she's already felt that way for years. Soon, it will just be her again, as alone as when she'd first arrived in Bordeaux with nothing but a bag and a story. No one had wanted her story back then, as much as they don't want it now, regardless of how it still breaks her heart. Gigi has no family, no connections, no tribe, no blood, aside from the pints she's given to this place. It's still just her. She has few acquaintances, fewer friends, no lover. There'd been a few men, once or twice over the years, to provide her with … what? What had they given her? Certainly not love.

Sometimes she wonders if she is damaged, missing an integral part, or perhaps she repels people. She does try. Ever since her assistant, Camille, left to go on maternity leave, Gigi is making an effort to be friendlier, less guarded to the extent that she'd had her new assistant send Camille a baby gift. After all, Gigi isn't getting any younger. She'll be sixty soon. There's no way she'll ever have a family again. It's physically impossible, but perhaps it's time to have something more than just work in her life. What that something is, she's not sure, but she's done what she set out to do with the vineyard. It's a success. Maybe it's time to enjoy life, try to … connect.

Her thoughts are broken by a sharp knock on the glass door. Gigi quickly opens the drawer in her desk before she looks up and pushes the documents back inside. Already, they've loomed over for years, what's another day or two? Then she swears she'll lay André to rest. Maybe, then, she can move on.

"Yes?"

"Madame, I'm so sorry to disturb you," the frightened-looking temp begins, then glances over her shoulder and puts a hand out as if trying to stop someone from rounding the corner. "I know you said not to disturb you under any circumstances, but there's a situation at the house."

Gigi stands suddenly. "Is it my husband?"

"No, no, madame. He's fine," she reassures her apologetically. "The security guard from the house would like a word."

Gigi frowns. "Let him in."

As soon as the girl drops her arm, he advances like a wall caving in. "Madame, there's a woman at the front steps of the chateau."

"A woman?" Gigi gives a false smile.

"Yes."

"And how did she get in?"

"She came in the main gate after the cleaners." He's panting as if he's sprinted the distance from the house.

"And where were you?" She tries not to act distressed.

"I'm sorry, madame. I was in the bathroom." His face colours as he whispers the final word. By his level of embarrassment, he must have been in there for quite some time.

"She says she wants to speak with you or Monsieur – that it's urgent."

"Who is she?"

He glances over his shoulder. "I didn't get a name."

Gigi tuts loudly.

"She said it's about your son?" He says it like a question, looking confused. It appears not everyone knows about André.

Gigi's jaw tightens as she puts her hand on the desk to steady herself and stares straight ahead. Behind the table, her legs turn to jelly. Once again, avoiding a situation has not made it disappear. Flushing the problem away may not have been enough. She should have called the number on that blasted sheet of paper straight away. This was no meaningless coincidence. Receiving the phone call from Marie-Hélène was a sign, a clue to pay attention, and Gigi is afraid.

Composing herself, she smiles. "Please show her into the salon at the front of the house. I'll be there shortly."

The guard nods once and leaves.

Gigi pivots to face the smooth, poured-concrete wall at the back of her office. Before she can stop it, her shoulders heave forcefully. Trying not to panic, she flees inside the bathroom and manages to close the door before falling to her knees and retching over the toilet bowl. Tears stream, the familiar anger lurches, picturing Marie-Hélène and their encounter all those years ago. Gigi's protective rage had erupted as soon as Marie-Hélène told her what she had done. Watching the colour drain from Marie-Hélène's face had felt almost gratifying. She must have felt clever, but Gigi had been the smart one that day. In the end, it hadn't taken much to get rid of her. Even André had been surprised that, when it came to it, a large dollop of money had been enough.

Gripping the toilet seat, Gigi roughly wipes her mouth with the back of her hand. She'd wanted nothing to do with Marie-Hélène then, and she wants nothing to do with her now. Standing, she runs the tap, wets a paper cloth and wipes her face clean. Then she washes her hands, adjusts her skirt, smooths her hair and gives her reflection a reassuring nod. She can do this, face Marie-Hélène one last time. It was like what she'd told André as a boy. "There will always be hurdles. All you have to do is jump high." If money is what Marie-Hélène wants, Gigi will oblige, this time with more stringent conditions. Besides, when André is officially declared dead in a matter of weeks, none of it will matter anyway. Marie-Hélène could try to destroy the family name, but there was no one left to care.

Feeling better, she opens the door and strides from the office, taking the path next to the vineyards. Inhaling, she can smell the sharpness of the vines. With the warm weather, flowering was earlier this year. In a matter of days, it will be time to thin the vines. Gigi has a good feeling about this year's harvest. Still, there's always the fear of going in too early, of the weather changing ... of unexpected events.

Making her way under the arch to the courtyard, she goes around the fountain, past the pruned trees. It's immaculate, as always – carefully tended. The marketing team wants her to open the chateau more to the public to increase revenue and brand-awareness. Until now, she's refused, but perhaps after Henri is gone and this little hiccup reburied, she should. She makes her way through the back door, past the kitchens, towards the hallway. Pausing at the salon door, she takes a deep breath, knowing whatever lies on the other side will be unpleasant.

"I don't have long," she says as she enters the room. "So let's get to the point."

"I'm sorry, could you repeat that?"

Gigi stares upon hearing the English response. The relief that it isn't Marie-Hélène floods her body to the extent that she finds herself suddenly smiling at the mystery woman. It only lasts a moment before she remembers that despite flushing it away, there's still a message from Marie-Hélène and this unexpected call is still about André.

"Who are you?" Gigi flips to business-like.

The apprehensive-looking woman swallows. "I'm Serendipity."

"And I'm Gigi, but I presume you already know that." She advances with interest. "Tell me, Serendipity, since I often confuse the two, are you the same thing as coincidence?"

The woman frowns at the peculiar question but answers anyway, "Serendipity is usually nicer."

Gigi nods. "Let's hope so.

Chapter 24

Doorstopping the Challants hadn't been part of the plan, but after Nicole had expressed concern, I'd decided to phone ahead to warn them of my imminent arrival. At the last minute, I'd changed my mind. I'd already made that mistake with Marie-Hélène. Giving her time to prepare had resulted in rehearsed answers, garbling and leaving me no further to the truth.

Now, I'm the one stuttering.

"How can I help you?" Gigi asks pointedly. It's peppered with unease.

Lost for words, I plonk down on one of the many tapestry-upholstered sofas. "It's hard to explain," I manage, at last. I'm about to ask her not to freak out, but I realise it will only alarm her further.

Gigi assesses me with one eyebrow arched. "Please try." She flashes a very brief smile that drops after a second.

I pull my bag onto my knee, take out a photo and hold it up.

Frowning, she turns to glance at the door, then looks

out the window. Clocking that the security guard is right outside the window, she steps forward gingerly.

"Oh, God, I'm sorry," I say, noticing her anxiety. Every muscle in my body is tense. "Believe me, I wish we were meeting under different circumstance." I frown. "I've no idea where to begin. So …" I swallow. "So I'll just say it. I was André's wife."

Both Gigi's eyebrows shoot up. She almost looks amused. "Is that right?" She advances and snaps the picture of our wedding from my trembling hand.

I watch as her eyes move towards it. It's slight, but I hear the air puff out from her lungs. *Was?* She turns to face me.

"He's dead."

This time, her legs falter. I shoot up from the sofa and grab her elbow before she drops. "I'm so sorry. I didn't mean to blurt it out that way." I manoeuvre her onto the sofa and crouch down next to her. Gigi puts her head between her knees for a moment. "Are you alright?" I ask. "Should I call someone? Christ, this really isn't how I planned it. I'm so sorry."

"Give me one moment." She raises her head a fraction.

I can hear her breathing in and slowly blowing out. I find myself doing it with her to help loosen the band that has tightened in my chest. When she finally looks up, I place my hand gently on her arm and look into her eyes.

"I'm so sorry," I repeat. "For shocking you and for your loss. I'm so very sorry."

I recognise the look she returns straight away – genuine pain. Gigi isn't what I expected. Then again, nothing here is.

Earlier, sitting in my car outside, I hadn't had time to

hesitate when I saw the van approach. As soon as the electric gates jerked open, I'd put the car into gear and, concealed behind it, followed it through the gates. Making my way wide-eyed along the snow-white gravel driveway, I thankfully avoided careering into one of the perfectly uniform trees lining it. Navigating the circular lawn, which was in itself a marvel, I watched the van disappear around the back as I came to a stop at the steps of the chateau. I refrained from tailing it further. You need to be very familiar back home before you let yourself in the back door. I assumed it was the same here.

Craning my neck out the window of the yellow car, I half expected Louis XV to pop his head of white curls out the front door and wave. My mouth formed an O as I attempted to take in all six sets of double-height windows on either side of the double entrance doors on the ground floor. The next floor was almost identical save for a vast balcony enclosed by ornate, twisted black metal. In place of windows on the second floor, double doors led outside. The roof tiles sloped over the top floor, encasing circular windows surrounded with decorative stone. I was gawping at the four turrets when I was interrupted.

The man skidded towards me, holding his chest and panting. Quite the commotion followed as I stepped out of the car to explain that I needed to see Monsieur or Madame with news of their son.

"Madame has no son."

I wasn't taking no for an answer and was fully prepared to lie down in the driveway if it came to it. In broken French, I assured him that Madame did indeed have a son and that I wasn't moving until I saw her. There was much gesticulating and tutting before he roughly grabbed something from his holster. I jumped back nearly two feet, thinking he was about to pull a gun. It was his walkie-talkie. Wiping the sweat off his upper lip, he'd rolled his eyes indignantly then spoke into the radio, beckoning for someone to come and watch me while he went to investigate.

Shortly afterwards, I found myself transported through the almost-white stone building into an impressive hallway beyond the front door. I had very little time to take in the sandstone tiles, high ceilings and monumental staircase before I was ushered through a heavy wooden door and warned with a pointed finger to wait there.

It was only then I wished I'd listened to Nicole. This wasn't the type of place where you amble up the driveway and ring the doorbell. This was ... Christ, what was it? Walking around the room, I tried to imagine how I'd describe it – antique furniture, gold mirrors, fancy lamps, massive fireplace ... it was ... well, it wasn't Ballycross, that was for sure. It was another world. A bit like being transported onto the set of *The Sound of Music*, awaiting a small blond boy wearing lederhosen to emerge singing tunes with his nanny. Not even for a moment could I picture my tousled-haired, Guinness-drinking husband here. Right then, I wanted to leave. I felt entirely out of my depth. The guard would hardly stop me, would he? Indeed the goal was to stop you coming in, not escaping. I was about to listen to my gut when the door swung open, and I got my first glimpse of Gigi.

"Again, I'm sorry I said it like that." I try to smile now. "I should have been more prepared." I watch while Gigi composes herself.

In the flesh, she's stunning, so much so that I find

myself staring at her face. Her hair is snow-white and bobbed, but instead of making her look older, it enhances her deep-brown eyes and sallow skin. She's familiar-looking. I'm sure I can see André in her – his eyes, his colouring. She looks so young that I have to stop myself from asking her how old she is. Her features are as dainty as her name, strengthened by heavily framed black glasses. On me, I'd look like a grandad – on her, they look chic. She's wearing a heavy gold chain around her neck, a plain white cotton T-shirt, a pleated skirt, flat shoes. Beside her, I feel enormous with my frizzy hair and unfashionable clothes. Gigi is so far from the terrifying monster Marie-Hélène described that it's laughable.

Despite the news I've brought, she seems oddly relieved, if that's the word. Judging by her earlier entrance and the way she'd first spoken, I wonder if she was expecting me to be someone else.

After a few moments, Gigi clasps her hands together. "Okay. It seems you started at the end." She closes her eyes briefly as if she still can't believe it, then turns to me. "Can you please tell me the start of the story, Serendipity?" She's softly spoken. The way she says my name is so familiar that I have to take a deep breath before rehashing my version of André.

Here and there throughout my tale, Gigi's eyes well. Once or twice she smiles, nods along. I hand her various photos while I speak and watch her trace her fingers over his image. It feels as though I've been talking for hours before she says anything.

"Did he suffer?" Gigi asks at last.

"A little," I answer truthfully. "In the end, it was fast. Too fast. It took us both by surprise, but André was … comfortable." I pause. "There was still so much we had

to do, you know? Still, so much he had to tell me, clearly."
I raise my eyebrows. "I … I just can't understand how I
didn't know about you or this life. I'm really struggling
to make sense of it."

"What did he tell you?" She tilts her head. Her actions
are incredibly refined, her voice like silk. It makes it hard
to imagine that she's anything but.

I grimace. "That you were dead."

Gigi makes a pained face.

"Further back than that, he said his father worked the
vineyards and that you were a pastry chef. He never spoke
badly about either of you." I'm trying to ease the blow.

She laughs hollowly. "Well, that's something. I
suppose some of what he told you was true. His
father *did* work in the vineyards, but he also owned them.
And I *did* bake. My mother was a pastry chef in Paris a
long time ago, so she taught me, I taught André."

"We run," I stop to correct myself, "*ran* a wine shop in
Ireland. Well, I still do. It's a patisserie too. It's small, but
we do really well."

She nods and swallows. "It sounds like a dream."

"It is. It's not anything like you have here. It's small.
We do okay."

"And how did you find out that what he told you
about his past wasn't true?" Gigi asks.

This time, I bend the truth. "I found his passport, some
old photos in his things. I knew I had to come. See it for
myself."

Gigi bites her lip and looks at the floor. There's a long
pause.

Taking a breath, I get ready for my turn.

Sensing it, Gigi stands and walks over to one of the
windows.

"I know he's gone," I begin, "but I feel like he wanted me to know about his life here. That maybe he couldn't find the words. Did something happen?"

Gigi stares out the window while I wait for her to answer. Finally, she turns to look at me, crossing her arms. Immediately, she seems guarded.

"It sounds like you were happy with André. It's rare. It's something to hold on to. Are you sure you want to know about the past?"

Her words echo both Bobby Cronin's and Marie-Hélène's, and I have to bite my tongue. I'm so fed up with everyone telling me the same thing.

Gigi makes her way back and sits next to me. "You must think that I don't seem shocked enough by all this."

I shrug, even though it's precisely what I'm thinking. Although Gigi is surprised, her reaction is a little too measured. "Not at all," I lie. "Shock is a strange thing. You must be relieved if that's the right word? I'm sure not knowing if André was dead or alive was torture."

"You've done your homework. I thought you knew nothing." Her eyes narrow ever so slightly, and I sense a change in her tone.

"I came across an article online," I explain. "It was the only one I could find about André." Then before I can stop myself, I say, "To be honest, I thought there'd be more. It seems strange. If someone was missing their son …" I trail off when I see a shadow darken her features.

"*I loved André!*" she hisses suddenly.

I startle. Noticing, she twitches.

"If you're suggesting I didn't try to find him, you're mistaken. I'm a believer in giving people what they want. Do you understand me?" This time, her tone is glacial.

I frown so intensely that it's a wonder I can still see

her from beneath my dropped eyebrows. I have no idea what she means. Although I get a distinct impression that I should.

"So why don't you tell me exactly what it is that you want?" Gigi asks so bluntly that it feels like a smack across my face. Her eyes are boring into mine. "I might be willing to give it to you if you're honest. I don't like games."

The penny abruptly drops. Oh my God, she thinks I'm after money.

"Sorry, just to be clear here," I snap, putting both hands up before she insults me, "I don't *want* anything other than the truth. How dare you! I've left behind my business and my home to traipse to France out of common decency. All to tell you that your son is dead." I shake my head. "The least you can do in return is to tell me why he told me *you* were dead. Why did he leave out the little detail," I hold up my forefinger and thumb, "of a vineyard, a big bloody chateau and –" I manage to stop myself before I say "a daughter". My heart is pounding so hard I can't finish.

Gigi nods curtly. "And that's all you want?" Her voice is authoritative.

"*Yes, that's all!*" I spit.

This time, I stand and walk towards the window to get away from her and check if my car is still outside. I'm starting to glimpse a side of her that I don't like, and I want to leave.

"I have a life in Ireland. If you think I'm after money, you can think again." Oh, Christ, I'm crying. I'm both insulted and hurt that this meeting, just like the one with Marie-Hélène, has taken a downturn. I turn and glare at her. "My husband is dead. I loved André, just like you say you did. I thought ..." I have to stop for a moment as a sob escapes, "that he loved me too. All I want is to know is why he lied!" I throw my hands up. "Can someone just tell me what the hell happened? That's what I want."

"To solve the mystery." She's quieter now.

I exhale impatiently. "If that's what you want to call it, then yes. You're certainly acting like there's a big mystery." I shake my head. "Actually, you know what?" I walk back towards my bag and take out the envelope containing André's death certificate. "I don't need this crap. Here," I throw it to her, "in case you need a copy. And just so you know, I didn't go looking for all this. It came to me."

Gigi's back straightens. "What do you mean *it* came to you?"

To hell with it. I've lost all patience now. "Marie-Hélène," I over-pronounce the name for effect. Gigi visibly convulses. "She's another person I'd never heard of. Remember her? Yes, I can see you do. She's the reason I'm here. I got an email from her. Oh, and by the way, she's as charming as you! I'm surprised you're not friends." I'm shaking with anger, but I notice Gigi's hand reach for the sofa's arm, where she squeezes the upholstery.

"Serendipity, please sit."

I'm breathing loudly, not sure whether to do as I'm told or storm out.

"Please," she asks again. "Let me explain."

Drained, I shrink onto the sofa.

"I need to apologise," Gigi says. "You're right. This was a shock. I'm sorry I questioned you. It's a habit. I ... how can I say it? When this is your life," she gestures around the room, "you're always sceptical of what people really want from you. Unfortunately, more often than not, it's money. André hated it." She smiles sadly. "He found it hard to trust anyone. I apologise. I see now I was wrong, and I've hurt your feelings."

I nod. "Okay, but still I think I should go. You know now about André, and really –"

"What did *she* tell you?" Gigi interrupts.

I'm not sure if I can trust her, but at this point, I have nothing left to lose. Hesitating, I resolve not to tell her about Nicole just yet. "She wanted to talk to André," I say, at last. "She hired a private investigator to find him, which they did, and then she sent an email. In it, she mentioned you and Chateau Challant. I did a little research and found the other stuff online about him drowning. I was so shocked that I ended up calling her, and we spoke. I told her André was dead, and that was it." I look down at my feet.

"Nothing else?"

I glance up, deciding to test her this time. "She told me she was pregnant and that you put a stop to their relationship – that you paid her off because she wasn't good enough for André."

Gigi doesn't flinch. "Is that all?"

"Is that not enough?" I open my eyes wide.

"And you believe her?"

"I don't know."

"Did you meet her?"

"Yes. She's in the city. In Bordeaux."

Gigi looks more astonished than when I told her André was dead. "Do you know why she went looking for André after all this time? What did she want from him?"

"Nothing. I don't know." I exhale impatiently. I don't like all these questions.

"I know what she wants," Gigi says. "It's what she's always wanted. Money! She must want more."

"Christ, can everyone stop talking in circles?" I throw my hands up in despair. "You know what? She said the same thing about you! I can't get a straight answer from her. I can't get one from you. What bloody happened? Did *she* do something? Did *he* do something? You're all acting like someone was …"

I could never have anticipated the next word that forming on her lips.

"Raped?"

My breathing slows, and I can hear the blood rushing in my ears as I stare at her.

"*She* accused him of rape," Gigi says bitterly.

This time, I clutch the sofa to stop my body from folding in two. "*No.*" I shake my head. "*No.*" It can't be. André would never do something like that and, yet, for some reason an ominous image of him as a vile heavy-breathing assailant pops into my head. I push it aside. "No. Not André."

Marie-Hélène is an evil liar. Is this why she'd acted so strangely with me? Her words flash in my mind. "A good man, but not to me." Is this what she'd meant? She's a bitch. André wasn't a *rapist*.

"They were together for about six months from what I can gather, maybe more. He met her in Margaux, he told me. She was a waitress." Gigi rolls her eyes. "So, they start a relationship. After some months, André tells her who he really is, that the vineyard is his or will be, one day. Suddenly, she's living with him. Of course, he didn't tell me that part. I heard it on the grapevine, so to speak. I have to admit, she was very pretty. Of course, no sooner does she know who he is then she wants to move things along … get married. The next thing André comes to me to tell me she is pregnant –"

"Oh my God, he knew?" I cut across her.

"Yes, he knew, but it was clear what Marie-Hélène wanted. He thought so too. To check if I was right, I went to speak to her. She told me that she was going to the police. That they'd argued the night before, that André had been drunk and raped her, beat her. She was bruised, with a black eye, scrapes down her body," Gigi closes her eyes at the memory. "She insisted she had two witnesses. Then she told me it had happened before, resulting in a pregnancy. Apparently, he was aggressive with her a lot. She had it all written down with dates ready to go to the police."

"*No.*" I shake my head.

"She threatened to take down the entire family name and André with it."

"He would never do anything like that. *Never.*" I can't bring myself to use the word *rape.*

Gigi shrugs and bites her lip. "I didn't think so either, but then –"

"What?" I shoot her a look. She can't be serious.

"She was *so* sure. I questioned the two other workers. The ones she said saw it. They hadn't seen that much, but they'd heard noises, heard her screaming … the bruises, the scrapes. I was afraid."

"*No,*" I repeat.

"André was devastated when I told him. So much so that he then started questioning himself. He kept asking if he *had* done it. He wouldn't stop saying it. They *had* argued. When she told him she was pregnant, he'd panicked, questioned her integrity. Afterwards, he said they'd made up, then 'made love'," she makes speech marks. "It wasn't clear in his mind. He'd had a lot to drink."

"*No.*" I'm still shaking my head.

"I tried to assure him that she was after money. So when I went to see her, I tested her. You have to believe me, I was trying to protect him. Maybe I was wrong, but without André knowing I offered her money. Enough for her to go away and never come back, on the condition that she had an abortion. She agreed. She was gone the next day. Before she left, to spite us, she told as many people as she could. I had to tell him what she'd done, that the rumours were out there and he should step away from the vineyards until they died down. He claimed staff started acting strangely towards him, ignoring him. He moved back up to the main house. He told me he felt trapped, hated, judged. He couldn't take it."

I'm still trying to make sense of it all. "So he knew she was pregnant?"

"Well, yes. *If* she was. I have a strong suspicion that she wasn't."

Except Marie-Hélène had been pregnant. Again, I have to stop myself from telling her, too confused to add another element.

Gigi exhales. "I'd never seen André so low. Not only about the accusation but also because she'd been pregnant. He felt guilty, ashamed. He blamed all this." Again, she gestures around the room. "He never wanted this life. Not knowing who you can trust, who loves you for who you are. He was so unhappy. He wanted to leave and never come back – go somewhere with no pressure, no having to conform. Somewhere like …"

"Ballycross," I whisper it to myself, and Gigi takes my hand. "Wait. So he faked his death? Is that not a step too far … ?"

"Perhaps he was nervous she might come back at any

269

minute looking for more, or someone else might. Once there's an accusation out there, whether or not it's true, it becomes you. She'd aborted his child. Accused him of rape. He'd lost what was important to him. I suppose it was a reality check. His father would never have let him go. So –"

"So?"

"So *I* let him go. I wanted him to be free. To find a life that made him happy. Sometimes you have to reinvent, start over, be reborn. I wanted to stop his pain."

My eyes are enormous. "Wait," I say, unable to keep up. "You knew?"

Gigi nods. "I knew he wasn't dead. Not until now!" She stifles a pained sob, then her entire face folds in anguish.

Chapter 25

Marie-Hélène

She's even more paranoid than usual. Her senses so heightened that when Nicole walks into the kitchenette, Marie-Hélène visibly startles, dropping her cup into the sink. It smashes.

"Maman? Are you okay?"

"Fine," she answers, gingerly collecting the broken pieces and throwing them into the bin.

Nicole grabs an apple from the bowl and bites down noisily. The sound grates. Feeling crowded, Marie-Hélène pushes past her daughter, goes to the sofa on the other side of the kitchenette and curls her legs up under her nightdress.

"Are you working later?" Nicole asks.

"Yes."

"I think I'll lie down for a while."

"Fine."

"Are you sure you're okay?"

"Fine."

Nicole shrugs at the third absent-minded response and

heads to her room. Exhaling, Marie-Hélène, rolls her eyes after her daughter. Nicole's sudden chirpy demeanour is beginning to bother her. Yesterday, Nicole hadn't batted an eyelid when she'd come home to find her with an enormous glass of wine in her hand to subdue her equally large hangover from the day before.

Thinking of it, Marie-Hélène stands suddenly, goes back into the kitchen and opens the cupboard. On tiptoes, she reaches back and retrieves the bottle of vodka hidden there for emergencies. Unscrewing the lid, she takes a slug from the now almost-empty bottle, anything to try and dull her paranoia. Taking a final sip, she replaces the cap, puts the bottle back in the cupboard, then moves stealthily back into the living room.

Glancing over her shoulder once in the direction of Nicole's closed bedroom door, she opens the drawer in the television unit and silently removes the plywood panel to retrieve the carefully concealed file. Settling herself back on the sofa, she opens it and attempts to focus. Since meeting Seren, her mind hasn't had a moment's respite. *Tick tick tick*. It's incessant. Of course, Marie-Hélène understands the reason. It's because she'd slipped up. In her defence, she'd barely realised what she was doing.

Perhaps she'd felt triumphant after meeting with Seren. She'd handled the grieving widow's persistent prying well – delicately, in fact. Aside from revealing that André had been weak, a grown man firmly under his mother's thumb, she had successfully managed not to tarnish Seren's memories.

Seren hadn't seemed all that grateful for the diluted version. Instead, there'd been a great deal of "I knew my husband" and "Not *my* André". She'd kept insisting that

André mustn't have known about the baby. Oh, he'd known all right, but he had tried to wipe it away as if it had never happened. Maybe she should have told Seren the real story. Marie-Hélène attempts to imagine Seren's face if she'd decided to lay it all on the table. Judging by her steadfast love for André, Seren wouldn't have believed her anyway.

More than once, Seren had issued the same disapproving look that Nicole gives her when she drinks. If only they knew maybe they wouldn't be so fast to judge. After Marie-Hélène told Seren that she didn't want her to meet Nicole, Seren had grown fractious. It was utterly ridiculous. André was dead! Then again, Marie-Hélène had met enough Irish holidaymakers over the years in Corsica to know that they were all about family – hoards and hoards of red-haired, freckly sentimental Irish, linking arms in search of the local Irish bar. How she'd endured mother after mother telling her about her six children, twenty-eight grandchildren, five sisters, three brothers. She should have known that Seren would try to latch on to Nicole.

In hindsight, that was another thing Marie-Hélène had managed well, telling Seren that Nicole didn't want anything to do with her. Who could argue with that? In truth, she hadn't even told Nicole that Seren had come to France. For good measure, she'd told Nicole that Seren had prevented André from having a relationship with his daughter after Nicole mentioned going to Ireland. That had put a stop to that stupid idea.

The remainder of the meeting with Seren is hazy in Marie-Hélène's mind. She can remember Seren telling her that she planned to return to Ireland and wouldn't see André's family in person. At least Marie-Hélène had been able to convince her of that much. It was a wise decision. After Seren left, Marie-Hélène changed her mind about having another drink and instead left too. She'd made a brief stop at the Supermarket to buy some more wine and then returned to the flat.

Sitting down with a drink, through unfocused eyes she'd searched the internet, then impulsively and half-giggling clicked the circular icon to connect the call to Chateau Challant. She'd almost hung up when she heard it ring, but then she'd had the daring thought that it might be gratifying to let Gigi know that a volcano was about to erupt.

An automated voice had brought Marie-Hélène in circles, pressing every button imaginable. When she finally spoke with a living being, the novelty had almost worn off. "I'm sorry, Madame Dubois-Challant is currently unavailable. Would you like to leave a message?" Again, she should have hung up, but she'd felt invincible reciting her name and number to the receptionist. It wasn't until the next day that she vaguely remembered making the call when she looked at her phone. Since then, she's felt sick.

"Follow the steps. That's all you have to do," the lawyer had advised.

So she had. Find André. *Tick.* Make contact. *Tick.* Get proof of his death. *Tick.* Wait until … No. Stupidly, she'd jumped a step ahead. Now, when Gigi saw Marie-Hélène's name on the message, she'd know something was coming. Still, Gigi would never guess what, and all because of a fortuitous encounter with a holidaymaker in Corsica. Closing her eyes, she revisits it, as she often does, just to ensure she hadn't imagined the entire thing.

Marie-Hélène had been serving a retired English doctor at the restaurant where she worked. The woman, who had been dining alone, had been eager to chat about anything from French wine to French peculiarities. Marie-Hélène actually enjoyed the conversation, so that when the woman offered to share a bottle of wine following her shift, she accepted. She regretted it, however, growing quickly bored. It became evident that the woman was using her as a sounding board for her entire life's grievances.

When she started on the French legal system, Marie-Hélène was about to make her excuses when the woman uttered, "For gain, never be surprised at how far people will go. Even your own flesh and blood. Especially your flesh and blood."

As if by magic, something clicked in Marie-Hélène's mind, making her back straighten. She continued to listen and was finally gifted the life-changing words, "*héritiers reservataires*" – reserved heirs. Originating from humble beginnings, Marie-Hélène had never happened upon the legal term that only holds meaning when there's some substance behind it. As an only child, all she'd been willed with was worthless jewellery and overdue rent.

"An outrage!" The Englishwoman leaned in closer to explain. "In England, we can leave whatever the hell we like to whomever the hell we please. But the French … ah, the French!" She rolled her eyes dramatically. "They have to be different! No matter if your children transpire to be enormous disappointments, as mine have. Regardless of how badly they treat you, they get practically everything. Just like that!" She'd clicked her fingers. "You can't bloody write them out. I was forever telling my husband to disinherit them, if only to make them see sense. It can't be done. The law protects them. You know what that means for me? More than likely, I'll end up sharing my house with grown-up children. Not only that, they take seventy-five per cent of my dear husband's legacy. Seventy-five! I'll be lucky if I don't starve to death. What's more, the wealthier you are, the more it hurts. I'm only thankful we didn't buy that vineyard all those years ago. Imagine me living out my days locked in a turret!"

It was the mention of the vineyard that sparked the memory of the spiralling towers of Chateau Challant. When the woman finished speaking, Marie-Hélène took a deep breath and decided, on the basis that she would more than likely never see her again, to seek counsel over something that had overwhelmed her for many years. Afterwards, Marie-Hélène replayed the woman's opinion on repeat before taking the first step in facing her demons. When she finally did, she knew it was time to retaliate.

Marie-Hélène has been plotting ever since. Of course, she'd had to remove her own emotions – try to see it from all angles by putting herself into each person's shoes. It took months of research to be sure about everything. At first, she'd gone to the library in the mornings when Nicole was at school, where she'd tried to pick apart document after document of legal terminology that she could barely comprehend.

Help eventually came in the form of a handsome law student she'd encountered at the library. They'd ended up in bed together, where he'd helped her decipher it further. Between making love, she'd attempted to explain the "hypothetical" situation to him. To do so, she'd come up with absurd character names. For the life of her, she couldn't remember now what they'd been. Ridiculous enough that they'd both found it difficult not to laugh. Mind you, her smile had faded fast when her legal lover disclosed her character's position in the "fictitious" scenario.

The English doctor had been spot on. Like it or not, French law granted specific inheritance rights to offspring. Historically, it had been to protect the family's interests from someone swooping in and making a claim over their inheritance. The part of the law that still amuses Marie-Hélène is that often the surviving spouse gets something of a raw deal – in that the estate of the deceased belongs to the whole family rather than any single member.

Opening her eyes again, Marie-Hélène cocks her head, listening for any movement from Nicole's room before opening the file on her lap. Flicking through it, she comes to the photo of her and André together, holds it up and smiles. There's a part of her that still imagines them together with their daughter. What kind of life might they have had? She'd been devastated when André accused her of getting pregnant on purpose for gain. Before that, just like Seren, she'd believed he was perfect.

"Do you think I know the secret to conceive on demand? *You did this!*" she'd shouted back. "Do you honestly think that's why I'm here?"

Not even André had known the real reason she'd originally come to Bordeaux. If she'd told him then, it would have sounded pathetic – juvenile for a woman in her mid-twenties to be searching for … what? … love? Certainly not money! How dare he! Afterwards, how they'd fought. She'd never known confrontation like it. He was paranoid, angry, so bitter that it had ended with her wailing, begging him to stop. "Please, André! Don't do this to me, please!"

The next day he'd left on business. It was the last time she ever saw him.

Gigi had come then, to tidy everything up fast. It was the first time they'd met. Naively, Marie-Hélène decided to tell Gigi everything, even what she'd failed to tell André, hoping that she might somehow understand. Instead, she'd been furious. What Gigi told her next shattered everything, completely destroying her and leaving her with no choice.

"You leave right now. Do you hear me? You stupid, stupid girl! Can't you see what you've done? André doesn't want you, and even if he did, this could never be. Here!" She'd thrust the piece of paper at her.

In all her life, Marie-Hélène had never seen an amount like it. She'd been so shocked that she'd taken it. To this day, she regrets it.

"This is what you're after anyway. Get rid of *it* for all our sakes but, most of all, for that baby. Nothing that starts out that way can ever be right. Do you hear me? I should know."

Marie-Hélène replaces the photo in the file and takes out the one of André and Seren that the private investigator had sent her. In other circumstances, if she wasn't so envious of her, she might have liked Seren. Seren had had a nice, uncomplicated life with a man they'd both loved. He hadn't hurt her. Once again, the thought strikes that perhaps she should have told Seren the truth if only to unburden herself of the sick, twisted lies. No, she couldn't risk it.

Flicking to the back of the file, she takes out the sheet of paper containing her notes. From afar, it's like a distorted family tree or a casting sheet. Years before,

Marie-Hélène had drawn it out, adding both hers and her daughter's names to the list of players in the drama. Tracing her finger over Nicole's name, she stares straight ahead in a trance. Once she knows the truth, Nicole will understand, won't she?

The lawyer had been clear. "You cannot stake claim to anything until that man is dead. There *is* no estate until he's deceased. So be patient. Although at age ninety-plus, how much longer could Henri-Dubois-Challant possibly have?" He'd laughed at that.

The lawyer was a greedy little man. Marie-Hélène had clocked that from the off. Then again, the hungrier, the better. He'd been willing to take the case under the proviso that, in time, he too would benefit.

"People like us, who can be patient, always win in the end." He said that a lot: *People like us.*

Marie-Hélène is nothing like him, but what was the point in explaining that this was never about wealth or status. The wealth would be a happy by-product only for Nicole. No. It isn't about money. What drives Marie-Hélène is the desire to inflict pain – the same pain that had been thrust upon her. Despising André for so long was a hard habit to break. Although, isn't that what they say? That there's a fine line between love and hate. Squeezing her eyes shut, she tries to relax by conjuring Gigi's smug face and how it will soon change when she learns the truth. Opening her eyes, she looks down at the page in her lap. Nothing can alter what's written on there.

"Maman?"

The door to the bedroom opens suddenly, causing Marie-Hélène to jump. This time, her paperwork spills to the floor.

"Are you trying to give me a heart attack?" She puts

her hand to her heart, then bends to retrieve the papers. "Creeping up on me! You know I hate snooping."

"What's that?"

"Nothing," Marie-Hélène answers, glancing up impatiently. "What's wrong?"

"I was going to ask … forget it." Nicole goes back into her room and closes the door.

Gathering the file, Marie-Hélène tucks it under her arm and retreats to the privacy of her room. Lying on the bed, she holds it against her chest before closing her eyes. How she adores French Law! With André officially dead, as his only child, Nicole automatically steps into his shoes as the beneficiary. Marie-Hélène has the one thing Gigi never wanted her to have – André's blood. The moment Henri Dubois-Challant closes his eyes for the final time, the real game will begin – one in which the winner is already determined. The biggest mistake you can ever make is to underestimate a person. Once upon a time, Gigi had made that mistake with Marie-Hélène. Now, as a result, she wasn't just coming for money. She was coming for everything.

Chapter 26

My legs are stretched out in front of me, resting on a cushion on top of the metal railings. Where I sit, my face is towards the sun. I've been here for over a week now, in this place where at last I'd allowed myself to pause for long enough to let the sun penetrate my skin, turn my limbs golden, thaw my soul, to simply breathe. In the distance, the view is of sunflower and maize fields. Closer still, the balcony sits practically on top of the vineyards, which I now know encompasses over ten hectares of walled farmland. It really is glorious – peaceful, still. It's warm but not stifling like it had been in the city. Here, the heat is different. There's more space for it to disperse, so it's less intense. Now and then, a light breeze sweeps past me, carrying fragrances of fruit, flowers, soil. It's hard to describe. If I had only one word, it would be *life* – the air is alive. Although he'd often tried, André never managed to convey its beauty – its vibrancy, how it fills every sense.

Inside the walls of Chateau Challant is a tiny world in itself. Within them, I feel free. Since discovering the truth,

I'd imagined that André had come from vastness, but I see now that his former world had once been smaller than mine. Over the week here, Gigi has revealed snippets about André's life. I'd known he'd attended boarding school in Bordeaux as a teen, but I hadn't known that he'd been homeschooled as a young child. Gigi has told me that they'd rarely mixed outside of the chateau, certainly not in the village. Life had been very much within the walls of this place. Everything had rotated around the vineyards. Yes, there'd been ponies, tractors, all the space he could ever have needed to run around – every little boy's dream. And yet had there been friends, other children with whom to play? I hadn't wanted to appear rude by asking. Aside from the summer André had spent in Ballycross as a teen, it seems as though his life had been somewhat insular – having known André, perhaps even lonely. If so, was it any wonder that he'd thrived among the comings and goings of our small Cork village, the people, the chat. I never imagined that anywhere could feel smaller than Ballycross, yet this place must have felt so to him. Had it? I wish he was here to tell me. How strange that I'm experiencing the longed-for freedom in what had once been my husband's world that I imagine he'd also felt landing in mine.

Being here, I've rediscovered André. I feel close to him again. I've found new things about him that I never knew, like how alike his father he was.

That first day I'd arrived, Gigi had led me to the top floor of the house to meet him. Henri's room resembles a hospital with round-the-clock nurses and every manner of machine beeping beside him. She'd bent to kiss his papery cheek, then plucked his limp hand from where it rested by his side and held it to her cheek. "They're very alike, *non*? Can you see it?"

I advanced a fraction to stare at the sleeping body, at what might have become the elderly face of my husband. Despite the tubes, the machines, his thin face, he was so familiar that my stomach lurched.

"I can see it," I nodded.

"In his day, Henri and André could have passed for the same person. If you could see his eyes, it would make even more sense."

I swallowed and smiled, glad that I couldn't glimpse the milky eyes of my husband's buried future. Dropping my gaze to the floor, I didn't want to look anymore at how André might have aged, how his skin might have sagged, at whom I would have loved in my twilight years. It was too painful.

I flashed my eyes up at Gigi who was staring lovingly at Henri. Next to him, Gigi looked more like a daughter. At a push, perhaps even a granddaughter. I struggled to imagine a time when they'd ever appeared right together. Eventually, Gigi turned to me. "Henri had his faults. He was far from the perfect husband or father, but with him this way, so very helpless, it's impossible not to forgive." She replaced his hand and patted it. "*À bientôt, Henri.*"

Thankfully, we didn't stay long. Being there conjured memories of André's final days. I'm no doctor, but I could tell that death was near. Once you know it, death is a sense, a smell, a change in atmosphere, a presence.

Gigi feels it too. At least she told me as much. "It won't be long now. He's very frail. I don't think you can ever be ready, can you? No matter how old or …"

"Young," I'd finished, smiling sadly. "No. You're never ready."

We'd shared a look then – between two women, still strangers, both with something huge in common.

André's similarity to his father isn't the only discovery that I've made. Learning that Gigi knew André was leaving France, possibly never to return, has been the most challenging revelation of all. If it's possible, maybe even more so the news that Marie-Hélène had accused him of rape. I keep trying to imagine how you could let your son leave, knowing that you might never see him again regardless of what he'd been accused of or how unhappy he was? But then, I'm not yet a mother, so how can I say what I'd do if faced with the same? I can't decide whether what Gigi did is the most beautiful display of altruism or if it's something else entirely.

I was further flummoxed when she revealed that it was she who'd placed André's belongings on the cliff to buy him some time and make it appear like he might have drowned.

"I wanted to leave it open so that he could return ... If I'd wanted to make it more realistic, I could have left a note, but I couldn't bring myself to do that, to put in writing what I already knew deep down – that he wasn't coming back."

"But how could you be so sure?"

"I knew André. This life wasn't what he wanted."

It was also Gigi who'd paid private investigators *not* to search for him, so she could demonstrate to her husband that she was doing everything she could. After she explained it, I sort of understood the rationale behind it. Although it sounds strange, the way she'd told it made sense. I believed her.

After she'd told me the truth, Gigi had thawed quickly.

After the visit to Henri, she took me on a tour of the estate. "You'll stay with me here at the chateau. Please," she'd encouraged, "you're family now."

"Thank you, but honestly I couldn't. You have enough on your plate with Henri being ill. I can stay in the village."

She wouldn't hear of it. "Nonsense. Then at least stay in one of the guesthouses. Besides, I'd like you near. We still have so much to talk about." She paused then, with a breathy laugh. "I get lonely. With Henri so sick, it would be nice to have someone to talk with in the evenings."

Again, I understood. It was exactly how I often felt back home. It was the never-ending evenings I hated most.

"He's been sick for more than a decade now – I should be used to it," Gigi told me, stopping under the arch in the courtyard that led to the farm, as she called it. "Can I be honest?"

"Of course."

Now that she knew I was no longer a threat, Gigi was an entirely different person. She oozed warmth just like André once had. "I think I'll feel relieved when Henri goes. Waiting is so hard. Witnessing his suffering."

"It's very hard," I agreed.

"I'll be a widow. Although at my age, it's natural. What happened to you –" Her voice caught. "My poor girl. What have you been through? And then to find out those cruel lies about André from *her*." She patted my arm. "There's some good though, *non*? It brought you here. How I've longed for family, and here you are."

Right then, I should have told Gigi about the baby or, more importantly, that she already has a granddaughter. Yet, in the same way Gigi couldn't bring herself to use Marie-Hélène's name, I was struggling to think about

Nicole. Instead, I allowed Gigi to lead me under the archway to the foot of the vineyards. Once there, my mouth dropped open.

"This is it. Where André grew up." She pointed down the rows of vines beyond. "This is the part André loved. The chateau, the ceremony, the pomp, all that comes with the land wasn't for him."

"Good with the bad," I whispered as every hair on my body had stood on end.

"What's that?"

I shook my head. "It was something my mother used to say." I turned to look at her. "That you have to take the good with the bad. That no one gets everything."

"I like that. When André was small, I used to tell him that he grew right out of one of those vines. That one day, I'd found him here, ready to be picked." There was a faraway look on her face.

For the first time, it dawned on me how tragic the entire story was. Gigi had lost her only son. André had lost his pride, his future, all because of Marie-Hélène. I hate her even more.

"It was a nicer story than the truth," she whispered, still staring ahead.

"The truth?" I asked. Could there be more?

Gigi shook herself back to present and stepped onto the path between the vines, beckoning for me to follow.

"The truth is, I arrived here many years ago to pick fruit." She glanced over her shoulder at me. "I left home in search of adventure. It's how most of us end up in this place unless you are born up there." She gestured behind at the chateau. "Henri was so handsome, just like André, but much older than me, as you saw. I was infatuated by him, by this place." She shrugged. "My father had died, my mother and I had very different ideas about life. She used to say, 'Georgine, life is not supposed to be happy'. Imagine! To her, it was about being responsible. I hated it. So I left at seventeen. The next thing I knew, I was holding a baby. I was a wife at eighteen, little more than a child myself. After we married, I found myself living the very life of duty I'd tried to escape. It was lonely. The vineyard always came first. Henri was always busy, and I was still locked in a tower, just a nicer one." She stopped walking. "You can see why I didn't want that for André. Raising him was a pleasure, but for many years I felt like little more than a nanny. My husband was a very private man with very few friends. There was no parties or social life, as you might imagine. No mixing with the locals. It was André and I, here, just the two of us."

"Wait, you were only eighteen when André was born?" I tried to calculate back. That made her …

"Fifty-nine. Don't tell me you thought more? Today has been difficult enough," she joked.

"I just assumed you'd be older because of André's age, but no, I mean, you look younger than me!"

"*Hah*. I like you, Serendipity."

"Did you ever see your family again?" I asked then.

"*Non*. André was my family. In many ways, André and I grew up together here, but I grew up realising that you take the bad with the good." She raised her eyebrows knowingly. "If I wanted to be part of this land, I had to accept the rest. This place is a privilege, but it's also a vocation. It can be a lonely life. André, well, he was more idealistic than me and perhaps braver. He wanted only the good."

"Was he … was his father …"

"Cruel?" she finished for me. "No, not cruel. Difficult.

Old-fashioned. Set in his ways. Antiquated. Disinterested. A recluse." She laughed sadly. "Truthfully, although I love Henri in my own way, I should never have married him. But then, I wouldn't have got André. Henri wanted a son to inherit all this and continue the business, but he wasn't much of a father. It made André feel like a commodity. After Henri became ill, the running of the vineyards fell to me. It was the happy surprise of my life. It feels like what I was always meant to do."

"I read that online. It looks like you've made a huge success of it."

"Yes. I've worked hard. I've achieved a lot for a woman, *non*?" She threw her eyes up good-naturedly. "And yet in my personal life … not so much. It's what André was terrified of, being alone. Perhaps he was right to be afraid. I'm as alone as I was when I first arrived."

"I am too," I'd whispered.

"Then we'll be alone together." She linked my arm. "Come, let me show you the rest."

Sitting here now, on the balcony of the guesthouse, I picture André. I'd been blown away when Gigi told me that she was putting me up where he'd once lived. Apparently, he'd chosen it as his own as his twenty-first birthday present. Unlike the chateau with its heavy beams, ornate antique furniture, enormous fireplaces and vast stone staircases, the guesthouse is small but comfortable. Knowing André, he'd chosen it for the breathtaking view alone. Nothing at the chateau reminds me of him, but here he's everywhere – in the air, in the fields, looped through the vines that grow just a stone's throw from where I sit. I can visualise him outside with his shirtsleeves rolled up, his face and arms tanned. He's smiling and, my God, he's so handsome, young, alive.

Much as Gigi claims, André hadn't wanted this life, I can't help but think that all along it was where he was meant to have been. Not with me, in Ballycross, but here. It hurts to think that I'd somehow robbed him of the chance. If he'd only told me the truth. I've thought about it a lot, tried to imagine how I might have reacted if he'd been honest. Would I have understood? Would I have nodded encouragingly at the news that he'd got his girlfriend pregnant, then ditched her? Would I have patted his arm when he told me his mother paid Marie-Hélène off to quash her alleged rape accusation?

What if André really had told me everything that the first day I'd bumped into him in Ballycross? Without knowing him, would I have believed him? Would we have still ended up going for wine? Would we have ended up together? Could I have loved him the same, not knowing if he was telling the truth if he was capable of rape? Because no matter how much you love someone, you'd still have to ask, wouldn't you? "Did you do it, André?" Would I have accepted it when he told me no?

Could he have told me in time, once we'd got to know each other? Would I then have questioned why he hadn't told me before? How was André to know that we'd eventually fall in love? Perhaps by then, it was too late to reveal his past. By then, he'd had more to lose. André had found peace, love, acceptance in Ireland. Can I honestly blame him for not wanting to threaten it? For me not to be able to look in his eyes and wonder.

Maybe Gigi is right. Once the word *rape, sexual assault*, or anything conjuring a man overpowering a woman is used, the seed is sown. By then, it's too late – opinions form, ideas take hold. And what if Marie-Hélène really did believe she'd been raped? As a fellow woman, am I wrong to call her a liar? Removing my hands from where they're linked over my increasingly prominent bump, I put them to my face. No matter what way I look at it, it's impossible. I suppose deep down, I know Marie Hélène is lying. She's the one damaging the victims who've actually been harmed, not me.

In one way, it's comforting to know that André had indeed been mourning something when we'd first met. I know now, he'd been mourning himself, who he'd once been, who he might have become.

"I'll love you until my dying day and beyond. I'll never harm you. Or hurt you. I'll protect you and trust you." André's vows. He'd sworn to trust me, and I'd done the same. André was innocent.

I haven't mentioned Marie-Hélène again since that first day. I'm afraid to bring her up again. Gigi has followed suit. Not for the first time, I have to physically push the thought of Marie-Hélène from my mind. I scrunch my eyes shut against the instant fury and irritation. In trying not to think of her, I'm now thinking of her. Worse still, I'm thinking of Nicole. She's texted me several times, but I can't bring myself to open the messages. I can't believe I'm actually ignoring a child, but what am I supposed to tell her? I'm stuck – tightly wedged into the middle of a hopeless situation, one that I'll have to face soon before Marie-Hélène comes knocking on the door of the chateau.

Nicole's last message had arrived the evening before while we'd sat at the back of the chateau eating dinner and sipping wine. Gigi never takes more than half a glass and savours it as if she's drinking gold. Which she could be, it's that expensive. She drinks only the best reserve from the vast cellars – another part of this operation that has seen my eyes out on stalks. Seeing how it all happens, what it takes to put a single bottle of wine on a dining table, is fascinating.

"Everything all right?" Gigi had asked as I'd glanced at my phone and made a face at the message. "If there's something you want to talk about –"

"It was just a friend from home." Once again. I'd missed the opportunity to come clean. Or was it that I was getting so comfortable here that I didn't want to disturb it?

I need to tell Gigi. I have to tell her both about Nicole and that I'm pregnant. She has a right to know, especially since she's been so open with me. At last, I feel like I'm in the right place, as if André has led me here for a reason. Since being here, I'm sleeping again. In fact, most of the time, I can barely keep my eyes open. It's as if André is lulling me, forcing me to rest, to take care of his baby. In turn, I feel like I've delivered him home. In truth, I never want to leave.

"Are you all right?" Cathy had sounded concerned when she'd called earlier. "I haven't heard from you in days."

"I'm fine, really." I almost hadn't answered. "I found out what happened."

Cathy was silent as I tried to explain it as best I could.

"So, in a nutshell, Marie-Hélène wanted money," I concluded. "I still can't believe she accused him of rape. That word! It's so horrible."

"Oh, God. I'm so sorry, Seren."

"He didn't do it. Obviously, he would never."

"No. No, of course not. Christ. Poor André. So, where are you now?"

291

"I'm still here. I … I'm staying on for a few days, maybe longer. I'm not sure."

"At the chateau?"

"Well, no. I'm in one of the guesthouses on the grounds. It's so peaceful here. I feel good." I told her about it, and she cooed in all the right places. "Finally, it all makes sense," I said, only to be met with silence. "Don't you think?"

"I suppose," she began, then I heard her take a breath through her teeth. "Except, putting his stuff on a cliff to make it look like he'd drowned? Would we say that was a step too far? Covering all bases a little too much?"

And, there it was. The rest made sense – why André hadn't told me, why he wouldn't want a child born out of alleged rape, why he'd like to leave and start afresh … why he needed to be dead to do that …?

I sighed loudly before answering. "Yeah, at first, I thought the same. But the way Gigi tells it, it makes sense." Did it? Was I trying to convince myself? "She knew that his father would just keep on looking for him. Wouldn't stop until he'd found him and brought him back. I think she'd felt pressure like that from her own mother, and she didn't want the same for André. This way, he could come back if and when he was ready."

"Yeah, I suppose it makes sense if we were living in the eighteenth century," Cathy quipped.

"Actually, this place is sort of like that." I was growing impatient. "Until you see it, Cathy, it's hard to understand …" I trailed off. "And is it so hard to believe that André might have been happier with me in Ballycross?"

"No. But couldn't he have had both? Couldn't he have stayed in touch with his mother, at least?"

"It's not that simple. This place is … complex."

"Yes, but –"

"How's home?" I changed the subject.

I should have known that Cathy would play Devil's Advocate. Despite her concerns, I feel strangely protective over Gigi. She's told me that me being here is finally allowing her to mourn the loss of André. It's the same for me. Being with someone who loved him like me is helping me too. I believe Gigi. What she's told me *does* make sense. To be a part of this life, you have to become it, and André had wanted to be something else.

I'm so lost in thought that when Gigi appears at the balcony door, I jump.

"I'm sorry, I did knock." She smiles down at me. "You look quite beautiful sitting there." She moves past me and rests her hands on the balcony's railings to stare at the view. "Beautiful, isn't it?"

"It's stunning. I could stay here forever."

"Then do." Gigi glances briefly over her shoulder at me and smiles. "Or for a while." She turns again so that her back is to me as she says, "At least until the baby is born."

Chapter 27

It's probably only seconds, but it feels far more when I blurt, "How did you know?"

Gigi glances back over her shoulder and smiles affectionately before turning to pull a chair closer. "I notice everything. I've always been observant. Too much so, possibly." She laughs gently as she sits, crosses one leg over the other, then leans forward. She cups her face with her hand in a perfect pose, with her elbow resting on her knee.

It would make a beautiful photograph. Once again, I'm astounded by her beauty. Her skin is luminous. With the help of the sunlight, I can make out intense flecks of amber in her brown eyes. I hadn't noticed them before now. Clearly, I'm not as observant as she is. Today, she's wearing a camel-coloured silk blouse with a matching skirt – a far cry from the nightie-like dress I have on.

She gracefully moves her hand from her chin to tuck her hair behind her ear, then continues, "A watcher, my mother called it. She used to say, 'Georgine, someday you'll find a purpose for your scrutiny'." She pouts and shrugs.

My eyes are narrow for one instant as I listen. I could have sworn ... Gigi continues before I get the chance to ask. Perhaps I'm mistaken.

"It turns out, it's been as useful in business as it has been in general life. I miss nothing." Reaching forward, she places the palm of her hand on my stomach. "Congratulations. It's good news, *non*? You are happy?" She sounds so like André that it feels almost as if it's him speaking.

I frown. "I think so. It's taken me a while to get used to it. It was sort of a surprise."

"It suits you. A pregnant woman has an aura."

"Exhaustion." I guffaw nervously. I'm so relieved that she seems happy.

"How long are you pregnant?" She removes her hand and leans back.

"Almost four months."

"You'll have an obvious bump soon." She makes an exploding action with her fingers.

I remove my legs from where they're still resting on the railings and sit forward. "I'm sorry I didn't tell you, Gigi. I was going to. It was just with all the other news I didn't want to overwhelm you."

Gigi smiles and nods once.

I lower my eyes. "And then I suppose I was trying to figure out how I felt about everything else, like Marie-Hélène. What she said about André. Ni–" I stop myself in time. "And then being here with you." I glance up unsurely. I'm babbling, but I need to explain how I'm feeling. "For the first time since André died, I feel like I'm with him again. It's so familiar here." How can I put it into words? "I feel so at peace here. I feel –"

"Home?" Gigi raises her eyebrows and smiles knowingly.

"Yes," I say, holding the palms of my hands out. "Back home, in Ireland, it felt like the walls were closing in on me. Everyone was smothering me." I roll my eyes. "Trying to help, but it wasn't helping. And then others didn't know what to say. They'd cross the road if they saw me coming. I couldn't bear the way my own friends would look at me. Like I was this lump of sorrow. I felt so wrong in my own life!" I exhale. "I was so angry with André for leaving me, angrier still when I discovered all this." My voice is animated before it turns serious. "I wanted to die. So many times, I wanted to just evaporate." I stifle a sob, look up at the ceiling and then swallow. When I look back at her, there are tears in her eyes.

"Do you know what it feels like to feel so misplaced in your own life?"

Gigi bites her lip and looks out at the fields. "I do. It's why I left Paris all those years ago. I felt so trapped. Here," she nods at the view beyond. "I found freedom. I was able to start again." She pauses and looks back at me quizzically. "Maybe André led you here. Maybe you're here for a reason."

I let out a laugh, surprised that she seems able to read my thoughts. "Do you really believe in that sort of stuff?" I ask, hoping she answers that she does.

"Do you?"

"I used to. I used to think life was on my side, that it kept sending me all these wonderful surprises."

"Just like your name?"

I shake my head and throw my eyes. "Yes, my stupid bloody name." I laugh again. "Then, André got sick. You know, until the day he died, I thought he'd pull through? So that when he did die, I was so *shocked*." I emphasise the last word. "And then all this. And here I am."

Gigi takes my hand. "Here you are. Maybe this is serendipity! You come here for another reason and find something else." Then she points at my stomach. "Is there anyone special at home? It's been what? Almost a year and a half since André. Time enough for another relationship if that's what you wanted?"

"Except another relationship isn't what I want, not really. Well," I correct, "for about five minutes, I thought there might have been someone. He was a friend of André's actually, but I was wrong. Maybe I'm too young to say this, but I can't ever imagine settling down with someone else. Not for anything serious anyway."

"Like me." Gigi tilts her head, and I raise my eyebrows. "Yes," she admits, "I've had a few lovers over the years. Henri didn't exactly live up to the stereotype of the French lover."

"André did!" I exclaim before my hand shoots to my mouth. "Oh, God. Sorry. I'm sure you don't want to hear that your son was great in the sack!"

Gigi puts her head back and lets out a genuine laugh. "Will I tell you a secret?" she whispers. "I think Henri might have been gay."

"Really?" I'm shocked.

"Or asexual. I'd be embarrassed to reveal how many times we actually 'made love'." Gigi makes speech marks.

"Oh, my God!" I cry. "And that was enough to get pregnant?"

"Once is enough, sometimes." Gigi looks sad.

"Not for us. We tried but didn't really try over the years, and then it was too late."

297

Gigi squeezes my hand, then stands once more to look out at the view. "I think you're strong. To go it alone, like that. I would never have been that brave."

"And yet, in your own words, you pretty much raised André alone."

"Yes. I suppose so."

"You did a great job. He was wonderful, Gigi. "

"Yes."

I'm suddenly at a loss for words, undecided whether to continue or allow Gigi time to digest this first piece of information before hitting her with more. Once again, I'm pleasantly surprised by Gigi. She's taken it so well, accepted the news of this grandchild so willingly that I feel utterly overwhelmed with admiration. Perhaps Gigi will be as welcoming to Nicole once she has time to process it. Knowing Gigi, she'll want to protect her granddaughter. My heart swells as the fog over my mixed-up feelings towards Nicole begins to lift. I've felt confused about how I should think about her since learning about the accusation, but I see now that none of it is Nicole's fault. I only hope Nicole will feel the same. Perhaps I won't have to tell her what her mother accused him of. Regardless, she's still André's daughter.

If Gigi can be so accepting of me, then I should be the same with Nicole. I'm actually in awe of Gigi's strength and pragmatism. At this very moment, I'm not sure I've ever admired anyone more than her – for protecting André, for allowing him to live the type of life he wanted, for being so ahead of her times, unafraid to rebuke tradition.

"I know it seems sudden," Gigi turns, "but I'd like you to stay for a while. Why not have the baby here in France? I can find you a good doctor. You must be due a check-up."

Goosebumps flood my skin as my heart lifts. Could I really do that? It had crossed my mind. After all, I'd left Ballycross not knowing when I'd return. It seems crazy, but …

"I'm actually due a check-up this week. I've been otherwise distracted, but I should see a doctor. Although I feel great." I smile broadly.

"Well, I know someone. I'll call this afternoon and get it set up. Are you sure you're comfortable here in the guesthouse? I wanted to talk to you about it."

"Very. It's perfect, Gigi." I look back through the French doors at the homely space. "I really love it."

"It needs some updating if you're planning to stay. It's due it anyway. This reminds me. Apparently, it needs new appliances. I spoke with one of the managers this morning. I can see now that he's right. The stove is as antiquated as Henri!" She gestures through the doors at the old-fashioned-looking stove.

"Don't worry, I haven't used anything yet anyway. It feels like weeks since I've prepared food or done housework! I'm getting lazy."

"Well, don't. Not until I get it fixed up for you. I think we should move you into the main house later, or at least the garden villa until we get it all sorted here. I'll help you pack shortly. All you have to do is rest and eat with me at the chateau until we have some new things organised. You'll feel more at home then."

Her eyes dart around the space. I can see her making a mental note of what I'll need.

"Did I tell you that André lived here?" Gigi glances behind. "Ah, yes. I did. It was his. It can be yours too for as long as you like, there's no pressure. I know he'd want you to feel welcome." She clasps her hands together excitedly. "We have some work to do! Some minor adjustments to make it cosy for you and the baby. It will be so nice to have a baby around again. I can help you, be a shoulder to cry on, a friend to laugh with ... if Ireland doesn't feel right for you anymore, maybe France is the answer?"

She smiles so warmly that my heart soars. It's similar to what Bobby Cronin once said to André about Ireland. I can't help thinking the meaning behind all the pain of the past few weeks has just been revealed.

I close my eyes briefly, trying to picture it; it's all I can see. Me, walking through the vineyards with the tanned chubby hand of our son in my own. Me, telling him all about his father. He'd speak French and get the chance to grow up in this magical place as André had. Gigi's still trying to convince me, although there's really no need. "I'm so nervous about what will happen when Henri passes, of what the next few weeks hold. He's so weak today." She pauses then continues. "It would make me more relaxed if I had someone to lean on in the coming weeks."

She looks so vulnerable, as daunted by the unknown as I'd felt before André died. I can help her – with the funeral, the aftermath, with all the little things that unexpectedly occur with grief. I've already been through it.

"It would be nice to take a sabbatical," I say with a grin. "To see what else is out there for me ... "

"And I'd love you to be my guest here." She sits back down and clasps her hands again. "Well, this is exciting. What do they say? One life goes, and another arrives," she muses. "Now, you'll have to forgive me if I rush and buy you a crib and some baby clothes. You deserve to be spoiled! Do you know what you're having? In France, we mostly find out –"

"A boy," I say.

"Ah," she claps her hands together. "Boys are so very loving. I'm so glad you feel you can be honest with me. No more secrets, agreed?"

It feels like a kick in the face. If this is to work, I have to tell her everything. My heart starts to pound. "Gigi?"

"Yes." She looks up, then frowns when she sees my face.

"There's something I need to tell you." My mouth goes dry as I struggle to formulate the words.

"Are you okay, Seren? You look like you've seen a ghost."

I shake my head. "I'm fine. It's not about me. It's about … you see, Marie-Hélène told me something else. I didn't tell you before because I was so shocked about what she accused André of that I felt sick …"

At the mere mention of Marie-Hélène's name, Gigi's jaw tenses.

"What lies now?" Gigi tries to keep her voice light, but she looks concerned.

"This is definitely not a lie. It's very … visual. I think Marie-Hélène plans on contacting you soon anyway ..."

Gigi's head jerks back. "She already called me a few days before you arrived. I was hoping she'd go away, that it was a mistake. What's this about?" Her back is now poker-straight, and she's holding her breath.

"Marie-Hélène didn't have an abortion."

I watch Gigi's chest slowly deflate. I could be mistaken, but she looks somewhat relieved.

"She's lying." She sounds assured. "No one would

keep something as revolting as that!"

I flinch at the description of Nicole.

"No. Not after what I told her about André," Gigi continues shaking her head. "No one in their right mind would —"

"What you told her?" My brow furrows. "You mean what *she* told you?"

Gigi blinks then dismisses me with her hand. "Yes, yes, of course, that's what I said. Did Marie-Hélène tell you anything else?"

"Like what?"

"Nothing would surprise me. The woman has a vivid imagination."

I shake my head absentmindedly. "No. There was nothing else."

It's a strange question when the other news is still so raw. What else could there be? For the second time in this conversation, something feels off. For some reason, my mind flashes back to the original email Marie-Hélène had sent. I'd need to look at it again to be sure, but now that I think of it, Marie-Hélène had been quite specific. I remember because Cathy gave me a hard time for not asking Marie-Hélène to clarify it when we first spoke on the phone. In truth, I'd been afraid to ask. I'd forgotten to question Marie-Hélène about in person. Not that she'd have told me anyway.

"Gigi?" I begin. "When Marie-Hélène first sent that email to André, she mentioned that *you'd* told *her* something about him, something awful, not the other way around."

Gigi exhales loudly and closes her eyes for a moment. "I really have no idea what you're talking about. Except to say, it *was* awful for her. I had to tell her that André didn't love her *or* want her baby. Then she accused *him* of rape," she says woodenly. "It doesn't get more awful than that."

I suppose she's right. For a moment I turn to look out at the fields. The vines are moving ever so gently in the breeze, so lightly that you can barely see it. I'm suddenly alert.

"There are so many sides to the story, aren't there? All except André's," I ponder. "But you're right, of course. What Marie-Hélène did was terrible, unforgivable. I can't deny that."

Gigi looks reassured. "Believe me, Seren. There's no child. Marie-Hélène is trying to play you for a fool like she did André and me. We can't let her win. She lied about André, and she's lying now. You have to see that. If she believes André raped her, she would never go through with a pregnancy. No one would have their entire life destroyed like that." Her voice catches unexpectedly.

I'm still staring at the fields. "I wonder why she didn't tell me?"

"About what?" Gigi frowns.

"That he'd raped her." This time I don't hide from the word as I turn to face her.

Gigi narrows her eyes. "Because she's crazy, maybe."

"Or maybe she was trying to save my feelings …" I trail off again. "Or maybe …"

"It didn't happen at all," Gigi finishes.

I'd been about to say the same thing, but with a different interpretation. Is it possible that Gigi is lying? It appears everyone is lying in some way. The shard of doubt that I've pushed from my mind reignites. The atmosphere begins to shift all around me. Even the light suddenly changes as if a cloud has passed over the sun.

"She's a liar, and she's lying again," Gigi persists.

I stand and walk inside to retrieve the envelope next to my bed. Rooting inside, I take out the sheet of paper, walk back, and hold it out to Gigi. She's followed me inside and is standing by the circular kitchen table.

"Her name is Nicole. She'll be eighteen in a few weeks."

For a moment, Gigi can't speak as her eyes move over the image and recognitions sparks.

"Marie-Hélène sent it to me," I explain.

Gigi's hand trembles as she takes the photocopied picture from my hand.

"And if you think the resemblance is uncanny there, in real life it's even more so. This *is* André daughter, Gigi. This is your granddaughter."

Gigi reaches for the back of the chair to steady herself, then slowly pulls it out and sits down. "How could she?"

She stares at the photo, and I put my hand on her shoulder. "I know this is a shock, Gigi, but I've thought about it a lot over the past week. I know what Marie-Hélène did, but this girl ... Gigi, she is *so* like André. She's wonderful." It's the same word I'd used to describe André earlier.

"You've met?"

I nod. "She's lovely. I feel sorry for her. Her mother is clearly deranged, but none of that is Nicole's fault. I know if André was here, if he knew about her, he'd want to get to know her despite the accusation." I wait for some form of response. When it doesn't come, I continue. I'm still standing behind her with my hand on her shoulder. "She's your family, Gigi. Your flesh and blood. It's like a part of André lives on. When you first told me about the rape, I thought I didn't want to see Nicole again, but when I see how generous you've been with me, I should be the same with her. By the sound of it, she's had a really terrible upbringing with Marie-Hélène. She could do with a family too. Like you said earlier, maybe the universe has somehow brought us all together." I can feel her shoulder shaking beneath my hand, her sobs vibrating through my flesh. "Maybe in time, you could …"

"No." It's barely more than a whisper. It's only when she turns to look at me that I realise she's not crying. She's laughing. "What a clever, clever girl!"

"Me?" I jerk my head in shock.

"No, dear. Marie-Hélène." As her hysterics subside, she says soberly, "Sit down, Seren. There's something I need to explain."

Feeling utterly confused, I do what I'm told. I watch her face contort while I listen to all about protected heirs and French inheritance laws. I'm unsure of the significance at first, but I gradually realise what Marie-Hélène is after.

"I underestimated her. She must have known that by being pregnant with André's child, she was carrying something valuable. It's the reason she wasn't honest with you. Can you see now that all her secrecy was because she didn't want to tell you her plan? Seren, she is using you. You are proof that André is dead. It has nothing to do with saving your feelings. I have to hand it to her. She is clever, but it's not enough."

"What do you mean it's not enough?" Once again, I'm disgusted with Marie-Hélène.

"You see, my husband's family favoured men." She smiles sarcastically. "Women were always second-rate. After Henri got ill and began losing his mind, I found documents in his office – his will namely." She's not even looking at me anymore – it's like she's speaking to herself.

"In a way, Marie-Hélène is right. When Henri dies, with proof Nicole *will* inherit in André's place. She'll be very wealthy. She'll even be entitled to earnings from the business, the vineyards, but she cannot touch the chateau or sell the land that comes with it." She tuts and wags her finger. "Very specifically, the chateau can only pass to a male heir." She scrunches her eyes closed. "If Nicole really is his daughter, I'll have to share what could be three-quarters of everything I own with her." She shakes her head in despair then puts her hands to her face. "It was always about money. *My* money. That's all people want."

My God, it's no wonder Gigi is upset.

She looks at me. "So, Marie-Hélène will hurt me. But I suspect she thinks she'll be entitled to more than she actually is. She is going to continue to destroy my life. She'll never stop. I rue the day that woman was born. "The girl must know. Nicole, is that her name? She's tricking you too, Seren. Do you really think she'd want anything to do us, except for money? In her eyes, her father *raped* her mother."

I scrunch my eyes and exhale. There's silence while it sinks in. I'm shocked that someone would stoop so low. Has Nicole tricked me too? No, Gigi has to be mistaken about that.

If anything, it makes me understand all the more why André didn't know who he could trust, why he hated the wealth. Marie-Hélène must have known all along what she was doing. She *had* been after money and a massive amount at that. I wonder suddenly if she already knew that André was dead when she contacted me? I remember Nicole telling me that Marie-Hélène had located André and then sat on the information for well over a year. If she'd hired a private investigator, there was every chance that she had been told more about us than just our location. The thought of someone snooping around in our lives, taking pictures of us without me knowing, sickens me. My God, had she been waiting for him to die? Right now, I wouldn't put anything past her. She must have been delighted when I told her he was dead. And then, there'd been all that talk about the death certificate! Gigi is right. All she'd ever wanted was proof that André was gone. It's the reason she was adamant about me not meeting Nicole. I feel like I'm about to be sick, immensely guilty for almost doubting Gigi, especially when she's been so kind to me. What the hell was I thinking? The poor woman.

"Oh my God, Gigi, I'm so sorry. I really had no idea, genuinely. There must be something you can do ... some way to fight it?"

"Alas, no. It's airtight, but at least I'll still have my home. That's one thing my husband got right. In the absence of a son, or indeed a male grandchild, it remains with me. Luckily, André produced a daughter and not a son ..."

I nod vacantly. "Yes. Until now."

Gigi's head swivels towards me. As gently as the breeze outside, her eyes settle on my stomach. "That would be a miracle, *non*? André was dead long before you became pregnant."

My face falls. Oh, my God. She's misunderstood me, but of course she has. I just assumed she knew that the baby was André's, but how could she?

"Oh, Gigi ... you've got it wrong ... I ... I used his sperm. He gave his permission before he died," I stammer as reality dawns.

Gigi's gaze moves from my stomach to my eyes as she,

307

too, starts to understand. Within me, I carry the heir to every inch of the view from the guesthouse's balcony and everything behind it – the fields, the outhouses, the cellars, the chateau."I want nothing. I swear to you, Gigi. That's not why I'm here," I stammer.

By the look on her face, Gigi doesn't believe me.

Chapter 28

Nicole

Nicole has stared at it long enough to be able to recite it backwards, yet still her eyes are drawn towards the sheet of paper resting on the threadbare bedspread. It's all there in black and white, a carefully drawn out set of emotionless, monochrome facts. How effortlessly the unbiased account now makes sense. Sitting cross-legged on her bed, she picks up the photocopied sheet of paper and once more scans the reason behind the mystery of her existence. All along, the answers to everything she'd never understood had been right there on that sheet of paper.

She'd found the original under the sofa, the day Maman had dropped the file from her hands. There'd been nothing terribly unusual about that. Maman's permanently shaking hands were always letting things fall. That same morning she'd smashed a cup in the sink. What had aroused Nicole's suspicions was that she'd never seen her mother with any sort of filing system before. Maman wasn't exactly the picture of being organised. Not only that, but after dropping the papers,

Maman had surged off the sofa, frantically collecting them. Under normal circumstances, she'd have asked Nicole to do it, citing exhaustion, telling her she wasn't getting any younger, her knees were terrible – any excuse. Maman must have been hiding something huge.

Earlier that day, Nicole had decided to confront her, demand the truth about her father, and plead an explanation as to why she was withholding information. Since meeting Seren two days before, her mind had been swimming to the point that she was practically drowning. She'd needed to understand precisely what was going on. Already she had got up three times from her desk, then sat back down before purposefully standing and whipping open the bedroom door. Maman jumped so high that she sent the contents of the file into the air, then brusquely accused Nicole of snooping.

Instantly Nicole changed her mind about asking. Maman wouldn't tell her anything anyway, and she didn't want to implicate Seren. She watched Maman curiously for a moment before retreating back into her room. Less than a minute later, she heard Maman's bedroom door close. Nicole waited as long as eagerness would allow before creeping back out and retrieving the sheet of paper that she'd noticed float beneath the sofa minutes before. Glancing at it, she felt butterflies stir.

She went to her room without further hesitation, quickly made a couple of copies on her printer, both sides of the sheet, then rushed to shove the original back under the sofa. Then she tucked her copies into her backpack and prepared to leave for work.

"I'm going to go now," she said as put her head around Maman's bedroom door five minutes later. "I'll be late, remember. It's a double shift."

"Okay. Give me a kiss."

Nicole went and bent to kiss her mother's cheek.

"You're a good girl, Nicole, considering everything."

Nicole barely batted an eyelid at the back-handed compliment. She was used to it by now. "I'll see you later," she promised and left.

It wasn't until her break that Nicole finally had time to remove one of copies from her backpack and focus on its contents. Only then did she begin to understand the significance of the words *"considering everything"*.

Seren was right. Maman was after money, but far more disturbing still was why. Sitting at the back of the restaurant next to a pile of used pizza boxes, Nicole scanned Maman's notes. Using her index finger to run her finger under each name then trace the lines connecting them, she whispered the additional information next to each person. She paused more than once to allow the story to sink in. Once she reached the end, she flipped over the page and read aloud the various legal-sounding terms. Some were accompanied by circled comments, questions, exclamation marks for emphasis.

Taking her phone from her jeans pocket, she typed some of the terms into Google then clicked the search link to help decipher the meaning. Satisfied with the definitions, she picked up the sheet of paper once again, then frowned intently at the last name at the bottom of the page.

"Nicole?"

She jumped almost as high as Maman had upon hearing aloud the same name she'd just read.

Her boss was standing there, tapping his watch.

For the remainder of her shift, her mind drifted back to the contents of that sheet of paper. Each chance she got,

311

she closed her eyes, trying to recall each name's position on the page. Later, walking home via the river, she stopped at one of the bridges to look out and give her brain a chance to catch up. Most of it made sense, if that was the word, except for one part. It was the presence of an additional line connecting one name to another that continued to throw her. She might have thought Maman had made a mistake only for the fact that it had been traced over several times. More worrying still was the word scrawled across the line between the two names.

It dawned on her as she stood there that if it was true, then what did that make her? My God, of what was she the by-product? Something so vile and unimaginable that it couldn't possibly be accurate. Could the man in her drawings, the same colourful man Seren had described, really be what was written on there? Nicole couldn't bring herself to even say the word. Is this what had given rise to Maman's fears about how she might turn out? Was this why her mother had worried endlessly that she'd end up sick? Because she was the product of a vile act. If it was true, how could Maman have gone ahead with the pregnancy? All to have a daughter who is "a good girl, considering everything".

Lying back on her bed now, Nicole is still disgusted by the answer to it all. She can't understand how Maman could be so conniving, so calculating, so cold. Maman must have only hatred in her soul so that in the end, she'd profit from Nicole presence as the last name on that page. So, this is why she'd been born. This is the reason her mother had kept her hidden away in Corsica until she was ready for … revenge?

"Soon, everything is going to get better. Both our lives

will change so much. All we have to be is patient."

Nicole replays all of Maman's vague statements. She understands their meaning now, but she'll never accept them.

Curling onto her side, she stares out the bedroom window. It's no better than being trapped in prison, even more so now that she knows the truth. There's little more than two metres to the next block of flats on the other side of the glass. She hates it here. She hates it all. Turning away, she traces her fingers over the mermaid image on her bedspread. Up until a few years ago, she was obsessed with mermaids. She'd spent years keeping an eye on the clear waters in Corsica in the hope of spotting one. Looking back, what had fascinated her most was that in all the books she'd read about mermaids, they were just as lonely as her, equally as trapped. She'd started drawing them then, spending hours perfecting what began as cartoon-like depictions and ended as lifelike images of women with billowing hair, complex scales and forlorn faces. Running her hand over the childish design on the bedspread, she sighs at something else that now makes sense.

She'd had to beg her mother for months to buy her the mermaid bedspread from the gift shop by the pier in Corsica. She'd almost given up hope when Maman arrived home with it, grinning from ear to ear.

"For you, little one. Today I received excellent news."

"Really?"

"Do you remember we went to see that nice man in France? Well, he wrote to me, and guess what! Just as I suspected, you're very clever. Enough to do anything you want! Someday you'll be rich."

Nicole had been around nine years old when Maman

told her that she'd been specially selected to get some tests to see just how clever she was. She'd made Nicole swear not to tell any of her friends in case they got jealous. They'd taken the ferry across to France and stayed the night at a hotel. Nicole had been so nervous about not knowing the test answers that she'd vomited in the square-shaped toilet in the hotel beforehand. In the end, the man barely asked Nicole anything. Instead, he'd wrapped a stretchy rubber band around her arm, squeezed it tight and told her to look away. Afterwards, she'd noticed little bottles of thick-looking blood on his desk. She'd waited outside the door, circling the round plaster in the crook of her arm with her finger while he spoke with Maman.

Maman had been so happy that Nicole passed the test that they'd gone out to celebrate at one of the fancy tourist restaurants that play music. That night Nicole had felt just like the other families.

When they were leaving, Maman had twirled her across the dancefloor then hugged her tight. "Always remember, Nicole, that there's a reason for everything. Even if you can't see it at the time. There's a reason." She'd held her at arm's length. "Say it! There's a reason."

"There's a reason!"

Maman's elation had been short-lived. She'd taken a downward spiral, staying in bed for weeks on end drinking, smoking, sleeping. After that night, she hadn't seemed as worried about Nicole anymore. Apparently, being "clever" meant you lost the right to a mother who gave a shit about you, who came to events at school, cooked pizza for your friends, got up in the morning to make breakfast.

There's always a reason, and this is Nicole's. The trip to France must have been for proof – evidence that she was who she was. It turned her stomach, making her feel dirty and used. No matter how many times she showers, she feels contaminated. Perhaps she should find a church. Maybe she should go to the cathedral and present herself as a product of sin. Once more, she traces the mermaid outline with the enormous sorrowful eyes, shell-like bra and curled tail. She can draw it with her eyes shut from all those years of practising, waiting alone for Maman to come home from work, expecting her to pop her head around the door to see if she was awake … alive. She never had.

Maman doesn't love her. Then again, how could she? All Nicole is, is a "reason" – a valuable commodity. In one way, she's part of a real-life fairy tale. One where the poor girl from Corsica with the threadbare bedspread, the thrift-shop clothes, the alcoholic mother ends up as the heir to a fortune so great that she'd been born solely to seize it. Nicole hates her mother. In fact, she hates them all – her mother, her father, Gigi, Henri … Seren?

Should Seren be on that same list? Indeed, after not contacting her for over a week, she almost deserves to be there. Sitting up suddenly, she grabs her phone where it's charging on the floor, opens her emails and clicks refresh. There's still no answer. For the past few days, she's checked it compulsively every few minutes. She can't come up with a valid excuse for why Seren hasn't answered it or her texts. What she has sent Seren warrants a response. Nicole has considered every eventuality – poor reception, preoccupied, gone?

Clutching at straws, she had gone online to find the number for Seren's shop in Ireland and dialled the number. The woman who answered told her that Seren was on holidays indefinitely.

"Hey," she'd said before hanging up. "You're French!"

"Yes."

"That's where Seren is. Maybe you'll bump into her."

Nicole doubts she'll bump into Seren again like she had that day in the city. Of all her theories, it's most likely that Seren is still at Chateau Challant and, having learned the truth, never wants to see her again. She could hardly blame her. Even her own father had wanted nothing to do with her. Why should Seren be any different?

If she wants to see Seren, she will have to make it happen herself. Giving her the benefit of the doubt, she considers that Seren still might not know. She may not have seen the email. Worse yet, what if Seren is in some sort of trouble? What if Gigi is as evil as Maman has indicated in her notes? If Seren has told Gigi about her, maybe they both think she is in on it too, that like Maman she also wants money. After all, who wouldn't? Who wouldn't want to be plucked from ordinary and rocketed to extraordinary? Not her. Nicole wants none of it, not ever. She'd been naïve to think that meeting Seren connected her to her father. André is dead, and now that she knows the truth, Nicole never wants to hear his name again.

Still, she owes it to Seren to tell her the truth. She's innocent in all this. The day they'd met, Seren had assured her that she wanted nothing from her but to talk. Now she can return the favour. After that, Nicole will leave France for good. Yesterday she'd contacted her friend in Corsica. For once, someone had been pleased to hear from her. Nicole hadn't told her much, just that she was planning a visit. Once she gets there, she'll figure the rest out. She'll find honest work there, enough to survive.

Nicole hears Maman's bedroom door opening. To be safe, she throws a pillow over the papers on her bed.

"I'm going to work!" Maman calls without bothering to look in at her. *"Nicole?'*

"Bye, Maman."

"See you later."

Nicole won't be seeing her later, nor ever again, for that matter. Standing up, she takes her bag out from where it's stored under her bed. She rolls the last of her clothes inside, and removes her savings from the mermaid ornament on her shelf. Stripping the bed, she goes into the kitchen and dumps the sheets, mermaid bedspread and the mermaid ornament in the bin. Back in her room, she surveys the empty space, then opens her wardrobe and takes out what she'd bought the night before. She'd had to ask one of the older guys at work to buy it for her. His eyes had been out on stalks when she handed him the money.

"A gift," she'd explained.

"Wow! This is good stuff. You must really like them."

Throwing her bag over her shoulder, Nicole walks into the living room and places the bottle of Chateau Challant on the table. She bends to check if the original page is still where she'd replaced it under the sofa. It is. Retrieving it, she places it under the bottle, along with a note.

I know everything. Then again, I did pass the "clever" test, didn't I? Without my blood, this is as close as you'll ever get to this place.

Chapter 29

Gigi

Her hand hesitates for a moment, floating mid-air next to the metal bolt on the guesthouse door. Seren is inside "resting". The atmosphere had grown glacial following the revelation that the baby is André's, abundant with acute awkwardness. Neither of them had known how to react.The entire time Seren had been telling her about Nicole, deep inside fury had bubbled in every cell of her body, but it had begun to fizz dangerously following the news that Seren was expecting André's son. She'd believed after the news of Nicole that things couldn't get any worse. If someone had rushed in and shot her in the gut, it wouldn't have hit so fiercely as the news of a granddaughter. Under normal circumstances and with the natural passing of time, it might have been happy tidings, but this situation is anything but routine.

She'd honestly thought that Marie-Hélène had made it up until Seren showed her the photo of the girl. It felt like a second shot, this time, straight to her heart.

The girl is André's daughter, all right. There could be

no denying the slightly crooked nose, that wistful look in her deep brown eyes, her dark features, the shape of her face. More disturbing still, Gigi could see Marie-Hélène in the girl's plump cheeks and slightly upturned top lip. It was a pleasant combination: André and Marie-Hélène, much as it pained her to admit it. It was like looking at a beautiful image in a magazine, only that the subject made Gigi want to scream.

If all that wasn't enough, it was tailed closely with the disclosure that Seren was expecting André's child. This third and final shot proved one too many, forcing Gigi's guard to slip. She'd managed to direct her anger at Nicole as if having a delayed reaction to the news of her existence.

"I know it's a lot to take in …"

"It's too much. That girl. I want nothing to do with her. *Nothing.* I swear if she ever comes here … "

Seren had appeared shocked by what she'd said in the heat of the moment, how vehemently she'd rejected Nicole, what she'd do if the girl ever showed up. She'd quickly managed to compose herself, but Seren still seemed wary.

The entire situtation is ridiculous. It's almost comical. Worse still, it's true. Not for one moment had Gigi considered that André could be the father of Seren's child. It was beyond belief, except that nowadays nothing was impossible. These days, there's a way to do almost anything – anything but change the past.

"Why? How could you possibly do that?" Gigi had found herself asking once she'd calmed. Even Seren hadn't been able to provide a clear answer. Gigi can't fathom why anyone would volunteer to have a baby by their dead husband. It's so morbid. Then again, it's

319

precisely what someone like Seren might do – someone who'd unconditionally loved a man about whom she'd known absolutely nothing. *Fool!*

While they'd sat there staring blankly at each other, for the briefest of moments Gigi had considered that, just like Marie-Hélène, Seren had uncovered what André's child would be entitled to and concocted a plan to come after it. Now, that was also ridiculous. Besides, the timing was off. Seren was already pregnant by the time she'd been contacted by Marie-Hélène. It was pure coincidence – that blasted word again. Gigi doesn't like what she can't explain.

Up until an hour before, for the first time in years, Gigi had felt as though she'd found a friend – a non-threatening companion with whom to shoulder the trials. It wasn't a bit like Gigi to be so sentimental, but lately she'd felt lighter, sure it was down to Seren's company. Gigi had enjoyed dining with her, walking the estate, chatting. She'd forgotten what it felt like to talk about nothing in particular. It was nice.

Seren loves it here. She appreciates it as much as Gigi does, and therein lies the problem. "I want nothing. I swear to you," she said. Gigi believes her, still the words had impacted. As pure as Seren is, she's not stupid. Just like those that came before her, Seren will end up wanting to make it her own. How could she not? Judging by Seren's aghast face, she's astute enough to realise that Gigi had felt instantly threatened. What she may not realise is just how far Gigi will go to protect what's hers. Seren will figure it out in time, possibly sooner than later.

Gigi whips her hand away from the antique bolt fixed to the outside of the door, stopping herself from swiping it shut. The lock has been there since the building was used as stables. Nowadays, practically all of the outhouses have been converted to dormitory-style accommodation to house the late summer fruit-pickers, the students, the drifters.

Feeling emotionally drained, Gigi sits at one of the benches outside and raises her face to the sun. It's quiet. Soon it will be abuzz. The workers will be arriving in a matter of weeks. Seren would have enjoyed seeing the place full, thronging with activity. The harvest was always André's favourite part. He'd described it once as spiritual, or was it sensual? Gigi knew what he'd meant – a mix of heat, passion, vibrance, young people working hard, tanned and happy, drinking wine in the evenings.

Looking back, is it any wonder he'd fallen for someone as beautiful as Marie-Hélène amid that bliss? There'd been others too, in previous years – harvest flings that would end as fast as they'd begun. This had been different. For a start, André had told her about the waitress he'd encountered in the village. "She's not like anyone else I've met, Maman. She's from Paris originally. I think you'll like her." Gigi had clocked it straight away by the way he spoke, flushed with love and youth and talk of a future at the chateau – the very place he'd claimed to smother him. For the first time, André had appeared settled, working in the vineyards. He'd even been getting along better with his father. That summer, for a time, everything had seemed perfect.

Looking back, it's hard to think that Gigi's only role had once been at the main house. She'd rarely ventured to the vineyards until she'd got wind that André had moved his new girlfriend in with him. One evening, spurred by curiosity, she'd walked almost to the very place she now sits, to where the workers congregated after a day's work. Standing well back, she'd observed them for a while before noticing the girl sitting with André. Her back had been to Gigi, but she could see her speaking animatedly while André laughed. Hovering at the side of the building, Gigi watched them together, flirting and chatting. Then André had got up to go inside and, for absolutely no reason, for she couldn't have known that Gigi was there, the girl had turned to look over her shoulder to meet her gaze. Gigi had held it for a moment before stepping back behind the exterior wall of the building. The moment had been enough to recognise the look of yearning in the girl's eye. Gigi had known straight away whom she was dealing with. Right then, she had accepted that she'd have to take certain unpleasant precautions to protect not only André but them all.

There's even more at risk now. Perhaps this time, she should be more definite in her actions. Glancing back at the door, she narrows her eyes. Maybe she should lock it and walk away. Then again, all Seren would have to do would be to use her phone to call for help. Perhaps what Gigi has already done will be enough. Standing, Gigi purposefully walks away, then turns left towards the vineyards instead of heading back to the office.

"It's a lot to digest, but give me time," she'd smiled reassuringly at Seren after collecting herself earlier. "Nothing changes, Seren. I meant everything I said." Then she'd pointed towards the partition at the far side of the open-plan room. "You're as white as a ghost. You need to rest. Will you?"

She stood, took her hand, and led Seren to the bed, gesturing for her to lie down.

"Please. You look exhausted. Look, these are complicated matters. In time, it will all work itself out. Leave that to me."

Seren plonked down on the bed.

"Do you want me to leave?" She looked up at Gigi. "I'll understand if you do."

Gigi tutted. "Silly girl. More than ever, I hope you'll stay. We really are family now. And look, I shouldn't have said what I did about Nicole. I was in shock. I feel terrible."

Seren nodded. "It's okay. I understand."

Had she? Earlier, it hadn't appeared that way. Seren's eyes had grown round after Gigi vehemently spat the words.

"It was a momentary slip. What can I say? I'm human."

"Gigi, I meant what I said. I really don't want anything from you. If you want, I can sign something … or … I'm just happy to know André's family at last and for my son to have a grandparent. You'll be his only one."

Poor Seren still didn't get it. There was nothing she could sign to take it away or change the facts. The law was the law. Over the years, Gigi had scoured for loopholes, employing, then firing countless lawyers who couldn't give her what she'd wanted.

"Just rest, my dear. I don't want any harm coming to my precious grandson, do I? I'll see you this evening." As she rounded the partition towards the kitchen, she paused momentarily. "I'll just get my keys from the balcony. I think I left them there. Sleep tight."

Gigi's feet move faster as she passes through the vines. Her skirt catches suddenly. She pulls it free, tearing the silk, but she doesn't stop. Her thoughts are muddled, morphing like a kaleidoscope filled with memories of a

323

lifetime of waiting. She'd come so close – carefully cradled this entire place in the palm of her hand until the day she could finally clasp her fingers shut ... now this. It's as though they've all waited until the eleventh hour to sweep in and snatch it away for her.

Over the years, she has been careful with her story, always staying as close to the truth as possible. Very little of what she's told are lies. Admittedly, there have been some, but there's a fragment of truth in most things. "If you're going to lie," a lawyer told her once, "make sure you stay close to the truth. That way, you won't slip up." So she had tried to. Everything she's described happened, in one way or another at one time or another. Gigi understands the emotions behind everything because she's experienced every single one.

As soon as she reaches the perimeter of the property, she lets them surge. They rip through her so that she finds herself screaming, clawing at her hair. Her body folds in two as she drops to her knees, so numb that she's unable to feel the dry soil beneath them. She is as hollow as when she'd first arrived here, broken and irreparably bruised. Who might she be today if she hadn't experienced what she had all those years ago? Why hadn't she fought harder then?

The moment Henri Dubois-Challant looked her in the eye and nodded once with approval, she was sure she'd found a future here. In time, her husband had proved to be as exploitative as the rest. Truthfully, no one had ever wanted Gigi, not really. All they wanted was to use her, to keep her at the bottom of the pile. Gradually, she'd learned how to climb. It had never occurred to her that she could be the one with the power until she'd laid eyes on Marie-Hélène – until the girl had looked her straight between the eyes, threatening Gigi's position here. Right then, something inside her had snapped.

* * *

"If you go, André, you can't come back. This life isn't something you walk in and out of as you please. Lord knows this accusation will destroy us all. It *will* destroy your father. What have you done?! There are two choices, stay and fight … or leave. Go and find the life you always talk about. What about America? But this isn't a revolving door. You have to understand that."

A few weeks before, André had come to Gigi to tell her that his girlfriend was pregnant. He'd told her all about the argument where he'd accused her of being after his money. He'd felt so bad about it. He was such a sensitive man. He'd explained that they'd reconciled and that as soon as he got back from his work trip, he planned on asking her to stay with him at the chateau to see if they could make it work for the sake of the baby. He'd wanted to let Gigi know out of courtesy.

Gigi had been frantic upon his return. "I went to congratulate her, André. I wanted to meet her for myself. I still can't believe the things she said."

She'd relayed the alleged attack in such vivid detail that he'd pleaded with her to stop.

"Please. I didn't. I would never. Let me talk to her."

"She's already gone, André. I was right. All she wanted was money. She doesn't love you. The woman is unhinged. She's spread the story everywhere. Everyone knows. We have to contain this, André. With someone like her, there's no telling what she could do. She'll probably come back. Like I've told you all your life where there is money involved …"

André had known the rest. She'd drilled it into him as

a boy – "No one will ever want you just for you."

After a time, hiding in shame, André had been adamant that he'd had enough of everything. Gigi had insisted that he step away from work and move back to the chateau for a while until it settled.

"They're treating me like I'm a sort of criminal. The way they're looking at me. I have to get away," André had confided in her.

Gigi had been genuinely astounded by the power of his imagination. But then, paranoia does strange things to people.

"Leave Henri to me," she'd assured him when he'd expressed concern that his father would never let him go or rest until he was brought back.

André had hugged her so tightly, so grateful for all that she'd done for him that she'd felt a pang of overwhelming guilt. She'd pushed it deep within and sworn that in the future she'd visit it as little as possible.

Since learning that upon Henri's death she'd practically be cast aside, Gigi had accepted she'd have to make a plan to protect herself. Marie-Hélène had been the impetus – a way to ensure that Gigi began her climb to the top of the chain. Getting rid of André had been her way to remain there. She'd made sure André had enough money with which to start a new life – a simple one, just like he'd always wanted.

"I didn't do it."

"I believe you, André, but Marie-Hélène was so sure. Will others be so fast to take your side? There are always people waiting to take people like us down."

"But the baby?" André had looked crestfallen.

"There is no baby. Not anymore."

* * *

Over the years, Gigi has consoled herself with the fact that if André had wanted to stay in France, he never would have left. He would have fought harder, questioned more. It was that simple. To this day, it still astounds her how readily he'd believed her. All Gigi had done was give him a reason to follow his dreams. André had seized it. The thought that he might be hated or lose his good name had been enough to break him. People see what they want to see. André chose to see something that wasn't even there. Gigi had been happy to learn that he'd had a good life in Ireland with Seren. Despite everything, Gigi *had* loved him. Otherwise, she would have found a more clear-cut solution for his disposal.

As she kneels in the earth, the thought strikes her that it had all been for nothing. André had died anyway. Perhaps it had always been his destiny. That said, she'd still have had Marie-Hélène to deal with and her daughter, and now she had sweet, innocent Seren. It's not yet midday, yet the sun is hot. Gigi's tears have dried with the realisation of what lies ahead. It's not over yet. Unlike André, she's willing to fight.

Gigi had got a distinct impression earlier that Seren suspected something. Especially when Gigi mistakenly referred to the fact that it was *she* who'd told Marie-Hélène something and not the other way around. She'd passed it off as a slip of the tongue. If everything else hadn't emerged, Gigi might have got away with it, but she can feel reality inching too close for her liking. What Gigi told Marie-Hélène that day was a different matter altogether, one that she'd sworn to take to the grave.

With Seren's never-ending news bulletins earlier, Gigi

had conveniently forgotten to help her pack up her things to temporarily move her out of the guesthouse. She ought to have reemphasised how important it was not to use any appliances, especially that old stove. This morning one of the Estate managers had stopped her primarily to discuss it.

"Madame. I see you have a guest in the old stables."

Gigi had stopped walking and turned.

"Yes."

"There hasn't been anyone staying in that particular one for some time," he'd said, twisting his hands nervously. "It's not safe. The stove needs to be replaced, urgently. It is on the list, but with no one there …" He'd trailed off. "If there was a leak with those low ceilings, it wouldn't end well. Please tell them not to even go near it." He'd shuddered. "In fact, the entire building needs work before the pickers arrive. The ventilation is poor, and if we were to be inspected … I've been saying it for months …"

Getting to her feet, Gigi wonders if Seren will make it to dinner later. The poor girl had looked exhausted. If she does manage to revive, Gigi will remain calm this time. She honestly hadn't meant to say that she'd murder Nicole with her bare hands if she ever set foot near this place. It was a just turn of phrase, of course. She'd better explain it again later to Seren, or perhaps there'll be no need. There's every possibility that flicking the forbidden pilot light and turning the stove to high before she'd left her earlier will give Seren the sleep of her life. Gigi had made sure to close the balcony doors to keep Seren nice and cosy and, just to be safe, she'd grabbed her inhaler from the table. With any luck, it's something from which the protected heir cannot be protected.

Chapter 30

I'm not sure how long I lie there, just staring up at the ceiling, moving my eyes from side to side in an effort to see sense. My mind keeps drifting back to Gigi's face. I can't stop picturing how it changed when she realised that the baby is André's. It instantly morphed into something resembling a rabid dog. Soon afterwards, she said that strange thing about killing Nicole with her bare hands if she ever came near this place or tried to take what wasn't hers to take. It had sounded like a warning. Had it, in fact, been meant for me? It wasn't so much the words as the way Gigi growled them through gritted teeth. My own mother had often threatened to murder me, but more out of concern than actual homicide, which is how this sounded. I think I'm in shock. It would explain why I'm still lying here pinned to the bed, pretending to rest as I've been instructed. I'm afraid to move, not to do what I've been told.

After Gigi said it, I tried to play it down, pretend like I understood. I'm no actress. I knew Gigi could sense I was trying too hard. It's difficult to believe that not an hour before I'd been basking in a warm glow of acceptance, elated at the possibility of a new life here in France with my son. Then I'd decided to come clean about Nicole. I wish I hadn't. Things had quickly gone from bad to worse. I'm an idiot. I'd failed to tell Gigi the most crucial part of the story in admitting that I was pregnant. For much of the conversation, we'd been on an entirely different wavelength. When she'd asked me if there someone special at home, she'd obviously meant the father of the baby. Going over it now, I'd made it sound like I'd had a fling, fallen pregnant and then realised it wasn't for me. "I admire you for going it alone." Well, the admiration had faded fast once I'd revealed how I'd actually managed to achieve my goal. Her mouth had shrunk so small that it was a wonder she managed to emit the murderous threats at all. Gigi had looked so threatened that I'd found myself repeating that I wanted nothing from her. The more I'd tried to deny it, the more it had sounded as though I did. Judging by the wry smile on her face, she'd thought so too.

Trying to forget it, I put my hands to my face. I feel suddenly ill. Taking a deep breath, I blow it out, then sit up slowly. My head tilts as I hear something. If I didn't know better, it sounded like a scream. Christ, I must be ridiculously on edge to be imagining things. Lying back again, I try to decipher if I'm nauseous from the pregnancy or if the sinking feeling is because of Gigi. Something feels wrong. Something is off. I push the thought aside. After all, I've been wrong before. Gigi is hot-tempered, surely, that's all. Even I know by now that she thaws as fast. Perhaps I should try to sleep. It might help to order my thoughts.

Gigi was genuinely concerned about me before she left, but I still can't shake the feeling that her reaction to everything was excessive. Yes, Marie-Hélène's actions are inexcusable. Personally, I'll never forgive her for what she did to André but is Nicole to blame? Has the dust not settled enough for Gigi to find it in her heart to even meet her granddaughter just once? I'm even more confident now that Marie-Hélène made up the accusation. I know why she did it too – for money.

I know Gigi wants to protect herself and the chateau, but there must be a way around the legal part. In my case, I'd offered to sign something, or better still, no one even has to know that it's André's son. If I'd never come here, no one would ever have known. I'm sure in time Gigi will come to see that, and it can all go back to the way it was. Still, I can't shift the feeling that Gigi no longer trusts me. She may be observant, but I'm good at reading emotions, and I'd sensed wariness.

Putting myself in her shoes, I try to reason how it might feel to have my family increase twofold and my fortune more than halved in the space of ten minutes. Of course, she must feel vulnerable. I've never been rich, so I can't claim to understand the responsibility that comes with immense wealth. Or is it paranoia? For some odd reason, my mind flits to a girl who was in my year at school. I can't remember what her parents did, but they'd had a swimming pool and a tennis court at their house. Half the class used to lick up to her so they could go back to her's after school for a swim. It was so obvious. I wonder if this is sort of the same thing – not knowing who likes you for you or for your swimming pool, or in this case, your chateau.

Before today, I'd never even heard of protected heirs.

331

To me, it sounded like something from a BBC period drama – one of those I used to love watching on a Sunday evening with my legs draped over André, trying to make him rub my feet. He'd hated those antiquated programmes. Now, I can understand why.

Once again, I try to focus. Even if it is true and Nicole had been born solely as an inheritance lever, it's still not Nicole's fault. Gigi's gripe is with Marie-Hélène.

My mind returns to when Gigi had been sitting at the kitchen table earlier. I'd thought she was crying. Instead, she'd been cackling to herself like a witch. I'm entirely torn now – between which of the two women/witches from André's past is less insane. Perhaps a game of *eeny, meeny, miny, moe* might be the best way to decide. I've always considered myself a good judge of character, allowing only decent people to become a part of my life – Jane, Cathy, Fi … André. I scrunch my eyes shut. How I wish he was here with me to tell me his side of the story. I try to picture him. Thankfully, he appears instantly. "Trust your gut." I wonder if André had once had to trust his. He was always banging on about instincts, making a fist and tapping his stomach for emphasis. "You know the truth by the way it feels," he'd say.

Suddenly, I know how I feel. Swinging my legs out of bed, I stand and reach for the envelope on the bedside table. I stumble backwards as the blood rushes to my head. Putting my hand on the wall to steady myself, I brush my hair back and fan my face. It's strangely warm. Coming out from behind the screen, I see that Gigi has closed the balcony doors. That probably explains it. Pushing them back open, I go outside and sit down with the envelope on my lap.

Earlier, two things Gigi said had struck me as odd.

One was right after telling me that she'd guessed I was pregnant – something her mother used to say to her. It wasn't the first time she'd said it either. I'd noticed it before. The second was when she'd implied that she'd been the one to tell Marie-Hélène something awful about André and not the other way around. I'd questioned her, asking had it not been Marie-Hélène who'd made an accusation. Gigi had cleverly explained it away. Now, I'm unsure. My thoughts are interrupted by my phone vibrating in my lap. I don't recognise the number, but I answer anyway.

"Seren? Jesus, where have you been?"

"Fi?" I ask, both relieved and distracted. "Where are you calling from? Listen, I'll have to call you back."

"I'm on Kevin's phone. *Wait!* Are you okay? I haven't heard from you in days."

Aside from a few quick conversations about the shop, we've barely spoken.

"I'm fine," I lie. "I'm just in the middle of something here."

"Okay, okay, but ever so quickly because it's getting creepy, Bobby Cronin has been in here maybe five thousand times a day looking for you. He says he can't get through to your phone. He needs you to call him as soon as you can."

I inwardly groan. I remember, after the mackerel incident, I'd blocked his number.

"I'll call him," I roll my eyes. I have no intention of calling Bobby – his original evasiveness is the very reason I'm sitting here now with what feels like fast-growing ivy wrapped around my neck. "I really have to go, Fi. I'm–"

"*Hold your horses, will you?* Did you get that email to your personal account?"

"What email?" I rarely check my own account. Everything usually goes through the shop.

"Some girl phoned here looking for your personal email address. She said it was urgent."

"Who?" I'm alert.

"She didn't say. She was French, sounded young. I told her that you were there, so she might run into you." Fi guffaws at her joke.

"I'll call you later."

I hang up and immediately press the email icon on my phone. With the poor reception, I have to wait for ages for the emails to download. There's a load of spam before I see her name. Not for the first time, I feel intense guilt for having ignored Nicole for the last week. I'd badly wanted to believe Gigi. So much of what she'd told me seemed genuine – she'd had an explanation for everything. André, torn apart by a cruel accusation, had run away to live in a world where he could be loved for who he was and not what he had. Except *this* had been André's world, and someone like me, someone honest, would have loved him either way, rich or poor.

All of a sudden, I can sense him so clearly. I know André is trying to guide me. Perhaps it's time I listened. I'm alert as another possibility materialises. What if André hadn't run away? What if he'd been pushed? I look down at Nicole's email.

I've tried to call you, but you're not answering. I'm really scared, Seren. I know I don't know you very well, but you're the only one I can speak to. Please call me. I found something. Maybe you did too, and that's why you're not calling me back, but please. All I want now is to disappear. I think it's best for everyone. I should

never have been born. I'm so sorry I was.

My hand flies to my mouth as I reread it. Simultaneously, the envelope falls from my lap, and the papers spill to the floor. Having now met all the women related to André, Nicole is the only honest one, and she's scared. The tears smart as I bend to grapple at the papers, reprimanding myself for being so selfish. Marie-Hélène must have told Nicole her side of the story. I have to make Nicole understand that André would never harm anyone. Should I add that her grandmother wants nothing to do with her – that she'd been solely born to secure gain? Oh, Christ, this is so far beyond my remit, it's laughable.

Glancing down, my hand hovers over a printed version of Marie-Hélène's original email. Picking it up, I reread it.

I wonder if your mother had not told me what she had about you, would it have been different? I may not have left as I did. But it sickened me to my stomach to hear it.

I was right, but what had Gigi told her? What really happened? Still, I don't know the whole truth. Gigi is lying through her teeth. What kind of mother sends her son away in case he ruins the family's reputation? Screw the family name! He was her son! Who was she really protecting? Him or herself? I stuff the rest of the papers back into the envelope. I don't have time to check the others now. I have to see Nicole.

Back inside, the air feels even denser. Despite the door being open, with the low ceilings, the atmosphere is stifling. I'm on my way to fetch a pen before I call Nicole to arrange to meet her when something catches my eye. Next to the stove, the pilot light is blinking red. I move forwards to the old-fashioned-looking appliance. It's like a mini-Aga sitting atop four curved legs. When I first saw it, it reminded me of a stove you might find in an antique shop. I haven't needed to use it. Anyway, up until now, I'd thought it probably wouldn't work. Earlier, Gigi had mentioned getting new appliances. How strange that this one has suddenly sprung to life!

Advancing, I can feel the heat exuding from it. I'm about to reach my hand out to turn it off when I stop, noticing how the wall around it is stained black. I'm confident that it wasn't like that earlier. Growing up in an old house, my father had been vigilant about ventilation and maintaining older appliances. As I stand there, abrupt lightheadedness hits me again. Am I being paranoid this time? As suspicious as one might be about someone trying to steal their fortune? Looking towards the steps that lead to the front door, I frown and glance back at the stove. This time, dread envelops me. I didn't turn it on, so there's the only person who did. But why?

Suddenly, I know. Closing the door, flicking the switch on a dodgy-looking stove … I'm not paranoid. This time, I don't hesitate. Perhaps it's maternal instinct, but I need to get out of here. Rushing to the bedroom, I shove my belongings into my bag at the same time as trying not to breathe for fear of inhaling something I shouldn't. I can feel my breath growing shallow. I peer over to where I'd left my inhaler on the kitchen table. It had been there the entire time I spoke with Gigi. Now, it's gone.

Panicked by one coincidence too many, I grab my bag and rush cautiously past the stove for fear it will explode. As I take the stairs, for one awful moment, a terrifying thought strikes. With trepidation, I reach for the handle, praying it opens. It does, and I grapple for the keys of the car in my bag. Climbing in, I throw my bag onto the passenger seat and reach for the spare inhaler inside. Pressing the tab, I suck in the gas like I've been trapped underwater. My hand is violently shaking as I put the key in the ignition, start the engine, and then shove the car into gear.

Gigi has made herself clear. She's given herself away more than once, but I hadn't been listening. What sort of person threatens to harm a child? Perhaps the same type who'd threaten a pregnant woman as soon as she sees her as a risk. Is that what Gigi was doing, trying to intimidate me? Or was she actually trying to kill me? I have no desire to stick around to find out. For the first time in my life, I'm actually afraid for my life.

Driving past the main house, I glance back through the rearview mirror. I understand now why André left. Now I'm going to do the same. Perhaps Bobby Cronin was right all along. I shouldn't have disturbed the past. Without André here to help me, I'll never know the truth. Maybe I'm not meant to know. André's history doesn't change the person I'd loved. Nothing can alter that.

Thankfully, the gate opens automatically. I don't even glance at the security guard as I exit and drive away.

When I'm a fair distance past the property, I pull in.

Tugging my phone from my pocket, I press the button to connect.

She answers straight away.

"I'm so sorry, Nicole." I'm out of breath. "I got … I …
"

"I was calling and calling." Nicole's voice sounds urgent. "I need to talk to you."

"I need to talk to you too. I only just saw your email. Otherwise, I'd have called sooner," I pause. "I know too, Nicole." I hear her exhale and then start to sniff. "Please don't cry, and please don't say you shouldn't have been born. Sometimes these things can be misconstrued. Maybe Marie-Hélène misunderstood the situation."

She's sobbing now. "I'm leaving. I'm going to go to Corsica, but I needed to see you first. I don't ever want to see my mother again, or *her*."

"Her?"

"*Gigi*." She spits the name.

"No, me neither. I've just left there."

"You've left?" She stops crying.

"It's a long story."

"But I'm here."

"Here?"

"I'm on my way to see you."

I sit forward suddenly. "Nicole, where exactly are you?"

"I'm in the village, just before the chateau."

"Stay there, do you hear me, Nicole? Don't go there. I'll come to you."

"Okay."

I can picture her nodding.

"I'll wait. I thought you wouldn't want to see me again. I feel so ... I don't know ... so wrong. So disgusting."

"Don't. No matter what your mother said, I know André didn't do to her what she said. I think she made it up, and I think Gigi wanted her to get rid of her baby, of you, to protect her inheritance."

"I know. That's all in the file I sent you."

"What file?"

"The attachment. It's my mother's notes – every detail of what really happened."

"I didn't see it. But it's okay, I'll be there soon." I go to hang up.

"Wait! What do you mean what my mother said André did to her?"

My eyebrows knit together. "You know. The thing." I can't bring myself to say it.

"What thing?"

"You know. *Rape*," I whisper, then pause. "Wait, I thought you knew? Gigi told me Marie-Hélène accused him of rape."

"*What?*" Nicole shrieks. "*No. There was nothing like that. Nothing at all like that.*"

My mouth grows dry. Instinctively I know that whatever Nicole tells me is going to be worse. As she does, the phone slips from my hand, but I still hear it.

"They were brother and sister. *André et Maman*. Gigi was mother to them both."

Chapter 31

Marie-Hélène

The view morphs from grey to green. Busy streets turn to landscape, all while she stares vacantly out the bus window. Every so often, she wraps her arms tighter around herself, drops her chin to her chest and squeezes her eyes shut as if she's in pain. She's neither injured nor sick. Instead, she's filled with profound internal misery. Her breath catches as she stifles a sob and angles further towards the window so that the other passengers can't see. Through her tears, the scenery blurs like the memories of the past. The only certainty she has is that her shameless actions have ruined everything. Marie-Hélène understands it now. Regrettably, so too does Nicole. She'd always intended to tell her daughter when she was old enough. On the day Nicole turned eighteen or the day Henri-Dubois-Challant died, whichever came first. In both cases, it would have been only a matter of weeks.

The moment she'd walked into the flat last night, her eyes had settled on the bottle of wine. Her first thought had been of joy. She walked towards it, not knowing or caring from where it had come. It wasn't until she picked it up to look at the label that she experienced a wave of horror. Rotating her gaze towards Nicole's closed bedroom door, she cautiously placed it back on the table. Then she saw the note.

Her heart was beating fast as she read Nicole's words. Only then did she notice the second sheet of paper. That time, she flatlined. Despite already knowing by heart the contents of the poisoned family tree, she reached down to pick it up, staring at it as if seeing it for the first time. In confusion, she glanced back at the table, searching for the rest. Why was there only this one page? The other part was missing. Rushing to her room, she pulled open the wardrobe to retrieve the file from under the pile of clothes where she'd rehomed it a week before. Spilling the contents onto the bed, everything else was there, except that one page. Panicking, she tried to replay the last few days. Nicole had started the week chirpier than usual then slowly descended into gloom. Marie-Hélène had been so busy licking her wounds after telephoning Chateau Challant that she hadn't asked what was wrong. Clearly, it had been this. The page must have fallen from the file the day she'd dropped it. Reading it this way, without Marie-Hélène there to explain the rest, must have come as a big blow to Nicole, as it had to Marie-Hélène the day she'd found out eighteen years before.

That day, Marie-Hélène had felt utterly deflated. She'd chosen to spend it relaxing on the balcony overlooking the fields. Usually, she loved spending time at André's. At his insistence, she'd recently moved into the converted loft space with him, right above where the pickers slept in the converted stables. They'd started to spend most of their time there anyway. She'd fallen in love with it. Next to the fields, André used to say, was where the real majesty of this place was, so different from the chateau yet equally as beautiful.

She'd met him a few weeks after arriving in Bordeaux when she'd taken a job at a restaurant in the village that included accommodation. She had happened upon the advert in the local paper. Before going for the interview, she hadn't decided whether to stay on in Bordeaux or return to Paris, but when they'd offered the job, she'd decided to give it a go for the summer at least. So far, nothing about her trip had worked out as planned until she'd met André. He'd come in alone for a bite to eat one evening. They'd chatted, flirted, then he'd asked her for a drink. She'd refused at first but then gave in. They'd been inseparable ever since. Up until when she told André her news, it had been the best six months of her life. His too, he'd claimed. They were in love. They had plans, then all of a sudden, they were going to be parents. It hadn't been part of the design, but they'd already talked about a future together, even marriage. This just accelerated their plans. They'd ended up arguing about it the night before. Although they'd made up, she kept replaying it. André had been unusually agitated, suspicious even. The surprise pregnancy had also come as a shock to her; his reaction even more so. Essentially, and most uncharacteristically, he'd accused her of trying to trap him for money. It had hit like a punch in the gut. They'd had a terrible argument where she'd ended up pleading with him not to say such horrible things. It had escalated fast, both saying things they hadn't meant.

In fairness, André soon saw sense, apologising profusely

for his behaviour. It was the shock, he said, a paranoia that had been instilled in him by his mother – could Marie-Hélène forgive him? Afterwards, they'd sat up discussing everything and what it would mean for them. While she'd sipped tea, André had had a few drinks, maybe a little more than usual, then they'd made love. In bed that night, he'd told her he was going away for a few days to see a distributor but that they'd talk more when he got back, make plans.

At the time, she'd felt better, but now in the cold light of day, she couldn't help wondering if she should be concerned. The only other time he'd acted oddly was when he'd told her that his father owned the chateau where he worked. André didn't like talking about his family. Marie-Hélène had never even met them. He'd kept the truth of who he was from her for months, claiming he just worked at a chateau in the region. She'd had no reason to question it. He'd usually meet her in the village after her shift at the restaurant. They'd take walks, go to her room, make love. When he finally told her which vineyard he worked at and that it would someday be his, she'd struggled to understand why he'd withheld the truth. When he took her to see it, it began to make sense. It was vast – like a self-contained kingdom. She'd been blown away by it, but more by his passion for wine and the land. Had his parentage made her love him more? At first, maybe a little, but she soon learned that appearances can be deceptive.

Gradually André had begun to open up. From what she could gather, his family were incredibly private, very insular – the complete opposite of him. He'd admitted often feeling lost, being devoid of choices, under pressure to stay and take over the business. By all accounts, he'd

343

had a lonely upbringing. He'd been homeschooled and then sent to boarding school, which he'd hated. He'd described it as going from one prison to another. Despite being warm and open, André had few close friends aside from those he worked with at the vineyard. But even with them, he was still the boss. He'd told her it was why he loved the summers so much. The casual staff didn't pander to him, but in the end, they left. There was no doubt that this place was in André's blood, but while he loved it, he still spoke about his own plans of one day owning a small farm, making craft wine, travelling the world.

Closing her eyes and clasping her hands over her stomach, Marie-Hélène concluded that the unexpected news had obviously made André feel even more cornered. She'd make sure he understood that she was only interested in him. In reality, she couldn't care less about his family or the vineyard as long as she had him. They could leave if he wanted to, start over elsewhere, anywhere, as long as they were together. He'd often mentioned Ireland. Maybe they could go there.

The last thing André had said before he left the next morning was, "We'll figure it out, okay? Maybe it will be more than okay."

It had reminded her of something her grandmother used to say, "Out of dark clouds, always comes sunshine." Mind you, she'd also told her that life wasn't supposed to be happy. Marie-Hélène had thought it grim until Grandmére explained it – that duty, following a greater plan, no matter how unfair it seemed, could end up bringing you great joy if you allowed it. Perhaps Grandmére had been right.

Sitting there, looking out over the fields, the beauty,

the life of Bordeaux, she couldn't help but think that perhaps fate had led her here. As soon as he got back, she'd tell André the real reason she'd come to this part of the world. It might make him understand that she, too, knew what it felt like to feel lost. For the first time ever, André had made her think that perhaps it was time to leave the past behind, to stop looking for what she'd never find.

She'd already been searching her entire life, but when Grandmère died, she had decided to look beyond Paris. It made sense to start from where the note had originated. Aside from an old, grainy photograph, the only clue she had was the scribbled note she'd found amongst her grandmother's things. There'd been a hint about a job at a vineyard, nothing more, and certainly not which one. She soon learned that people passed into the vineyards, took work for a few months, then left, never to return. It was futile.

Marie-Hélène had been so deep in thought sitting on the balcony, imagining her future, reconciling her past, that she'd hadn't heard anyone come in. The woman must have been standing there for quite some time before she looked up. As soon as she did, she knew exactly who it was.

Gigi didn't give her a moment before she was launched on her, spitting rage. It took Marie-Hélène several minutes to comprehend what was happening.

"*An abomination!*" Gigi's words hit with force. "*A dirty, filthy, disgusting sin!*"

Marie-Hélène tried to stand, but her legs gave way, melting beneath her until she was slumped to the ground in shock.

"*You knew, didn't you?*" Gigi raged on, barely giving

her a moment to answer. *"You knew he was your brother!"*

My God, Marie-Hélène had never experienced anything like the agony of those words, the realisation of what they meant.

"What are you talking about? What are you trying to say?" And then, as reality dawned, "No. I had no idea. I swear. Oh my God, I think I'm going to be sick. I swear to you –"

"Then, why are you here?" Gigi stood over her.

"To find you." She could barely breathe.

Gigi began pacing, muttering wildly to herself. "She wouldn't listen. I kept telling her I wasn't ready, but she wouldn't listen. No, but she knew best, but I wasn't ready –"

"For what? To be my mother?" Marie-Hélène glanced up. "Is that what you're talking about? Are you talking about Grandmère?"

Gigi didn't answer. She stopped pacing and stood silently, shaking her head from side to side.

Looking at Gigi was like staring at a younger version of her grandmother.

"I didn't know!" Marie-Hélène pleaded. "How could I? I came here looking for you. Grandmère is dead."

Gigi didn't react.

"She died a few months ago, and … I don't know … she wouldn't tell me much. I wanted to see for myself. I had this vision of you, I –"

"Well," Gigi splayed her arms sarcastically, "do I live up to your expectations?"

Marie-Hélène closed her eyes and shook her head. "I'd given up. I tried some vineyards, but no one had heard of you. I was only going to stay until the end of the summer, but then I met –"

"*Your brother!*" Gigi shrieked.

Marie-Hélène flinched then fixed her eyes on the ground.

"Aren't you a clever girl, Marie-Hélène? I suppose when you met André and realised that all this will be his," she gestured out the window, "you must have batted those pretty lashes."

"No. It wasn't like that. I can't even –" Marie-Hélène looked up suddenly. Her entire body was shaking. "Does André know?"

"I saw you a few weeks ago with him. Right here, sitting on the benches outside," Gigi went on, ignoring the question. "As soon as I saw you, I suspected it was you all right, but it wasn't until I heard your full name that I knew for sure. André came to me this morning before he left to tell me your news." Gigi clapped her hands together. "Before that, he had been calling this year's summer fling simply 'Marie'. This morning, when he referred to you in full as Marie-Hélène, I knew it was time to intervene. André's gone now, but he asked me to tidy up this little situation." Gigi laughed bitterly. "Forgive me if I don't congratulate you on your pregnancy. Were you trying to trap him? It might have worked if you weren't *related!*"

"Does he know?" Marie-Hélène pleaded again. "Does he know I'm his –" She couldn't bring herself to say the word.

Gigi tutted. "I don't think André needs to know the finer details, do you? The thought alone of your love-child was enough to turn his stomach even without the news that it's inbred." She smirked coldly.

So, this was her mother – the one who'd abandoned her as a toddler. Until then, Marie-Hélène had felt almost sorry for the girl who'd been barely fifteen having her. When Marie-Hélène had turned the same age, she'd tried to imagine a baby growing inside her belly. She'd gone so far as to stuff pillows up her sweater to see how it might feel. It hadn't felt right. Grandmère had given her so little information through the years that it had made her ravenous for more. She'd built her mother up to be something exceptional ...

"How did you know where to find me?"

"The letter."

Gigi rolled her eyes. "She kept sending me pictures of you. For years she wouldn't stop. I never responded. I meant what I said in that letter. I didn't want to be found then, and I still don't. I gave birth to you, but you are not, nor will you ever be my child."

The tears were streaming openly down Marie-Hélène's face. "I wanted to tell you was that I understand why you left. You were so young."

This time Gigi's face contorts. "Understand? I was fifteen! There's not much to understand. I was a child – a child who'd just buried her father, a child who was –"

"Who was he? Who was my father?"

"Who knows?" Gigi shrugged. "I bet she told you that too, did she? That I was promiscuous? Is that the word she used? I bet it was." She closed her eyes and breathed loudly before recovering. "Now," she clasped her hands together, "your time here is at an end. André wants you gone by morning, as do I. We need to wipe out the fact that you were ever here. You need to dispose of that baby. There's no place for a child like that in this world. Imagine how it would turn out! It probably wouldn't even survive." She removed a cheque from the pocket of her skirt and thrust it at Marie-Hélène. "Get it done.

Leave, and don't ever come back."

"I have to speak to André. Please. Let me explain –"

That time Gigi had been clear. "If you don't leave, I'll have to tell him what you are. Take it from me – if he didn't want you before, he certainly wouldn't want you now. Aside from it being illegal and immoral, brothers and sisters rarely get along. Now, go, or I'll call the police, and every person in the world will know what you've done. Abort that child."

"Like you should have done with me?" Marie-Hélène could barely see through the tears.

"If you want to put it like that, then yes, but no one gave me a choice. Consider it a gift."

Marie-Hélène catches a glimpse of her reflection in the bus window. It's as dejected-looking as the day she left Chateau Challant and fled to Corsica. Afterwards, she'd felt so alone, so hurt, so afraid, so helpless – but when it came to it, she couldn't go through with it – abandon her child as she'd been abandoned, reject anyone or anything, no matter what it was, as cruelly she'd been cast aside. She kept waiting and waiting until it was too late. Until there was no other choice but to have her baby, do her duty – wait in fear for the arrival of the "abomination".

Nicole had been perfect: a beautiful, even-tempered, gentle, artistic child, yet still Marie-Hélène's allowed her anxieties to overshadow Nicole's entire childhood. She'd wanted to love her wholly, to ignore what she was, but it was there every single day. The worry never left. What if someone found out? What if there was something wrong inside Nicole? What if ...? The questions drove her demented, slowly transforming her into what she now is – a pathetic, selfish, obsessed, bitter drunk. Yes. She knows it. Through the years, she'd tried to convince herself that everything she was doing was for Nicole, but truthfully she'd been driven by hate. She'd wanted revenge, a way to take back all that had been stolen from her, to make Gigi pay with the one thing she would do anything to protect – her wealth.

If only she had realised sooner that the best reprisal would have been to become nothing like her mother. The only real stigma in it all was that she, too, ended up dismissing a daughter who only wanted to be loved. She should have confronted it all long before now. She should have forced herself to face André in person all those years ago instead of leaving Bordeaux like a criminal. Had Gigi told André everything in the end? Is that why he'd left France, laden with shame at what they'd done? It's something she intends to ask. It won't change anything, but nonetheless she'd like to know if it was the real reason he hadn't wanted her. She'd like to know that she hadn't disgusted him like Gigi said before he even knew the truth. Then perhaps she'd see that she hadn't imagined that he had loved her once, if only for a few months. Maybe it hadn't all been in her head. Believing that he'd rejected her before even knowing had hardened her irreparably, making it impossible for her ever to trust another man. It might be nice to move on, to forgive André so they could both be at peace.

That morning, Nicole's friend's mother confirmed by phone that Nicole was on her way to Corsica. At least she'd be safe there. As soon as she can, she will follow her, explain to her daughter about the genetic testing and how she'd needed to know. It was the English doctor in Corsica, all those years before, who'd advised her to take Nicole to get tested, to find out for sure. Oddly, instead of quashing Marie-Hélène's anxieties, the "clever test" only served to deepen her anger. In hindsight, finding out for sure had been the worse decision of her life. Now, all she wants to do is assure her daughter that she is perfect, regardless; she always was. Then she'll beg for forgiveness and spend the rest of her life trying to make it up to her. But first, she needs to pay a visit to her mother.

Chapter 32

Through the discarded phone on my lap, I can hear Nicole calling my name over and over. "I'm here," I say, coming to and picking the phone back up. "I'm coming."

I arrive at the village with practically no recollection of the short journey to once again meet with my husband's daughter. Is that what I should still call her? Or is she now my husband's sister's daughter? His niece? Oh my God, this can't be happening. It cannot be true. This has to be a mix-up, another bizarre lie. Please let it be that.

The thought of it makes me retch. *They were brother and sister. Brother and sister. Brother and sister.* I can't stop replaying the words, but instead of Nicole's voice, it's some ominous tone vibrating in my ears. My heart pounds as I reach the village square, park the car and switch off the engine. Everything around me slows, making me feel detached, like I'm trapped on the other side of a glass wall, watching another version of myself. But no matter how much I shout or bang the glass, I can't stop what's happening. I must be in shock. I've spent much of the past few weeks in a similar state, but honestly, this news is perhaps most disturbing of all.

I close my eyes, take a deep breath, then peer over the steering wheel. Nicole is leaning against the fountain with her head bowed so that her hair is concealing her face. Her legs are crossed, extended in front of her, and her hands are clasped like she's praying. Perhaps she is. Her leather jacket is beside her on the wall, and there's a camping-style backpack by her feet. She could be any other tourist until she glances up and I see how young she looks. For a moment, we just stare at each other before her face contorts and her chest heaves. I'm out of the car before her tears have a chance to fall. She feels tiny, fragile in my arms as she exhales against me, her body vibrating silently. I can't decipher what I'm feeling but, whatever it is, this child is feeling the same. Right now, she is the only person in the world who understands.

"*Shh,*" I comfort her, smoothing her hair. The village is quiet, with few people to witness the agony taking place at the monument – those who do, keep walking. "It's going to be okay," I manage eventually.

"Is it?" Nicole pulls away and sits back down with a thud, once again allowing her hair to hang over her face. I place my hand on hers, and she peers across at me. Once again, I'm blown away by how like André she is. Under normal circumstances, it might have felt comforting – right now, not so much.

"Are you sure?" I ask, hoping she isn't.

Bending down, she unzips the front pocket of her backpack and takes out a well-worn sheet of paper. "This is what I sent you." She places it on the wall and smooths it out. Then she slowly points at the various names, runs her finger along the lines that connect them while watching my reaction to see if I'm getting it. I nod as I follow the lines, the dates of birth, where they were born. Then she turns the paper over.

Frowning, I lift it and read before setting it down again.

"I don't know what to say."

"Me neither."

"They didn't know, did they?" I ask, closing my eyes and taking a breath.

We both exhale at the same time.

Nicole shakes her head. "I don't think so. How could they? Maman must have turned up in Bordeaux looking for her mother and not realising started a ... you know, with ..." She gestures at me.

"With André," I finish. "It's one hell of a coincidence."

Her features fold again. "It's disgusting."

I want to disagree with her, but I can't. Even if André and Marie-Hélène didn't know, it's still unimaginable.

"*Incest*," she spits the word. "That's what I came from." The statement is followed by a sob. "I shouldn't even be alive. I should have been destroyed."

"Please don't say that." I place my hand on her shoulder. "It's not true, Nicole."

"But it is true. It must be the reason Maman was always worried about me. Maybe there's something wrong inside me that I don't even know." Nicole can hardly catch her breath.

I rub her back until she relaxes, circling the palm of my hand on her back like a baby.

"She took me for tests in France, you know? She called it a 'clever test'!" She laughs humourlessly. "They must have confirmed it. That I'm ..." she searches for the word, "inbred? Maman only kept me because she knew that I'd be worth something someday. It must have been an added bonus when André vanished. Maman must have been happy! She needed him dead to benefit most from. She was never trying to find him for me. It was all a lie. I hate her. I hate them all. Look!" She points at the sheet of paper again – at the same words I'd learned that morning.

"Protected heir." I pause, wondering if I should go on. "I know. Gigi told me about it when I told her about you."

"And?"

"She was shocked." I exhale. "More than shocked, in fact. I can see why now."

"Can I ask you something?"

I nod.

"If it was you. If it had happened to you. I mean, if you'd somehow got pregnant with your brother, would you … would you get rid of it?" She looks as bereft as I feel.

"Honestly, I don't know, Nicole." I don't want to upset her anymore than she already is.

"What about for money?"

"No! Definitely not for money." I grimace. Thinking for a moment, I turn to her, "Nicole, are you sure there was nothing about André harming your mother? Gigi was particular. She told me that André left because Marie-Hélène accused him of rape and that your mother wanted money to keep quiet about it. There was absolutely nothing about them being … related." I choose a milder word. I'm still trying to decide which story I prefer: André as a rapist or André bedding his sister. Both versions are repulsive, but I'm hoping it's one versus the other and that both aren't true.

Nicole puts her hands to her face, exhales loudly, then drops her arms by her side. "No. There's nothing like that.

You can see for yourself. Maybe Gigi made it up to cover up the real story? Maybe she didn't want anyone knowing that she'd had a baby so young." She shrugs and points at the paper. "If it did happen, why would Maman leave it off here? It's a big part of the story to omit. Everything else is there."

I bite my lip and nod again. "True. Your mother never mentioned it to me either. I knew she was hiding something that day. I can't believe it was this. Christ, Gigi must have been only a child having your mother."

"The notes say she was fifteen when she got pregnant. Sixteen when she gave birth." She points to the paper again.

Tilting my head, I think back to what Gigi told me about her childhood. She'd mentioned that she and her mother hadn't seen eye to eye. How trapped she'd felt. That her mother had been all about duty.

"She ran away when my mother was about two. Maman used to say that if it weren't for her grandmother, who knows where she would have ended up." She smiles sadly and looks around. "Gigi ended up here."

I shake my head in dismay. "Then met a wealthy man, got married, had André. And all was well until Marie-Hélène showed up and ruined it for her."

We fall silent for a while.

Eventually I ask, "Does your mother know where you are? Does she know you know?"

She nods. "She does by now. I left a note. After this, I'm going to Corsica for good. My friend's parents invited me to stay. I'll get a job." Her shoulders slump.

My head shoots up. "For good? Really? Are you sure? Do you want me to …" I trail off before I say something stupid. I can't ask her to come with me.

"It's okay. I don't want anything from you, Seren. I just thought you should know the truth. I bet you wish you never met me."

"I'm glad I did." Am I? Right now, I'm so confused, so numb, that I have no idea how I feel about anything. I'd wanted to get to the bottom of André's past, to know that I hadn't imagined my life with him. Now I wish I'd never come here. At this very moment, I'm not even sure I still love him or his memory or whatever I've been chasing. Is it the same thing? Just this morning, I'd been willing to give up my whole life in Ireland to start a new one here, all to stay close to his ghost. Everything that's happened has made me realise that I have only one priority now: my son. I have to get the hell away from here.

"There's something I have to tell you, Nicole. It's the reason I need to leave France today. Right now, in fact. As soon as we're finished here."

She listens wide-eyed as I explain everything that happened with Gigi. Her eyes flit to my stomach when I come clean about the baby. I tell Nicole how Gigi had threatened to injure her if she went near the chateau and how strongly I believe that she'd purposely tried to harm me this morning after learning about my pregnancy. "I need you to swear that you won't go near her. I don't trust her. Because of me, Gigi knows about you, Nicole, and she knows what Marie-Hélène is after. I know you're angry with your mother, but you should warn her too. I was terrified earlier. I think Gigi was actually trying to kill me, or at least send me a clear message," I pause to shake my head in disbelief. "She's unhinged. I don't feel safe in France now. And it's not just me I have to think about now." My hand settles on my stomach as I finish.

"May I?" she asks.

357

I nod, and she places her hand next to mine.

After a moment, she says, "I understand, Seren," followed by, "I wish I'd had a mother like you."

I put my hand on hers. "He'll be your brother." I dip my head to meet her eyes, but she looks away.

"He?"

I nod.

"He doesn't need a sister like me. Please don't tell him, okay? Don't tell him I exist. I want to forget it myself. I'll have to hide it for the rest of my life."

"Don't say that. You're perfect." I have to fight back the tears. If I give in to them, they may never stop flowing again. "They didn't know, Nicole. I think it sounds worse than it actually is – after all, they were only half brother and sister. Put it out of your head. And I *will* tell him about you. You can come to meet him someday."

She doesn't answer. I'm not sure I even mean what I'm saying. Once again, I stop myself from asking her to come with me to Ireland.

If I could only pause for long enough, I might hear the person on the other side of the fictitious glass trying to tell me not to leave her here. If I'd only look.

We stay that way for a while, sitting there while she tells me her plans.

"It's all Gigi's fault," Nicole says after a while. "It's all on her. If she hadn't left Maman as a baby, maybe none of this would have happened. I hope Gigi or Georgine, or whoever the hell she is, gets what she deserves. Sooner rather than later."

I don't disagree. The atmosphere has gone flat. When there's nothing left to say, I stand and make my way to the car. She follows.

"You'll stay in touch?" I ask. "And promise me you'll

contact your mother as soon as you get to Corsica. And swear to me you won't go anywhere near Gigi." I throw out instructions as if I'm her mother. I have no right.

Nicole shuffles the loose stones on the ground with her boots. I lean into the car and get my wallet. Opening it, I take out a couple of hundred euro notes and hand them to her.

She looks at them flatly and takes a step back. "Thanks, but I have everything I need."

"I know, I just … I'm sorry." My eyes fall to my feet.

Chapter 33

On the drive back to Bordeaux, Nicole's disappointed face haunts my thoughts. She'd looked utterly let down. I shouldn't have left. I'd realised it almost as soon as I'd driven away, and yet I still hadn't turned back. *Brother and sister. Brother and sister. Brother and sister.* It's too much to take in, too far-fetched to fathom, but it makes sense. I have to think of myself now, my baby. I have to get home to Ireland. *She's still his daughter.* I push the thought aside. *But what kind of daughter?* I shake my head, getting annoyed at myself. *It's not her fault.*

I'm almost in the city when I indicate and pull the car off the road. Catching a glimpse of my face in the rearview mirror, I scowl at my reflection.

The feeling that I'm never going to see Nicole again won't leave me. After sharing so much, in the end, the farewell had felt stilted, so final. Sitting here, I run over it again. Nicole had insisted that she didn't want a lift back to Bordeaux. She'd told me she would catch the bus straight to the airport, that she wanted to be alone, to have time to think. Still, I can't shake the sensation of dread deep inside, like something else is about to happen.

I should have insisted that she come with me. I could have at least made sure that she got on the flight to Corsica, but she'd been so adamant. *Why?* If I hadn't been so focused on getting out of France as quickly as possible, I might have asked.

She'd hardly go to see Gigi after what I told her, would she? Oh, Christ, I don't want to even think what I'm now thinking. Should I call Marie-Hélène? In truth, I'm scared of her too. Maybe she didn't know that André was her brother, but her later actions were deplorable. How could she use her only daughter that way – for money? I can't trust someone like that any more than I can trust Gigi. I think back over what Nicole had said earlier about it all being Gigi's fault. *"I hope Gigi or Georgine, or whoever the hell she is, gets what she deserves. Sooner rather than later."*

As I replay Nicole's words, something resonates, and I feel a chill run up my spine. I grab my phone off the passenger seat, dial Nicole's number, and drum my fingers against my knee while I wait for her to answer. It rings out. *"Dammit."* I bang the palm of my hand against the steering wheel. Staring ahead, I recall Nicole's email. I open it on my phone, this time clicking on the attachment. It's identical to the sheet of paper she'd shown me back at the fountain. I reread it, then resting the phone back on the passenger seat I open my bag and pull out the envelope containing the files I brought with me to France. I remove the one I'm looking for and trace my finger over the word. My eyes scan across. Reading it to myself, I frown, pick up my phone and cross-check it against the email, then freeze.

Oh my God, I was right. Earlier back in André's

apartment, there'd been two things that had struck me as odd.

First, Gigi had slipped up by revealing it was she who'd told Marie-Hélène something shocking about André. When I'd questioned her about it, she'd tried to cover it up. I'd believed her, but I know now what she must have told Marie-Hélène was that André was her brother. I'm still wondering about the rape part, still unable to understand why Gigi added it to the story. From Marie-Hélène's notes and my meeting with her, as far as I'm concerned Gigi fabricated it. But why? Was the idea that they were siblings not enough?

The second thing was the way Gigi spoke about the things her mother used to say. I'd been about to check it earlier in André's apartment, but then I'd been distracted by Fi's call, Nicole's email, and finally the small matter of almost being the victim of intentional gas-poisoning. With all the commotion, it had slipped my mind until now. Slowly the reality of what it means dawns on me. As much as I'd like this nightmare to be over, it isn't, not yet. I'd been right to leave Nicole earlier, if only for a while. Over the past few months, I've learned something about myself. To think, to see sense, to regard the person on the other side of the glass, I sometimes need to step away. I can see clearly now. I know what I have to do. With the phone still in my hand, I close the email and click into my contacts. Taking a deep breath, I press the green phone icon.

"Hello?" he answers straight away.

"Bobby. It's me, Seren."

"Christ." I can hear him sighing with relief. "I couldn't get you at all. I've been worried sick. I didn't know you'd actually go to France. Fi told me. Jesus, if I'd known –"

"It's okay, Bob," I cut across him. "I don't have much time. Can you listen? I'll explain properly when I'm back. I need –"

"You're coming back?" he interrupts. He sounds relieved.

"Yes, but listen, Bobby, I need you to do something for me. I know everything, okay? But I need you to tell me what André told you in his words. I know what you said before, Bobby, and I get that you were trying to protect me, but you're the only one who has André's voice in this. I need to hear it now, please. It's important. In fact, it's *life and death* important. Do you understand?" I finish, then hold my breath in the hope he'll cooperate.

"This is what André was afraid of. This is why he didn't want you to know … are you sure you're okay? Jesus, can you just come back? If I'd known –"

"What do you mean this is what he was afraid of?"

"*That woman*," he growls.

"I met Marie-Hélène, Bob. She's bats, but I think –"

"Not her," he says. "The mother."

"Gigi?"

"That's right. She's the one who's to blame. Do you know about the …" Bobby trails off.

My stomach knots while I wait.

"About the rape?" He coughs the word.

I'd been waiting for him to say that André and Marie-Hélène were half-siblings. "Yeah," I nod. "Gigi told me what Marie-Hélène accused him of, but I don't –"

"It *didn't* happen, Seren. André swore on *your* life. He'd never have done that unless he was sure. After all the fuss, André tried to find Marie-Hélène, but she'd vanished. He couldn't believe what she'd accused him of. She was very normal, he said – a nice girl, like. The

363

pregnancy was a surprise, but he was okay about it. He went to his mother to tell her that the girlfriend was expecting – looking for advice, like. Then he went off for a few nights with work. The next thing he comes back and the girlfriend is gone. Apparently, there's an accusation. Apparently, she wanted money for an abortion and then some. His mother kept saying that it would destroy the family, ruin them all. It would be best if André left for good. He was young, and I suppose you think your mother knows best." He gives a humourless laugh. "She told him everyone was starting to talk, that the rumours were spreading. She didn't want him working in the vineyards. She threatened to tell his father. He was afraid –"

"Did he ever mention who Marie-Hélène was to him?" I cut across impatiently.

"What do you mean?

"Think, Bobby," I urge. "Was there anything about them being somehow related?"

"André and Marie-Hélène? No! Nothing at all like that. Where did you get that from? In hindsight, he said he knew very little about her, really. He thinks that's why he couldn't find her."

Oh, my God! André hadn't known. He'd still thought he'd been accused of rape.

"But here's the strange thing," Bobby's still talking. "Years later, you know what André told me? That there'd been a rumour doing the rounds when he was a teenager. He'd asked his mother about it, but she told him it was bullshit. That it was people out to get them. Sounds like a desperate paranoid yoke."

"*What was it?*" I want to reach down the phone and smack the words out of him.

"Well, people were saying that the father had been

married before and that she'd died in childbirth and that Gigi," he pronounces it G.G., "was actually the second wife, that she wasn't André's real mother at all. Shortly after he asked her about it, she packed him off to boarding school just when he had started making a few pals in the village, get a bit of freedom. Sounds like a miserable childhood. They never left the chateau, apparently. He made the most of it, I think, but he said it was like a prison. Being allowed to come to Ballycross for that summer as a teen – the one when he met you was a massive deal for him. He said he'd never known freedom like it. It's probably why he came back here. Sounds to me like she wanted André away from mixing with the locals. I suppose with distance André started to hope that maybe there was some truth in it – that she wasn't his mother after all. Wishful thinking, maybe – she sounded like a right weapon. In the end, he decided that she wanted him out of the way because of money or inheritance or something. I suppose that legal shite with a will happens all the time, doesn't it?"

"Not to this extent," I sigh, dropping my head to the steering wheel and squeezing my eyes shut.

It's worse than I'd imagined. Gigi had concocted two entirely separate sets of lies – one for André and a separate one for Marie-Hélène, both equally as damaging.

Nicole was right. It's all on Gigi.

Now, I'm even more sure about my theory. More than once, I'd noticed how when Gigi repeated something her mother said, she used her full name. *"Georgine, life is not supposed to be happy,"* and *"Georgine, someday you'll find a purpose for your scrutiny ..."* In Marie-Hélène's notes, it's the same. But I'm the only one with a copy of André's birth cert, and the name I've just read on there is

Georgette Dubois-Challant. No matter how similar they are, no one confuses their real name – no one, not even someone as despicably creative as Gigi. André's real mother was called Georgette, not Georgine. At one point, there must have been another Gigi – one who'd probably died in childbirth just like the rumour André had heard. One who'd been replaced by what I can only imagine was a far lesser version. One who'd taken her role to the extreme.

"I think he was right, Bob. I don't think she was his birth mother," I say urgently.

Marie-Hélène had been duped by her own mother. She'd never accused André of rape, and they weren't brother and sister because "Gigi" or Georgine wasn't André's real mother. Gigi had told a sick lie to get rid of Marie-Hélène, safe in the knowledge that she'd abort the baby – if left be, that baby would someday become a protected heir.

The rape story must have been created to shame André into leaving France, never to return, hitting him where she knew it would hurt. Gigi was right in what she'd said earlier. "It was always about money. *My* money." And she'd have done anything to protect it, cleverly covering all bases. She could never have imagined that Marie-Hélène would keep the baby. To be honest, I can't understand it either. Had she really kept Nicole solely to gain wealth? I'm beginning to doubt it when suddenly it hits me like a ton of bricks.

"Oh, my God! She knows!" I exclaim, remembering what Nicole had told me earlier. If Marie-Hélène had taken Nicole for genetic testing, it must have revealed that André wasn't her "uncle". I can't be sure, but I think Marie-Hélène is planning to be the one who finally gives Gigi what she deserves.

"S-heren? Are you still there?"

I'd almost forgotten about Bobby.

"Sorry, I am. I'll explain later. I have to do something." I pause. There's one more thing I want to know. "Why didn't André go back and just oust Gigi if he suspected she wasn't his real mother, do you think? Why didn't he fight for what was his?"

There's a long pause. "He was ashamed of the rape part, even though he knew it wasn't true, but, you know, people can be odd as hell. They believe what they want. Maybe he hadn't wanted to risk it. And like I told you before, he wasn't happy in France. A few years back, he did a bit of searching on the internet, and he found the same article you must have, saying that he'd gone missing after a swim – presumed dead. There was no swim, S-heren. He knew where he wasn't wanted."

With relief, I start laughing or crying. I'm not sure which, but I sound hysterical. "Why the hell didn't he tell me, Bobby? Why didn't he tell someone what she'd done? Why … what about his father?"

Bobby interrupts my rambling. "In his own words and pardon my French, André's father was a right bollix. If I was to hazard a guess as to why André didn't tell you, then I'd say it's because he no longer cared. He was as happy as a pig in shit here in Ballycross, and he had a future with you." Bobby coughs nervously. "You were far more valuable than the past."

Chapter 34

Gigi

She's dressed for the occasion – something elegant, demure. She has the distinct feeling that someone will be dropping by later. With so many new family members, it's hard to imagine who it might be. The daytime security guard confirmed that Seren had left earlier that day in a rush and, as yet, hasn't returned. Gigi had gone immediately to the guesthouse, wrapped her scarf over her mouth and crept inside to switch off the stove. The entire wall behind was a blackened mess. For a brief moment, Gigi had considered lying on the bed and allowing herself to fall into a never-ending sleep.

After everything she'd been through, it seemed too simple, too defeatist, especially for someone who believed that where life and death is concerned, you should feel the struggle, embrace the fight. Gigi is ready to do so. She has given everyone at the chateau the evening off so that aside from Henri and his nurse, she's alone. The security guards are gone, and for once, the gates of Chateau Challant are wide open.

She'd visited Henri earlier, spoken with him alone after asking the day nurse for a moment of privacy. Once the nurse had left, Gigi had sat in the high-backed chair next to his bed. Taking his frail hand, she'd traced her fingers along the bulging blue veins, wondering if she could stop the flow of blood if she pressed them hard enough.

"You never loved me, did you, Henri?" Gigi said it like a statement. "I never told you the whole story, did I? Not that you would have cared, or believed me. Not when my own mother didn't." Then, she leant forward, whispering the truth to him, forcing herself to relive the still vivid nightmare. When she finished, she sat back. It felt good to get it off her chest.

Resting her head back against the armchair, she closed her eyes, revisiting the first day she'd met Henri when he'd walked purposefully towards her in the vineyard, stopped in front of her to look her up and down, then asked, "Do you like children?"

"Yes," she lied. "Very much."

Without another word, he nodded once in approval and indicated that she should follow him. She trekked in silence back to the main house behind his straight-backed wooden form. She should have felt nervous, except there was something safe about him. Henri was a real man, not like the boys from Paris or the sweat-drenched men from the vineyards. That said, it was the chateau that impressed her most. She gazed about in awe at the furniture, the staff, the grandeur.

When they reached the staircase, Henri pointed to the top. "The nursery," he gestured.

Again, she tailed him up the stairs, not knowing what was expected of her. He pushed open the heavy door at the top of the stairs, and Gigi glimpsed a cradle inside.

For a second, an intense wave of nausea hit, threatening to overcome her, but she swallowed it back. Before she knew what was happening, Henri had placed the bundle in her arms, and she'd looked down to see André for the very first time. He was tiny, perhaps as small as the other slippery, wet, wailing baby that had been thrust upon her once. Instead of feeling horrified as she had then, this felt different. This baby was quiet and clean and staring straight at her.

"He was such a beautiful baby. I did love him, Henri." She'd opened her eyes to look at the elderly man. "It could have been so different if you'd tried to include me in your life, even a little. That was all I needed. But I'd never be *her*, would I? Do you remember how long it took you to even ask my name? It must have been a week after you plucked me from the vineyards to care for your son. You were so shocked that we had such similar names, weren't you? Do you remember?"

"Georgine." She'd stood up straight to answer him clearly.

Henri had blinked several times as though he'd seen a ghost before finding his voice.

"Georgette?" he'd whispered.

"No. It's Georgine."

"Gigi," he'd responded hollowly. "I'll call you Gigi." He'd turned and left the room.

"I looked just like her, didn't I? A younger version, of course. Just like your precious Georgette, but I wasn't her, was I, Henri? You never cared less who the hell I was." She squeezed his hand hard. "Do you remember you used to come and sit for hours in the nursery just watching us? It was like you were trying to see someone else. Like you were trying to change me into her."

Gigi had been fascinated by him. Henri was handsome, strong, mysterious. It took her years to realise that he was empty, barren and broken from his loss, still mourning the wife he'd tried ro replace. Foolishly, she'd thought she could fill him. Sometimes he'd smile at her, and she'd feel intensely proud that she must be doing a good job with André. Caring for *this* baby was easy – there was no housework or having to listen to her mother, no working in the patisserie, no wanting to put a pillow over the baby's head for destroying her life.

She loved her bedroom next to the nursery. It felt like a hotel – one of the ones she used to pass by in Paris, dreaming of escaping inside. Instead, she'd escaped here. Not once did she ever think about what she'd left behind in Paris. In fact, she never wanted to think about it again. By then, she'd heard the tragedy of Madame Dubois-Challant dying in childbirth. One of the other staff members had whispered it to her early on. They'd proceeded to tell her how shocked the staff had been when Monsieur – once considered the eternal hermit bachelor, had arrived home one day with his equally reclusive bride. They were notoriously private – had told no one about their practically secret marriage. They soon gathered that Georgette was an old family friend from a town somewhere near the Belgian border. As an only child, Georgette had refused to marry Henri until after the death of her parents, whom she'd nursed dutifully. It wasn't until after their passing, and with no remaining family on earth, that she'd finally agreed to marry Henri and assist him in producing an heir. Less than a year after arriving at Chateau Challant, Georgette had once again seamlessly fulfilled her duty. There was an heir, but she was gone. Gigi wished she could have died in childbirth, just like Madame. But she hadn't. Instead, she'd run away, found herself here, and now she never wanted to leave.

At first, the other staff members had treated her as one of them until Gigi made it clear that she had far more significant responsibilities, her own room and a "special" relationship with Monsieur.

A year later, Henri asked her to marry him "for the sake of the boy".

After considering it, she'd accepted on two conditions. One: André must never know that she wasn't his real mother. Henri had seemed moved by this. He'd agreed, mistaking the insurance policy she'd concocted for genuine adoration for his son – a son with whom he'd struggled to bond. In Gigi's naïve mind, a wife could always be discarded, but as André's real mother, she could stay here forever to be treated like royalty, issuing orders to the *new* staff Henri had promised. That way, no one would ever know that she'd been plucked from picking grapes. It would be as though she was always meant to be here. And two: there would be no more children. She never again wanted to go through what she'd endured in Paris. *Never.* He'd agreed to this demand almost too readily. He had what he needed, and so would his son.

André would have a mother, always, and it would ease Henri's guilt over his anger at his son for taking away his precious Georgette. Truthfully, an untarnished slate had suited Henri as much as it had served her. Henri was old-fashioned, not wanting anyone knowing his business, attempting to take down his dynasty, come after his money, blackmail him with idle gossip. Yes, the conditions had suited him too. Besides, Gigi was the only mother André knew. How would he ever know that there'd once been another? Georgette hadn't been there long enough to make an impression beyond the staff at the house. She'd swept through the chateau, then vanished as fast, paving the path for Gigi.

The union took place in one of the rooms downstairs – just them, the priest, one witness, no dress, no celebration.

Over time, Gigi imagined that Henri might change – that he might grow to love her. It wasn't until she was in her mid-twenties that she knew he never would, and it was purely a marriage of convenience. He'd never dealt with his grief. Instead, he'd acted in haste and perhaps spent a lifetime regretting it. By then, it was too late for the truth.

Henri had no interest in her, sexually or otherwise. He cared only for the vineyards, was only too happy to stay hidden behind the walls of the chateau rotting away. Still, all was not lost. She was the lady of the house, and she loved it here. Some day, perhaps sooner than later, her already ancient husband would die, and she'd have the last laugh – it would be hers.

As promised after the wedding, Henri filtered out the old staff so that eventually no one who mattered remembered that for a short time, there'd once been another Madame – a different Gigi to before.

They'd managed the lie all those years by keeping themselves to themselves, by carefully selecting who was allowed inside their walls. Well, there'd been one time when André was a boy, and he'd told her that one of the older vineyard farmers kept telling him about his real mother who'd died when he was a baby. She'd sat André down and told him the truth – that people were jealous and they'd do anything to trick you for money, and if he ever mentioned it again, he'd be sorry. The senile farmer left the next day quietly, and André went away to school. By the time he returned, the few local friends he'd made had no interest in the privileged young man from the chateau. They'd moved on. Although it's what she'd planned, Gigi had experienced a pang of guilt. To make up for it, she'd sent him to Ireland for summer – to the most insignificant town she could find.

This place had become her world. She'd accepted life as a living ghost, as odd as it had been, as hurt as she'd often felt by her husband's coldness – safe in the knowledge that better things would come in time.

Then, she'd uncovered the paperwork to say it would never be hers, not really. The fear of losing the only life she knew reared its head once more. Upon Henri's death, it would all pass to André – the boy who didn't even want it in the first place, who moaned about wanting a normal life. She'd be cast aside, especially if he ever found out that she wasn't his real mother.

Poor André could never understand his father's aloofness. Over time, Henri's resentment towards his son morphed into acute awkwardness. Once again, Henri had left it too late to mend the relationship or to even try. Similarly, his mother's bitterness confused him when all he wanted was a nice, normal family. Well, if he wanted normal, let him have it. Gigi could help him achieve it. When Marie-Hélène showed up, threatening everything, she'd found a way to make things work in her favour.

* * *

Sitting here now, on the balcony of the house, Gigi feels calmer than she has in a while. Far more so than she had following the initial news of her ever-blossoming family. It's almost laughable now. Earlier, the ever-extending branches of the family tree had whipped into her flesh like a punishment she didn't deserve. After all, she's been more than selfless throughout her life, raising a child that wasn't hers, taking over the business when Henri lost his mind. Admittedly, she'd loved that part of her life. It made the rest bearable. Now, it would have to be enough.

She'd said goodbye to Henri earlier. She'd stood next to his bed, slowly leaned over him and whispered, "Till death do us part." Then she'd kissed his lips so hard that she was sure she'd tasted blood. She hadn't been sure if it had been hers or his.

It's over now. Perhaps that's why Gigi feels at peace. If she's right, it should be soon. In preparation, she'd asked the kitchen to lay out some simple platters of food on the balcony, along with their very best vintage – something easy to swallow. The entire day, she's felt aware that something is coming, or indeed, someone. She's sure of it. It could be Seren. What a surprise she'd turned out to be. Will she be brave enough to return, or had she understood Gigi's earlier warning at the guesthouse loud and clear? Gigi likes Seren. She's romantic and genuine – sentimental people always fell in love with this place. Seren certainly gave the impression that she'd like to stay, perhaps raise her little test-tube baby here. Once the penny drops, all this could be her son's … yes, it might be Seren.

375

Then again, it could Marie-Hélène. Will tonight be the night that Marie-Hélène appears, to reveal that she cleverly kept the baby? If she didn't hate her so much, Gigi might feel proud. Leaning back, Gigi considers it. Indeed, she'd weaved quite the intricate puzzle. She doubts there is anyone in the entire world who could decipher it. Indeed, poor Seren had struggled to know what to believe. At times, she'd had trouble remembering it all herself. Mind you, there'd been vital elements of truth. She'd rarely if ever, called André her son, and sadly, someone had been raped, just not Marie-Hélène. André would never have done something so vile. He'd just been too weak to question her.

The gravel crunches below. To make things easier, she'd left the back door slightly ajar. The lights are on to guide them upstairs to this room. Whoever it is will find her. The sky over the estate is breathtaking tonight, blazing with every shade of orange, red, purple. Hearing the stairs creak, she takes a sip of wine, allowing it to roll over her tongue, before swallowing. It's like heaven. She closes her eyes to capture the flavour of what could be the last thing she'll ever taste after having to dramatically alter her goals.

Someone is in the room beyond now. The footsteps pause when they notice where Gigi is sitting on the balcony with her back to the door. Unable to stop herself, Gigi turns. It's so unexpected that, for one moment, she loses the power of speech.

"You must be Nicole. It's a pleasure to meet you," she says, at last.

Seren was right. In the flesh, Nicole is even more like André.

"I had to see for myself," Nicole advances fast, and Gigi startles. "I had to see the face of the person capable of ruining so many lives." Looking down at her, Nicole is trying hard not to cry.

"Sit down, please." Gigi gestures, nonplussed, at the empty chair.

"No. Just answer me. Why did you do it? How could you?"

"How could I what?"

"Pretend that he was her brother. *You sick … bitch*."

Gigi raises her eyebrows in astonishment. "I'm impressed. Finally, someone knows. Did you figure that out alone?"

"I can see now," Nicole continues undeterred. "I can see now why my mother was so angry. First, you abandon her. Then when she finds you, and you destroy her life. All those years, you let her believe that she'd had her brother's baby. It ruined our lives!"

"My, my!" Gigi claps sarcastically. "You *do* know everything. Bravo! Did you get help?"

"*Seren!*" Nicole spits the name at her.

"Seren?" Gigi raises her eyebrows further this time.

"Yes. Seren is on her way here right now. She called me from the airport. She was going to leave France, but she decided to come back. You won't get away with it. Any of it."

Gigi looks relieved. "Oh, I'm so glad. I knew Seren would see sense. That's marvellous news. The party can't proceed without her adult supervision. I bet Seren told you not to come here alone, am I right?"

Nicole narrows her eyes defiantly. "Yeah. She told me you're dangerous. But all I can see is a little old bitter woman. What are you going to do, gas me? Like you tried to do to her. Poison me? Shoot me?" Nicole quickly surveys the contents of the table. "You're pathetic. I'm not afraid of you."

Gigi laughs at her gutsiness and shrugs. "I like you, Nicole. You remind me of someone. Sit, please. Let's talk."

"Yeah. Let's talk." Nicole remains where she is, shaking with adrenaline. "Let's talk about how you ruined *both* my parents. I could have had them both. I never even knew my father. I never got to meet him because of you."

Gigi exhales impatiently. "Do you really want the truth, Nicole? Or would you like a nice version – one that a child like you can handle?"

"Fuck you, old lady! I want the truth. Like, why did you tell him Maman accused him of rape? He was innocent. What sort of sick person does that?"

"Very well." Gigi nods, calmly pouring some more wine into her glass. She needs to bide her time until Seren gets here. "Yes. I told André that. The truth is, I needed him gone. When Marie-Hélène showed up here, she provided the means for me to make that happen. If she hadn't come looking for me in the first place, then who knows what might have happened? You see, just like you, Nicole, your mother should never have been born."

"But I was."

It's barely a whisper, but they both turn at the same time.

"Maman?" Nicole's chest deflates with a sob when she sees her mother materialise at the balcony door.

"I'm so sorry, Nicole. I should have told you. I should have told you everything." Marie-Hélène's shoulders are slumped. "I thought you were gone to Corsica. I'm glad you didn't leave."

"I had to see it. I wanted to … it was a lie," Nicole begins wildly. "It was all a lie. André wasn't your brother. I'm not – I'm –"

Marie-Hélène nods and smiles sadly, "I know. I know he's not. I believed *her* at first," she shoots Gigi a glare, then turns back to Nicole, "but I've known for a long time that André wasn't my brother or *her* son. She's a liar. You were always perfect, Nicole, regardless. I know that now. You *were* supposed to be born. I was the one who was broken. I'm so sorry." She bows her head for a moment, then meets Nicole's eyes. "Let me fix it now. We can go wherever you want." She extends her hand to Nicole. "We can –"

"It really is lovely to see you, Marie-Hélène," Gigi interrupts. "I'm not surprised, though. Ever since your phonecall, I've been expecting you. Haven't you changed? Age is a terrible thing, isn't it? It doesn't suit you at all. Not to worry. Now, all we need is Seren, and the family will be complete."

"Seren?" Marie-Hélène frowns, ignoring the rest.

"Yes, dear daughter. After all, it was you who summoned her all the way from Ireland." Gigi claps again. "Did she not tell you? Seren is pregnant! And with André's baby!" Gigi throws her head back and laughs when she sees Marie-Hélène's face. "Surprise! You weren't expecting that, were you? So all your clever plotting and planning was in vain. She's having a boy, and that trumps everything! Isn't it amazing what they can do nowadays – a baby from the grave!" She pauses to take in Marie-Hélène's dropped jaw. "Oh, dear, I've shocked you. Here –" she points at the glass of wine, "have a drink. Seren tells me you love to drink. Apparently, you drink *all* the time." She pouts, then jeers.

379

"And I hear you've been having trouble with your mental health. Why don't you tell your mother all about it?"

Marie-Hélène moves towards Nicole and puts her arm around her. "I don't care anymore. Nothing you say matters. You can't hurt me."

"Look at you with your daughter! Beautiful. Are you not going to tell her that the only reason you had her was to get your hands on this place? Let's be honest."

Marie-Hélène grimaces and turns to Nicole. "It wasn't like that, Nicole. I didn't even know for years about the inheritance. That was a mistake, but I had you because I … I didn't want to reject you like she'd rejected me. It was my –"

"If you say duty, I'll vomit," Gigi says. "So like your dear grandmother."

Marie-Hélène whips her head around. "I came to ask you how you got rid of André, but I know what you told him now." She shakes her head with disgust. "You told him that I said he'd raped me. How could you do that to an innocent person? You bitch! I would never … I loved André. You couldn't bear the thought of it, could you? Of anyone finding out that you already had a daughter or that André wasn't yours. Grandmère was right. You're nothing but a selfish bitch."

Gigi glares at her, then bows her head. For one moment, she considers telling Marie-Hélène the truth, but it would only delay the inevitable. Besides, Gigi doesn't want sympathy now. It's far too late to explain that no one ever wanted the truth nor believed her when she'd told it. Instead, they'd been happy for her to carry it with her all her life. Not once had it ever left her. In fact, it had defined her. Never again would she let anyone take anything from her. Eventually, she looks up at her daughter and her granddaughter, narrowing her eyes at the fruit of the truth – the produce of the night of her father's funeral when his friend crawled drunk into her bed and raped her.

Fear, grief, disbelief had pinned her there in silence while he pressed his mouth to her ear and told her never to tell, that no one would believe a whore like her. He'd been right. No one had believed her. Her own mother had been as shocked as Gigi when her stomach began to swell. She'd tried to make it go away, knocking herself into walls, but the "punishment", as her mother called it, wouldn't leave. And then the birth, feeling her body torn in two. It had been almost as harrowing as how it got in there in the first place. Afterwards, her mother had pushed the baby at her throbbing breasts while Gigi sobbed in pain. After a year, she'd hated that baby more than she hated herself, but there was no point in telling them now. It was too late.

Summoning the former fury, the years of agony, the face of the man that ruined her life, the image of the daughter she never wanted, the husband who rejected her, the mother who didn't believe her, the child who was damaged for eternity, Gigi stands.

"I never wanted you. You ruined my life, do you hear me? I never loved you. I wanted you dead!" Gigi screams the words while Nicole and Marie-Hélène stare wide-eyed. *"You make me sick. Why couldn't you leave me alone? You had to turn up here, trying to retake my life. And still, you can't leave me alone. You knew what you were doing, having that child,"* she jabs her finger hard at Nicole's chest, *"but you'll never get any of it. Do you hear me?"*

She's shouting so loud that Nicole and Marie-Hélène glance nervously at one another. She won't stop. All the while, Gigi is backing towards the railings, still yelling, glancing towards the upstairs windows where Henri sleeps and his nurse watches. *"All you want is my money. And you'll go this far to get it!"*

"I did want it," Marie-Hélène takes a step forward. "I'll admit that. I wanted to make you suffer like you hurt me, but I don't want it anymore. I have my daughter and my pride. That's enough for me." She nods reassuringly at Nicole.

"Liar! You're willing to kill me for my money!" Gigi's eyes are wild, her hands flailing everywhere. She has to make this work. *"This is your fault!"* she screams and points at Nicole, attempting to spur them into action. She flies at Nicole and grabs her, pulling her closer. It's so fast that Nicole careers towards the railings with Gigi gripping on to her T-shirt. She won't let go. There's an enormous clatter as Gigi pushes against her and a section of metal dislodges to hang mid-air from its bracket.

"No!" Marie-Hélène launches herself into the scuffle, grappling for Nicole.

For a moment, Gigi is winning as she manoeuvres herself into position. It will be fast. It's over now anyway, but she won't lose. She'll be gone, and they'll get the blame for her death. They'll never see a cent.

Chapter 35

A scream. A shout. A name.

As a body plunges to the ground, the last sound that rings through the lavender light is the name *"Nicole!"*.

I hear it. I catch it, and my blood runs cold. Nicole wasn't supposed to here. I'd told her not to come. Why hadn't she listened? Curiosity? Intrigue? Anger? For a moment with the woman who'd destroyed so many lives. It's my fault. I should never have left her earlier. Nicole is the only reason I've come back. Oh my God, what have I done?

Earlier, after piecing it together, I'd phoned her back immediately. This time she'd answered. "It's not true. She wasn't his mother. Gigi wasn't André's real mother." I'd been speaking fast, trying to relay what Bobby had told me, what I'd begun to suspect. "I'm coming back. I'll be there as soon as I can. Do you understand? Wait there. Please. Don't move. Do you hear me? I'm so sorry, Nicole. I panicked. I shouldn't have left you. Wait there for me." I could hear her muffled sobs.

"I have to tell Maman. She needs to know. I have to tell her it's a lie."

"Nicole, I think she knows. I'll explain when I get there. I have to hang up now so I concentrate on driving but I'm coming to get you right now. Just wait there. I'm coming to get you. We'll talk to Marie-Hélène together. Okay? Just wait. We'll drive straight back to tell her. Okay. Wait there."

Nicole hadn't waited. I'd driven back to the exact spot where I'd left her earlier, expecting to find her in the same place, sitting by the fountain. When she wasn't there, I'd tried her phone a hundred times before trying Marie-Hélène's number over and over. Then panic set in – the image of an angry, confused girl wanting to see it for herself – to witness the place that held more value than people's lives. I'd driven towards it slowly, dread inching through my body, wanting to turn back, but knowing that it was where I'd find her.

I'm a fool. I'm an idiot for thinking that she wouldn't go there, to be so close to it and resist the chance to glimpse it, confront the woman who'd now tried to ruin us all. I'd parked at the gate, thinking how strange it had been that it was open. Then I'd got out, begun to inch up the driveway on foot. I could see the darkened figures on the high balcony above, and even though I couldn't make them out entirely, I'd known who they were. The colours in the sky had been changing, as fast as my heart and my breath. I'd almost left, trying to convince myself that I wasn't part of this mess. But I am part of it. I could no longer deny how I'd come to care for my husband's daughter or how I knew that she was meant to be in my life. She was a part of André – of the man who was still my everything.

* * *

As soon as the scream sounds, when her name echoes, when I hear the thud on the gravel – I know that I've realised it too late. With every shred of strength that remains, I run to her, praying it's a nightmare and more than anything wanting it to end.

Epilogue

Six months later

The house is full – people buzzing in and out of rooms as they so often do at these things: fussing, chatting, laughing. I can hear it from where I've escaped for a few minutes to sit in my chair, to look out at what I now call home. It has always been my home, but for a while, I forgot. Ballycross is in my blood. It was in André's blood, perhaps more so than Chateau Challant ever was. It's in my son's blood. I smile down at him, wondering, as I so often do, how I'd ever questioned if this child was meant to be born. He's almost three months old now. In a short space of time, he has fitted into my life, slotted himself into my heart, filling it once more in a way that I never thought possible. More than ever, it's made me realise that some people, despite how they make an appearance into the world, are meant to be. No matter what length of time they have on earth, some people are here for a reason.

He's getting tired now, so I lift him over my shoulder, where he turns his head and nestles into my neck as if he was specially made to fit right there. I suppose he was, in

387

a way. I'd longed for him without even knowing what I'd been longing for. I listen to his little grunts as he settles, kiss his head softly once, and then look back outside as his breathing quickens. I love that noise. André would have loved it too.

I'm thinking of him again – about my husband, the father of our son. I wish he was here with us today. He'd have been so proud holding his child over the font in the church as the priest called out his name. Instead, I looked on with enough pride for us both, flanked by the two Fairy Godmothers, Cathy and Jane.

Yes, we figured it out in the end. We're all friends again. Granted, they'd had little choice but to forgive me, bandage me up again, fix me once more, after I'd returned from France more bashed up than I'd left. It took almost an entire day to fill them in on the whole thing with all its complexities. It's taken me far longer to process everything and decipher what drove the women of Andre's life to that point. Gigi: greed. Marie-Hélène: revenge. Me: grief. Nicole …

Nicole had been the most innocent of all. I still wonder what might have happened if Gigi's plan had worked, and either myself or Marie-Hélène had been blamed for "pushing" Gigi off the balcony.

The police found a letter after they took her away – a detailed note filled with lies, describing how we'd all been in cahoots and that she'd been in fear of her life. I'd featured heavily. In it, she'd claimed that I'd purposely got myself pregnant to stake claim to "her" fortune. It said that Marie-Hélène and I had been working closely together. I had to hand it to Gigi – it was brilliant but utterly psychotic. Now, in the cold light of day, I can see precisely who Gigi was all along. I never have to worry about her again, though. Where she's gone, I doubt she'll see the changing skyline above the vineyards of Chateau Challant again.

I still wonder how Gigi knew that one or all of us would come that evening. Then again, I think many of us possess a sixth sense to alert us to impending doom. I'd felt it that night too – I'd known that Nicole was in danger. It baffles me to think that if Gigi couldn't have everything, she'd been willing to go so far to ensure no one else would either. When I think about it, and believe me, I try not to, I remind myself that people, like life, will never fail to surprise me – sometimes for better, sometimes for worse. That I'd allowed myself to be fooled by Gigi, if only for a moment, still makes me shudder. I was wrong about her, so very wrong, but I was also wrong about Marie-Hélène.

Resting my head back, I close my eyes and savour the feeling of my son's soft skin next to my face. I'm a mother now. They say you never truly understand until you are one. Now, I understand. There's plenty that Marie-Hélène failed at. There's an awful lot that she should have done differently, but no mother deserves what happened to her. I can only feel her pain now and understand the worry she must have felt, the rejection, and the suffering. It's no wonder she wanted revenge, and no surprise that she turned to drink. I think of her often. Sometimes I picture what she and André might have been like together as parents to Nicole, as a family.

Poor Nicole. I inhale sharply as her image enters my mind. Nicole didn't deserve to lose her mother that way, just as Marie-Hélène had come to her senses. In the end, she did what any mother would – what I too would do, now that I am one. Marie-Hélène had stepped in front of

Gigi, pushed Nicole from harm, and taken the fall.

"There you are." It's Jane, followed by Cathy. "Tired?"

"Always," I laugh. "But happy."

Jane gently cups the baby's head with the palm of her hand. "This little guy played a blinder today! What baby doesn't cry at their own christening? He's so bloody cool, like his father."

"I second that." It's Cathy. "Good job, little man."

They've been fantastic. I honestly couldn't have done any of it without them – the remainder of the pregnancy, preparing for the birth, the actual delivery, especially that part, one on either side, each holding a leg, cheering for me. It had been as perfect as it was going to be without André there. Come to think of it, everyone has been fantastic – everyone understood the reasons why I'd want to have my husband's baby.

"I'm sorry I doubted you." Cathy had told me through tears on my return from France. "I think a lot of this mess is my fault. I pushed you away."

"I did too," Jane had been bawling crying. "It was all too much. I'm so sorry, Seren. We didn't give you time. We didn't think that you might know what was actually best for you."

We'd been lying on my bed together. The three of us in a row, holding hands, making amends.

"I didn't know what was best. I hadn't a bloody clue what I was up to, but I think I know now."

I'd put my hand on my bump before Jane had followed suit and then Cathy. "We're your family. We always will be. This is your home."

"I know."

I do know it now. I know that so much of grieving is trying to find what your life is afterwards. I know that even if you're precisely where you're meant to be, you'll feel lost before finding your way again. I also know that I'll never stop missing André. For the rest of my life, I'll wish he was here with me. I'll never stop telling our son about him or imagining what he'd be thinking or what he'd say, or how it might have been. Above all, I realise that all the time in the world would never have been enough. Even if he'd lived for another hundred years, I'd have wanted more.

André gave me the best eighteen years of his life. Every second of my time with him was pure. I understand now why André didn't tell me about his past. In fact, I'm thankful – glad that we didn't waste a moment of our precious time together on what ultimately made me question everything about him. Because I did question him. I wondered, I doubted. Not because I didn't love him or trust him but because I'm human. I'm happy he wasn't here to witness it. In the end, André and I had exactly the life we were meant to have here in Ballycross, and for that I'll be forever grateful. He died knowing that I loved every molecule of him, that I adored every moment. Although everything that happened after his death was devastating, perhaps it distracted me from my pain. It gave me a focus and now it has left me with the greatest gift of all.

"It's nearly time." Jane breaks my thoughts.

"Oh, it is." I glance at my watch and smile. "Will you take him?"

"I will." Another voice from behind.

"Thanks, Bobby." I smile.

391

Bobby is the godfather. Someday I know, he'll teach him to fish and do all the things that André might have. I hand over the sleeping bundle.

"You want us to come?" Cathy asks.

"Nah. I won't take long." As I get up, she pulls me in for a hug so tight that I can barely breathe. "We love ya. Don't we?" She lets go, looking to the other two for affirmation. There are enormous tears in her eyes. She opens her eyes wide to suck them back in.

"Ah, we do," Bobby answers first, and Jane raises her eyebrows, gives me a knowing look and bites her lips together to stifle a laugh.

Frowning, I shoot her a warning look while Bobby, still holding the baby, obliviously settles himself into the chair I've vacated.

"Well, I love you all too, and you." I lean over the chair to pat the baby's head.

"Who's that? Who do you love?" Jane whispers in my ear, pinches my side.

I poke her sharply in the ribs before walking away. I'm no fool. I know what everyone's saying behind my back and others to my face, telling me that Bobby Cronin is mad for me. Even Marian Cummins stopped me on the riverwalk last week to ask if the rumours were true.

I'd thrown my eyes up to heaven. "No. Marian. We're friends. Just friends."

"But that's where it always starts, dear." Her teasing smirk had been wiped away when Tiny started circling by her feet, then crouched in preparation for one of his infamous dumps.

Marian is in the kitchen now getting stuck into the wine. I might have a glass or two myself when I get back. Lately, I'm very into Italian white, but I'll always have a place in my heart for those French reds. I wave as I pass Marian on my way to the front door. Everyone I care about is here today – all my friends from Ballycross with its small-town gossip and simple ways, just how I like it. Only Fi is missing, but she'll be back to work a few months after her baby is born. I'm so glad that I'll have her in my new mother's group. I know we'll never stop laughing together about motherhood. In the meantime, I've a new girl arriving in her absence. Honestly, I've no idea how long she'll stay, but I'm hoping it will be for a very long time.

I pull open the door and step outside. It's bloody cold out today. Shivering, I cross the road. I'm almost at the row of shops where we're due to meet when I spot her. The bus must have come early. Her back is to me, and she's sitting on the same bench her father once had sat on. As soon as she turns, I know my chest will collapse, and I'll start sobbing. I'd wanted her to come back to Ireland with me immediately after Marie-Hélène's funeral, but she'd insisted on going to Corsica for a while. Her friend's family had come to France to be with her for the funeral. They'd seemed like kind people.

After losing her mother, she'd needed time to heal, forgive, process, and breathe – a break to decide her next move. I hadn't wanted to push her, but I'd still phoned her every day just to chat until she'd told me she was ready to come.

She's waving now. I can still see traces of André, but it's faded a little over time so that mostly I just see her. Nicole's face lights up as mine crumbles, and she laughs as she strides towards me.

Then she's in my arms.

"It's so good to see you!" I hug her.

"You too. How is my baby brother? Little A.J.?"

"André Junior is very excited about meeting you in person!" I grin, wiping my tears.

"Just so you know, I'll be speaking French to him – someone needs to," she says.

"*Mais, oui. Bien sur.*"

"Pathetic," she says, grinning, and looks around. She seems so grown up. The time away must have done her good. She's lost so much, and yet, like me, she's still here. We're here together. "I think I'll like it here." She nods in approval.

"I know you will."

Before I take her hand to lead her home, I glance back at the bench overlooking the sea where André once sat. The wind picks up, blowing my hair over my face, but through it I see him. He'll always be there looking out at sea, keeping watch over his family, what he left behind, his legacy. André Dubois-Challant lives on. I smile suddenly at everything the past brought me and all that the future holds. If I want to be exceptionally sentimental, which I still can be, of course, old habits die hard. I might say that André orchestrated it all from afar so that although I'd lost him, I gained my very own family – something to live for. Or maybe things just happen, unfolding as they ought to. Either way, I win.

I wonder what else will unfold as life ticks on? I'll have to wait and see, but I'm not afraid anymore, now that I understand that no matter what happens, it just keeps going until it doesn't. The past two years almost crushed me alive, but I'm still here. I survived. Of course, there's bound to more heartache, sorrow, mixed with endless joy, immense pride as I watch my son and my stepdaughter pave their path in the world.

Whatever they decide, it's their decision. It may, or it may not involve a chateau in Bordeaux. If they choose to accept what is already theirs, the future will be mapped out, or like their father they might let serendipity decide. Chateau Challant is theirs now that their grandfather is dead. He'd hung on until Gigi was well out of the way. Their portions will be kept in trust until they're twenty-one. For now, it will continue to operate under a board of directors, or so I'm told. It's nothing to do with me, really. Except as any mother might, I'll be sure to push plenty of bottles of Chateau Challant in my little country wine shop.

Other than that, all I have to do is to love both of my husband's children, navigate them through life until they are of age to know what they want. I suspect I'll lose Nicole to the draw of France sooner than A.J., or who knows, maybe she'll remain in Ballycross, become a "Ballycrosser" like her father. A Ballycrosser, who, like the rest of us, never leaves. Sure, why would you? It has everything you might need right here. It's certainly enough for me.

A thought came to me last night in bed. A very enlightened, incredibly handsome, wonderfully selfless Frenchman once said that if we were born understanding the feeling of loss, then the world might be a better place. Perhaps it's what made André the man he was.

He'd known loss from the moment he was born. I've known it too. But I understand now that if you're lucky enough to be standing after some of the unexpected events that come along, threatening to shatter your world, then stand tall. There is life on either side of loss, so live. Find the light. As cruel as life might sometimes seem, there is always light. It comes in many different colours. If it's too dark right now, wait it out. Eventually, you'll see it.

I did.

FIN

Acknowledgements

Writing *Unexpected Events* has proved to be a fantastic, unexpected event in itself. I enjoyed every moment of creating this story from the first moment I imagined a chateau in Bordeaux, France. Let's say the research was delightful as my husband and I worked our way through several full-bodied French reds! As usual, there are many people to thank, and I'm so grateful to have reached the point where I can do just that.

To all at Poolbeg Press, in particular Paula Campbell. Thank you, as always, for the support, encouragement and laughs. To the typesetters, designers, proofers, thank you. There wouldn't be a book without you.

To my marvellous editor Gaye Shortland for the hugely encouraging words of praise and for putting up with all my ridiculous mistakes. Thank you for improving my story.

To my initial readers: Jane, Lucie, Nicole and Susan – you guys are so important in this process – my sincerest gratitude for your friendship and help. Please stick around!

To Dom from the Parting Glass, Enniskerry, for providing the wine and the information! Quelle Surprise is loosely based on your beautiful shop – the best haunt in town!

To my loving husband Mal, who patiently listened to *Unexpected Events*' rather intricate plot again and again without once nodding off. Your belief in my babble (and me) is outstanding! Someday … xxx

To Martha, Bruce, and Gertie. I've said it before, and I'll say it again – you are my reason for everything. Thank you for emptying the dishwasher, bringing me tea, the walks, the chats, the laughs, and for understanding how important these books are to me. I'm the luckiest mother ever. Gertie, this book is dedicated to you. As the littlest, you waited patiently for "your" book. Here it is. You've promised me this will be my best yet! Make it happen, my lucky little charm!

To Wilbur, my steadfast writing companion whose world I destroyed by getting him a baby brother in the form of Blue – I'm sorry! I'm looking forward to writing my next book with my two best pals by my side. (The puppy will be calmer by then, I hope.)

To my sister-in-law, Jenn, who helps me plot, gives me the wildest ideas and helps with any legalities.

To my parents, John and Amy Small, for all your support and love, as always.

To my parents-in-law, Cyril and Dee Dee Cuffe. Our times spent in Cork with you are my very favourite. So much so, Ballycross is loosely based on Crosshaven, which has proved a haven for us. Thank you for everything.

To the authors who inspire me, thank you. To the readers who make me want to continue writing, I hope you enjoy *Unexpected Events* as much as I loved writing it. To anyone who has supported me, it took me a very long time to get here, with plenty of bumps along the way, but I am living my dream – long may it last.

Until next time … this time next year, Rodney!

Printed in Poland
by Amazon Fulfillment
Poland Sp. z o.o., Wrocław